Deal With Death

Deal With Death

by

ENDY

This is a work of fiction. All of the characters, organizations, and events portrayed in this novel are either products of the author's imagination or are used fictitiously.

www.melodramapublishing.com

Library of Congress Control Number: 2007943733
ISBN-13: 978-1934157121
ISBN-10: 1934157120
First Edition: October 2008
10 9 8 7 6 5 4 3 2 1

Acknowledgments

As always, l want to give thanks to most high. Without Him I am nothing; with Him I can do all things! I thank Him for blessing me with the craft from which it flows.

First I'd like to say that if I have forgotten to acknowledge anyone, please don't take it personal. I am human. Charge it to my head because my heart is truly innocent.

I want to thank all of the readers who continuously support me! I appreciate all the support and feedback. Don't think a day goes by that I don't appreciate YOU the readers!

I'd like to thank the wonderful staff at Melodrama Publishing! I gotta give credit where credit is due. You are the backbone to the company and although you're not seen you are definitely appreciated! So I am extending my thanks to you personally.

Crystal L. Winslow (CLW) You are truly an amazing person. I have nothing but love and respect for you. I am most appreciative to be with a publishing company like Melodrama, where the authors are treated respectfully and fairly. Thank you, CLW, for the free advice and for being sincere.

I give much thanks and love to my two precious daughters, Briona and Len-da. Once again the two of you have been patience and understanding when I am in a zone trying to bang out these books. My time is limited, but you know in the long run this will pay off for all of us. Thank you for continuously making good grades and showing me what mature young ladies you are. I am proud to say that the advice I have constantly given you is paying off in a big way. I love you!

To my mother and father: George and Frances. Again thanks for being patient with me and putting up with my mood swings stemming from my extreme focus on honing my craft. Thank you for being my safety net when I don't even realize half the time that it is there. I love you for being the loving and supporting parents that you. Most can't say that they have both their parents in their lives, which makes me appreciate you that much more. I love you both more than words can express.

To my brother, Daraine. I love you and miss you very much. Although miles may separate us, it will never separate the love that I have for you.

To my extended family: Thanks to all of my family in Jersey for the continuous support! Thanks to my family in the south for spreading my name in the dirty! Tracey, Lakeda and Sadeka, thanks for spreading my name in GA. I see ya work and it show!

Once again Eric you have always been there for me and constantly showing me what a true friend is. The great advice and encouragement can only come from a true friend like you. Thank you!

To my close friends who are always there no matter what. Thank you: Sonya (NJ), Shells (KS), Shelley (GA) Janice (NJ), Lloyd & Kells (MO) Tasha & Byron (KS) Tamiko (NJ) Thanks to all of you for still having my back!

Hey Rica (Reno) Brian (Cali) Sonya, thanks for the continuous support. Thanks for spreading my joint throughout Continental airlines! Hey Ty Goode, thanks for having my back even when I think you're not there. Keep grinding it's gonna happen!

Special thanks to my good friend Denise (GA) What's up girlie, you know you my peeps! I miss you and I love you! Hey Denitra, Raynice. Luv you, girls!

To all my peeps at Linden Pop Warner . . . You knew I couldn't stay away. Coach Freeman, I forgot you last time but I didn't forget you this time. Thank you so much for being a genuine person who cares as much as you do. Hey Johnny Mae, you know you my girl! Anita here we go again, you gonna milk me for all I'm worth this time I know it . . . lol. Coach D. Brown, you're another one I forgot, thanks again for being a lifelong friend. We go way back! What's up Coach Parker? Mona I have to give you a shout out, because you pumped my book hard. Thanks Mona. To all my fellow coaches: Michele, Tarsha, Monique, M. Crump, & Tonya, thanks, ladies, for a great season. First place on all three levels! It has never been done . . . Big L rocks the house! Lol. Coach Huggins, hey girl! Thanks for spreading my name in Maryland! Thanks for the support! That's all I'm gonna say . . . lol . . . Shout outs all across the board to all the cheerleaders on all levels, football players and the rest of the coaches and staff.

To all the book clubs who have read my joints and pumped my name: C2C, Rawsistaz, DaReview, Locksie from ARC, The Urban Book Source, Delta Reviewer, Urban Reviews, just to name a few. I want to thank you all!

Thanks to all the book stores that sold my joints. Special thanks to Source of Knowledge and Black Vision books. Big Thanks to all the street vendors. What's up Nelson from the BX? The book vendors are the truth behind the sales of the books. Thanks!

To my fellow label mates: Storm, what's up girl? Kiki, you know you my peeps! Luv you both! Kiki you are my real sister! Jackie Simmons, what's good? Linda Brickhouse, special thanks to you. Thanks for being a genuine person. No one knows just how blessed you are.

Ms. Toni, thank you so much for continuously showing me that STL love! You are one of the hardest working sisters in this business. They just don't know the pull you have. Nardsbaby, it don't take a CSI agent to know that you show luv and support. Hot Chocolate, hey gurl! Thanks for having my back like you do. Lady Scorpio, what's up sista? You are everywhere! LOL . . .thanks for the support, great conversations and just being a down chick! One! Chini's girl, thanks for the support and showing the luv. To all the book clubs that review my books and show continuous support, thank you! Ty from DaReview, that for keeping it real!

To all my fellow authors Thanks for the support, genuine luv and advice.

Again, if I have forgotten anyone, please don't take it personal. My head is all over the place and my age is catching up to me . . .lol . . .So I know I have forgotten someone. But I am sure you will tell me and I will put you in the next joint! Charge it to my head!

Oh yeah. Hi haters, I see you!

Behind every successful person there is a hater! So here's to you, haters. I raise my glass because with you hating on me, it only makes me stronger. Oh yeah, do me a favor, when you hate make sure you know what you're talking about before you open your mouth. LOL!

One!

Prologue

She was a hard-core crack addict who sat on the floor as she held the bowl of a crack pipe, filling her lungs with the thick, white smoke. Removing the pipe, she pinched closed what was left of her badly decayed nose in a desperate attempt to keep the smoke from escaping. Heroin had helped to eat away the bottom half of both nostrils from years of snorting the poison. When she was out in public, she wore a bandage to cover the gruesome sight.

She closed her eyes as her head began to spin. Her chest got tighter the longer she held in the smoke. Her face became pale when she could no longer hold on. She released what was left of the smoke from her lungs, and she began to cough and gag as she tried to regain regular breathing. She leaned over and scooped up a large portion of heroin and snorted it heavily. The burning sensation caused her to wince in pain as blood ran from her nose. Her eyes bulged out of her skeletal head as she reloaded the pipe's stem. She had a strong urge to urinate, but the crack in the pipe seemed more important. She simply released the yellow liquid right where she sat; indifferent to its mixture with the bowel movement she'd had hours earlier.

She had been diagnosed with cancer, so she knew life would pass her by. That was why she'd plotted—and succeeded—in robbing a big-time drug dealer earlier that day. She knew her life was limited because she had made a deal with the devil, better known as Death. Since true death was already staring her in the face, it really didn't matter.

She heard footsteps coming her way and she snorted the heroin faster in response. She struck three matches before she managed to light the pipe, shoved it into her mouth and sucked on it as the cocaine melted. The blood now flowed from her nose like water from a faucet. She just wiped it away and continued with her suicide mission.

The dealer's crew walked in and surrounded her. They knew she was half dead before they even got there. The dealer raised his gun as his eyes began to tear. *BOOM!* Her blood splattered all over the floor. The crew members collectively shook their heads at the pitiful pile of flesh. This woman had once been the dealer's mother.

Chapter One

HOW IT ALL BEGAN . . .

"What the hell?" the man asked, sitting up in the bed.

"What is it, honey?" his wife inquired.

"That smell. It seems like it got worse."

It was a scorching, sticky summer night in Newark, New Jersey, and the man had the window fan on like he always did at night, trying to get some relief from the stuffy bedroom. But on this night the fan pulled a horrible stench from the outside air right into his bedroom.

He got out of his bed and walked over to the window. After turning off the fan and removing it from the window, he peered out the window while holding his breath. He figured the odor must be coming through a broken window directly across from his bedroom window. He could hear dogs growling, but he noticed that the growling dogs didn't sound like the average dog.

"I'm calling the police," the man told his wife. "I can't take this shit anymore. Something's not right."

It was well after midnight when the station got the 911 call.

"911. What's your emergency?" the dispatcher asked.

"There's some God awful smell coming from the abandoned house next door," the man complained. "And you know this is the same house where all those damn drug dealers and addicts hang out."

"How long ago did you notice the smell, sir?"

"It's been there for about two days, but now the smell is unbearable. My wife and I can't even sleep."

"OK, sir. We are sending the police to investigate now. Please stay on the line until they arrive."

Police radios buzzed loudly as several officers stood below a ladder looking up at a fellow officer. The officer on the ladder removed a handkerchief from his pocket and placed it over his nose and mouth to lessen the horrible smell coming from the window. He peeked into the window and shone his flashlight into the room. A Rottweiler suddenly jumped at the window and scared the shit out of him, causing him to fall off the ladder and land on the other two officers below. Other officers came running to aid and assist.

The dogs were going wild. Their barks were deep and loud, and it sounded as if they were trying to break out of the room. Fortunately for the officers, the windows were too high for the dogs to jump out. The sergeant had been called to the scene and was en route.

"What the hell?" the head officer asked as he watched the other officers gather themselves together.

"There are dogs up there," the officer who fell responded. "We know there's a dead body in there too. Don't you smell it?" he asked, rubbing the bruise on his leg.

"Yeah, I do. Go get that leg checked out," the head officer said as he removed his gun from the holster. "Gimme your flashlight," he ordered no one in particular.

The acting officer in charge climbed the ladder and held on with the same hand that was holding the flashlight. His other hand held his gun, cocked and ready to fire.

Once he reached the window, he could hear the wild dogs growling ferociously. He peered in the window as the dogs jumped at the window again. He shone his flashlight in their eyes as the stocky canines stood side by side. Blood covered their snouts and the officer could see flesh and clothing hanging from their teeth. The smell was a combination of decaying flesh, urine, and feces. He gagged at the stench.

There, in the corner, was what looked like the body of a male.

"We got a dead body in here! I only see one, but who knows what else is in here? Call animal control," he yelled down to the officers below.

About an hour later, the dogs had been tranquilized with darts. Investigators, EMTs, and other officers swarmed the house. The body of a teenage male lay on the feces-covered floor. Raw steaks had been tied to the body to encourage the dogs to feed. The medical examiner estimated that the man had been dead for weeks.

Sergeant Terrell Tilmond, the handsome, tall, black police sergeant walked out of the building. The air outside wasn't any better, but it was a big difference from the horrible stench that was on the inside, and he welcomed the outside air into his nostrils. He looked around and it seemed everyone in the neighborhood was standing outside. He looked at his watch and it was four AM. Were the people of this neighborhood that nosey that they would get out of their beds at four in the morning to see a dead body? He shook his head and answered his own question. Hell, yeah, they were, and they had gotten out of bed. He walked down the steps to greet his lieutenant, who was walking toward him.

"So what's the story?" Lieutenant Dickson asked.

"We got a dead body and tranquilized dogs."

"Dogs? What happened?" The lieutenant placed a lit cigarette to his lips.

"From what I can tell, someone wanted to make sure the boy was dead. They tied steaks to his body and let the dogs loose on him, I guess to get rid of the body, so to speak."

"Shit! What the fuck is this, some kinda cult sacrifice?"

"A cult in this neighborhood?" Tilmond laughed. "He was dead before the dogs got to him. He has three bullet holes to the chest."

The lieutenant looked up to see the EMTs pushing a gurney with a black body bag on it. He and Sergeant Tilmond walked over to it.

"Let me see," the lieutenant ordered.

The zipper on the bag was pulled down to expose the face of the dead teen. The horrible odor immediately assaulted the lieutenant's nose.

"Shit!" He turned his head away to get a gulp of fresh air, then he turned back to look at the body. "He doesn't look eaten to me."

"Zip it all the way down," Tilmond instructed.

When the EMT exposed the body, all the color drained from the lieutenant's face.

The legs of the young man had been eaten down to the bones, leaving hanging flesh and exposed veins. A chunk was missing from his abdomen, to which a piece of the steak was still tied. The intestines dangled outside the body, and the inside of the stomach was visible.

"Get him outta here! Jesus Christ!" the lieutenant exclaimed. He turned to Tilmond. "This shit has got to stop! Bodies are turning up all over this city, and no cases are being solved. It's like we got people on the inside working with these damn hoodlums. Tilmond, I want you to lead up some of these cases and close 'em!" And with that order, the lieutenant stormed off, hurrying to leave the horrible sight behind him.

෩෩෩෩

THREE DAYS LATER . . .

Grunting echoed throughout the empty apartment after each slapping sound. Three bullies were beating a twenty-something-year-old man named Cutty. Cutty sold drugs for a known drug dealer named Death, but he had recently been caught selling his own product on the side.

The streets below were busy with midday activity. The apartment was on the second floor, above a music store. The store's music was so loud that you could feel the vibrations from the bass through the floorboards. Death owned the store and the apartment. He made sure the workers turned the volume way up on the store's system, so no noise from the apartment could be heard on the streets.

Death sat on the windowsill of the front window watching the streets buzz while his three henchmen—Ibn, Jamal, and Dean—put in work on the young man.

Cutty was tied to a metal table. His face was disfigured and deformed. The huge swelling of his cheeks almost looked to be pulsating, like the big toe on Jim Brown in the movie *I'm Gonna Git You Sucka*. Cutty felt no pain at this point because he was numb from the beatings. His eyes were swollen and all he could see through the slits of his eyes were blurry figures. He knew that this day would come when he sold the bag of his dope to a police officer two weeks prior. The cop was on Death's payroll. Cutty tried to avoid running into Death by getting low, and had his sixteen-year-old brother push both his own product and what was left of Death's product. His plan was to take the bread he had saved and blow town. Cutty didn't know that he'd sent his little brother from the frying pan straight into the fire when the boy delivered the money to one of Death's crewmembers. Cutty had hoped that because he paid up they would turn down the heat.

Unfortunately for him, the crew had been out looking for Cutty for two weeks, since the sale to that cop. When Cutty's brother came to them with the money from Cutty's package, they took the boy to Death, who tortured him until he gave up Cutty's location.

Ibn, Jamal, and Dean stood over Cutty, trying to catch their breaths. All three were weed and cigarette smokers, so breathing didn't come easy for them. Cutty turned his head and focused his blurry vision on the body that lay atop a sheet of plastic on the floor in the corner. He cried silent tears for his dead brother. The boy's mutilated body had been laid out like a picnic lunch for Cutty to see when they brought him into the apartment.

Death turned his attention away from the window and looked at the three men.

"Y'all old heads need to give up them cigarettes. That shit's gonna kill y'all."

"Yo, I'm good," Dean said. "We been beating this niggas ass for, like, an hour now. Shit, I'm tired as hell!"

"Dude, seriously, it's only been"—Death looked at his platinum iced Movado watch—"like ten minutes."

"Bullshit! You can't be serious," Ibn said in disbelief.

"Word? You on some bullshit, man?" Dean asked, waving his hand dismissively. He put his hands on his waist and walked in a circle.

Jamal was bent over with his hands resting on his knees, still trying to breathe. He was the one who smoked almost two packs of cigarettes a day.

"Frankly, I don't give a fuck how long we been beating this nigga. I'm done," Jamal said. He stood up straight and retrieved a cigarette from the pack in his pocket.

The three men were all in their late fifties, the oldest of Death's team. They came highly recommended by Death's brother Terrell. Death liked the men because they had reputations and résumés that went back to the early seventies. They were good at what they did and got paid well for their services. There were times when Death would contemplate whether the men needed to go into retirement. Because of their ages, he figured they might be getting too old to put in the type of physical work he needed them to do. But then they always stepped up to the plate when it came time to put in work, changing his mind.

Death chuckled at the men whom he referred to as Three the Hard Way, because they reminded him of the three actors that played in the movie. Ibn, Dean, and Jamal were stuck in the seventies. They even sported short afros with long sideburns from that era. Their style of dress was somewhat of that time as well. They often brought comedy to the team and relief to the sometimes-stressful business. And although their appearances were humble, they were not to be underestimated. The three of them were, in fact, ruthless and dangerous.

Death looked over at Cutty and frowned when he remembered the reason why he was there. He watched as Cutty stared at his brother's body in the corner. The boy's legs and arms had been severed from his torso. Blood had created a pool under the body parts and threatened to run off the plastic and onto the floor. Death stood and straightened his Marc Jacobs dress pants over his gator-skin shoes.

"A'ight, squeeze off on this punk and stop that blood from staining my hardwood floors," Death stated. He pointed at the body in the corner, then he walked toward the door and turned to face the men. "Yo!" he called out.

The men looked at him.

"Wait until dark this time. I don't want no shit like the last time. I had to pay that fuckin' cop fifty thou to back up off of me." He eyed them with intensity.

Dean waved his hand at Death to dismiss him.

"Play with me if you want," Death warned. He turned on his heels and walked out of the apartment.

Half the time the three men didn't pay Death any attention. They respected him more than they feared him. They were old school and felt that they knew more than he did about the game because of their years of experience.

Death was not easy to get along with, much less work for, but truth be told, he was *that* nigga. His revenue ran deeper than a well. His product's potency could not be touched. The fear with which he blanketed the city was total. When you worked for a cat like Death, you did what he said to do, and made serious ends in the process. Every once in a while, though, there would be a cat who thought he was smarter than Death and would try him. Ultimately, Death would have to bring the pain. He always told his team, "You always got to stay two steps ahead of these motherfuckers."

Once down onto the streets, Death rubbed his hand across the sea of waves on his head. Death was his street name; the name given to him when he was younger. As a boy he was fascinated with death. It amazed him how the living could close their eyes and never wake up. It thrilled him as a teen to watch living creatures squirm and suffer before dying. He would torment cats, dogs, mice, and insects. When he took his first human life he was only seventeen-years-old. He loved the rush it gave him to watch a victim beg for his life. Death never used any of the hard drugs he sold, and he only smoked weed once in a while. He didn't need drugs, because he was sure that no drug high could top the feeling he got when he took a life.

As a child Death was always the bully in school. He used his size to intimidate the weak. He was a tall kid who grew into an even taller man. Death had a muscular yet slim frame, but his six-feet, four-inch height and unapproachable face was what he used to intimidate others. He was a fairly good-looking man with jet-black, wavy hair that was cut into a fade, and a mustache that graced his caramel-colored skin. And no matter what the weather, Death was always dressed to impress. After all, he was an entrepreneur.

Once he built his reputation in high school, he had a following of over half the students in the school. Death was a smart kid and became quite bored with school, but he loved to be there to control the other students, who showered him with gifts and money to keep themselves in his favor.

Death came from a large family where he was exposed to drug dealing at an early age by his older brothers. They grew up in Trenton, New Jersey before moving to Newark when Death was thirteen-years-old. As a result of his family's involvement with the game, he was very familiar with the streets.

When he graduated high school, Death became a permanent fixture on the street corners. Once he was brought on by his friend Wiz and fully in the drug game, Death infiltrated his competition's crews until he gained their territories. He used force to accomplish everything.

As Death stood on his block, his right-hand man, Bear, approached him. He had been waiting downstairs as the lookout. Bear acquired his nickname because he was as ugly as a bear. Bear was a skinny man who stood at just six feet. He had big, red lips that were attached to his blue-black skin. His wide nose spread across his face, and his Herman Munster-like eyes instilled fear in many. Most who found out that his name was Bear thought it was quite comical because of his small size. But

Bear was as ruthless as they came. He had the strength of three average-sized men, and he could easily snap a man's neck with the quickness.

The two looked over the street scene as the hot sun beat down upon their heads. Three of the neighborhood kids ran up to Death. They knew who he was and what he stood for. Their parents—and those of most of the kids in the neighborhood—purchased drugs from his crew. Every time Death was in the area, he would always give the neighborhood kids ten dollars to spend at the corner store. He did this because he knew what their parents did with their money. Death considered himself the Black Robin Hood. This was his sick way of thinking that he gave back to the community.

"What's up, fellas?" He towered over the three little boys, all of whom appeared to be around eleven-years-old.

"What's good, Death?" a brave little boy asked as he stuck his hand out for some dap.

Death cracked a smile and dapped the young boy.

"Yo, can you put me down on your team?" he asked.

Death looked at Bear and they both laughed.

"How old are you, little man?" Death asked.

"I'm eleven, but I'll be twelve in two weeks. I'm strong in my spot, and I'm ready. Just ask my boys. They can tell you I'm ready! Right, y'all?" He looked to his friends for backup.

The other two boys weren't as bold as their friend, and they only came with him because he called them punks and they didn't want to be labeled as that.

"Listen, little man, come see me when you turn thirteen, and then I'll hook you up." Death rubbed the boy on the head and then handed them each ten dollars. He had an age limit on recruiting new runners.

"Good looking out!" Although the little boy wasn't feeling the response that Death gave him, he accepted it anyway and happily accepted the money, knowing that day he would be thirteen would come soon enough, and he would be put on with the notorious Death.

Suddenly a stolen black Porsche GT2 bent the corner a block away, squealing on two wheels. Everyone on the street looked at that corner. A masked male holding a MAC-10 hung out of the passenger window as the car raced up the street at top speed. Midway up the block, the gun-toting bandit began to buck. Death knew that the shots were intended for him, so he grabbed the young boy and put him up as a shield to block the bullets. Bear pushed Death out of the way and took cover behind a parked car while he pulled out his 9 mm pistol and fired at the Porsche. Bullets shattered the glass of the nearby stores. People screamed and ran for cover while others hit the deck, covering their heads with their hands. Death bobbed and weaved while still holding the boy in front of him until he was able to get behind a parked car as well.

Shots came from the second-floor apartment over the record shop. Ibn, Dean, and Jamal heard the shots and began to retaliate. One of their bullets hit the gunman square in the middle of his forehead. The car continued to speed up the street with the dead gunman hanging from the passenger window. Once the car was gone everyone lifted their heads or came out from their hiding spots, making sure the coast was clear. It seemed as if time had stood still in just the few seconds that the shooting happened.

"You all right, little man?" Death had the nerve to ask the young boy.

The boy didn't respond. His body lay limp in Death's arms. Death looked down and saw two bullet wounds in the center of the young boy's frail chest. He laid the boy on the cement, stood, and brushed dirt from his pants. A woman that had ducked down behind the car next to where Death took cover began to scream when she saw that the young boy had lost his life to stray bullets. Police sirens blared up the street in the direction that the Porsche had traveled minutes earlier, while several other squad cars double-parked to give assistance to the injured.

"You see that clean shot right between the eyes?" Ibn asked Dean and Jamal.

"Nigga, you crazy!" Dean looked at him. "That was my bullet that did that punk in."

Jamal began to laugh. "Neither one of y'all clowns touched him. That was all me," he stated proudly.

"Here we go. You know damn well you couldn't shoot an elephant if he stood still and let you," Ibn clowned Dean.

"You talking Ibn? You know you got that Parkinson's disease and can't hold your dick steady to take a piss!" Jamal jumped in. Dean burst into laughter.

"Well we gonna see when they pull out the bullet whose gun it came from," Ibn said, holding up his .45, not seeing the humor in Jamal's statement.

Ten minutes later several officers were questioning any witnesses who would come forward about the incident. Most did cooperate with the officers, purely because the young boy had lost his life. The only information anyone could give the officers was that a masked gunman hung from the passenger window of a black Porsche and rained bullets as the car drove up the street. No one could give a description of the driver or the gunman. No one got a look at the license plate of the vehicle either.

Death stood in his store, making sure the employees were all right and checking out how much damage had been done. He walked over to the broken storefront window and looked out onto the cluttered streets. Sergeant Tilmond looked up from the notes he'd been taking on his notepad and peered at Death standing in the window. Death held his gaze and slowly gave a nod of acknowledgment. The sergeant placed his pen and pad back into the inside pocket of his suit jacket as he continued to hold Death's gaze. He then shook his head and walked off.

Chapter Two

"Let me get the matches," Nina said as she held out her hand, all the while examining the rock of cocaine in the stem. The two women used the stem from the crack pipe to get high. They never used the whole bowl. They thought it was a better direct hit.

Jackie was busy searching the pockets of her blue jeans for the matches. She had just taken a hit from her stem and was tweaking badly. Her mouth twitched and moved from side to side as her hazel eyes stretched as wide as they could go. Sweat poured from her forehead due to her confusion. She seemed to have misplaced the matches.

Jackie was five feet five with a dark complexion. She had been Nina's best friend of fifteen years. She was a pleasant-looking large woman with micro-braids and a mild case of acne. Most people would never think she smoked crack.

Nina was a dime piece in her own right. She was definitely model material. At five feet seven her olive complexion was blemish-free. It appeared as if she wore foundation, but she didn't. Her shoulder-length hair was always on point, without a strand out of place. Nina never missed her two-week appointment to get her hair done. She had the perfect set of lips—not too full and not too thin with just the right amount of pucker to them. "Dick-sucking lips" was what men said about them. She also had the perfect body with child-bearing hips, but she did have one flaw to that beautiful face of hers—her nose. For the last two years the inside of her nose would shed dead skin, and on occasion scabs would grow. She wasn't worried about it, though, because they were located inside her nostrils and out of sight.

At forty-years-old, Nina was a drug addict, although she didn't exhibit any of the physical signs. She was a functioning addict. She was always dressed neatly, and although her weight fluctuated and once neared the weight of a fiend, it never quite made it there. Nina made sure of that by monitoring her intake of crack cocaine and making herself eat meals.

Nina had two teenaged sons, and because she kept herself up, never did anything illegal to get drugs, and always went to Jackie's to blast off, she believed that she did a great job at hiding her addiction from her sons. Nina had an inner demon, though, that kept her on his leash, and after years of using, she still refused to face those demons from the past.

"Where the matches at, Jackie?" Nina asked again. She was ready to take her hit.

Jackie tried to talk, but couldn't. She would open her mouth to speak, but her lip control was lost from years of sucking on a glass dick.

Nina sucked her teeth as she waited for Jackie to find the matches. Nina's patience was beginning to run thin, as her own anticipation for a hit was getting the best of her. She wanted that almighty blast too. She eyed Jackie with hatred. Nina knew she had to have used the matches to light her own stem. Now, all of a sudden, Jackie couldn't find the matches. This was something that Nina went through every time they got high together. Nina often would want to get high alone because of Jackie's bad habits, but she hated to get high alone. Jackie was what Nina called a match hog. As many books of matches and lighters that Nina would bring, Jackie would always seem to misplace them, or use them all up.

When Jackie would bring the match up to the stem to take her hit, the air she breathed from her nose would always blow the match out, which made her have to light more matches. It was a wonder she was able to smoke at all with the way she wasted matches. If that weren't bad enough, Jackie would light four matches at a time, when only two would be required, in Nina's opinion.

While most slept at night, the dark demons were awake—the "night crawlers" as the drug dealers would call them. Drug addicts of all kinds would roam the streets all times of the night as if getting high all day wasn't enough. If a crack smoker had a good amount of money or a hustle, they could get high for days straight as long as the money lasted without a meal or sleep. But there was definitely something about the night hours that brought on the extreme urge to pollute their bodies with drugs.

It was around two in the morning on a Friday, and the two women sat at the kitchen table in Jackie's studio apartment. She lived in the basement of a two-family home. Jackie and Nina both knew they had to go to work later that morning at eight AM, but the way they were blazing, it was as if it were a Friday or Saturday night. They had been smoking all night, like they did every Thursday night after they got their checks. Sometimes they would actually make it to work on Friday after staying up all night.

"Come on, Jackie, damn!" Nina was agitated.

She stood carefully, holding her stem steady so she wouldn't lose the rock she'd just loaded into it several minutes ago. She began to move things around on the messy table, trying to locate the matches.

"Unh ... he-here ... they ... unh," Jackie grunted, trying to let Nina know she found the matches as she held them out to Nina with shaking hands.

Nina snatched the matchbook and tore off two matches with one hand, never setting the pipe stem down. After she lit the match from a burning candle that sat atop the kitchen table, Nina proceeded to smoke her rock.

The euphoria invaded her body and calmed her craving almost instantly. Nina began to swallow the smoke, not ready to release it yet. After several seconds, when she was no longer able to hold her breath, Nina released what little smoke there was from her mouth. That's when she put her share of rocks into a folded playing card and began her ritual. She walked over to the sink and washed the dirty dishes. Nina was a cleaner, and when she smoked crack, it sent her cleaning senses into overdrive. Jackie, however, couldn't lift so much as a fork when she smoked.

HOURS LATER . . .

After scraping their pipe stems for residue and the last hit of the night, they cleaned them and decided to take a break. On the last run that Nina made, the young dealer told her that he was out of coke, and he wouldn't be back out there until that afternoon. With no other means to cop, and neither woman having a car, they decided to wait it out. They searched the kitchen for fallen pieces of crack. Once all the crumbs— whether it was coke or food—were finally gone, the reality set in that there was no more to smoke.

They settled onto the sofa and stared into space. Jackie was the first to fall asleep. It took Nina a little longer. Although she nodded off, it wasn't the sleep taking over. It was the heroin. She needed the dope—a downer substance—to balance her high because crack made her paranoid. She hated that feeling, so she chose to snort heroin. That wasn't the only reason she used, though. Nina had a past that constantly haunted her, and heroin was a way to escape.

Nina laid there with her eyes closed, but never fully asleep. When she heard the apartment building come alive with doors slamming and people talking, she knew the streets were coming alive as well. She got up and decided to go out on the block in search of more crack.

Chapter Three

The early morning sun was already sending out vicious rays of heat. Nina looked up at the brightly lit sky and squinted. She felt like a vampire who had just been exposed to the sunlight. It burned her eyes and she knew that it was going to be a hot day. As pedestrians hustled about the streets, trying to get to their destinations, Nina desperately searched the corners for the early bird dealer. It was already apparent that neither she nor Jackie were going to work that day.

The corner bodega was open as people went in and out to purchase breakfast sandwiches or to simply buy the morning paper. Nina stood on the corner, looking back and forth, shifting her weight from one leg to the other, still searching for that morning score.

Nina wasn't craving heroin at that moment, but she needed to snort it to calm her nervous stomach. The anticipation and craving for the crack was starting to get the best of her. She stepped around to the side of the building and pulled out one of the packages of heroin that she had purchased just last night. She carefully looked around and used the bent corner of a matchbook cover to snort two hits to each nostril.

A shiny, olive green Acura Legend pulled up to the curb soon after Nina walked back in front of the store. The windows were rolled up, but you could still hear the muffled sounds of 50 Cent blaring from the speakers. Nina's stomach began to do flip-flops. She knew who the owner of the vehicle was. She smiled when he got out of the car.

"What's up, Nina?" BJ asked as he stepped onto the sidewalk.

"Hey, BJ, how you doing this morning?" She continued to smile, then dropped her voice to a whisper when a woman came out of the store. "BJ, you got anything on you?"

"This is yo' lucky day. I just picked up what was left of my package from one of the young boys this morning, so I got a little something in the car. Wait right here. Let me grab some blunts, and I'll serve you." BJ went into the store.

Nina felt like taking a shit. It was the same feeling she got every time she was about to take that first hit of crack. That was one of the reasons why she snorted the dope to keep her stomach settled, but it wasn't working. Chills ran up and down her arms. Beads of perspiration formed on her nose, and her head felt hot. Her hands shook, and every minute seemed like an hour. She looked in the store window at least ten times to see what BJ was doing before he appeared in the doorway of the store.

A navy blue Mercedes Benz with tinted windows drove down the street and passed the store. BJ looked at the car with piercing eyes. Nina didn't notice the vehicle. Once the car turned the corner, BJ came out of his daze.

"Come on." He beckoned Nina as he stepped around the back of the car. He looked again for the Benz before he hopped into the driver's seat. Nina was so anxious that she beat BJ into the car before he even had his hand on the door handle. Once inside it felt nice and cool. *He must have been driving with the air conditioner on,* she thought. She was right. As soon as he started the car, the cool air hit Nina smack in the face. The smell of vanilla from the fragrance tree that hung from the mirror filled the immaculate automobile. BJ pulled into traffic and slowly drove down the street. He made two lefts and then a right into a dead-end street. He parked at the curb and left the engine running, then reached into the middle console and pulled out a plastic bag half-filled with ten-dollar valves of powder cocaine, and a few small envelopes of dope. He tossed the baggie in Nina's lap.

"Pick what you want outta there," he said.

She looked at him in confusion. "I just want three and one."

"Get six of whatever, and pay me for four." He winked at her.

Nina smiled at the generous offer. She picked out four fat capsules of powder cocaine that were packed to the brim, and two bags of heroin. Just by looking at the capsules she knew when she got back and cooked the cocaine that the rocks were going to be fat. She placed them in her jeans pocket and refolded the bag. BJ unzipped his pants and removed his dick. Nina stopped folding the bag and stared, wide-eyed, at his large manhood. It lay on his leg like a fat sausage, and he wasn't even erect. She looked up at BJ's face.

He sat there confidently and stared back at her.

"You know what to do," he said. "You should know me better than that. I don't do shorts or freebies. So it's on you, baby girl."

Nina looked at the bag of drugs, and then back at his dick. She was not the one for turning tricks, at least not willingly. She had not reached that point in her drug career to stoop so low.

She reached into her pocket and removed one capsule and a bag of dope, and put them back into the plastic bag.

"So, you ain't giving up no brain, ma?" BJ asked in shock. He just knew he was going to get an early-morning nut before he took the drive to DC, where he was going to cop his next shipment.

"No, boo-boo, let me explain something to you," Nina retorted. "I may be a lot of things, but a whore is not one of them. You got me fucked up with them other bitches. Just because I like to get my head right don't make me no fiend. Frankly, you gotta be out of your fuckin' mind if you think I'm gonna suck you off for some coke! I don't give a shit how you rolling, you'll never get me to suck your dick for some get high." Nina was pissed. She tossed the bag of drugs and two twenties onto his lap. Just before she got out of the car, BJ grabbed her arm.

"Keep smoking coke and snorting dope, and the day will come when you will be glad to drop to ya knees to suck my dick," he said arrogantly.

Nina's blood boiled. She snatched her arm away from him and opened the car door. Before she could even get out, a hand grabbed her arm and snatched her out of the car. At the same time, the driver's side door was opened and BJ was also dragged out of the car, and slammed to the ground. Neither of them realized what was happening.

BJ tried to get up while reaching for his gun, but the attackers were ready for him. One of them hit BJ in the back of the head with the butt end of a .45. Nina was tossed to the ground as well.

"Stay there," Dean warned her.

By the look on his face, Nina knew he meant business. BJ fell back to the ground, hard. He grabbed the back of his head as blood seeped through the broken skin. A kick in his side lifted him partially off the ground. He grunted loudly.

"What the fuck, man?" he yelled with his dick still exposed.

A stomp on the side of his face slammed BJ's head into the pavement. While Dean watched over Nina, Ibn and Jamal continued to beat BJ to a pulp. Death stood and watched, smoking a cigar as if he was watching a professional boxing match. He didn't blink once as he continued to oversee the beating. Finally, he spoke.

"You was gonna get you a litlle early-morning nut, huh?" He laughed.

BJ lay on the ground as blood ran from his bruises. He was grunting and breathing hard. He was barely conscious. He thought about how he shouldn't have parked his car on the dead-end street, how he usually watched his surroundings. BJ thought he took care of Death that day when he did the drive-by. But the most overshadowing thought on his mind was that he should have never served Nina in the first place, being that he usually didn't serve. He left that up to his runners.

Nina scurried to her own feet. Dean grabbed her arm and Nina cringed, not wanting the man to touch her.

She was escorted over to where BJ lay. She turned away at the sight of the beating BJ had taken. She looked dead into Death's eyes and lowered her head. She was very familiar with the man they called Death.

"Look at me," Death said sternly.

Nina slowly raised her head until her eyes met his again. He had cold, black eyes that could cut through your heart like a razor. His eyebrows protruded over his deep-set eyes like a shutter.

Nina felt short of breath and nauseous. She thought about how she had left Jackie on the sofa, asleep. She thought about her boys, and what would they do without her if Death decided to kill her. She thought about how if she had taken her ass to work she would not be in the position she was in then. All of these thoughts, and many more, went through her mind. Her main thought was of how Death had finally caught up to her after she had been ducking him for such a long time.

Tears welled in Nina's eyes. She really believed she was going to die. Death continued to stare deep into her eyes, almost hypnotizing her. She was frozen in place. She couldn't move, or even blink for that matter. She wasn't sure that if she opened her mouth words would even come out. She was scared shitless, literally, because she couldn't hold it anymore and defecated on herself. She had known this man since she they were younger. She is older then Death, but as he grew into manhood he is now one of the most feared men in Newark. And she feared him even more than most people because she had been on the run from him for a long time.

Death wrinkled his nose as he smelled the foul odor of shit coming from Nina's body. He grabbed her by the neck with one hand. The force of his grip caused Nina to see stars immediately. He forced her to look at BJ, who still lay on the ground in pain.

Ibn pulled a syringe from his pocket. He removed the rubber top and squirted out a little of the liquid substance inside, just to make sure the needle wasn't clogged. Jamal and Dean held BJ down. A hand was placed over his mouth to muffle any sound that was sure to come out of his mouth.

Nina felt weak in the knees. She didn't know what was about to happen.

"You missed, nigga," Death said to BJ as he stood over him.

BJ widened his eyes when Death leaned over to talk to him.

"See, what you don't understand is that I am untouchable, nigga. You can't kill me, 'cause I'm already dead. Death by lethal injection, bitch!" He laughed.

Ibn slammed the needle of the syringe into BJ's eye, causing him to scream out in agony.

Death simply snickered.

Word on the street was that the dead gunman from the earlier drive-by was BJ's right-hand man. When you saw one, you saw the other 100 percent of the time. Naturally, the driver would have been BJ. This was what Death believed, anyway.

The substance in the needle was pumped into BJ's eye. He squirmed about and screamed, but it was a wasted effort because of the force that was holding him in place.

"You see, I'm like a thief in the night, except I don't steal nothing but life. I'm like the Grim Reaper. Fuck with me and lose your life." Death continued to laugh.

"Naw, man, you like the devil, and this nigga just sold you his soul," Dean added.

"Word! These motherfuckers don't know when they fucking with me, they fuck around and make a deal with death!"

As Death talked, Nina watched as a white substance bubbled up and around BJ's mouth as his body began to twitch around. Everyone stood around watching BJ's discomfort.

Death saw Nina trembling. He rubbed her face gently with the back of his hand. Nina's whole body became tense, and his touch sent a creepy feeling throughout her body. She wished she ran while his attention was on BJ, but she knew she couldn't escape Death.

"Yeah, that cat just bought his own ticket for a one-way trip to death." Death stared deep into her eyes. "Need I say more?"

Nina shook her head. Tears continued to fall from her eyes and saliva began to build up in her mouth. She tried to swallow the liquid, but the force was unbearable. Nina lunged forward and threw up all over BJ's dying body.

Chapter Four

Sergeant Tilmond exited his car in the parking lot of the AMC movie theater in Linden, New Jersey. His tall, muscular frame glided across the asphalt. He wore jeans, a fitted cap, and a pair of Timberland boots, which made him look like the average thug, instead of a police officer. He walked into the theater and up to the cashier. Revealing his badge, he was given a free ticket to the matinee of *Ocean's Thirteen*. He purchased popcorn and a soda, and then walked to the theater that played his movie. He stood there for a few moments as his eyes adjusted to the darkness, then surveyed the theater. There were four other people scattered throughout the theater, and the previews had already started. He saw the man whom he had come to meet. He was seated way up at the top. Tilmond sighed and climbed up the stairs. Once he reached the last row, he walked down the aisle of empty seats until he reached the man. The man had his foot propped up on the back of the chair in front of him.

Tilmond took the empty seat next to the man and placed his popcorn and soda in the holder on the armrest.

"You getting sloppy," Tilmond said to the man.

Death looked over at him and held out his fist for a pound. Tilmond bumped his fist against Death's and picked up his cup of soda.

"Why we gotta meet here?" Death finally asked.

"Because for one, it's private and secluded. You know I can't be seen with you. Two, I get to see a free movie in the process."

"Free? How you get in for free?"

Tilmond cocked his head to the side and looked at Death with a raised eyebrow.

Death turned his attention back to the movie screen. Tilmond had the benefits of being a cop, so he got a lot of things for free. He had the advantage over the average Joe.

"I see you brought your boy with you?" Tilmond asked, referring to Bear, although Bear was not sitting near Death.

"I don't know what you talking about." Death played it off.

"He's sitting down there in the corner." Tilmond pointed to a nearby, dark corner. Death laughed. Tilmond was on point.

"I know that's your boy and all, but sometimes your right hand don't always need to know what your left is doing."

Death just rolled his eyes.

They both watched the movie previews before Death spoke again.

"Why we gotta see this particular movie? We could have seen something that was gonna benefit the both of us."

Tilmond twisted his lip and shook his head.

"Look, this movie *will* benefit you. These same cats did parts one and two of this movie. You could learn a lot from these jokers. They know how to be a team, unlike the niggas in the game today. These cats right here are the real gangstas."

As Tilmond spoke, Death held up his hands like he was playing a violin, indicating that he didn't want to hear the song Tilmond was singing.

"A'ight, Todd, take my word for it," Tilmond said, calling Death by his birth name. "Niggas get buck when they paper don't stack right," Tilmond warned.

Terrell Tilmond was Death's older brother. He was the oldest of four boys and two girls, with Death being the baby and having a different father because their mother remarried. Death was thirty-five-years-old, and Tilmond was older than him by fourteen years. Before Death was even born, Tilmond was in the game, and by the time Death was two, Tilmond had the drug game on lock in Trenton, New Jersey. During his time on the streets, Tilmond was both ruthless and very well respected. When he reached his early thirties, he was well established and financially stable until the near-death experience of his then three-year-old daughter. That was a reality check for him. He began to worry about his family's safety and became paranoid, thinking that someone was always watching him, trying to take his spot. With that type of stress and pressure came mistakes, mistakes that cost him a lot of revenue.

Tilmond was a smart man and had never spent a day of his life in jail. At that time, he decided to relocate his family to Newark, New Jersey, where his siblings had moved years before. Once there he began to search for another occupation, one that would provide a decent paycheck to continue to take care of his growing family. He only had a high school diploma, and had never held a legitimate job in his life. He worked several odd jobs before strongly thinking about taking the test to become a cop. He struggled with the idea for quite some time while living off the money he had saved. His wife was then pregnant with his second child, and he knew he had to do something fast.

Tilmond worried about the reputation that took him years to build. Becoming a cop would surely label him a sellout. After countless conversations with an acquaintance who was a corrupted cop, he decided to take the offer his friend presented to him. The friend told him he would be able to get him in. So Tilmond became a cop and worked on a team of corrupt cops. That way he would keep his street status, but still be able to earn a living for his family without worrying about their safety.

"You know these jokers got team players," Tilmond commented, referring to the characters in the movie. "Everybody got a lane, and everybody plays their lane, unless otherwise instructed. Y'all cats can learn something from them. There are no haters on the team, and everybody makes paper in the process. Y'all cats got too much drama. Everybody wanna run shit, and the ones that ain't running shit is plotting to get the nigga that is."

Death laid his head back on the seat and snored loudly, pretending to be asleep. Tilmond shook his head and continued to eat his popcorn. He knew Death was hardheaded. He had always been a spoiled, stubborn kid because he was the baby of the family.

"A hard head makes a soft ass," Tilmond said, looking straight ahead.

"Rell," Death called him by his nickname. "I'ma grown-ass man. I know what the hell I'm doing. I was born into this shit, remember?"

"Yeah, but you sloppy as hell, Todd. I know you better then you know yaself. Don't forget, I raised you, boy."

"Aw, damn, here we go with the I-know-you-better-than-you-know-yourself speech," Death said with irritation. "Oh, and let's not forget the I-raised-you-like-you-were-my-son bullshit. When you gonna let that go, Rell? I been hearing that shit all my life! Damn!"

"Until you get it. You throw too much loot away on protection, Todd. I can't keep covering for the stupid shit you do. You're 'bout to fuck it up for all of us. The cats on the force are starting to think you're more trouble than the paper you pay them. I know you losing bread by the pound, as much as we cover your shit up for you. After that little stunt you pulled yesterday they gonna want to increase the taxes."

"What stunt?"

"The shoot out on the ave?" Tilmond looked at him with a raised eyebrow.

Death laid his head back on the seat again and rolled his eyes. He was tired of his brother's bitching. He loved Terrell and had nothing but respect for the OG, but he was a grown-ass man and was tired of the constant lectures.

"Listen, man, I got this."

"Oh, like you had that shit yesterday?"

"Yo, that wasn't my fault!" Death sat up and looked at Tilmond.

"Oh, yes, it was. I'm sure you did something along the way to raise that kinda reaction toward you, Todd. Shit just don't happen for nothing."

"That's bullshit, Rell, and you know it!" Death was getting pissed. "Listen, man, tell the boys that it wasn't my fault, and as far as taxing me more, I ain't with that."

He turned his attention back to the movie. Tilmond just shook his head, not saying a word. Both watched the movie in silence until Death spoke again.

"Oh, shit! I know that cat. That's the dude who played in *The Departed*," he said, referring to Matt Damon. "Now those cats were some real gangstas!"

Tilmond shook his head again.

"Todd, what did I tell you about glorifying violence?"

"Rell, chill, aight?"

"No, Todd. I've been talking to you about that shit since you were a kid. That's not the answer to everything. That's not the way to handle every situation."

"You killin' me, Rell!"

"Yeah, and you killing me. Violence only begets more violence. You should only use violence when necessary, and if necessary. If you need to use it, use it quietly and cleanly," Tilmond schooled.

"Oh my gawd! Stop beatin' me over the head, Rell!"

As far as Death was concerned, Terrell failed to realize that those were the old days. Nowadays, all the young boys knew was violence, so therefore Death had to play the game in order not to be played.

"So is that how you still handle all your business?"

"What are you talking 'bout, Rell?"

"I'm talking 'bout that cat BJ, who we found in the empty lot over in Westside Park. I told you we would handle that, baby bruh."

"I got this, Rell," Death repeated.

"Listen, if you need me to help you organize your business, you know I'm here for you."

"Same ol' Rell, always want to be in charge. That's a'ight. I'm good. You just keep doing what you do for me, and get this side paper I'm paying you."

At times Death thought his brother was jealous of him, jealous of his status, the status Rell wished he could still have, but had given up because he got scared.

"The money is in the duffel bag under the seat. I'm out, big bruh." Death stood and prepared to leave.

"You ain't gonna watch the rest of the movie with me? I think you need to see this joint," Tilmond urged.

"Naw. I can't make no paper watching movies all day. Always love." He gave Tilmond a pound.

"Always love," Tilmond replied as he watched his brother descend the flight of steps. He checked to make sure the money was in the duffel bag under his seat, and then he sat back to watch the remainder of the movie.

≈≈≈≈≈

THREE WEEKS LATER . . .

Nina barged into the room. The bedroom door hit the wall with a bang.

"Y'all get up and clean up this funky room!" Nina yelled at the top of her lungs.

She stood in the bedroom that her two teenage sons shared, and it looked like a pigpen. Shoes, clothes, plates with old food stuck to them, and empty soda cans were scattered all over the floor. Nina was a neat freak, and to stand there in the middle of the junk pile was killing her.

"I didn't work this hard for y'all to lay around!" she continued to scream at Malik and Marquis. "Y'all run the streets all night and think you gonna come up in my shit and lay around all day? No! Hell no! And, Malik, get ya ass up and find a damn job or something! You are old enough to go out and support yourself. You are not a baby anymore!" She turned and left the room, but just as quickly returned. "And you better not be out there selling no drugs, either. If I find out you selling drugs, you gonna find yaself living on the streets!" Nina left again, this time slamming the door shut. The force knocked a picture of the teens' father, Wiz, to the floor. It landed with a soft thud atop a pile of dirty clothes. Wiz was doing a twenty-five-to-life sentence for at least one murder that was on file. He had already served fifteen years.

"I guess we both know why she wildin' this morning?" Malik asked his brother.

"Yeah, I know," Marquis, who was seventeen, responded, looking up at the ceiling.

The boys knew that Nina acted like that whenever she needed a fix. Nina still thought they didn't know about her drug habit. The boys would talk to each other about it, but had never mentioned it to their mother.

"I don't know why she always screaming on me," Malik complained.

"She aight Malik, man. You know how she get sometimes," Marquis replied.

"Mark, please! She really got a lot of shit with her, telling me I better not be slinging dope. If I was hittin' her off with a bag or two, I bet she would be good with me selling."

Marquis thought about that and sat up.

"Malik, man, come on! That was foul, and you know it."

"As foul as it may sound, you know I'm telling the truth."

Marquis just shook his head and lay back on the bed.

"I'm really starting to get tired of this shit. And the fucked up thing 'bout it is she think we don't know she getting high, like we stupid or some shit. How do you think I feel when I'm huggin' the block and niggas be coming up to me like, 'Yo, ya moms just copped from me'? That shit burns me the fuck up!" Malik stood and stretched.

"Don't say that, Malik! Man, that's still our moms." Marquis came to his mother's defense. "She worked hard to raise us by herself. We need to respect that. I mean, yeah, I wish she wasn't getting high. But at least she ain't like them other skeezers out there, selling they bodies and shit. And she don't look like the rest of the skanks walking around, all skin and bones."

Malik gave Marquis the screw face. "You stupid as hell. She got you brainwashed. I ain't gonna let her continue to beat me over the head with the I-worked-hard-to-raise-y'all-by-myself bullshit. Pops left her in good hands before he went to the pen. She chose to do what she do, and struggle doing it."

"Yeah, but she still had to do it by herself," Marquis reiterated.

"Mommy is a fiend. When was the last time you looked at her real good? Her shit is starting to sag. Her nose is getting fucked up on the inside. All she doing is hiding behind a fake mask. But, trust, that shit is gonna come out sooner or later," Malik warned before walking out of the bedroom toward the bathroom.

The boys were right about the reason for Nina's behavior. She was in need of her morning dose of heroin. She was waiting for the dope man to hit the block so she could cop before going to work. She could see from her third-floor apartment window, and he still hadn't shown up yet. She would not be able to go to work if she didn't get her dope. When she didn't get it, she was a beast. She didn't notice her steadily changing behavior, though. Most junkies didn't.

Since running into Death, it reminded her of why she feared him. The secret that she had held for over eighteen years still ate away at her insides. Drugs seemed to be a way to escape the nightmares and thoughts of the past. First she had started snorting cocaine, then the mellow high of heroin, and once she met Jackie she had started smoking crack. The dope high helped her to sleep, but since witnessing the cruel way BJ had lost his life, she upped her intake of heroin. Her urge for the drug was stronger, and it didn't take much to piss her off.

Nina picked up the ringing phone as she walked into the kitchen. The clock on the wall read six forty-five AM.

"What?" she yelled into the phone, thinking it was one of the many fast girls that called the house for the boys.

"Damn, Nina, what the hell is ya problem this early in the morning?" Jackie asked.

"I swear to God, I don't know what is wrong with my sons. I bust my ass every day, working to keep a roof over their heads and food in this bitch. And all I ask them to do is keep their room clean. I'm 41 years old and I don't need this shit," Nina vented.

"Girl, you preaching to the choir. You know I feel you. I told you to start putting your foot in they asses! Girl, you raising niggas without a father. You got to be as hard as a nigga to raise a nigga," Jackie schooled.

"Yeah, I guess you're right," Nina agreed.

"So you *are* coming to work today, right?" Jackie sounded suspicious.

In fact, Jackie had been suspicious of Nina for the past two weeks. Nina had not come over to her place to smoke with her since that brutal day. Outside of work, they had not spent any time together. Whenever Jackie would call her, Nina simply told her she didn't feel like coming out. Jackie began to think that Nina was smoking crack without her. Nina's behavior made Jackie's fiendish mind jealous.

Jackie was a selfish addict. If she thought that Nina was getting high without her, she would play Nina close all day. She would go so far as to spend the night at Nina's house, just to make sure that if Nina did cop something, she was gonna get a hit of it. What Jackie didn't know was that Nina was not smoking with anyone, or even by herself for that matter. Nina was only using heroin, so there was no need to go to Jackie's house. Nina never told Jackie what had happened that day with BJ.

Jackie was stone broke and couldn't wait until payday. She knew that Nina always had money stashed, and eventually Nina would treat her to a get high. Nina was not a selfish addict and would share with Jackie openly. Even in times when Nina could just cop from her side of town and go home to use, she wouldn't. She would catch the bus to Jackie's and share her wealth with her. This was why Jackie knew something wasn't right with her.

"I don't know if I'm coming to work," Nina whispered, not wanting the boys to hear. "If I don't get me some diesel, and I mean quick, I ain't gonna be able to get off the floor."

"So you ain't gonna get no coke with that?"

"Jackie, how you sound? I don't want no crack. I need the dope." Nina's voice was shaky.

"Sick, huh?" Jackie noticed. She knew all too well the effects that heroin had on a person. She'd watched Nina many a time when she tried to kick, and knew how sick she would be from it.

"Come on, Jackie, don't play yaself. You know the deal. The pain is kicking my ass right now. I just need a bag to get me through the day."

"Who you think you talking to, Nina? You know damn well a bag ain't gonna do shit for you."

"Bullshit!" she whispered. "I ain't hooked like that, Jackie. All I need is a bag a day. I just choose to use more. Really, I could go with a bag every other day," Nina bragged, clearly in denial of her addiction.

"And my name ain't Boo-Boo the Fool, Nina. You ain't *been* on a bag-a-day habit in years. I'm with you just about every day, and last I saw, you got at least a three-bag-a-day habit, and it's getting worse. So don't blow smoke up my ass. You hooked, and you know it. Just like me. I know I need cook up every day. I ain't gonna play myself by saying I don't, because I love to get high."

"Well, regardless of what you think, Jackie, I can kick this thing anytime I want. I've done it in the past. And let's get it straight: You and me are two different people."

"Yes, we are, and let me set *you* straight. You still getting high, and downplaying the situation ain't gonna change that." And with that, Jackie hung up.

Nina sucked her teeth at Jackie's comments as she hung up the phone. *Who does she think she is? As much coke as she smokes, I know she ain't talking 'bout me*, Nina thought.

The pain in Nina's legs and stomach was becoming unbearable, and the sour taste in her mouth had her stomach turning. She had gone cold turkey several times in the past, but it was never this bad. And to think, her last bag was last night around eleven.

Nina could feel the burning sensation in the back of her throat as the acid from her stomach traveled up her esophagus, even as saliva filled her mouth. Running to the bathroom was not an option at this point. She leaned over the kitchen garbage can and vomited into it. When she was done she straightened, grabbed a paper towel off the counter, and wiped her mouth. Her head started to spin and her body was weak. Malik stood in the doorway of the kitchen, staring at her.

Nina stared back at him. "Whatchu looking at?" she asked.

"Why don't you go get some help?" he finally asked.

"Help from what, Malik?" She frowned in confusion.

"Come on, Ma." Contempt shone in his eyes.

"'Come on, Ma', what?" she yelled.

"Nothing." Malik rolled his eyes before he walked away.

Nina turned to look out of the kitchen window and she saw the person she'd been waiting for. He was standing on the corner talking with another man. Her stomach began to do flip-flops. Nina rushed into her room and threw on her house slippers before dashing out the front door.

Malik watched her run out the door. He walked into the kitchen and looked out the window. He saw his mother dash across the busy street, dipping in and out of traffic, not realizing that she could have been hit by one of the speeding cars. To his amazement, Nina was in her housecoat and slippers with a headscarf tied around her head, heading over to the dope man's car to purchase.

All who knew Nina knew she wasn't the type of chick to be caught dead in anything less than perfect attire. That day was the first time Malik had ever seen his mother look the way that she did, let alone leave the house looking like that.

"Yo, ya mother is losing it," Malik said as he walked back into the bedroom, pissed.

"What are you talking about?"

"I'm talking 'bout how your mother is out there on the block right now in her bra and panties."

"Huh?" Marquis was perplexed.

"Mark, go to the kitchen window and see for yaself if you don't believe me. She out there coppin' dope as we speak! Man, I know niggas gon' be in my shit for this." Malik shook his head in exasperation.

Marquis reluctantly walked out of the bedroom and toward the kitchen just as Nina came bolting through the front door. She had a look of desperation in her eyes. A layer of sweat coated her neck, and her breathing was short but hard. She was so focused on her mission that she blew right past Marquis, not even acknowledging him standing there. She practically ran into her room and slammed the door.

Malik was right, and Marquis couldn't believe his eyes. *She would have never gone outside like that before,* he thought.

Marquis returned to their room to look over the college classes that he wanted to take in the fall. He had plans to go down to the college that morning to register. He had contemplated taking some summer courses just to get a jump on the four-year college term he was facing. He was also going to run downtown to apply for a job at Dr. Jay's, the sports store near the school. But now his thoughts were focused on his mother and it was only going to get worse.

Chapter Five

"Yo, Malik, ain't that ya brother right there?" Justice asked as he pointed to Marquis, who was walking up the street.

Malik leaned forward and looked where Justice was pointing.

"Yeah, that's him." He leaned back onto the building, trying to stay in the shade while surveying the area.

The weather was hot and sticky. Kids ran up and down the busy street. School was out for the summer, and every kid took advantage of that. The corner store had air conditioning, but the store didn't seem to stay cold because the door opened so frequently.

"College boy!" Justice yelled to Marquis.

A smirk appeared on Marquis's face as he approached the crowded corner.

"What up, y'all?" He walked past Justice and slapped hands with the other crewmembers, then gave Justice some dap. Marquis didn't care too much for Justice, but tolerated him because of his brother.

"Yo, college boy! What's up, man?" Justice asked again, seeming to want all the attention.

Marquis just threw up his head with a sarcastic smirk on his face. It was funny to him how the fake, wannabe hustlers were the loudest ones on the block. In reality, they were just "yes" boys. They all had to answer to somebody and Marquis knew better. He was more educated in the game and had more heart than any dealer that was out there on the block, because he was an observer. He educated himself by watching and listening while growing up. But the street corners weren't in his plans. He had a better hustle, and that was going to college.

"What's good, man?" Jeff asked.

"I'm good, B," Marquis replied.

"Yeah, you a college boy now. I hear you, man. Go get that education so you can be a doctor. We need a doctor in the hood to take care of these niggas that's gettin' popped." Justice laughed and revealed the butt of the .44 he had in his waistband.

"Hell, yeah! Word!" several of the other cats standing out there chimed in.

Marquis laughed sarcastically. "Yeah, I feel you." He decided not to waste his time correcting them and explaining that he wasn't attending college to be a doctor. He wasn't big on telling his business, and he felt that the less someone knew about him, the better off he would be.

"But frankly, I prefer gettin' money this way," Justice said, pulling a grip from his pocket and showing it to Marquis.

"Yeah, I see you." Marquis nodded while laughing to himself. He thought that Justice was ignorant and Malik was stupid for getting caught up in the hype of it all, especially following the lead of a loudmouth like Justice.

Justice ran the four corners, and Malik worked for him. Justice had his crew thinking that he bought weight from Death himself and was doing big things. But in reality, Justice only worked for Death. He talked loud and bragged even louder, which left a sour taste in the mouths of most people with whom he came in contact.

Justice recruited some of the cats from the neighborhood to sell his work so that he could sit back and collect the dough. Death didn't care what Justice did, as long as he had his bread by the end of the package. Each runner made twenty dollars on every bundle sold, which consisted of ten bags of capsules. There were three runners selling for Justice. The younger boys made twenty dollars for the day as lookouts.

Death had the best product out there, and each of his crew members was in competition with each other. They all tried to outsell each other, running up to cars to get the sale first—all except Malik. He made sales from where he stood in front of the store. He refused to chase cars for the sale.

An old Ford pickup truck, loaded with junk, backfired as it drove by the corner on which the boys stood. Most of those in the area ducked when they heard the noise, mistaking the exhaust pipes for gunshots. Marquis shook his head at the mistake.

A kid named Money burst into laughter after seeing some of the crew members' reactions to the loud noise.

"Ay-yo, y'all niggas some punks! Y'all check your pants for shit stains," he teased. They all clowned each other while Marquis looked at Malik and gestured with his head in a direction away from the group.

"I'll be back," Malik told his crew. He followed Marquis away from the group to a spot where they couldn't be overheard. "What's up, little bruh?"

"I just registered for some classes for the summer."

"That's what's up, baby bruh! Did I ever tell you I'm proud of you?"

"Yeah, all the time." Marquis smiled. "Man, why you be with that nigga Jus?"

"I don't be with that clown." Malik looked back at the corner where Justice and the rest stood, still clowning each other. "I'm just tryna get a little loot. I got something in the works right now, anyway." Malik wasn't feeling Justice, but his boys made bread with him, so he jumped on board. Malik actually had a plan of his own and needed to use Justice to bring it to fruition. He had to do what he needed to do to get what he wanted to get, even if that meant dealing with Justice and his braggadocio ways.

"Real talk, you don't need to be in that niggas shadow! You can do your own thing. If huggin' the blocks is ya thing, then cool. But at least be ya own man," Marquis advised.

Ain't this some shit, Malik thought as he chuckled at his brother, *the little brother telling the big brother what to do.*

"You just finish college and let me worry about the block." Malik draped his arm over his brother's shoulder.

Marquis may have been the younger brother, but he was definitely the bigger brother in size. He was six feet three, two inches taller than Malik. They had gotten their height from their father.

"Check this out. If this is something you have to do, then I feel you. Get ya hustle on. But at least do you and step off from this clown. I heard y'all's stash got robbed and Death was coming for y'all's heads," Marquis said.

Malik laughed. "Who told you that shit?"

"Don't matter who told me. You just watch yo' back. Coward-ass niggas like Justice will flip the script, and the next thing you know, you'll be the one taking the fall for the team." Marquis was serious.

"Naw, man, that shit ain't gonna never happen like that. I'm always one step ahead of that punk-ass nigga. Death claimed he already knew who lifted the stash, and that the next time that shit happened, then he was coming through dumpin'. But trust, baby bruh, it's just a matter of time, and I'ma be out," Malik assured him.

"A'ight. Do you, Malik," Marquis stated.

Malik hated that he had to take his orders from Justice, but it was necessary in order for him to follow through on his plans. Justice was weak and didn't know how to run a team. There was no team player concept with his crew, because it was a dog-eat-dog world out there. The money that they made varied, and some days they didn't make much. Malik didn't like how it went down because Jeff and Brian, his fellow crew members, were his best friends, and the situation out there on the blocks often played them against each other.

Marquis worried about his brother day and night. Several cats they'd gone to school with had already lost their lives to the streets. The very same dudes that Malik ran with had already been to jail at least once. He hated that his brother dropped out of school, only to stand on the corners and sell the very same drug of which their mother was a victim. He wanted so much more for his brother because he had always looked up to Malik. Malik had always taken care of him since their father wasn't around.

Marquis always talked to Malik about changing his life.

"Malik man, why don't you just at least try to go back to school? It's never to late."

"School? And be in what grade Mark, tenth? Come on man that's over. I ain't going back to school."

"Come on, you can go to night school. They have classes to take the GED exam. I'm saying you at least need to get your diploma," Marquis reasoned.

"Diploma? I don't need no diploma for what I'm doing."

"No but you need a diploma to go to college, Malik. Man we can be in college together and do something no one in this family has done. You and me a team."

"I ain't going to college. Yo, where is all this coming from all of a sudden?" Malik was curious.

"Because you ain't gonna get no where out here on the streets but dead or *in jail man. And I don't want either for you." Marquis was serious.*

"Psst, now you sound like your mother. I told you she got you brainwashed." He pointed at Marquis.

"Our mother don't have to tell me what you and I already know. What about all them cats that you idolized?"

"What about them?" Malik asked nonchalantly.

"Where are they now? You see what happened to them right? Times ain't like they used to be and ain't no life in the life you tryna live big bruh. Fast money leads to the end of your life fast."

"You sound like a TV commercial. Go 'head with the 'drugs are bad for you' bullshit." Malik waved his hand at Marquis.

Disappointed, Marquis decided to hit Malik where he knew it would hurt. "You just like Wiz and you see where Wiz is right now. He was out here tryna play king pin, but that ain't hold no weight and now he sitting behind bars doing life." Marquis waited to see his reaction.

Malik looked at him with death piercing eyes and then suddenly he smiled.

"I ain't nothing like that coward ass nigga. The difference between me and him is, he got caught. That ain't gonna never happen to me because I gotta plan that's gonna change the game forever!"

Malik was also a hothead, and it didn't take much to get him going. He had no love for their father Wiz either. Sometimes Marquis felt that maybe Malik was hurt because he felt their father abandoned them, and their mother got high off drugs because she didn't know how to handle any pressure. Little did he know that Malik was quickly building a secret hatred for the woman who brought him into this world. He was more concerned about the street rep he was trying to build for himself than loving his mother.

Marquis was totally different from his older brother. He was a good student and had goals he wanted to reach in life. He was street smart as well as book smart. He was very observant, and he analyzed a situation before he reacted to it. He was a thinker and very mature for his age. Marquis was the total package, and he was Nina's favorite. She always spoiled him and protected him more than Malik. Although both boys had the same father, Malik was the spitting image of Wiz. Seeing him always reminded Nina of when Wiz left her to take care of the boys alone.

Unfortunately for Malik, this made Nina treat him differently. As a result, Malik dropped out of high school at age sixteen, and strayed farther into the street life, looking for the love he didn't get from his mother.

HOURS LATER . . .

Kurt the Conductor was walking up the middle of the street. You could hear him a mile away, pulling his convoy of grocery store carriages. He had three carts tied together with extension cords. In the first cart he had aluminum, steel bars, and panels. In the second carriage, he had an old air conditioner with other aluminum parts, and in the third carriage, which he called the caboose, he had everything that he owned. There was an overcoat, a blanket, a pair of old rubber rain boots, newspapers, and other trinkets.

"*Woo-woo!*" he recited, sounding like a real locomotive. "The express is coming through! *Woo-woo!*" He did that all day while he hauled junk. Everyone knew Kurt. He'd collected junk in the neighborhood for as long as most could remember. He hauled more junk to the junkyard than the yard received from any other customer in a week. He had a rapport with the junkyard owner, and when times were really bad, Kurt could go down to the junkyard and get an advance up front. The owner knew that Kurt would come through to make up for the money he'd been given.

Kurt was a master of many things. He had the brains of a genius, but lacked willpower and drive. Kurt liked quick chump change because he liked to say that pennies added up too. Kurt could—and would—fix anything for pennies. If it was broken, you paid Kurt a few dollars and he'd fix it. He was good with his hands. In the winter he shoveled snow. In the spring, he swept and washed windows. In the summer, he did everything. And in the fall, he raked leaves.

Kurt was homeless and an addict of many things—meaning, whatever he could get his hands on for a high, he used it. Kurt had even removed the Freon from the air conditioner and inhaled it to get high before he loaded the air conditioner into the carriage.

"Fellas! What's up?" Kurt asked as he parked his train next to the curb where Justice and his crew stood. He looked and smelled exceptionally funky that day. Not that he didn't smell most days, but that day he seemed to reek extra foul.

"What up, Kurt?" Justice and some of the crew members asked.

"What y'all fellas holding out here today?"

"We got that murder dope, and that freeze-rock," Brian told Kurt.

"Yeah? Who gon' let me get something on credit? It don't matter which one of y'all young gunners step up first."

The four boys looked at him like he stole something, and then burst into laughter, all except Justice.

"Man, you better go 'head with the bullshit, Kurt!" Jeff said. "Ain't nobody got time to be fucking around with your foul-smelling ass today, as hot as it is out this motherfucker." Jeff walked away, fanning his face in an attempt to escape the smell.

"Heeey, come on, fellas," Kurt sang. "I got a shitload of work I'm taking down to the pound now. You know I'm good for the bread. I'll hit you on my way back."

"Conductor, how you sound? I'll tell you: Like a fuckin' fool if you crazy enough to think we gon' let you hold something until you get back," Justice finally said. "Raise up, man."

"Aw, so y'all gon' do me like that? As much loot as I done spent with y'all? I thought y'all was my peoples! I see how y'all do ya peoples." Kurt walked back over to his train, complaining all the while.

Malik walked out of the corner store. As soon as he stepped onto the sidewalk, he got a whiff of Kurt's odor, which still lingered in the air like fog.

"Damn, Kurt!" Malik exclaimed. He pinched his nose to block the vulgar smell.

"Malik, my man! What's up? Let me hold something till I get back?" Kurt pleaded.

"Man, I told you to raise up!" Justice snapped.

"Yo, man. Chill. I owe him a little something," Malik lied. "I got this."

"Yeah, right." Justice wasn't convinced. "I don't know why you keep fucking with that bum-ass nigga, but if you pass off to him, that shit's coming outta your pocket."

"Chill, man! Damn!"

Malik actually didn't owe Kurt anything. He knew Kurt through his mother. Kurt was nice to him and his brother while they were growing up, and he had always looked out for them. While the other teens clowned Kurt, Malik saw past the filth and the odor. He actually had many conversations with Kurt. The older man gave Malik great advice and knew about anything Malik wanted to talk about. Malik repaid the favor by taking up for him in times of need, and this was definitely a time of need. It wouldn't be the first time that Malik had to take a loss of twenty to forty dollars here and there. For Kurt, he didn't mind. Malik guided him away from the corner for privacy.

"You need a bath bad, man," Malik told him.

"Yeah, I know. What's up? You got something I can hold till I drop off this shit?"

"Yeah. Here, man." He handed a glassine envelope to Kurt.

"That's why I fucks with you! My man!"

"Yo, you better chill out, askin' these cats to let you hold something, because the first time you don't pass off, they gonna kill ya ass," Malik warned him.

"I'm good for it, though. You know me. If I don't come back with the money today, you know I will get it to you tomorrow."

"Man, Kurt, you can't play that shit with these cats! I'm telling you."

Malik looked at Kurt. He definitely could see the hard life lines that were deeply embedded in his face. Each line probably told a story of his past, and how he ended up the way he did. Kurt was good friend of his fathers. Kurt always talked with him and Marquis watching out for them. Malik begged Kurt in the past to let him help clean him up so that he could live a better life, because Malik saw what Kurt could be capable of, and it was much more than being a junkie. He didn't understand that Kurt liked the life he lived. He didn't have a bill to pay, and he got food from the food bank and churches whenever he was hungry. He worked around the neighborhood, doing odd jobs and transporting junk, and got paid for it. He felt this was a better life than going through the everyday hassles of finding a job, and then trying to keep the job, trying to pay the rent, and pay all the other bills. He preferred to spend his money on drugs instead. Kurt loved to get high, and he couldn't work a nine-to-five gig while he got high. It was just like water and oil—the two just didn't mix.

Malik turned his head while Kurt opened the package of heroin and snorted it in one stroke with no concern of his surroundings or who might be watching. Malik had never watched Kurt snort, because he always thought about his mother, and it made him weak. Malik couldn't stand the idea of his own mother being addicted to heroin, but he had no problem selling it to anyone else. It was just the life of the streets.

"Oooooh!" Kurt grunted and snuffled, sounding like a pig. "Yeah, boy, that's that shit right there! Good lookin' out!" He licked the remaining residue from the envelope. "*Woo-woo!* All Aboard!" *Sniff.* "*Woo-woo!*" Kurt chanted his usual chant as he walked away from Malik. He got his train going and chanted all the way down the street.

Kurt was like a godfather to Marquis and Malik. He made a promise to Wiz just before he got locked up that if anything ever happened to Wiz that he would take care of Nina, Marquis and Malik. Little did Malik know Kurt had more pull on the streets then he revealed to him.

Chapter Six

Nina walked into the apartment and plopped down onto the couch. She had a rough day at work. She worked in downtown Newark in the Gateway Building and had to run out for lunch to buy a bag of dope from one of the dealers on Broad Street. She barely made it through the day anymore as her addiction got the best of her. She was fighting the urge hard, even at that very moment. Jackie didn't speak to her all day at work, and it bothered her. She thought about what Jackie said and decided to prove her wrong. Nina knew she could quit if she wanted to, and she decided on her way home from work, while riding the bus, that she was gonna do just that. But the last bag of dope she snorted had been at lunchtime, and she was already ready for another.

She'd bought two bags that morning and snorted one before work. She snorted the second when she got to work, and the third that she had purchased at lunchtime. She opened her wallet and looked inside. She was down to her last sixty dollars, and it was only Tuesday. She thought about how if she had only paid fifty dollars on the light bill instead of the total sixty-five dollars that was actually due, she would have had an extra fifteen dollars to spare.

Nina shook her head, trying to clear the thoughts of even considering purchasing more drugs. Her check for the week was gonna be short a day because she didn't go to work on Friday, like she didn't most weeks. She would just go in on Saturday sometimes to make up for the day missed. It was getting harder and harder for her to maintain her job. Just yesterday she had been called into her supervisor's office and put on probation for too many days missed from work. She had exhausted all of her sick and vacation days for the year. Nina kept telling herself that she could handle getting high and working. After all, she'd done it for years and managed to maintain. She didn't—or wouldn't—realize that she was starting to lose the grip she thought she had on her addiction.

Marquis walked out of his bedroom and saw his mother sitting on the sofa. He noticed that she didn't look well.

"What's up, Ma?" He sat down next to her.

"Hey, baby." She rubbed his leg. "Did you go register for classes yet?"

"Yeah, I'm all set. I went and put in an application with Dr. Jay's downtown, and they hired me on the spot too. So I can help you out around here."

"That's good. You're a good son." She smiled and rubbed his face.

There was an awkward silence as they sat there.

"Ma, can I ask you something?" Marquis asked, breaking the silence.

"Of course you can."

Nina stared at her son, admiring his facial features. He was growing into a handsome adult. He was taller than she'd expected him to be. He was lean with muscular arms and legs due to the many hours he played basketball. He kept his hair cut low, which showed off his waves. He had the same perfect, pointy nose like hers, and the whitest set of teeth she had ever seen. A thin mustache graced his top lip.

"Ma, you know I love you, right?"

Nina shot him a sideways glance. "What are you up to, boy?"

"Nothing, Ma, just listen." Marquis cleared his throat as he prepared himself to say what has been on his mind lately. "Well . . . Ma, I know you are using," he blurted, not knowing what was going to happen next.

Nina just sat there and stared at him in shock. She really didn't think that he knew. She knew her boys weren't that naïve, especially Malik, but she thought she had been extra careful.

"What are you talking about?"

"I'm talking about the drugs, Ma. I know you are doing drugs. I've known for a long time."

"Yeah, OK. So what are you thinking?"

"I'm thinking that I don't like it. I've never liked it, and I don't understand why you do it. But—" He stopped her from interrupting him with a gesture of his hand. "I know you've had it rough raising us. You know I love you for you, no matter what. But I can't help but see how it is starting to get the best of you."

Nina kept her gaze on Marquis, whereas he couldn't keep eye contact with her. She loved him so much, and she could see how it was hurting him to even speak about the subject. It also made her proud of him to come to her and speak about it. It showed his maturity, as well as his genuine love for her.

"Son, you have no idea what I've gone through to raise you and your brother alone. I've sacrificed so much, and no matter what anyone tells you, they will never understand why I do what I do. Most people who don't understand will do nothing but judge. You can't judge me unless you walked in my shoes. I'm saying all that to say that yes, I use occasionally." She grabbed his hand and held it.

There it was again. She was manipulating him with the I-raised-y'all-by-myself speech that Malik hated.

"Ma, me and Malik are old enough to help you now. You don't have to struggle anymore."

"Yes, you're both old enough. However, you're going to start college and all I want you to do is finish school. Don't worry about me. I don't want you to have to worry about getting a job to help me. Get that job to help yourself. I can take care of me. As for your brother, he is a waste. He is gonna die right out there in them streets. I have already accepted that."

"Don't say that, Ma! He is your son too, and he loves you just as much as I love you. He cares about what happens to you too. True, he may express his love differently, but maybe if you look at the message instead of the delivery, you can see that. I think if we help him to find another way, he can succeed too," Marquis said with sadness in his heart.

"Come here, son." Nina pulled him into her arms just as she used to when he was much younger.

"Malik is hardheaded, and I've done all I can do for him. He just turned nineteen and he thinks he's grown. He's out there on them streets selling drugs, and he thinks I don't know. The same drugs that I use from time to time," she said, being careful not to let on just how much she used.

"Y'all's father was of the streets, and it landed him life in jail. When I look at your brother, all I see is your father. He looks like Wiz, acts like Wiz, and is even starting to sound like Wiz; therefore, in my mind, he *is* Wiz. He is heading nowhere fast, and I can't concern myself with that, because my heart will be torn apart, just the way it was when your father did what he did to me."

Marquis lifted his head from his mother's shoulder. "Ma, so you punishing Malik for what our father did to you?"

"What? No. What are you talking about?"

"By the way you talking, you saying that because Malik reminds you of our father, and our father hurt you, that you giving up on him. That's what it sounds like to me."

"Well, that's not what I'm saying."

"I mean, I know our father sold drugs, but what did he do so bad to you that you despise him like you do?" Marquis was serious.

Nina had never talked to the boys about their father and the relationship they had. She had never told them how their father was her first love. There were a lot of things in her past that the boys didn't know about, and she preferred to keep it that way. The secrets that lay in her past were buried deep within her, and she refused to bring them out for them. These deep, dark secrets were keeping her in the state she was in.

"Nothing that you should even worry about," Nina commented.

"Naw, Ma, I'm not taking that for an answer. I have a right to know what happened to you and my father. Why are you keeping it from us?"

"I've kept that part of my life from y'all because you didn't need to know about it. I was trying to protect y'all. Your father left me high and dry to defend y'all, and raise y'all on my own."

"Ma, he's in prison! It wasn't like he did it on purpose. I heard he left you with a grip before he got locked up." Marquis tried to defend his father. He had heard the story from Kurt. In the streets his father was labeled a legend for his time. Deep down inside, Marquis was proud of that, although that wasn't the life he wanted to live. Maybe that was why his mother fought against Malik so much, because she thought that Malik was trying to follow in their father's footsteps.

"Who told you that?" She frowned at him.

"Kurt."

Nina was pissed. "Kurt needs to mind his damn business and keep his mouth shut," she snapped. "Wiz didn't leave me much, and the little that was there when he went to prison wasn't enough to raise y'all up to the ages you are now."

Wiz had actually left over $300,000 in the safe in their condo. Instead of budgeting the money, Nina continued to live the lifestyle she had grown accustomed to, along with getting high. She blew through the money as if there wasn't a bottom to the safe.

"I tried to talk to him about the people he kept close to him. I didn't trust none of them, and sure enough, they turned on his ass. So to me, he walked out on his family, and I cannot forgive him for that."

"Just to let you know, I'm gonna try to get in touch with him." Marquis closed his eyes and waited for the explosion.

"Why?" Nina asked, shocked.

"Because he is my father, and I want to see him. I would do it for you too, Ma. You never took us to go see him when we used to ask you. So, now I'm older and I can do it myself."

"Well, you do what you feel you need to do. I don't want to know shit about it."

"Why you never took us to go see him Ma?"

"For what? Wiz left me with y'all to fend for y'all. There was no need to go see him. He made the choices he made knowing that it could end up the way that it did. But he wouldn't listen to me so no, I didn't take y'all."

"Ok so that explains why *you* didn't want to see him, but that doesn't explain why me and Malik couldn't see him." He grabbed her hand. "I remember you told me one time that you missed your father and wished he was in your life."

"Mark, my father died when I was a young girl in the army," she interrupted him. "He didn't do anything stupid to get himself killed or jailed!" Nina was growing irritated by Marquis's questions.

Marquis stood to his feet also growing irritated with the conversation. "So grandma couldn't take us or someone else from the family? I mean we don't even know our father side of the family."

"Mark, those people never liked me and trust me the feelings where mutual. It was Ok with me. But when your father went to prison not one of them would help me and they knew y'all where small children. So to hell with all them, Wiz included! I'm done with the whole conversation." She stood and left the room, leaving Marquis standing there, dumbfounded.

Marquis couldn't believe his ears. Why was his mother so bitter toward his father? What was she holding on to from the past that she couldn't tell him about now that he was older? It was obvious there is more to it then just Wiz going to prison. Maybe his father would be able to tell him. He was going to try to get in touch with his father because there were so many unanswered questions. Also, at this point, he wanted his father in his life. If that meant that Marquis would have to visit him in prison to get to know him, then he would.

Chapter Seven

It was three thirty AM and Nina found herself tossing and turning in her bed. She was determined not to go out and get a bag of dope. She wanted to overcome the urge to use, but there was a nagging desire digging into the pit of her stomach. She sat up in bed and wiped a massive amount of sweat from her face. Her neck was soaked, as well as her T-shirt. Her body ached something terrible not to mention the migraine she had. She felt like she was going to vomit and shit at the same time. Her hands shook and her skin felt clammy and cold.

"Fuck this," she said aloud as she jumped from the bed.

She went to her closet and pulled on a pair of jeans and a shirt, which read, "It Can't Get No Better Than Me." She slipped into her white, three-inch sling-back sandals, and she went over to her dresser and looked in the mirror. Her hair had sweated out and looked a hot mess all over her head. She combed it back into a very neat ponytail. She examined her nose and pulled the shedding skin that hung from it. She left her bedroom and tiptoed down the hall, trying to avoid waking the boys, whom she thought were asleep by now. She carefully grabbed her keys, which sat on a small table by the door. She opened the door quietly and stepped into the hallway. Once outside, she began her search for the heroin she so desperately needed.

She walked down the street with her usual confidence, her shapely hips swinging from side to side. She held her head up high as if she was Miss America taking that walk after just winning the pageant. But at that time of night, cars honked at her, thinking she was a streetwalker.

As she approached the corner where she usually copped her stuff, she noticed that her dealer wasn't there. In fact, none of the usual boys were out that night, which was unusual. A couple of the drunks passed a bottle of poison back and forth and stared, awestruck, at Nina as she approached the corner.

"Hey, lady," one of the men said.

"Hey. Anybody holding out here?" she asked.

"What you looking for?"

"I want to get a couple of bags." Nina looked around.

"Why you put that junk in ya body? You such a pretty lady, and you gon' mess your body up, fucking with that poison," another drunk said.

Nina just sucked her teeth at the man. He had some nerve to tell her about her drug use when he was obviously an alcoholic.

"Yes, you too pretty for that. Hey, ain't you my man's . . ." He snapped his fingers, as if he was trying to think of something. "You know that young boy . . . my man . . . what is his name?" He turned to one of the other men. "He be with Justice," he clarified.

"Oh, yeah, I know who you talking 'bout. His name is Malik," the second drunk chimed in.

"Yeah, that's it! Ain't you Malik's mother?"

Nina didn't answer. She simply walked away from the men. They didn't have what she wanted, and she saw no use standing there, holding an irrelevant conversation with them. Her mind was on one thing, and that was getting some heroin.

She walked down the partially deserted street, asking anyone that she came in contact with if they had any drugs. Disappointment was starting to settle in. The thought of not getting what she needed to calm the savage beast within was becoming inevitable, and Nina began to feel sick. She stepped off the curb to cross the street. A navy blue Benz stopped short, almost hitting her. Nina was so preoccupied with figuring out where she was going to cop some drugs that she failed to look before crossing the street, and stepped out in front of the fashionable car.

She stepped back to let the car pass, not recognizing the car because of her disoriented state. The driver allowed the car to roll up to her and stop. The car windows were heavily tinted. The back window lowered and a cloud of smoke escaped the car. The strong smell of weed assaulted her nose. A man leaned forward and the streetlights exposed his face.

Nina gasped when she realized it was Death. He looked her up and down, undressing her with his eyes.

"What's up, Nina?"

"Hey," she said, barely above a whisper.

She had managed to avoid running into him since the incident three weeks prior. She had been looking over her shoulder ever since. She hated that the past would always haunt her as long as he was alive, and she often thought about having him killed. She never forgot that day when he told her that she owed him. She knew then that one day he was going to come for her to pay up, but she just didn't know when.

"You looking for this?" He held up an envelope of dope and smiled his perfect smile.

Chill bumps invaded her entire body when she saw the package. Nina knew the dope was good because Death had the city on lock with the potent drug. She stared at the package as if in a trance.

"You want it?" he asked her again, breaking her out of her zone. He waved the bag back and forth to get her attention.

"I need two," she said in a raspy voice. Her mouth was like a bale of cotton, and she couldn't swallow.

He pulled his hand back into the window and brought it back out again, exposing two bags of dope. Nina simply dug her hands down into the front pocket of her tight jeans and pulled out a twenty-dollar bill. She handed Death the money and he took it, but pulled the hand that held the drugs back a little. He laughed when she tried to reach for it and missed. Nina's hands were shaking so badly at this point that she would have dove headfirst into the car just to get her hands on the drugs. Death played with her like this two more times before he finally handed the drugs to her.

Nina turned on her heels and took quick steps to make it back to her apartment building three long blocks away, leaving the Benz sitting in the middle of the street. She could hear Death's sick laughter fading behind her. Her shoes sounded like trotting horses as her heels hit the pavement in quick steps. Gas was quickly building in her stomach and Nina farted with each step as she rushed to make it to her apartment. She ran into the four-story building and took the steps two at a time to her third-floor apartment.

The Benz continued to cruise up the street at a slow crawl. Death turned to the passenger who sat beside him in the car.

"So what you're telling me is that you think you're good enough to have your own blocks?" Death asked Malik.

"No doubt. I'm that nigga," Malik said with confidence.

"You that nigga, huh?" Death laughed. "Naw, kid, *I'm* that nigga. You feel me?" He looked at Malik with serious eyes.

"Oh, no doubt. But dig. What I'm tryna tell you is that some of these little niggas you got out there have no clue how to run ya business. They don't have no respect for the customers. I've watched them niggas run away a lot of sales because of the disrespect. I mean, addicts are people too. Am I right?" Malik spit game.

"Yeah, I feel you. They are the customer, and good customer service should be displayed." Death sounded like a manager of a corporation.

"I'll tell you this. Keep doing what you doing with that kid Justice. Put in some serious work, get your feet wet. You know what I mean? I know Nina's your mother, but I ain't gonna show you no favoritism. So let me see what you workin' with, and come see me in about a month. I may break you off something."

"A'ight, Death, but this conversation never happened between us. Cool?"

"That's a bet," Death said, giving him a pound.

The Benz pulled over to the curb and Malik hopped out of the car. He stepped back and watched the piece of fine art drive away, then walked home, deep in thought. It pissed him off the way Death clowned his mother. Not to mention how she had displayed her fiendish ways. *It's only a matter of time before she'll be just another victim among the walking dead of the night*, he thought.

Once Nina reached the third floor, she stopped right there and sat down on the steps. She tried to open one of the paper baggies carefully as her hands continued to shake uncontrollably. She didn't have the steadiness to even scoop up a portion with her manicured nail, like she did at times. That night she pinched one nostril shut and stuck her face into the envelope. She took a huge snort, almost inhaling all of the substance into the one nostril like Al Pacino in the movie *Scarface*.

When Nina raised her head, she had powder circling her nose. She pinched the other nostril closed and snorted the remaining dope. This time when she raised her head, she tilted her head back so that she could feel the drainage leaking down the back of her throat. It was as if the drug soothed her aches and pains immediately. The heroin was definitely high quality. Nina licked the remaining dust that sat on the envelope. She licked the tip of her finger and rubbed it across the tip of her nose to remove what heroin was there before sucking the residue from her finger. She wiped her nose with the back of her hand then wiped under her nose with her fingertips to remove any substance that was still visible inside her nostrils. She accidentally scratched a scab that had formed in her nose, and blood ran.

Nina never heard the footsteps that approached her floor until it was too late. She looked up and right into the eyes of Malik, who had been standing there the whole time, watching his mother snort dope.

Nina rubbed her nose, sniffing, and stood silently. Her eyes were glassy and her mouth was shaped like a smile turned upside down.

"I thought you was in the bed," she commented before walking down the hall to their apartment.

Malik followed her, not saying a word.

Chapter Eight

Nina sat in the break room at work. She was supposed to be reading the magazine that sat in front of her, but she was in a dope nod instead. Some of the other girls she worked with sat in the break room as well. They looked at Nina from time to time, nudging each other to look at her. Her head would sometimes get as close as one inch from the tabletop, but she never touched it. She would open her eyes, pull her head back up, and turn a page in the magazine, only to do the same thing again.

After her break, Nina went back to her desk and put on her headphones, ready to take the next incoming customer service call. She logged into her computer and waited for a call. When it came, she began her ritual of helping customers with their problems. Several times the customer hung up on her because she went into a nod while on the phone, which made them think she had hung up on them. Several other times Jackie woke her up from her nods by throwing paper clips at her from her station.

After several more minutes of this behavior Nina's supervisor, Mr. Wall, called her into his office.

"Nina, have a seat." He pointed to the chair directly in front of his desk.

She sat down and rubbed her hands together. She felt cold. Mr. Wall was an overweight man with a receding hairline. His pale face was in desperate need of some sun. His thick mustache seemed to grow up into his nostrils, and he breathed heavily because of his obesity.

"Nina, it has been brought to my attention that you have been very inattentive lately. You were seen sleeping at your desk, and we're starting to get complaints from customers about you hanging up on them—"

"I don't hang up on the customers, Mr. Wall," Nina interrupted him.

"Hold on now, Nina. Let me finish speaking, and then you can speak. Your team lead sat and listened in on two of your phone conversations, and she states that you fell asleep on both calls while talking to the customer. Now you were one of my best representatives at one time, but in the last few months your stats have dropped considerably. I am not sure what's going on with you, or if you need to talk to someone about any problems you may be having, but you are on probation for constantly being late and taking too many unscheduled days off. These new incidents put me in a very bad position as your supervisor. Sleeping on the job is intolerable and grounds for termination."

"What?" Nina panicked. "But Mr. Wall, I *am* a hard worker, and you know that. I have just been having problems with my oldest son. He has been hanging in the streets and I sit up at nights, worrying about him until he gets home. I don't get much sleep and I can't control him, so it is taking a toll on me," she lied.

"I'm sorry to hear about that, Nina. I can understand what you must be going through. But why didn't you come talk to me?"

"I am trying to handle it myself." She let the waterworks fall from her eyes.

Mr. Wall handed her a napkin leftover from his McDonald's lunch.

Nina wiped her eyes and blew her nose. When she looked in the tissue, there was a blood clot sitting in the middle of the mucus. She folded the tissue, hoping Mr. Wall hadn't seen it.

"Listen, Nina, you have no more time left to take off. But what I can do for you is give you two days off with no pay for a family emergency. But you must find a solution to your problem and get some rest. I am also scheduling a drug screening for you when you return. I have exhausted all of my efforts, as I have someone I have to report to as well. If you don't make some changes, then I am going to have to let you go. I'm sorry, Nina," he said sincerely.

Nina stared at her lap until she felt liquid run from her nose. She thought it was snot until she wiped it and saw that it was blood. Mr. Wall quickly handed her more tissues, and she began to wipe away the blood.

"Are you OK?" Mr. Wall was alarmed at the blood coming out of her nose.

"Yes, I will be fine. It's the stress. This happens when I'm stressed," she continued to lie.

"Do you need for me to get you to the hospital?" Mr. Wall was now standing and very concerned. He was naïve about drug addicts and had no clue of what the signs were. Unlike him, most of the girls that worked on the floor knew. They either had family members who were addicts or lived in the neighborhoods where the fiends dwelled. A couple of the women brought this to his attention, which was why he had scheduled a urine test for Nina.

"No, Mr. Wall, it will stop. I just have to go to the bathroom and put cold water on a paper towel, and put it over my nose." Nina stood, holding the napkins in place against her nose. "Can I go now?"

"Yes, yes, please, and take care of your problem, Nina. I would hate to have to let you go, but I will. You have two days. I'll see you back here on Monday. Good luck!" he called out after her.

All Nina could think about as she walked out of his office was that she wouldn't get paid until Friday, and she didn't have a dime to her name to get her supply while she was off for two days. She was already thinking of a way she could get the money to get more dope.

ର୍ପର୍ପର୍ପର୍ପ

Death's silver Benz pulled up to the corner. Justice was leaning up against the building in his usual spot, drinking a Red Bull. He wore long jean shorts that looked like (men's Capri jeans) with a cotton blue and white Rocawear short-sleeved shirt. His white ankle socks just peeked over the top of the low-cut, tri-colored blue Nikes. He stood upright and walked over to the car. Death sat in the front passenger seat while Bear drove. The tinted window lowered, exposing Death's face, which was covered by a pair of designer shades. The crew began to walk away from the corner because they feared him, all except Malik, who continued to stand there. Justice leaned forward and rested his hands on the sill of the car window. He could feel the ice-cold air from the air-conditioner hit him in the face, bringing relief from the heat.

He and Death talked low enough so that even Malik couldn't hear the conversation, and he only stood a few feet away from the car. Once their conversation was over, Malik saw Death pass something to Justice, who then put it in his pocket. Justice stood and began to backpedal away from the car. Malik looked at Death and gave a slight head nod. Death did the same, and then he rolled up the window and the car pulled off slowly. The big-bodied Benz bent the corner and was soon out of sight. Several seconds later Jeff and Brian returned to the corner, slowly looking around.

"What's up, man?" Malik asked Justice.

"Nothing. It's all good," he responded, letting them know that Death didn't have anything to say about them.

Once Jeff and Brian heard that, they relaxed. They tensed up every time Death rolled up onto the block, worrying that they had done something wrong.

Ten minutes passed and the crew was laughing and talking again when Brian saw his aunt Juanita coming up the street. She sashayed her rail-thin body as if she was a runway model. Her clothes hung on her because they were three sizes too big.

"Hey, nephew, what's up?" she sang to Brian as she reached the corner.

"What's good?" he responded.

"Tell me something good. Let me get two caps." She danced in place, counting the money out in front of him.

"How much you got?" Brian asked, knowing that she always came up short on money when she came to cop from him. He would then have to make up the difference. Juanita made sure she reminded Brian every time she came to cop that she was his aunt. She made sure she used that against him in order to get drugs on credit, or without enough money to purchase.

"I got enough." She continued to dance and count the money as if she was hearing some imaginary music no one else could hear. She was fidgety and tugged at her shirt. She worked her mouth like she was chewing gum, when in fact she didn't have any in her mouth.

"A'ight, hold up. I'll be back." Brian went away to go get the drugs from the stash.

"Juanita, what's up?" Justice asked her with a smirk on his face.

"What's good, baby boy? How you doing?" She never looked up from counting the money for the umpteenth time while dancing around. It seemed as if years of using the drug had done something to her nervous system.

The rest of the crew just looked at her and shook their heads.

Juanita was a fabulous addict. You couldn't tell her she wasn't a dime piece. Back in the day, yes, she was, but nowadays she qualified as one of the worst-looking females on drugs. She had teeth missing in the front and liver spots all over her face and body.

Brian came back to the corner and handed her the two capsules, took the money from her, and began to count it.

"It's right, boy! Whatchu counting it for?" Juanita was offended.

"A'ight, auntie! Damn!" Brian put the money in his pocket.

"A'ight, y'all. I'll holla at y'all later, OK?" she sang. Juanita began to walk off when Justice called her.

"Yo, let me holla at you for a minute." He steered Juanita away from the others.

Brian removed the money from his pocket and counted it anyway. He didn't trust his aunt because she was slick and a master of trickery. She was a fiend, after all.

Chapter Nine

Juanita walked at a quick pace, practically running while her bony hips moved from side to side as she put extra swing in them. She was five feet eight, weighed all of ninety-five pounds, and walked with confidence.

"Hey, Juanita!" Kurt yelled to her.

"I ain't got time, Kurt. I'll see you later." She waved and kept it moving.

"Oh, so it's like that, huh?" Kurt yelled back, but didn't get a response. He knew that walk of Juanita's, and he knew she had some crack. She had told him that the next time she got some, she was gonna hit him off because he had shared the wealth with her the last time he copped.

Juanita walked alongside a raggedy house that looked as if the wind blew hard enough, it would collapse. This house was the worst house on the block and was known to all the drug addicts as "The Shack." The front windows were boarded up. It was also her house. That was one of her hustles. She would seek out addicts who purchased drugs and would talk them into coming to her house for a free high.

The house had once belonged to Juanita's mother. It had been paid for years ago by her father. When Juanita's parents died, they left the house to her. Once Juanita became addicted to drugs, she let the house go to hell. Back taxes on the house were near $70,000. The state confiscated the house; however, the lack of upkeep over the years required that the house would have to be torn down. No one would buy the house if they had to invest hundreds of thousands of dollars to rebuild. Repairs for the home were out of the question.

In the meantime, Juanita took it upon herself to move back into the house. Kurt climbed the light pole and illegally hooked up electricity in the house. There was no running water and the bathroom toilet had been backed up for months, sending out a smell that would wake the dead. That odor of garbage, dirty clothes, and sewage permeated the entire house.

Juanita cut through the backyard and climbed the broken brick steps. She walked in through the filthy kitchen. Dishes were piled in the sink and looked to have been there for months. Roaches crawled all over the dishes, countertops, and walls. A mouse walked around on the counter, looking for scraps, and didn't run when she walked past. Juanita headed straight for the rear bedroom and shut the door behind her.

The bedroom had a mattress on the floor, three folding chairs, and a coffee table. Juanita sat down on one of the chairs. Shauna and Patrice were in the other two chairs. The two women had been desperately waiting her return, ready to smoke the crack that Juanita had gone out to purchase.

Juanita pulled the six capsules from her pockets and placed them on the table. The other women looked at her like they had just hit the lottery. They knew that they only had enough money between the three of them to get two caps.

"How you get six bottles, Juanita?" Shauna asked. She scratched a scab on her arm.

"Don't worry about how I got it. Just be glad I got it," Juanita told her as she opened one of the capsules and placed a rock on her homemade pipe made out of a soda can.

"I know that's right, Juanita." Patrice laughed. "This bitch over here, asking questions and shit! Fuck all the questions. Let's just say grace and get high."

Juanita laughed at Patrice's joke.

No one said a word while each woman lit her homemade pipe. Shauna was the first to finish her hit. She sat there as the effects of the crack invaded her body, then she frowned. Something didn't taste right. She swallowed the smoke and felt a burning sensation in the back of her throat.

"Juanita, who you cop this shit from?" Shauna demanded.

"I got it from my nephew." She looked for her lighter on the table.

"Why the hell would you go cop from Justice and 'em after we just robbed his stash last weekend?"

"Stop bitchin', Shauna! That nigga don't know who took that shit," Patrice said as she filled her homemade pipe made out of a piece of a TV antenna and took another hit.

Shauna waited a few moments before speaking. "This shit got a funny taste to it. Y'all don't taste that?" She looked at the stem from a pipe in her hand as if she was going to see what made the crack taste funny.

There was no response. Juanita and Patricia just kept smoking.

"No, for real, y'all tryna tell me this shit don't taste funny?" Shauna asked again.

"Damn, Shauna! You fucking up my high! Justice gave me four extra caps for free, 'cause he say I'm one of his loyal customers. So stop bitchin'. The shit is free!" Juanita was getting aggravated with Shauna's whining.

There was more silence while Patrice and Juanita continued to smoke. Shauna just sat there, not wanting to smoke anymore because of the bitter taste that was starting to give her a headache.

"I heard Death put a bullet in one of them boys of his 'cause he wasn't watchin' the shit anyway. So he don't know we took that shit. OK?" Juanita croaked as she tried to hold in the smoke.

"This shit ain't right. It taste funny, and we can't even go back and get another package," Shauna continued to complain.

"Shauna, you fucking up my high!" Juanita yelled.

"Well, if you don't want your shit, I'll take it." Patrice held out her hand. She was greedy and sneaky. She would—and had—stolen from her own mother. She'd jack a cripple and a blind man for their shit if she thought she could get a blast.

Shauna stood. "Well, y'all can have my share. I ain't feeling this." She walked out of the bedroom and out of the house. It didn't sink in to Juanita's and Patrice's heads that their get-high buddy only took one hit and left. All they knew was that they only had to split the crack two ways instead of three.

Once outside, Shauna's stomach felt queasy and her mouth began to water. She felt like she had to throw up, which she thought was strange because that had never happened before. She walked up the street and the queasiness turned into severe pain. She threw up mostly greenish-looking liquid. Once she finished, she felt a little better.

Shauna knew something was definitely wrong. She believed that Juanita had purchased a bad package of crack. After about thirty minutes or so of leaning up against the side of a building, she tried to get her bearings together so that she could go back to Juanita's, but she was sick and feeling weak. She wondered if Juanita and Patrice were feeling the same way she was.

It took another thirty minutes before Shauna was able to make it back to Juanita's house. When she walked into the bedroom her stomach turned all over again. Juanita and Patrice were both lying on their sides. Their eyes bulged, blood leaked from their eyes, and vomit ran from theirs mouths. They were dead.

ာ ာ ာ ာ

ONE HOUR LATER . . .

"Yo!" A young boy called as he ran up the street.

Malik looked in the direction of the boy. Jeff and Brian walked up next to Malik as they looked at the young boy running toward them. Justice continued to lean up against the building, unfazed by the young boy approaching.

"Yo, man . . ." The boy bent down to catch his breath. "B, man, ya aunt . . . ya aunt just got put into the meat wagon . . ." he gasped.

"What? What are you talking 'bout, little man?" Brian questioned.

"Ya aunt Juanita is dead, man. I saw them coming outta her house with two body bags, and put them into the ambulance. Everybody was standing out there. So I asked them what happened and they said that ya aunt and Pat OD'd."

Brian frowned as if he didn't understand what was going on. He'd just seen his aunt only a couple of hours or so ago. All she bought was two caps. How could she OD on two caps of crack?

"Come *on*, man!" The boy took off running again.

Brian and Jeff took off behind the boy. Malik stood there with a perplexed look on his face. Juanita only smoked crack, so he couldn't figure it out. He turned to look at Justice and saw that the news didn't faze him. Justice continued to lean against the building, smoking a Black & Mild cigar. He never made eye contact with Malik. It almost seemed like he was avoiding it.

Malik looked at the ground, put his hands in his pockets, and walked over to Justice. He leaned against the building next to him.

"That's fucked up what happened to Juanita," he said in a matter-of-fact tone.

"Ay, that's how the shit goes. It's a gamble every time you put this poison in ya system. It's like playing Russian roulette." Justice shrugged.

Malik continued to stare at Justice until Justice looked him in the eye. Justice gave Malik the screw face. "What's up?"

"You gave Juanita some bullshit, didn't you?" Malik asked.

"Fuck how you sound?" Justice was on the defense.

Malik shook his head and walked off in the direction the others were running.

Chapter Ten

Marquis left the college building as soon as he finished his last class of the morning. He planned to take the walk to downtown Newark, to his job at Dr. Jay's. As he descended the steps, he spotted an attractive young lady sitting on them. They both made eye contact and she simply lowered her head back into the book she was reading, although she had held eye contact longer than usual. Marquis continued to stand there until she looked up again. This time he smiled at her and she blushed and smiled back at him. He walked over to her and stood in front of her two steps below where she was sitting.

"How you doing?" he asked.

She looked up at him and was hypnotized. "Hello," she said.

"What's your name?"

"Shea." She couldn't stop staring at him.

Marquis smiled. "Why are you sitting here?"

"I have some time before my next class, so I thought I would sit outside. I love the summer sun." She smiled and stood.

Her beauty mesmerized him. Shea was a petite girl, only five feet three. Everything on her body was petite, but full for her size. Her shapely body was a turn-on for Marquis.

"What time does your class start?"

"In about an hour and a half."

"Hour and a half? You're gonna sit out here in the hot-ass sun for that long?" he asked in surprise.

"Yeah. Why? You wouldn't sit out here?"

"Hell, no," he said, and meant it. Shea laughed at him.

"I could go home. I live like a few blocks from here. But to hell with that." She shrugged and lowered her head. Frustration crossed her face.

Marquis bent down a little to try and look into her face. Shea looked up into his eyes. Marquis could see sadness there.

"Did I say something wrong?" He was concerned.

"No, it's not you." She shook her head.

"Well, I have a little time. You wanna go get something to eat?"

"Sure, why not?" Her smiled suddenly reappeared.

Forty-five minutes later they were sitting at a booth by the window in McDonald's, enjoying a meal and laughing and talking. Marquis thought Shea was such a smart girl. They both were the same age, but she was taking pre-law classes, and had her work cut out for her by the way she ran down her curriculum to him. He admired how she was one of the very few inner-city girls who weren't interested in the street life and all that came with it. She wasn't the average young teenager who was only concerned with buying the latest clothes and materialistic things. Shea was very familiar with the street life, but she chose not to live it, just the way Marquis did.

Shea lived with her mother and her stepfather. She was an only child, and her mother was very overprotective of her.

"So, how does it feel to be the only child?" Marquis asked.

She just shrugged and looked out the window at the people walking by.

"You don't know?"

"It used to be a good thing, when my mother and my real father were together. I mean, even when my mother and I were alone, it was OK. I loved my father to death. I was his little girl, you know what I mean?" She looked at Marquis.

Marquis nodded to let her know he understood. He adored her for the simple fact that she was a chick from the hood, but very well spoken.

"But being an only child did have its disadvantages at times. I used to get lonely sometimes. I got tired of playing by myself."

"You didn't play with the kids outside?"

"Yeah, I did, whenever my mother would let me. But trust she was right out there with me sitting on the stoop watching. I didn't get much play time with the other kids. Plus we moved so often that when I did make friends at school, we would move away."

"What about family? Didn't you have cousins your age?"

"I only know a few family members." Shea looked out the window again. "For a long time I would ask my mother about my grandmother, aunts, uncles, and cousins. She would always tell me that we would go see them soon, that they lived too far away. When I was fourteen my mother finally told me the real reason why I didn't see my family. She had to tell me the truth. This was before she met my stepfather," she said, chewing on a fry.

Marquis sat patiently and waited for her to speak again. He was done with his food, so he basically sat and watched her eat.

"She told me that she became pregnant with me when she was a teen, and that her parents threw her outta the house. My mother loved my father with all of her heart and refused to listen to my grandfather, who told her not to see my father again. So she decided to just leave, at their request. My father was a drug dealer at the time."

"Word?" Marquis looked surprised.

"Yup." She nodded. "My parents are from South Carolina, and back then I guess my father was some kinda big-time dealer. He loved my mother, although she wasn't his only girlfriend. My mother was underage and she had been a virgin at that. But do you know what my father did when my mother came to him with her suitcase in hand?"

"What?" Marquis leaned forward with interest.

"He simply told her, 'Well I guess we're gonna be a family now.' He then put his arms around my mother, and walked her into his house."

"That's what's up!" Marquis took a sip of his soda and sat back in his chair.

"They stayed there for about another month or two. My mother couldn't finish school. She was so sick while carrying me. Now I don't know for sure, and to this day, my mother still won't come clean about it, but I think my father got into some kinda trouble, and that's why we moved all the time. I think he was on the run."

"That's deep." Marquis shook his head. "So they got a divorce? Where is your father now?"

"He's dead. He got shot in a barbershop chair. I was twelve-years-old when we went to his funeral. I mean, it wasn't nothing for him not to come home some nights. I was used to that. He said he was working, so I believed him at the time. I mean I knew what my father did. I wasn't stupid. I saw all the money he had. I watched TV and heard things too. So it wasn't like I didn't know. But I knew that to be his job. He always bought me whatever I wanted, and we never wanted for anything. So when he hadn't shown up for two days, I figured he was working until my mother started crying hysterically after one of my father's friends, my godfather Ezel, came to visit. The next thing I knew we were going to his funeral. My mother never told me that he was dead. She was a mess and cried all the time. Ezel's girlfriend came and stayed with us. She told me that my father had died. I didn't believe her, though."

"Why?"

"Because I just knew my daddy was coming home."

"So when you found out it was true, what did you do?"

"We went to the funeral four days later. As we walked in, everyone was hugging me and my mother. Everyone was crying. My father had a lot of friends. It was packed in that church. So we went up front and there he was, lying in the casket. My mother was falling all over the casket and when they pulled her away, she fell to the floor, kicking and screaming. And even then I didn't believe it. When I walked up to the casket and looked at the man they said was my father, I was convinced that all those people were on some kinda drugs. That man that lay in that casket was not my father." She shook her head, staring off into the distance as if she remembered it like it was yesterday.

"He looked like his face was swollen. His forehead was misshapen, like it had a hole in it and they tried to fix it. He had dark circles around his eyes. Naw, that wasn't my father."

Marquis could see the sadness on her face. He could feel and understand her pain, since he missed his father too. Although his father wasn't dead, he might as well have been because he was not there and hadn't been around for fifteen years.

He leaned forward and held one of her hands. They were smooth and silky. Shea never looked him in the eyes. She looked back out onto the streets and continued to talk. Marquis could see her eyes becoming glassy.

"I stood there, staring at this man until someone walked me to my seat. To make a long story short, the reality of my father being dead didn't hit me until one month later. That's when it hit me in my dreams one night that my father wasn't ever coming back. He came to me in my dreams and told me to be a good girl. I woke up screaming, and I think I must have cried for hours. My mother came and held me for the rest of the night. We cried together." Tears dropped from her eyes.

He handed her a napkin from the table. "I feel your pain," Marquis told her. "So are you and your stepfather . . . I mean, I know he could never replace your real father, but it must be nice to have a father figure around, right?"

Shea rolled her eyes and sucked her teeth. "Fuck that asshole. I hate that man with a passion!"

"Huh?"

"He whoops my mother's ass, and he used to hit on me. But my godfather told that jackass if he ever put his hands on me again, he would be eating dirt."

"Damn!" Marquis couldn't believe his ears. "Why don't y'all just leave him?"

"My mother is too scared of him. Every time my godfather would help us out, my mother would only run back to my stepfather. My godfather gave up on helping my mother. So that's why he told his dumb ass he better not touch me again."

"Yo, that shit is crazy. Why don't you just go live with your godfather?"

Shea shook her head again. "Uh, no. That will never happen. My godfather is still farting around in the game with his old ass. Plus, he would never let me live with him. He is the one who encouraged me to stay in school and do well."

"So why don't you go home during the day between classes?"

"Sometimes my stepfather comes home during the day. Now you see?" She smiled.

"Yeah, I do. Well, I really want to spend more time talking with you, but I gotta be getting to work. I'll walk you back to the school." He put the wrappers and garbage onto the tray.

"OK." Shea stood.

Marquis put the garbage in the trash can and placed the tray on top. He walked back over to their table where Shea was lacing the strings on her pink and white Jordans.

"Shea, you never told me how your father died," he said.

"The men took him out back of the barbershop in the alley and shot him six times in the chest, and then hit him in the head with a sledgehammer," she said matter-of-factly. "You know, they found out the barber helped set up my father."

"That's fucked up!" Marquis opened the door for her.

"Tell me about it. But my godfather took care of that ass, the barber too."

The two walked out into the muggy air, heading toward the college. Marquis had a feeling that Shea might just be the prefect woman for him.

Chapter Eleven

Malik and Jeff returned to the corner where Justice still stood. He had served a customer and was getting ready to walk into the store when the two approached.

"What happened?" Justice asked.

"Just what little man said. Juanita and Pat are dead. They OD'd," Jeff replied. He walked past Justice and into the store.

Malik leaned against the building and eyeballed Justice.

"What, nigga?" Justice gave Malik the screw face again.

"What's up, Jus?" Malik asked in an even tone.

"Fuck you talking 'bout?"

"You don't want it, motherfucker." Malik called his bluff and raised up off the wall.

"Correction, *you* don't want it!" Justice pulled up his shirt to reveal his gun. "I'll make the hollow tips rain out this bitch!" he bragged.

"You gonna have to use that motherfucker, because you ain't got nothing else," Malik challenged him.

Just as Justice was gonna step to Malik, Jeff walked out of the store. He looked at the both of them and could feel the tension.

"What's up, y'all?" He walked over and stepped in between them. He faced Justice and eyeballed him, letting him know that he was down with his boy Malik.

"*Woo-woo!*" Kurt came up the street chanting his usual chant, interrupting their beef. That day his carts were empty. "Fellas!" he yelled at the crew standing on the corner. "What's the word of the day?" He smiled, exposing gray teeth.

"The word of today boys and girls is BATH! Can you say it with me?" Money clowned.

Justice joined in on the laughter. Malik was deep in thought and didn't respond.

"That's a good one, son!" Kurt laughed along with them.

"Yo, Conductor, you ain't hauling no junk today?" Justice asked.

"Since when you've known me not to work? I made my run this morning. Yeah, got me a big score. Shit, I made fifty bucks today so far," he bragged.

"Fiddy beans? Nigga, that ain't no real bread. You gonna snort that up ya nose in one hour, then what you gonna do? Come see me when ya grip look like this." Justice pulled his stack from his pocket and showed it to Kurt.

"I ain't even mad at you, young'un." Kurt was mesmerized by the cash, and he began to drool.

"Conductor, you heard what happened to Juanita and Pat?" Jeff asked, breaking him out of his trance.

"Hells yeah! I just saw them earlier today."

"Yeah, man, so did we. That shit is crazy!" Jeff shook his head.

"They said they OD'd," Justice said.

"Sheeee-it!" Kurt dragged out the word. "Them sisters ain't OD on no crack."

"So what you saying, Conductor?" Malik finally spoke.

"I'm saying they crack smokers, not dope jokers. Whatever they had was tampered with." He danced and did a spin.

"So you saying somebody put some shit in the crack?" Jeff was interested.

"That's bullshit!" Justice was becoming afraid. He knew he had given Juanita the package Death had passed to him.

"No bullshit, boy, that's real shit," Kurt said while watching a young teen girl with a fatty walk past. He scratched his matted beard.

"How you figure, Conductor? What, you a doctor now?" Justice continued to challenge him simply for his own satisfaction.

"Oh, yeah. I'm a doctor of love. Y'all know that song? Dr. Love . . ." he began to sing loudly. Not surprisingly, most who knew Kurt already knew he could sing his ass off.

"How you know, man?" Malik interrupted Kurt's performance. Although he spoke to Kurt, he looked at Justice, who would not make eye contact.

"How I know? How I know?" Kurt repeated himself as he spotted a cigarette butt that still had a couple of tokes left on it. He picked it up and walked over to a nearby garbage can.

"Let me get a light, somebody?" he asked while examining the butt. Malik threw him the lighter he had in his pocket.

"How you know, Conductor?" Jeff asked again.

Kurt put the cigarette butt in the corner of his mouth and clicked the lighter. He covered the flame to protect it from going out.

"I know . . ." He held his head high and dragged deeply on the cigarette. "I know because I seen that kinda shit before," he finally said, releasing a long stream of smoke through his nose. "I know the difference between a heroin overdose and polluting your system with garbage. And those sisters was polluted with garbage. Probably some synthetic, man-made shit. They said they eyes was bleeding. Since when y'all young niggas know crack to make ya eyes bleed?" He spoke around the cigarette in his mouth. "Huh?" he looked at them with one eye closed, trying to keep the smoke from going into his eye.

"I ain't never heard of no shit like that before." Malik walked away and into the store.

Justice tried to play it off when, in fact, he was spent. Death had given him the vials and told him to give them to Juanita, or one of the other two women, whenever they came to cop. He said they did something for him and he wanted to reward them for it. Now, to add insult to injury, Justice could possibly be blamed for the murder of the women because he gave Juanita the crack.

"What happened with Shauna? Ain't nobody seen her since that happened?" Justice asked, in hope that Shauna hadn't talked to the police.

"I don't know," Jeff responded by shrugging his shoulders before walking away to serve a customer in a car by the corner.

"Nine times outta ten, she was with them. Them sisters is stingy bitches," Kurt responded, remembering how Juanita had dissed him earlier.

"So where she at, then?" Justice asked.

"Nigga, I don't know! Why, you writing a book about it?" Kurt cracked.

Justice didn't see the humor. At that moment he was ready to get up with Death to see what the hell was going on.

"Yo, Conductor!" a man called out from across the street in his Ford F150 truck.

"Yo!" Kurt replied.

"Yo, man, I need you to come to the crib and hook up this stove I just bought." He pointed to the huge box that sat on the back of the truck.

"You headed home now?"

"Yeah. You know where I'm at, right?"

"Yeah, yeah, I know where you at. I'm on my way!" Kurt walked over to his train and grabbed the first cart, pulling it behind him. "I'm out, fellas! Gotta go make this money! *Wooooo . . . wooooo!*" He walked off down the street, bopping to his own tune.

ഝഝഝഝ

Nina stepped off the bus and onto the sidewalk. She was dope sick. The humidity of the hot day hit her smack in the face once she was off the bus. She felt a little better once she got on the bus because of the nice, cool, air-conditioned ride. Now she felt ill all over again. The bus pulled away from the curb, leaving a polluted trail of smoke behind it. Nina tried to hold her breath to keep from breathing in the toxic fumes. Blood seeped from her nose. She wiped her nose with the back of her hand and looked at it.

"Shit," she said to herself. The nosebleeds were coming more frequently, along with migraine headaches.

She was about to cross the busy street when she spotted Bear standing at the driver's side door of the Mercedes.

Nina turned to walk in the opposite direction when Bear called out to her. She reluctantly crossed the street and walked over to the car. Bear opened the back door and she got in. Death sat there with a smirk on his face. She felt the sweat running down her back.

"What's going on, Nina?"

"Hey, Todd," she said, calling him by his government name.

"You know you owe me, right?"

"Yeah, I know. You won't let me forget." She rolled her eyes at him with newfound courage.

"What did you say to me?" Death was not feeling Nina's slick mouth.

"Todd, listen, I'm dope sick. I don't feel good, and I don't have time for the bullshit. What do you want from me?"

"Oh, is that what's wrong with you? Here, let me scratch that little itch you got." Death pulled open the ashtray that sat in the console in the back of the armrest. He reached inside and pulled out a bundle of ten envelopes of dope wrapped in a rubber band. He pulled three envelopes from the stack and returned the rest to the ashtray before closing it.

Nina's stomach did flip-flops. A small amount of sour liquid rushed into her mouth. She swallowed it back down and tried to compose herself. Sweat ran down the sides of her face and neck. The car's air conditioning did nothing to stop her sweats. Chill bumps ran up and down her arms, and she began to shake a little.

"Here." Death passed her one envelope. Nina wasted no time snorting the contents of the envelope.

"You know what time it is, don't you?" He smirked.

Nina looked up from the envelope. Powder coated the rim of her nose.

"Come on, Todd! Them days are over. You can't be serious!"

"Serious as shit. Them days ain't gonna never be over." He laughed.

The days they were talking about were after Wiz went to prison and Nina had spent all of the money he'd left in the condo. She'd started to stress and her addiction was getting the best of her. As usual Death was there to save the day. But of course, his rescue came with a price.

In the past Death was in love with Nina, but he had since lost that love. Using his power to its advantage, Death now enjoyed manipulating Nina. He would make her do all kinds of sexual favors for him when needed. Sometimes, depending upon his mood, he would even let Bear have his way with her. It was all a part of being in control. After the last time she had been forced to sleep with Bear, Nina had vowed that was something she would never do again. And she had avoided Death for many years. But it seemed that Death always caught up to her at the right moment, when she needed a fix. And with Death holding what he knew about her past over her head, she had no other choice but to obey him.

Bear knocked on the window and Death rolled it down.

"What's up?"

"Did you tell her?"

"Oh, yeah, Nina, Bear wants some company tonight." Death smiled at her.

Nina looked up at Bear, who was stooped down looking into the car. She could see all the sweat dripping down his black face. All she could do was envision the last time she had to lick his asshole after he failed to wipe himself good from taking a shit. She suddenly felt sick again and began to gag.

"Bitch, don't throw up in my shit! If you gotta yak, then you better do it in ya purse or open the fucking door." Death knew the reaction most had when using heroin. "Let's ride," he instructed Bear as he passed Nina another bag of dope.

Nina had been a functional addict for many years. Back in the day, before she became an addict, she was one of the prettiest girls of her time. Every dude in the neighborhood wanted to be with her. Nina wouldn't give it up to anyone, though. Her grandmother had raised her, and she had ruled Nina with an iron fist. Nina had a curfew, and her grandmother made sure she stuck to it. After Nina graduated high school, her grandmother couldn't afford to send her to college, so she made her come work with her at the factory. She kept a close watch on Nina. One day her grandmother's arthritis acted up terribly and she sent Nina to the store alone. This was the day Nina met Wiz, her sons' father.

Wiz was older than her and he was already established as one of the well-known drug dealers in the neighborhood.

Since Death's older brothers wouldn't let him hang with them, he had begun to hang around Wiz. Wiz was much older than Death, and he considered Death to be a younger brother. In reality he let Death hang with him because he liked the grind in the young man. Death had respect for Wiz and he idolized him. Wiz let him be a man, and brought him on. Although Death's much older brothers where in the game, Wiz taught him first hand.

Death had always had a major crush on Nina, although she was older than him by six years. He was the only boy that could come to Nina's house because her grandmother played Pokeno with Death's grandmother, who had lived in Newark all her life. That was one reason why Death's parents moved there. The older women would send him on errands to the corner store for them while they played. He was sort of like family to Nina.

Nina used to tell Death that when he got older she would love to date him. Death held on to that promise in the hopes of finally getting with her. But Wiz ended all that.

When Nina went to the store for her grandmother that fateful day, Wiz and Death were outside the store. Nina took one look at Wiz and fell instantly in love with him. Wiz not only drove her home from the store in his brand-new convertible Mustang, but he also paid for the groceries. Wiz was a good-looking man and a gentleman on top of it. He was confident and bold. When he brought Nina home, her grandmother was sitting in the front window and saw her get out of the car. She almost flipped her wig until she saw Death with them. Wiz brought the bags of groceries inside and charmed the housedress right off Nina's grandmother. Wiz was a smooth talker and a smart man. He knew just what to say, how to say it, and when to say it. Before long he was allowed to visit Nina without Death tagging along. He gave the old woman money every time he came by until she finally allowed Nina to go out on dates with him. Of course Death wasn't thrilled about the situation.

Death's world turned upside down when he got word that Nina and Wiz were a couple. He never forgave his friend for it, and he secretly held animosity against Wiz for years.

Two years into the relationship, Nina moved in with Wiz. They were the couple of the hood. Both men and women envied the two, as everyone wanted to be in their shoes. They had it all—good looks, money, and the finer things in life. Things couldn't have been better for Nina until the day when she, Wiz, and Death took a ride through the city.

Wiz suddenly pulled the car over to the curb and jumped out. Although Nina hadn't been exposed to too much violence in her life, she did know what Wiz and Death did for a living. Wiz never brought it home, so she was OK with it.

On this day she watched as Wiz walked over to two men with Death on his heels. The men were chilling on the front step of a multi-family home. Wiz grabbed a handful of one man's braids with a gloved hand and threw him to the ground. Death suddenly pulled out a .38 snub-nosed gun with black tape wrapped around the handle, and held the other dude at bay.

Nina didn't know what was going on, and she couldn't make out what Wiz was saying to the man. Wiz pulled out a .32 and pistol-whipped the man. Nina was shocked. She had never seen anything like that in her life. Blood flew everywhere as she watched the man she loved with all of her heart beat this poor man to a pulp. She saw rage in Wiz's eyes, and that frightened her. She didn't recognize the man with whom she had fallen in love.

After Wiz beat the man until he no longer moved, he let his body drop to the ground. Just when Nina thought it was over and sat back in her seat, expecting Wiz to come back to the car, he did something that, oddly enough, turned her on. Wiz grabbed the man by his bloody shirt, lifting his body partially off the ground, stuck the gun to his forehead, and pulled the trigger. Brain matter and skull fragment splattered from the back of the unconscious man's head and hit the ground. Wiz dropped the body and then stood directly over it and fired three more bullets into the man's face. He then walked away from the man, leaving him sprawled on the steps. Before Death walked away, he pumped bullets into the other man.

When Wiz and Death came back to the car, Wiz was covered in blood. His eyes looked demonic, and he never looked at Nina or said a word to her. He simply passed Death the gun over the seat and told him to get rid of it.

Nina, in turn, looked at him with dreamy eyes. He drove off as if nothing had happened. That's when Nina knew how powerful he was, and that was when she fell even more in love with him. She knew that she could go to jail for not telling the police about the murders she had witnessed, but the love she had for Wiz would make her cover for him in any way she could. She would take what she saw that day to her grave.

Death saw how Nina's love deepened for Wiz over time, and he plotted to take care of it. Death was out of control and his jealousy of Nina and Wiz's relationship got the best of him. No one ever found out who snitched on Wiz and got him twenty-five to life in prison, but Nina knew. Yet Death held something over her head that could put her away for life as well. And so Nina made a deal with Death many years ago in order to keep her freedom.

But little did Nina know a deal with Death was for life and Death was about to make it much worse for her.

Chapter Twelve

It was seven PM when Marquis walked out of Dr. Jay's. He was on his way to the bus stop when someone called his name.

"Mark!"

He turned around and saw Malik. Marquis waited for his brother to catch up, and they walked to the bus stop together.

"Whatchu doing down here?" Marquis asked.

"I came to pick you up. I got here early, so I went to get me something to eat at that Muslim joint over there on Branford place." He held up a bag of food.

"How you figure you come to pick me up, and we catching the bus home?"

"I figured you needed an escort." Malik laughed.

Marquis laughed as well. "I hope you at least got me something to eat too?"

"Yeah, you know I got you, little brother."

The bus pulled over to their stop and Malik and Marquis exited through the back door.

"I'ma go in the store and get me a soda. You coming?" Malik asked him.

"Yeah."

They both walked to the corner store. They spoke to several people that roamed the streets. A fiend walked up to them.

"You holding anything?" the fiend asked as he walked backward in front of them.

"Naw, man. Shop closed," Malik said simply. The crew had finished their work and had to wait until Justice got the re-up.

"Shop closed? Come on, man! Ain't nobody got nothing out here?" the fiend asked desperately.

"What I say, man? Shop closed!"

Marquis tapped his brother on the arm. Malik looked at him with a frown.

"Come on, man, don't do it like that," Marquis reasoned.

"Man, fuck him!" Malik walked away.

"Look, man, right now they're waiting for the re-up. So you gonna have to go somewhere else, a'ight?" Marquis told the man.

"Damn!" The fiend lowered his head. "Thanks, man." He walked away with his head still hung low.

Marquis waited for Malik to come out of the store. After a few moments Malik walked out carrying a bag with two sodas in it.

"Malik, man, you can't talk to the customers like that."

"What? Come on, man! Let me do what I do. You don't know nothing 'bout this here."

"I know enough to know that if you treat your customer's right, they will be loyal customers. It don't take a rocket scientist to know that."

"Psshh!" Malik brushed past him. He knew Marquis was right. In fact, he had used that same line on Death to try to get put on his own blocks. But since Death dissed him, he didn't give a fuck about it anymore. He was bitter and displayed it to the customers.

"Malik!" Marquis yelled after him.

Malik turned and waited for Marquis to catch up, then the two started their walk home, shoulder to shoulder.

"Listen to me," Marquis said. "What I'm telling you is some good shit. People like dude back there"—he nodded back in the direction of the store where the fiend had been—"niggas like that will turn on you when they are mistreated. Don't let their state of body and mind fool you, bruh. Trust and believe that if you catch a fiend at the wrong time, he will shut your whole operation down with just one phone call, snitching you out."

Malik didn't say a word as they walked, but he was listening.

"You swear you know shit. Just 'cause your ass go to college don't make you street smart. When you attend the School of Hard Knocks, then you can come to me." Malik smiled.

"Don't need the School of Hard Knocks, brother. I've watched this shit in these streets for too long. Trust I know what I'm talking about. Maybe you need to attend the School of Marquis Boyd. Class starts tonight. When we get in the house, I'ma school your ass." Marquis laughed.

They crossed the street, laughing and talking with each other when the silver Mercedes pulled over to the corner ahead of them. Both teens looked at the vehicle, knowing who it was. They were quiet and kept walking, but their pace slowed down considerably because they were on alert. The back door opened and their mother got out of the car. The Benz pulled off, leaving her standing there. The brothers looked at each other and continued to stand on the sidewalk across the street. Nina leaned up against the mailbox on the corner and nodded. There couldn't have been a more terrifying sight than to see a well-dressed woman in a dope lean.

Malik was pissed and it showed on his face. Marquis handed his book bag to his brother and trotted over to his mother. He grabbed Nina by the arm and helped her across the street. The whole time she talked loudly and cursed him out, but Marquis kept dragging her along.

Once inside the apartment, Marquis took her to her room and laid her on the bed. He walked into the kitchen where Malik stood looking out the window. Marquis grabbed his food from the bag and put it into the microwave.

"You want me to heat up your food?" Marquis asked.

"No, I lost my appetite," Malik said. "I can't deal with this anymore, Mark. I think I'm gonna get my own place."

"What?" Marquis was shocked. "You can't leave!"

"The hell I can't. I can't deal with this shit with her no more. She's a junkie, and she ain't tryna do no better. Pretty soon she gonna be out there like the rest of them. I ain't feeling that shit, Mark. One day we gonna come home and our shit gonna be padlocked." He rubbed his hand over his face.

"Naw, man. Ain't no way in hell I'm gonna let that happen!" Marquis was confident.

"Bullshit, Mark! How you figure you gonna stop it? I'm around them motherfuckers every day, all day. When they want that next high, they will do anything to get it. The shit ain't that easy to kick." He turned to look back out of the kitchen window. "You know what happened today?"

"No. What?" Marquis removed his sandwich from the microwave and sat down at the table.

"Brian's aunt Juanita and Patrice died of an overdose today." He turned to look at Marquis.

"Word?" Marquis looked up with a mouth full of sandwich, not believing his ears.

"Word, and the fucked-up thing about it is that I think I might know who did that to them. But the point I'm tryna make is, Mommy's out there just like them. Who's to say she won't get some bad shit and we come home and find her dead? Man, I can't deal with that." Malik was frustrated.

Marquis could see the hurt in his brother's eyes. He felt bad and wanted to make the whole thing go away. He also struggled with the idea of Nina's addiction, but he made excuses for his mother because he was so close to her.

"You know, that's the second time I've seen her with Death, and I don't have a clue what the fuck that's all about," Malik continued. "All I know is that now I don't trust that nigga. I was gonna try to get down with him and get my own blocks, but that sheisty motherfucker may try some bullshit with Ma if I do."

Marquis replaced his sandwich on the wax paper in which it had been wrapped. He too had lost his appetite envisioning his mother lying in her bed after an overdose.

"We gotta do something. We gotta get Ma to a rehab," Marquis said.

"*You* get her to a rehab. I'm done."

"Malik, no! Man, you can't turn your back on our mother! What's wrong with you?"

"You can't make her get clean, Mark. She gotta wanna do it. If you take her to detox, she can leave on her own if she wants. Brian said Juanita had been to detox twelve times, and every time she walked out and came home, only to get high that same day."

"Malik, man . . . for me, man . . . just don't leave yet. Big bruh, just don't leave yet. I can't do this without you. Don't leave me, man. I need you," Marquis begged with serious eyes.

Malik looked at his brother and his heart felt for him. He loved his brother to death. They were very close, and he was proud that his brother wasn't the man he was.

"A'ight. For you, man, I'll stay." He grabbed Marquis by the neck and pulled him in for a brotherly hug.

Chapter Thirteen

The two-year-old boy opened his eyes and looked at his mother, who lay there in the bed with him sleeping. He climbed out of bed and walked over to the partially open door. His diaper sagged in the back due to the amount of times he had urinated in it. It was four in the afternoon. He walked into the living room and stood there, looking at the television that was on. A commercial of puppies advertising dog food played on the screen. He watched the puppies while scratching his head full of big curls. Once the commercial went off he went over to the window and pulled back the curtain. He stood on his toes and looked out at the activity that went on outside. Across the street he could see children playing in the lot. They ran with the ball up and down the grassy lot. He smiled as he watched them.

He went over to the door and tried to reach the doorknob, but couldn't. He walked over to a small stool that sat next to the sofa and was being used as an end table. He dragged the stool over to the door and climbed on top. From watching his mother, he knew that the little piece that was on the doorknob needed to be turned in order for the door to open. He turned it and then turned the knob. The door partially opened, but then hit the stool that the boy had placed there. He climbed down, moved the stool, and pulled open the door. He opened the screen door and walked out onto the porch. The air was warm and the breeze that blew felt good on his shirtless belly. He climbed *down the stairs and stepped onto the sidewalk.*

He could no longer see the kids because the parked cars were blocking his view, but he could hear them clearly as they yelled and played. He stepped down off the sidewalk and walked in between two parked cars. He ran out into the street, toward where the kids where playing.

A car's tires screeched loudly . . .

Nina sat straight up in bed. Sweat covered her body. She was breathing hard as she looked around the room. She was still fully dressed in her work clothes, and she didn't even remember coming into the house. She got down on her knees and began to cry, deep and hard. Her chest was tight and breathing became difficult for her. She began to pray with all of her might.

"Father in Heaven, I beg of you to help me! Please, help me! I am so sorry, Father! Please do not punish me!" She continued to cry.

Marquis ran into the room when he heard his mother's cries. He got down on the floor with her and held her in his arms. Nina cried uncontrollably, holding on to her son. Marquis began to cry with her, not knowing why she was crying. All he knew was that his mother was hysterical.

"I didn't mean to do it. I didn't mean to do it," she kept repeating.

Marquis looked down at his mother as she lay in his arms and continued to cry. He could see that her nose was starting to decay. A scab was in one of her nostrils, and the outer rim of her nose was peeling. Reality set in. The drugs that his mother snorted were affecting her worse than he had thought. He helped his mother to her feet and laid her back on the bed before calling Malik on his cell.

"What up, Mark?" Malik answered.

"Yo, man, it's Mommy! I'm 'bout to call an ambulance to come get her. I think she's hallucinating, or overdosing, or something!"

"I'm on my way." Malik disconnected the call.

TWO HOURS LATER . . .

The brothers sat in the waiting room of the hospital. Marquis had his head in his hands. He was so exhausted. He only had about one hour of sleep, and he had to go to school in three hours. Malik sat with his head resting on the wall. A doctor came into the waiting room and walked over to the brothers.

"Your mother is going to be fine," he told them.

"What's wrong with her?" Marquis asked, standing up. Malik stood with him.

"Your mother may have been hallucinating, which often comes with drug use. I can't say for sure. Her blood pressure is a little high, but other than that she can go home."

"What about her nose?" Marquis inquired.

"I have prescribed some cream for her nose sores. She has been informed that if she continues to administer drugs through the nose, that it is quite possible that the sores can get infected. We have also given her pamphlets on drug use. She has admission papers that she has two days to use, for her admittance into a detoxification program. It is her choice. We have informed her of all avenues to go into recovery."

Malik shook his hand. "Thank you, doctor." "Thanks," Marquis said, sitting back down.

"I will have the nurse send her out as soon as she signs the release papers. Goodnight, fellas." The doctor walked away.

≈≈≈≈≈

Malik was sound asleep in his bed and Marquis sat on the bed in Nina's room, talking with her. It was six in the morning and he had not slept since returning home. He had about an hour to get dressed and get to his first class. Nina lay there and looked at him as he spoke.

"Ma, you can't keep doing this to yourself. When I saw you on the corner last night, looking like a fiend, I almost lost it. I never want to see you like that again."

Nina didn't reply. She simply lay there and took in all that her son was saying.

"Ma, you gotta go into detox. I mean, I don't know what I would do if I lost you. I can't even imagine life without my mother. Today Juanita and Patrice died of an overdose."

Nina frowned. She hadn't heard about that. She had grown up with Juanita and Patrice. She couldn't believe they were gone.

Marquis saw her expression and confirmed the news. "Ma, they are gone, Ma. We will never see them again. Do you understand? I thought we were going to lose you tonight." Hurt was written all over his face.

"I'm not going anywhere, baby," Nina croaked. Her voice was deep and raspy due to her dry mouth.

"I thought you were going into a convulsion, and it was gonna lead to an overdose. Ma, I been reading up on heroin," he blurted out.

"What?" She looked at him, surprised.

"In the hospital they have all kinds of information on drugs. You have a lot of pamphlets that we brought home too. Ma, I want you to seriously consider going into a program and getting clean," Marquis suggested.

Nina shook her head while she rubbed the back of his hand.

"Ma, I know you said a person shouldn't judge another person. I know you said no one can tell you about you unless they walked in your shoes, but I can't understand why you would use drugs. Nothing is that bad to start using drugs," he said sincerely.

Nina cleared her throat. "You will never understand, and I wish I could tell you, but I can't." She looked away as one tear fell from her eye.

"Ma, you can tell me anything."

"No, baby. Not this. I . . . I . . . Mark, I'm gonna try to kick this thing. I'll go to detox," she agreed as tears stained her face.

Marquis did everything he could to stay awake in class. It killed him to do so. He also had to go to work that evening. He figured he would have to skip the rest of his classes for the day and go home to take a nap before work. He looked up at the clock on the wall and it read nine thirty AM. He put his books in his book bag and walked out of class while it was still in session. Once outside he enjoyed the warm and inviting breeze as he began the walk across campus. He heard someone calling his name, and he turned to see his favorite person, Shea. She was looking exceptionally lovely that day.

"Hey! Where are you going?" She leaned in and gave him a kiss on the cheek.

"What's up, Shea? I'm really tired, and I can't even keep my eyes open in that boring-ass class. I was thinking about running home to take a nap before work."

"Mark, you live all the way up the hill. By the time you get home and get to sleep good, it will be time to come back downtown. I live four blocks away. Come to my house and you can lay on the couch," she offered.

"Where are your parents?"

"They're at work, silly." She smiled.

"What about your classes?"

"They're just summer classes. I can get the work from a classmate."

"I thought you said your stepfather comes home sometimes?" he asked.

"He does, but today he's at a site in South Jersey. He does construction, so he won't be coming home early today."

Since their first meeting the two of them had been hanging out together on campus. They'd only talked on the phone a few times, but their special time together was spent at lunch every day. They would go to McDonald's and other nearby restaurants. After they ate, they would sit and talk until it was time for Marquis to go to work.

"How are you doing in your classes?" Shea would ask.

"It's all good, boring as hell though," Marquis complained.

"So what do you do when you're bored?" she looked at him sideways.

"What?" Marquis smiled. "What are you looking at me like that for?"

"I'm saying I've seen your classes and there aren't that many dudes in your classes. So I'd like to know what do you do when you're bored?" She eyed him suspiciously but playfully.

"Come on, I ain't thinking 'bout them girls in those classes," he continued to smile. He was flattered by Shea's display of jealousy. He thought it was cute. "You're the only female on my mind." Marquis kissed her on the lips.

"Yeah OK, I was just checking. Don't let the pretty face and the proper English fool you son, because I can thump with the best of them." Shea used her homegirl voice.

Marquis burst into laughter.

Marquis adored Shea, and Marquis could tell she felt the same way about him.

"You're so cute," he said playing with her hair.

Shea gazed into his eyes. "So why don't you have a girlfriend again?"

"Come on," he laughed. "I told you why."

"So tell me again."

"Are you serious? You don't remember what I told you?"

"Yeah I know. I just want to make sure your story is the same."

"Oh so that's how it works. You playing games," he said.

"Games? Me? Naw son, I don't play games."

"OK enough with the hood rat talk," he told her.

"What? I thought that's what you wanted. A ride or die chick. A chick that would have her mans back."

"Shea," he looked at her seriously. "I like you because you aren't all of those things. I can probably have any hood rat I want, but why? I want to be with you because you are smart. You have a goal in life just like me. We have so much in common and I love the way you speak proper English. I don't need a woman to stand behind me. I want a woman to stand next to me and I see that in you," he said sincerely.

It was true they did have so much in common, one thing being they had both managed to escape the harsh reality of the hood by not letting it consume their minds, and their plans for the future.

"So you sure your stepfather is not gonna come home?"

"No Marquis. Don't you trust me?" She smiled at him.

"Well that's a whole other story." He put his arms around her shoulders.

"Don't get smart." She punched him in the stomach playfully. "You can come over if you want to."

"OK, if you say so. I don't want to be the reason that you fail your class."

"Trust me, boo-boo, not you or nobody else is gonna be able to make me fail at anything. Come on, let's go." She winked at him and wrapped her arm around his waist.

Shea lived on the first floor of an old, two-family home. The outside of the house didn't look inviting, but once inside, it was like stepping into a whole new world. The immaculate apartment was stylish.

"Have a seat, and I'll get you a pillow and a sheet." Shea walked out of the room.

Marquis watched her hips sway as she walked. He looked around the living room and placed his book bag on the floor next to the couch. He sat down and smoothed his jeans with his hands. His body sank into the huge, plush pillows. He laid his head back and the comfort of the cushions almost sucked him in. Shea returned with a sheet and a fluffy pillow.

"Stand up," she ordered.

Marquis stood and watched her as she covered the sofa with the yellow sheet. She placed the pillow on top of the sheet, then she walked over to turn on the window air conditioner.

"There. It should be cool in here in no time. Would you like a blanket, just it case it gets too cold?"

"Naw, I'm good. I probably wouldn't feel it anyway." Marquis sat down again.

Shea continued to stand and watched him remove his Timberland construction boots. Marquis lay down and looked up at her. He grabbed her hand and pulled her down onto the couch with him.

"Mark, what are you doing?"

"Just lay here with me. I'm not gonna do nothing," he assured her. He was telling the truth. His mind and body were so exhausted that having sex with Shea was the last thing on his mind. Shea positioned her body in front of his and lay on the pillow with him. Her ass was pressed up against his dick. Marquis draped his arm around her waist and relaxed his body.

"Can you wake me up at four?"

"I better set the clock on the radio, because I may fall asleep myself." Shea got up, set the alarm on the stereo system, and then returned to the comfortable spot next to Marquis on the sofa. They lay together until they both fell asleep.

About four hours later Marquis felt Shea kissing him on the neck. He thought he was dreaming at first, but when he opened his eyes, he realized it wasn't a dream. He accepted the attention she was giving him. She continued to plant wet kisses along his neck and ears. Marquis was not a virgin, and he could tell that neither was Shea. She played the innocent little girl, but the way she fondled his hard-on showed him that she wasn't.

"What are you doing?" he whispered when she began to unzip his jeans.

She simply looked at him and smiled, never saying a word. She removed his stiff dick and played with it.

"You better be careful with all that in your hands. It may just bite you," Marquis said, looking down and enjoying her hands on his dick. Shea slid herself down, her face inching closer and closer to his rock-hard erection.

Marquis knew where she was going, and as horny as he was, he wanted nothing more than for her to put it in her mouth. But he really liked Shea, and he didn't want to think of her in that way. He wanted to really build something with her. He didn't want to consider her as one of the little whores from the neighborhood. He wanted something more. He grabbed her shoulders to stop her from going down on him.

"What?" she asked as if she was an innocent child.

"You don't have to do this," he said seriously. "I really came over here to take a nap, Shea. I didn't come for this, and I don't want you to think you are obligated to do this. I'm good with just being here with you."

"But I like you too, and I want to do this. I want to feel you inside me. I haven't had any in a few months, and I am tired of pleasing myself."

"Come here." He pulled her up toward his face. She lay partially on top of him. "In time that can happen. But right now let's just take it one day at a time and get to know each other, for real." He looked deep into her eyes.

Shea smiled. "Wow! I have never met a guy who just wanted to get to know me personally. When they would say they wanted to get to know me, they wanted to know what was in between my legs. You are such a sweetheart, Marquis."

He smiled at the way she pronounced his name. She dragged out the R sound.

"Come on. Let's go get something to eat before I have to go to work." Marquis put his now limp dick away and got up from the sofa.

Malik watched his mother walk into the Trinitas Hospital Substance Abuse Service Center in Elizabeth. She was going to admit herself into the seven-day detox program. Marquis had class and couldn't go with them to drop off his mother. Nina had asked Malik to stay outside. She didn't want him to come in with her. She wanted to do this alone.

Malik asked the cab driver to pull up to the corner. He looked out of the rear window of the cab just to make sure his mother wasn't gonna walk out. He was no stranger to how an addict had all kinds of tricks up their sleeves. They couldn't be trusted, even if the addict was his mother. He waited for about five minutes while the meter on the cab was still running. Nina never came out of the building. He was relieved to see that she was going to go through with it.

⋈⋈⋈⋈

ONE WEEK LATER . . .

Malik and Jeff met up and were on their way to the block to start work. As they approached the corner, they saw that the police had several of the crew up against the wall, frisking them. The two teens decided to fall back and watch from a distance. Several other observers stood on the other three corners, watching. Some yelled obscenities at the cops.

"Damn, yo!" Jeff shook his head.

Malik just looked on and didn't say a word.

"I wonder what's up with that?" Jeff asked.

"Hell if I know," Malik responded. Malik couldn't figure out what was going down because he knew that Death had an enormous amount of cops on his payroll. There were times when the crew would be standing on the corner, right in the middle of a sale, and a squad car would ride by. They would nod their heads at the officer and he would do the same, and continue to roll past.

While the crew was frisked by one cop, a second officer walked up to the third officer, who was watching over the crew, and handed him a brown paper bag. The officer looked in the bag. As far as Malik could tell, it was the stash they used to sell to customers. Neither Malik nor Jeff could make out what was being said, but from the body language of the police officers, they could tell they were trying to get answers about what they had just found.

Justice was the last to get searched when the officer found the gun he always bragged about stuffed down the front waistband of his jeans. The officer removed the gun, passed it to another officer, and handcuffed

Justice before escorting him to the backseat of the patrol car. After several more minutes of interrogation, the officers let the rest of the crew members go. The cops got back into their cars and pulled off with Justice.

When the coast was clear, Malik and Jeff walked over to the crew, who was discussing what had just happened.

"That was some bullshit! I thought we was protected!" one of the runners named Hanif shouted.

"Word up! That shit was a setup," Money concluded.

"What up, Malik?" Brian asked when Malik and Jeff came over.

"Yo, what happened?" Malik asked.

"Man, we was just standing here and them bitches just rolled up on us. They was roughhousing us and the whole nine," Brian complained.

"Word," the rest cosigned.

"Yo, they got Jus," Money added.

"He had his heat on him, and you know they gonna try to burn him on that shit," Hanif said. "And you know they gonna pin the stash on him that they found too."

"We gonna have to get up with Death and let him know what's up," Malik stated.

"That's on you, homeboy. You next in line after Jus," Brian said.

"How you figure? I'm just a regular nigga, just like y'all." Malik did not want to rank second behind Justice.

"Naw, man, you definitely the man," Jeff chimed in. "You can run shit better than Justice. We always took direction from you, even before we got down on these corners."

Malik stood there, deep in thought. The last time he spoke with Death, he was trying to get his own blocks, but since then he had decided to do his own thing. He knew someone was going to have to tell Death about Justice if he didn't already know by now. They wouldn't be able to eat if they didn't have product to push. Nobody else was going to do it, so Malik knew it would have to be him.

He walked over to one of the few payphones left on the street. Nowadays most of the payphones had either been removed or torn down by the neighborhood kids. The majority of people carried cell phones, making the boxes useless on the corners. Malik retrieved a few coins from his pocket and used them to dial Death on his business cell phone. He let it ring until he got the voicemail. Malik knew not to leave a message.

Death had a system, and the cell phone number he gave to the boys was strictly for business and emergency purposes. When any one of his corners called the business line, they were to let the phone ring until the voicemail came on. Then either Death would have someone call back, or he would send someone by the corner to check on his crew.

Death looked at the business cell phone as it rang. He saw that it was Justice's block's pay phone number calling. Little did the crew on the block know that Death was already aware of the situation. His phone had been blowing up since the incident started. He put the cell phone back in his pocket and sat there in the church basement, listening to an old white man call off bingo numbers.

Death was bored out of his mind. He had called his brother for a meeting, and the one thing he hated most was the crazy meeting places his brother picked to meet. Sergeant Tilmond had instructed him to come to an old church in Clark, New Jersey. They were in the basement of the church, and it was Bingo Night. There were fifty old people in the church, all trying to win the night's jackpot. The elderly man who called the numbers looked to be a hundred-years-old, due to the many wrinkles that graced his face. Death watched as the man's hand shook horribly when he tried to read the ball that he retrieved from the basket. He looked over at his brother, who had at least eight boards in front of him and seemed to be in deep concentration.

Death turned around and saw that Three the Hard Way had made themselves comfortable, and were trying to play the game as well. Death just shook his head at the trio. He brought them along with him because he'd sent Bear on another assignment.

"Come on you old, crinkled motherfucker," Ibn mumbled.

"Leave the man alone. He can't help it 'cause he old. You ain't gonna win anyway, motherfucker," Dean told him.

"Bullshit if I don't! Call my number, you wrinkled bastard," Ibn snarled.

The three older white women who were sitting at the same table were offended by the trio's use of foul language. Not to mention the fact that there were only a handful of blacks in there in the first place. The three old ladies gathered their boards and chips and removed themselves from the table.

"See? Look what you did! You done ran the old biddies away. I was gonna try and get me some pussy from one of 'em." Jamal laughed.

The other two laughed along with him. People began to turn around and glare at them for disturbing the game. Even Tilmond raised his head and gave them an evil look.

"Rell, let's get this over with so I can get these clowns back to the hood," Death said. "You know damn well they ain't got no manners, and they damn sure don't need to be up in here with all these crackers."

"B-5," the old man said into the mike.

"Oh, you old fart!" Dean yelled. The man had just missed calling the number Dean needed to have Bingo.

"*Shhh!*" others in the room responded.

"Rell, man, why you have to meet me here? Damn!" Death was growing inpatient.

"Listen, don't blame me for bringing those knuckleheads inside. You know damn well how they are." Tilmond looked over his boards.

"I can't leave them fools outside either. Never mind all that. What's up with the sweep on my corners?"

"Sweep?" Tilmond asked as if he didn't know what his brother was talking about.

"Don't play yourself! You know damn well what the fuck I'm talking about," Death hissed.

"That sweep had nothing to do with my team, Todd. That came from my captain."

"OK, so why the fuck would your captain send pigs to sweep my corners?"

"Your corners? Come on, bruh, you renting those corners. I have no idea what happened, but give me a few days and I will have some answers for you."

"Why am I paying you, Rell? You supposed to have my back, man! Where was the motherfuckers that's on my payroll? They couldn't stop that shit?"

"Todd, I said I don't know what happened. As soon as I find out, I'll let you know." He gave Death an I-am-the-oldest-so-listen-to-me look.

Death sat back in the folding chair and played with a chip.

"N-24," the caller announced in a shaky voice.

Several people in the building grunted out in disappointment. It was getting down to the wire. At any moment there was bound to be a winner.

"Do you realize how much money I lost? Those faggot-ass cops hit every last one of my blocks and cleaned me out!" Death was serious.

"I'll take care of it."

"You need to take care of it, Rell. Ain't no way in hell I'm gonna get these niggas to pay more in taxes to be protected with this kinda shit happening."

"B-6."

"Bingo! Motherfuckin' Bingo! Yeah!" Dean yelled at the top of his lungs. He stood with both fists held in the air like he'd just won the heavyweight title of the world. He jumped up and down in celebration while the elderly people in the room panicked. They were afraid of the big, black man who looked as if he was going to rob the place. Dean ran up to the front with his winning Bingo board. He approached the old man, who was now ready to shit his pants.

"Where my money at?" Dean yelled at the poor man.

The man was so shaken that he couldn't even speak.

"Go get your boy, Todd." Tilmond eyeballed Death.

Death snapped his fingers and directed Ibn and Jamal to retrieve Dean. He looked back at his brother as if to say, "I'm that nigga." Tilmond shook his head.

"Get them clowns outta here. I'll call you later." Tilmond dismissed him.

Death rose to his feet and straightened out his pants. "It's all love," he said in a low tone.

"All love," Tilmond said, returning the sentiment.

Chapter Fourteen

The pay phone rang and Malik ran over to answer it.

"Stay there," was all Death said to Malik. Several minutes later the Mercedes pulled over to the corner.

"Get in," Death ordered.

Malik was shocked because no one else was in the car, and Death was driving. Malik hopped in the front seat, but not before telling the crew he would be back. Once in the car they drove in silence until Death spoke.

"I'll have somebody come by here tomorrow to drop off some more work. By then, Justice will be back on the block. Until then, y'all niggas got a day off."

Malik looked over at the big man and couldn't believe his ears. As hard as they worked for him—not to mention the amount of bread that their blocks pulled in—and this was the best way this nigga could rap with him? Malik was heated.

"No offense, Death, but I can handle the blocks. Just get me the work, and I'll show you what I'm working with. In fact, you told me to prove it to you, and then you would consider giving me my own blocks." Malik didn't really want that now, but he was testing Death, just to see how much game he had with him.

"Naw, my dude. Right now is not the time to be training niggas."

"Training? I think you got me fucked up with somebody else. I don't need no training, but it's cool. It's on you, man." He glanced out the window. "You can let me out right here."

Death pulled the car over to the curb. "Tell the rest of them little niggas to be on the block tomorrow, and the work will come through."

Malik didn't say a word. He hopped out of the car and walked back to the blocks.

Death liked Malik, and after the conversation they just had, he was feeling him even more. Malik was about his paper, and that was the type of nigga he needed on his team. He would seriously consider putting Malik onto his own blocks.

Once Malik made it back to the block, he saw that the crew was waiting to hear what he had to say.

"What up, Malik?" Brian asked.

"Yo, Death said he gonna send somebody through tomorrow with the work. He also said y'all got the night off."

They all looked at each other in confusion. They were sure that Death was going to let Malik step up to the plate.

"So, you ain't gonna take Justice's place?" Tim asked.

"Naw, man, but trust, I'm good with that. So I guess I'll see y'all tomorrow." Malik didn't want to talk about it anymore. The crew left, talking excitedly about going to a Chinese restaurant.

Malik contemplated his next move. He damn sure wasn't going to sit around and wait on nobody to eat. It was only a matter of time anyway before he and Justice bumped heads. Now was as good a time as any to step up his game.

"Yo, Jeff, Brian! C'mere," Malik called to his boys.

"What up?" Jeff asked as he and Brian approached.

"We need to get some heat and quick."

"Why, what's up?" Jeff wanted to know.

"Yo, I ain't feelin' this whole situation, and you know I don't trust that nigga Justice. I been thinking about breaking out on my own, and if I do, are y'all down with me?"

Jeff looked at the ground. Brian spoke first.

"No doubt," Brian agreed.

"You mean, you want to go against the grain? I mean, I ain't tryna go up against Death, man," Jeff said with concern.

"Listen, Jeff, we don't work directly for Death, so that nigga could care less. That nigga Jus gotta take the fall, because it's on him to get his crew together. I ain't nobody's flunky. I'm 'bout to do my own thing." Malik was serious.

"I'm ya man and all, but seriously, who you gonna cop from?" Jeff inquired.

"Don't worry 'bout that. Leave that to me."

"So where you gonna get heat from? 'Cause frankly, I always wanted to be strapped," Brian chimed in.

"I'll get with Kurt. He knows everybody. I know he knows where we can get a couple of burners from. Y'all got the loot to spare for it?"

"Hell, yeah! I'm straight," Brian said.

"Yeah, I'm good," Jeff replied.

"Bet! Then it's on. I'll let y'all know when we gonna make that move."

ෞෞෞෞ

One night after his first talk with Death, Malik had met up with his cousin and they took a ride. His cousin was doing big things, and was putting in work for a cat named Luke. Luke was in direct competition with Death, but Luke worked the other side of town. Rumor had it that Luke's product was more potent than Death's. Word was that Luke had crossed the border into Death's territory and shut down his shop. Since Malik's cousin was down with this young team, Malik felt that the benefits were better than being under Justice, and he felt that he could make paper with no problems.

Chapter Fifteen

Justice walked out of the county jail where he'd spent three days in lockup. He'd known that Death would post bail all along. He looked around, trying to focus in the blinding sunlight when he spotted Dean, who was leaning up against a car, waiting on him. Dean looked like a pimp straight from the seventies.

Dean wore a lime green and cream dress shirt over his lime green pants. His hat was a lime green brim with a cream-colored band. With his sunglasses, you couldn't tell Dean that he wasn't dipped. If it was the seventies, then he would be on point, but it wasn't, so he stuck out like a sore thumb.

Justice descended the steps and walked over to Dean. Dean looked the boy up and down and put a cigarette in between his lips. After lighting the cigarette he gestured for Justice to follow him, not saying a word. Justice trailed him as they walked to the next block where Ibn and Jamal waited in the car. Dean opened the back door for Justice and the teen slid in next to Jamal. After Dean hopped into the front seat, Ibn pulled into traffic.

No one spoke during the ride. Justice was about to die of smoke inhalation because all three men were smoking with the windows cracked because the AC was on. Justice rolled the window down to get relief from the cigarette smoke, and Jamal almost lost his mind.

"Little nigga, you must be crazy? Roll up that goddamn window. Don't you see we got the AC on?" he yelled.

"Man, I can't take this smoke! I need to get some air."

"I tell you what, little nigga. If you don't roll up that window, you gonna be tryna find some air after I put a hole in your little lightweight ass," Jamal growled.

Ibn and Dean shot him venomous looks. Defeated and outnumbered, Justice rolled up the window.

They drove for another ten minutes before they turned into a small parking lot located behind a chain of stores. They all exited the car and Justice was escorted to the front entrance, next to the record shop. Fear immediately invaded his body. Justice knew from the past that the empty apartment above the record shop was the place where Death took niggas to torture and kill them. He stopped in his tracks just as Jamal opened the door to the steps that led to the apartment.

"Fuck is wrong with you? Move it," Ibn bellowed. He gave Justice a push to help him into the hallway, and they all climbed the dark stairwell.

When they walked into the apartment, Justice noticed that the front room had a loveseat and a small table. This brought him some relief, as he remembered the apartment not having any furniture. Ibn pushed him again so that he would follow Jamal into the next room. Once in the room, Justice saw Death sitting in his usual spot on the windowsill, looking down onto the streets.

Death turned around to greet them.

"What up, Jus?"

Justice nodded his head in acknowledgment. His mouth was extremely dry, and forming words at that point was almost impossible.

"I smell chicken," Ibn said. "You got something up here to eat?"

"Yeah, it's in the kitchen." Death laughed at Ibn. He and the other two were always hungry.

"Hells yeah! That's what I'm talking 'bout. I'm hungrier than a yard dog." Ibn left in search of the chicken.

"Yeah, man! I'm so hungry I could suck a sandwich through a straw," Dean exclaimed. He and Jamal was right behind Ibn.

Death turned his attention to Justice. "So, what did you tell them?"

"I ain't tell them nothing," Justice rasped.

"A'ight, but they did question you, right?"

"Yeah. They tried, but I ain't no snitch."

"What I tell you 'bout holding heat out on the blocks?"

"I thought it was all good since we had them pigs on payroll."

"We? *You* ain't got shit. I pay them motherfuckers to protect my investments," he said, pointing a finger at himself.

"My bad, but you know what I'm saying, though." Justice tried to reason with his boss without pissing him off.

"I know what you said, Justice. A'ight, check it. I'm gonna move you to a different location. In your absence I let my man Malik run the blocks, and he got it on lock." Death watched Justice's reaction.

Justice showed no emotion. He had to play it hard. He had to play like he wasn't bothered.

"It's whatever, man. Just as long as I make paper, I'm cool with whatever." He shrugged.

But Justice wasn't cool with it at all. His insides were boiling over. He was heated! He felt like maybe Malik set that shit up so that he could take the fall, and that way Malik could step up in his spot. He always thought Malik was jealous of him.

Death continued to tell Justice about the new area where he was going to grind. Justice got madder by the minute as Death spoke.

One of Death's head men, AP, walked into the apartment soon after.

"What good?" Death asked.

"It's all good right now," a cocky AP shouted, slapping hands with Death.

"Yo, this the cat I was rapping to you about." Death pointed to Justice.

AP looked at Justice with a screw face. Justice looked him up and down, not impressed. AP was a cocky, confident dude, and it showed. He was flashy and wore a lot of jewelry.

"So he'll be through the block tomorrow. Put him to work. He know the script," Death said.

"No doubt, Death. I'ma put little dude to work for sure. He gonna grind. You know how I do it!" He gave Death dap.

Justice wasn't feeling AP at all. AP kept looking at him when he talked, and the way he looked at Justice, he knew there was gonna be some issues. Justice felt that working for AP was an embarrassment because it was a demotion to his position, and he knew his street rep would be shot.

AP stood there with a stupid smirk on his face. When Death finished giving AP his direction, AP gave Death dap.

"Yo, son, I'll see you on the block tomorrow. Be there at seven AM," he said to Justice before leaving the apartment.

Justice just looked at AP. This didn't sit well with him. *He* was used to calling the shots. *He* was used to falling up on the block at whatever time he wanted, because he knew Jeff, Brian, and Malik had shit covered. Now he would have to be the low man on the totem pole again, and take orders from a clown like AP.

Jamal walked back into the room with a chicken leg in one hand and a cigarette in the other. He had a napkin tucked into the top of his shirt so as not to get food on it. Death shook his head.

"A'ight, so you know what you gotta do, Justice. Is there anything you want to discuss?"

"Naw . . . well, yeah. You know Juanita OD'd off the vials you told me to give to her. Did you know that the shit was tampered with?"

Death looked up at Jamal, who was still in the room. Jamal looked back at Death and raised an eyebrow.

"Your point is?" Death asked.

"I'm saying, is that shit gonna come back on me?"

"You worried about something?"

Justice didn't say anything. In fact, he already thought he'd said too much at that point.

"Listen, all you did was pass her a couple of extra vials. Unless you ran your mouth, nobody knows that. Right?" Death cocked his head and glared at Justice.

Justice wouldn't meet Death's eyes.

"Naw, it's all good. Don't nobody know," he said.

"Good."

The front door opened and two more of Death's security men entered. They dragged a man whose mouth had been taped shut and dropped him to the floor next to Justice. Justice jumped up out of his chair. He looked down at the man and could see that he had been beaten. His heart began to race.

Jamal immediately spread plastic on the floor and sat a chair atop it.

Justice saw this and his bowels turned to water. He just knew he was going to release them any minute. He was scared out of his mind.

"You want me to take him outta here?" One of the security men nodded at Justice. Ibn and Dean walked back into the room.

"Naw, I think he might like to see what happens to people who betray Death." Death smiled.

The man lay moaning and groaning on the hardwood floor. He sounded like he was trying to talk, but you couldn't make out the words.

"Call down to the music shop and have them turn up the music," Death ordered.

"We'll tell them when we get downstairs, unless you need us here," another security man said.

"Yeah, do that for me. We got this. Y'all can bounce." The two men turned and walked out of the room.

Jamal walked out of the room and returned within seconds with some rubber gloves and aprons. He passed Dean and Ibn each a pair of gloves and an apron. Death stood and walked over to the man that lay on the floor.

The man was lifted into the chair. He seemed to be inebriated because his body slouched in the chair.

"So you wanted to leave my team, huh?"

The man shook his head. He could barely keep his head up because he had been drugged. Jamal grabbed a spool of duct tape and taped the man to the chair.

Death positioned himself in front of the man. "Once you're in, you're in, son. Didn't I tell you that from the rip?"

The man tried to talk. Death nodded to Jamal and he peeled the tape back from the man's mouth.

"I got a family, man. I can't keep living like this," the man slurred.

"You ain't think about your family when you was gettin' money, so why now?"

"My wife said she would leave me if I didn't get outta the game," he struggled to say.

"You's a bitch-ass nigga! You let your bitch tell you how to be a man? Bleed this nigga. I got some place I need to be." Death was irritated.

The tape was reapplied and muffled the man's screams. As if on cue, the volume rose on the music in the store beneath them.

Jamal pulled a scalpel from the pocket of his apron and carved one of the man's eyes out of his head. The man screamed and moved the chair around as he tried to stand up. Dean and Ibn came to Jamal's aid and held the man in place. The other eyeball was removed and placed on the table next to the first one.

Justice did everything in his power to hold back the tears that sprang to his eyes. He refused to blink because he knew if he did, the tears would fall. He tried to look away from the torture.

Death walked over to Justice. "You a'ight?"

Justice didn't say a word. He just nodded his head. The stone face he thought he had on earlier was now gone.

"Listen, I'm not a mean cat. This nigga made a deal with Luke, our competition. He was getting ready to jump ship and get put on with that nigga. Now you know that ain't how the game is played. So there was only one thing to do—death by lethal injection." He laughed.

Death looked at Justice and was satisfied that he got the general idea on what not to do. He ordered Ibn to drop off Justice while Jamal and Dean continued to torture the man in the chair.

Fifteen minutes later Justice was dropped off in his neighborhood. He walked down the sidewalk with his head hung low. He was in deep thought. Fear still swam around in his body. He played the part of a cold gangster, but he wasn't as hard as many thought. What he experienced today was something that changed his heart. He feared dying, and he knew that working with Death ultimately meant death. He realized he had sold his soul to the devil himself. He knew now he was in it for life. He didn't want to play the game anymore, and he knew he had to do something to get out from under Death's command. But what could he do?

ന്ദന്ദന്ദന്ദ

While Justice had his meeting with Death, Malik did as he was told and oversaw the blocks until Justice returned. Bear came through and called Malik over to him.

"What's up?" Bear greeted in his deep voice. Sweat poured from his face like a river. Bear hated the heat.

"What up?" Malik replied.

"It's all you. You got the blocks. Death said you the man from this day on out. It's up to you to get ya own crew, and when the bread is short, it's still on you." He wiped a mound of sweat with a towel he was holding.

"Word?" Malik thought for sure that Death wasn't gonna let him run the corners. He didn't know what to do, because he had already put the bug in his cousin's ear to put him on with Luke. *Damn, now what am I gonna do?* he wondered. "Anyway, when can I get up with Death?"

"Why?" Bear inquired.

"I need to holler at him for a minute," Malik replied, irritated by Bear's nosiness.

"I'll get word to him. In the meantime, get money." Bear got back into his car.

Malik watched as the car pulled off. He walked back over to where the fellas were waiting.

"Yo, what's up, man?" Brian asked eagerly.

"Death gave me the blocks," Malik said.

"I knew it!" Jeff replied. "Yeah, nigga!" He punched Malik in the arm playfully.

"Did y'all niggas forget about us stomping for Luke? Y'all out here celebrating and shit. So what are we supposed to do about that?" Malik asked.

"Man, I say fuck Luke! We already got our shit established. We already set up, nigga. Just accept victory and let's get this paper!" Jeff replied.

"I'm with that," Brian agreed.

"Yeah, but I had my cousin talk on my behalf and shit. How that shit gonna make him look?"

"Listen, Malik, man, I know that's ya family and all, but y'all niggas ain't that damn tight. If you was, then he woulda put you on a long time ago. He knew you was out here starving, and he didn't hit you off not once," Jeff stated.

Malik thought about it. Jeff was right, but Malik struggled with getting on board with Death. Would it still be the right thing to do? After all, he did witness how Death treated his mother, and he didn't like it one bit.

"I don't know, man, but I told Bear that I wanted to holler at Death, so we'll see what's up."

"Well, until that happens, it's time to celebrate. That nigga Justice gonna be tight when he step up on the block and see you running shit." Jeff laughed.

"Hell, yeah," Brian joined in.

"Naw, son. We ain't celebrating until shift end," Malik said. "Right now we 'bout to get shit poppin', 'cause I ain't tryna be Death's bitch for long. I'm gonna save my money and start my own shit. Now if y'all niggas down with me, then y'all need to start stackin' ya loot too. We can be partners in our business." He stared at them seriously.

"Word, I'm with that." Brian nodded.

"I'm in," Jeff agreed.

"A'ight. Get them other niggas, 'cause we 'bout to have a meeting. I'ma show y'all motherfuckers how to really grind."

Chapter Sixteen

It had been weeks since any of the crew had seen Justice. Malik had the blocks jumping. He was a natural-born leader. Under his leadership everyone seemed to feel less stressed. Ibn came every morning and every night to drop off the product and pick up profits from sales, and the revenue continued to rise since Justice had left.

Malik had his crew on point. They worked in shifts. He hugged the blocks more hours than any of them, making sure everything ran like clockwork. Malik even came up with a system to beat the police, who always came through the block trying to catch them slipping.

Malik had six crew members, two runners per shift. Jeff and Brian were the most experienced, so he split them up into separate shifts. First shift started at seven AM and stopped at four PM. The next shift started at four PM and ended at twelve AM. The third shift—the graveyard shift—was from twelve AM to seven AM. Malik had each shift member rotate the corners every hour.

Packages were no longer stashed behind buildings, in paper bags, in garbage cans, or in drain pipes. They were now stashed primarily in mailboxes. No one in the neighborhood mailed anything anyway, so the postal workers would never come to empty the box, plus, they feared the corners.

Malik requested that an old car be parked on one of their corners. It had to be legal, with correct papers on it. The car also had to be operable, so that it could be moved around from time to time to seem like it really belonged to a resident in the area. This car was used as a stash spot. Product would be stashed underneath the bumpers, and the backseat of the car.

Malik came up with a system that worked for them during the day. He took ordinary tennis balls and partially cut them. Because they were hollow inside, the balls still appeared to be intact. Each runner had two tennis balls—one cut and one uncut. When a customer came to purchase, one runner would put the drugs into the cut ball and toss it to the runner who was serving the customer. It appeared that the males were playing ball, because when there wasn't a sale, they would toss around the uncut balls to each other or against the buildings in case any police were observing.

One day soon after Malik had taken over the blocks Marquis came on the block to talk to Malik, who was standing in his usual spot. They both leaned up against the building. The sun wasn't quite as hot as it had been the day before, so it was a pleasant day. Everyone seemed to be out that afternoon enjoying the weather. The local kids had even opened the fire hydrant down the street. It seemed that the word spread fast because kids from everywhere came to cool off in the city water.

"'Sup, baby bruh?"

"What up, man?"

"Why you not at school?" Malik asked.

"Didn't have to go. We're having a two-day testing. I'm only part-time, so I stayed the whole day yesterday to do my testing and completed it all."

"Oh, so you have the day off?" Malik raised an eyebrow.

"Yup."

Both of them continued to stand there in silence, watching the scenery. The two runners tossed the ball back and forth to each other across the street, trying to pass the time. Brian came out of the store and saw Marquis. He walked over and shook his hand.

"What up, Mark?"

"What's good?"

"Gettin' this money," he responded before returning to his corner.

"So, what's on ya mind?" Malik asked.

"How do you know something's on my mind?" Marquis looked at him.

"Come on, bruh, I lived with you all ya life. We joined at the hip, so when you think it, I feel it. Feel me?" Malik looked at him.

"Yeah, man. You know I been chillin' with this broad I met at school."

"Oh, word? You hit that yet?"

"Come on, man, that ain't why I kick it with her. She cool as hell, and I really like her. But she lives with her mother and stepfather. That nigga is fucked up in the head. I believe he treats her badly, and her mother don't say nothing 'cause she scared of him. It's like when I first saw her, she used to look sad all the time. But once we got to know each other, it's like I make her happy when we're together."

"So what's the problem? I'm not getting it." Malik observed an unmarked car as it bent the corner from down the street.

Marquis looked up and spotted the same vehicle. "Narcs," he said.

"Yeah, I see 'em."

Malik put two fingers in his mouth and whistled a high-pitch whistle. Brian picked up a two by four piece of wood that leaned against the building behind him. The other two runners trotted over to him. One held the tennis ball while the other stopped in the street. The three were playing stick ball by the time the Narcotics patrol car reached the corner.

The black windows hid the identity of the undercover cops, but Malik still stared at the car and was not moved by them in the least. He and Marquis never moved from their spot. The runner that was in the street moved out of the way so that the car could pass and then returned to his spot, pretending to play ball. The undercover car made a quick right at the corner, drove halfway up the block, and busted a U-turn, but Malik had already peeped around the corner of the building to check the whereabouts of the vehicle.

He made a fist with his hand held high in the air to let the crew know to stay in their spots. When the unmarked car reappeared on the block, everyone was doing exactly what they were doing when it first drove through. The car sat at the corner for a few minutes with the windows still rolled up. Everyone ignored it as if it wasn't even there.

The car turned right and went down the street to where the children had the open fire hydrant.

"So, back to what you was saying," Malik said.

"Oh yeah, I mean when I'm with her it's different from any other chick I've been with. Me and Shea have intelligent conversations. You feel me?"

Malik nodded that he understood but kept his focus on the surroundings.

"I'm saying, I wanna hit it bad as hell, but then again I have so much more respect for her."

"Sounds like that broad got ya nose wide open, baby bruh."

"You got me fucked up. No broad will ever have my nose open," Marquis defended.

"Ok, so, you saying all of this to say what then?"

"I'm saying I got a lot of respect for her and I don't want to dog her out cause she ain't like them other chicks I fucked with . . ."

"OK I get it," Malik interrupted Marquis. "So what's the problem?"

There was an awkward silence.

Malik spoke up. "Listen, baby bruh if you feeling this broad the way you say. Then wife her. I mean ain't nothing wrong with that. You a good dude."

"Yeah I hear you," Marquis agreed.

"But whatever you gonna do, just make sure you don't let this broad get in the way of school."

"No doubt," Marquis said as he observed the undercover cops as they had come back and parked down the street.

"Malik, since you holding it down, you shouldn't be seen out here all the time. You don't think they know your face?" Marquis nodded in the direction of the undercover cops.

"Oh, you know about the streets now?" Malik laughed.

"Naw. I'm saying, they know you running this."

"Mark, I change my clothes at every shift, and most times I go in and get some sleep for a couple of hours when Jeff out here."

"I feel you, big bruh, but they still know ya face. They know, man, I'm telling you. Now if it was me, I wouldn't be out here all the time. I mean, you got Jeff and Brian for that. I would observe from a distance, and then I would roll through and chill every now and then."

Malik smirked at his brother. "Leave the streets to the street niggas. I got this, Mark." He punched his brother in the arm playfully.

ᏃᎧᏃᏦᎧᏃᏦᎧᏃ

Death, Bear, Three the Hard Way, and several other members of

Death's squad sat around a large oak table in the dining room of one of Death's three homes.

"A'ight, first I want to tell y'all that business is good. Every team has been very profitable. We haven't had any major problems that we couldn't solve until now. But there is one slight issue I will tell y'all about before I get to the real shit. I talked to my peoples downtown for the second time, and they ain't happy with us right now. They say we gettin' sloppy with how we handle our business. Them motherfuckers is tryna go up on us in taxes for the shit."

"What?! They already taxing us enough, and you mean to tell me they want more. Naw, man! Them pigs getting greedy is what it is," Trey said.

"Word up!" the others agreed.

"Hold up!" Death tried to calm them down. "Yo, I feel y'all niggas 'cause I'm getting taxed too. I mean, I got blamed for them clowns rolling through the block dumpin' on Central Ave. I got blamed for that body they found in the lot, and I got blamed for the shit you did, Mike," he pointed to another dealer.

"Yo, man, my shit was clean!" Mike protested.

"Naw, fam, it wasn't clean at all. The dogs was still there, and so was the body."

"Listen, man, the dogs weren't fed for over two weeks. They was hungry and ready. I was coming back to get 'em," he defended.

"Well, homeboy, you didn't go back soon enough. The cat's body was still intact, and not only that, you left evidence."

"Yo, I don't know what happened then. Do they know anything about who did it?" Mike was concerned.

"Naw, because the motherfuckers y'all don't want to pay more money to covered the shit up! Y'all niggas fail to realize that even if they don't lift prints to link them to anyone, they still got detectives and investigators on the case. So we pay these crooked motherfuckers to keep them niggas at bay, so that they *don't* find out who did the shit," Death scolded. "So the harder they gotta try to hide shit, the more time is spent, which means the more money we gotta pay. Simple as that!"

The men in the room began to grumble. They didn't like what they had just heard, because Death had just told them in so many words that they were going to pay—period, whether or not they wanted to.

"Yo, I know y'all bitch ass niggas ain't complaining?" Death asked as he stood.

Everyone became silent.

"Yo, listen, we gotta come up off of the bread, plain and simple. If you don't want to let loose of the bread, then just let me know 'cause we can handle it right now, before we go any further," he said as he clasped his hands in front of him.

The men looked around at each other, knowing that none of them were going to speak up—all except one. Demetri was Death's second cousin. They grew up together and were pretty close, but just like Death, Demetri had a temper and was just as hard as his cousin. Death and Demetri got into arguments often, but because they were family, they always came to a truce. After Demetri did a ten-year stint in prison, he became a hardened criminal. When he came home, Death put him right on as one of his top men.

"Come on, man, how you sound?" Demetri exploded. "That shit is stupid. Seriously, cuz, you can't be serious. Either them motherfuckers gonna take what we give them, or we need to take care of the ones who got a problem to send a message to the rest. You feel me? 'Cause I ain't with coming up outta my pockets no more than I already am. Next thing you know, we'll be working for them motherfuckers." He frowned.

"D, you missing the point. In order to keep doing what you do and be comfortable without any conflicts, you gotta pay to play."

"Todd, man, come on! You ain't even hungry no more, man. Oh, so now you eatin' good, what, you getting soft? What happen to the hunger and grind you had in you? Nigga get some bread and then he turns political and shit, with your head up them motherfuckers' asses. Typical nigga! Now you a house nigga?"

Hearing his government name called out in front of everyone stirred the monster inside Death. He stood there, trying to remain calm and cool.

"We'll talk on the side 'bout this," he said, dismissing Demetri.

Death knew where the conversation was gonna go with his stubborn cousin, and he preferred it was done when everyone had left. Most times their arguments would get really heated and they would come close to fistfights. Death knew that was where this one was headed. Demetri stunted in front of everyone, and to add insult to injury, he had called Death by his birth name. Not that some of his crew members didn't know his given name, but they knew not to use it. Rumor had it that Death had injured many people for calling him by his birth name. Only a chosen few called him Todd.

"Fuck that!" Demetri growled. "Let's do this now, 'cause frankly it ain't just me who ain't feelin' this shit. These niggas scared of you, but I ain't. So let's do this now!"

Death's level of patience had reached the point of no return. Without hesitation he pulled a .45 out of his shoulder holster and planted one right between Demetri's eyes. Blood splattered onto the table and on the man sitting next to Demetri. As the back of Demetri's head exploded, the force of the bullet caused his chair to fly back, and Demetri's body landed on the ground, feet up.

Death calmly put the gun back into the holster and sat down. All in the room were wide-eyed and stuck on stupid. They knew Death was ruthless, but most hadn't seen what he was capable of because he always had his henchmen take care of his dirty work. If they hadn't been sure before, they definitely were now.

"Dump his body where it can be found, and get word to his mother that he must have gotten hit by a stray bullet," he told Three the Hard Way. The three men shook theirs heads in disappointment.

"Now, who has a problem with me?" Death asked calmly.

No one said a word. In fact, no one moved a muscle, not even the dude who had Demetri's blood and brain fragments on his clothing.

"A'ight then. Stop bitchin' and let's get to the reason why I brought y'all here. I brought y'all here so that I can let y'all in on what is about to happen. My squad leaders, y'all play a very important part to my plan whereas security, your risk is much higher." Everyone wondered what could be worse than what had just transpired.

"I know y'all know that nigga Luke," Death continued.

They all nodded.

"Well, he is my new problem. This nigga been shootin' his mouth off, talking 'bout he gon' take over. He been kickin' up dust all over the place. Word got back to me that he is cocky and confident that he can take over my territory. This nigga said my time is up, and that I need to go into retirement." Death laughed and the others laughed nervously along with him.

"This punk said I am over the league age. He said I need to sit down and let a young, up-and-coming nigga make his bread. Picture that shit?"

The room started to buzz. Death held up his hand to silence them. "Now, I heard this young clown got a squad of young gunners that will lay yo' moms on her back if they thought she was gonna say something out the side of her neck. I'm very sure this cat is gonna try me. I was told that his coke and dope can top my shit. But that, I ain't worried about. I know that nigga can't fuck with my shit. How many times we step on the shit?" he asked Bear.

"Three or four." Bear held up three, and then four skinny black crooked fingers that looked like burnt sausage links.

"Tell them niggas only step on it two times, and watch how my shit blow that niggas shit out the water," he instructed Bear. Death turned his attention back to his crew members. "See, muthafuckas kill me, yappin' and shit. I step on my shit at least three or four times, and it is still the hottest shit on the streets," he bragged.

"Word up," one man said. The rest chimed in with agreement.

"So what's up, Death? What you want a nigga to do?" Cleff asked.

"Easy, Cleff. I got my goons for that dude. What I got for you and the rest, I'll fill y'all in on later. Right now I need security beefed up." He looked over at Dean, Ibn, and Jamal, and they simply gave him a head nod.

Everyone continued to give him their undivided attention. Death explained to the crew that he was gonna start recruiting more muscle. He wanted everyone there to keep their ears and eyes open. He wanted to make a move on Luke before Luke made a move on him. The element of surprise was his plan.

Death's ego got the best of him because for the first time, he felt as though Luke might be a challenge for him. He knew the code of the streets. He knew if he showed any signs of weakness it was a wrap for him. Death knew that the day would come when he would have to retire, but he was not ready yet, so he would defend his title by any means necessary.

But Death may have bitten off more than he can chew.

൜൜൜൜

THREE WEEKS LATER . . .

Nina sat at the kitchen table looking through the classified ads in the newspaper. She had been home from detox for seven days and had not found another job yet. After admitting herself into the program, she lost her job because she didn't notify them. "No call, no show" went on record as her reason for termination. Jackie had made several attempts to reach her and was only told by Marquis that Nina had gone away. Jackie knew from experience what that meant, so she simply asked him to have Nina call when she got back. She herself was on her last leg at the job. Since Nina stopped smoking crack altogether, Jackie found a new get-high partner and had been missing a lot of days at work. She, too, found herself on probation for the same things for which Nina initially received probation.

Nina applied for unemployment, not knowing how long it would be before she found a new job. Malik was very helpful and gave her money to pay the bills for the apartment. She didn't like that he was selling drugs full-time, but she welcomed the money. Marquis also kicked in to help out around the house, but Nina wouldn't take his money. After all, he only worked part-time, and he needed his money for school and transportation.

Nina felt good. It had been a long time since she felt so refreshed. Unfortunately for her, she wasn't able to keep herself up the way she used to due to lack of money. She had to do her own hair, and ended up cutting her nails because she could no longer afford to have them done at the Chinese nail salon. There were times when Malik would offer the extra money to send her to the hair and nail salon, but she refused. Despite all that, she still remained neat and clean.

Frustrated, she folded the paper and sat it on the table. The same job openings had been in the paper all week, with maybe an exception of one or two new ones. She found out from unemployment that she was denied. Nina decided to take a nap because she had been getting up early every morning to go job hunting.

As Nina stood to make her way to the bedroom, the doorbell rang she walked over and looked through the peephole. She opened the door and smiled when she saw her friend Jackie standing there with a dirty duffel bag on her shoulder. Nina noticed for the first time that the drugs had begun to take a toll on Jackie.

Jackie had lost some weight, but it wasn't enough to make her appear that she was using. She was still overweight, and apparently she had been walking around for months with the same braids in her hair, because the new growth was extremely noticeable. The braids that hadn't fallen out already were merely hanging on by threads of hair, and the new growth hairs had twisted themselves into knots that appeared to be dreading. Jackie no longer saved enough money to get her hair re-done. Jackie also had bags under her eyes from lack of sleep. She no longer had the self-control to keep up her appearance the way Nina had managed to do when she was getting high.

"Hey, girl! Come in," Nina said. They embraced each other and the odor hit Nina in the nose. It was evident that Jackie hadn't bathed in a few days.

"You look so good! Not that you didn't before, but you have a calm glow to you now." Jackie was her usual loud and fabulous self. She walked in and sat on the sofa, making herself comfortable. Nina sat next to her.

"Where you been, girl?" Nina asked.

"Here and there. You know me." Jackie laughed nervously.

"Yeah, I know, but I came by your apartment and someone else answered the door, said you didn't live there anymore."

Jackie lowered her head.

"What's wrong, Jackie?" Nina was now concerned.

"Well I got put outta my apartment."

"You did?"

"Yeah, I was two months behind, but you know how that goes." She shrugged. "But what I didn't expect was my family to act all funny with me when I asked to stay with them."

"Your mother won't let you stay with her?" Nina was surprised. She had always known Jackie's mother to be there for Jackie whenever she needed help.

"Girl, my mother been acting funny for a while now. She started listening to gossip about me and came to her own conclusions."

Jackie talked as if her family was wrong for not taking her in. But she failed to tell Nina that she had burned her own bridge with her mother by stealing anything at her mother's house that she could get her hands on. So it wasn't the rumors that turned her mother bitter. It was Jackie and her fiendish ways.

"So where are you staying?"

"Oh, well, I stayed with my sister a couple of days. Then I stayed with my aunt a couple of days. You know, I bounce around so no one can say that I'm there for too long. I figure if I only stay a short time, then they won't have a problem letting me rest my head there if I ever need to come back."

"Yeah, I know what you mean, girl," Nina said.

"Nina, you are my best friend and I know you are tryna stay clean and all, but I really need a place to stay. Is it all right if I stay here with you for a few?"

"Say no more, Jackie. You know you my girl, and I will do anything I can to help you. But you can't bring any drugs in my house."

"I know. That's why I didn't come to you first. I knew you were tryna get yourself together. I am so happy for you. I will only be here for a few days," Jackie promised.

Nina smiled at Jackie and wondered if accepting her into her home was the right thing to do.

They sat laughing and talking for a half hour, something they hadn't done in a long time. Nina was enjoying their time together, but it was becoming difficult for Jackie. The monkey on her back was getting the best of her, and she was ready to get down to the other reason she was at Nina's. She wanted to borrow money to go get high. She had her new boyfriend downstairs waiting on her so that they could go cop. Her plans to use Nina's apartment as a smoke place went out the window when Nina told her she couldn't get high there. Jackie wasn't worried, though. They could always find a place to smoke, just as long as Jackie got the money.

"Hey, girl, I was wondering if you had any money I could borrow until I get my unemployment check?" Jackie lied.

"Jackie, girl, I ain't got a dime. You know if I had it, I would lend it to you, but I don't. Malik is taking care of us right now. I applied for unemployment and they denied me. They didn't deny you? " Nina asked.

"Nope. So Malik got a job?" Jackie tried to change the subject when in fact she already knew the answer. She had copped from his crew several times.

"No, girl. I wish! He out there on the block, and as much as I hate it,

I'm glad he is taking care of these bills for me right now, or else we would be on the streets."

"I feel you. Well, let me go. I'm gonna go to this job interview. Nina, girl, I promise I won't be a bother. I probably won't stay here all the time, but at least I know I can leave my stuff here and come lay my head when I need to." Jackie stood. She didn't need to stay there any longer than she had to because Nina didn't have any money. Jackie knew her boyfriend was going to be pissed because of the amount of time he had been waiting, and because she was going to come back to him with no money.

"Oh, OK, Jackie. Be careful out there," Nina said to her as Jackie walked out of the door in a hurry.

Nina shook her head. She knew Jackie wasn't going for an interview. She knew the fiend in Jackie, and she was definitely on a mission to get some crack.

Truthfully, Nina was jealous that Jackie was getting high. The undercover fiend in Nina was still lurking below the surface.

Chapter Seventeen

Nina walked into the office of the counselor that had been assigned to her while she was in detox. She didn't have any intention on coming to see the counselor, but after still not having found a job, she found herself becoming depressed and ready to use again. She had met with the counselor once for a brief moment in the hospital. Today was her first official meeting.

"How are you today, Nina? Have a seat," the counselor instructed.

Nina took a seat in the old chair and folded her hands on her lap. She looked around at the pictures on the wall. In every picture the counselor was with a different person. There were so many pictures that you could barely see the wall behind them. She saw the woman's college degrees, awards, and other important documents that were framed and hung on the wall, and the woman's desk was full of files and papers.

"Just give me a minute while I finish writing this report," she said, never looking up.

"OK," Nina responded as she noticed the name plate that sat on the desk, which read Nilda Reed.

Once Mrs. Reed was done with her paperwork, she shoved it into a file and laid her pen on the desk. Her skin was fair, with a few freckles located on the upper part of her cheeks. She had sandy brown, shoulder-length hair, pink lips, and gray eyes. Nina had already pegged the woman to be bi-racial. Mrs. Reed searched through the files on her desk, removed a file, and opened it. She read the contents for a moment, then placed it on the desk in front of her.

"As you know, my name is Mrs. Reed. We met at the hospital, right?"

Nina nodded, not saying a word.

"OK, good. You also know that I have been assigned to you. I see that you've been released from the detoxification program"—she paused to look at the paperwork—"hmm . . . a month ago. You were supposed to have come to see me two weeks after you got out of detox."

"I know." That was all Nina said, because she didn't know what else to say. She really didn't want to be there, and had she found a job, she wouldn't have been.

"Well, how do you feel?"

"I feel OK."

"What have you been doing since you got out of the hospital?"

"I've been looking for a job."

"Good. Any luck?" Mrs. Reed wrote something in the file.

"No."

"How does that make you feel?"

"Frustrated." Nina was honest.

"I'll bet it does. That's a normal emotion for this type of a situation; however, in your case, the important thing is: How are you going to handle it without relapsing?"

"I don't know. Mrs. Reed, is there any way you can help me find a job? My bills are falling behind and I really need to work to keep myself busy."

"I understand, Nina. However, I can't help you find a job. But I can give you resources to help you find a job." She reached into the file cabinet behind her and handed Nina several pamphlets for job programs that helped people with job searches.

Nina looked at the pamphlets and burst into tears. Her throat became tight, and her head began to hurt.

"Oh my God! Are you OK?" Mrs. Reed asked while running to Nina's side and handing her a few tissues from the box on her desk.

Nina cried in her arms for what seemed like an eternity. Mrs. Reed felt bad for Nina, but she didn't know why. All she knew was that Nina was crying tears from deep within. She knew those tears too well. Those were tears of a hurt soul, tears that only a person who was battling demons could produce. Mrs. Reed had been a counselor for drugs addicts for over fifteen years. She had helped hundreds of addicts find themselves again so they could go on and live better lives. She now hoped she could help Nina.

Mrs. Reed waited patiently until Nina had calmed down, and then she lifted Nina's head. "You are holding back, Nina, and I want you to let it go for me today."

Nina moved her head from Mrs. Reed's hand.

"I'm fine. I just get frustrated, and looking for a job is starting to frustrate me more."

"Well, Nina, then we need to talk about that. I mean, if you keep holding your feelings inside, making yourself frustrated, then you may turn to drugs again in order to free yourself from frustration. Everything is gonna be all right. Trust me."

"Have you ever used drugs?"

"Uh, no, I haven't, Nina. Why do you ask?"

"I thought so. Mrs. Reed, there are not enough degrees in the world that will teach you how it feels when using. You will never know the emptiness inside when you have nothing else to turn to but drugs for comfort. You have no idea how hard it is for me right now to hold on to the little bit of sanity that I have left, and not turn back to my comfort zone of using drugs. So how can you sit there and tell me that everything is gonna be all right? How can you tell me to trust you? I don't even know you. But yet and still, you want me to open up to you so that you and all your other bougie college friends can share war stories about us poor, drug addicted, helpless people while you sip on an apple martini! No! Hell no! I won't subject myself to this bullshit. Thank you, Mrs. Reed, but no, thank you." Nina stormed out of the office, leaving Mrs. Reed behind to think about her own past.

Although Mrs. Reed had never used drugs, she had been affected by drug use firsthand. Mrs. Reed had watched her father's addiction to drugs until she was ten-years-old when she found him dead in his bed with a needle sticking out from his arm. She had nightmares for years after that. When she turned seventeen her twin brother overdosed on heroin, leaving her alone. Five years ago, she lost her only child to a drug overdose. So, no, she might not have known what it was like to use drugs personally, but dealing with family members who used was just as painful.

Mrs. Reed sat back down at her desk. She tapped her pen against the desk and stared off into space, thinking of Nina. She accepted the challenge.

"OK, Satan, it's on!" she yelled in the empty room. "This battle is not mine, and you know whose it is. Let's see what you working with."

She looked in Nina's file and jotted down some information before closing it. Then she stood and pressed the intercom button on her phone.

"Yes, Mrs. Reed," the secretary answered.

"I'm going to be out of the office for the rest of the day."

"OK."

Mrs. Reed quickly grabbed her purse and left the office.

An hour later Mrs. Reed pulled in front of the building where Nina lived. She retrieved Nina's address from her purse and got out of the car. Once she reached Nina's apartment, she knocked on the door.

"Who is it?" Marquis asked, peeping out of the peephole.

"I'm here to see Nina.

"Who are you?" he asked.

"Can you please tell her Nilda is here to speak with her?"

"Hold on." Marquis knocked on the partially opened door to Nina's room. "Ma?"

"Come in," Nina said.

"Ma, some lady named Nilda is at the door for you."

Nina sat up in the bed. "Nilda?"

"That's what she said," Marquis said and walked away.

The door opened and Nina looked at Mrs. Reed with confusion, but she waved her in. Mrs. Reed walked into the neat apartment and made herself comfortable on the couch.

"Mrs. Reed, what are you doing here?" Nina asked her.

"Well, Nina, I didn't want our encounter today to end like it did. You never gave me a chance. We have more in common than you know. No, I've never used drugs, but I have been surrounded with them all my life, and lost some loved ones to addiction. Let me help you, Nina."

Nina stood there, looking at the floor. She didn't know what to say, so she didn't say anything.

Mrs. Reed pressed forward. "OK, Nina, do me one favor. Come with me somewhere, and after we go, if you don't want to continue your sessions with me, then I will understand. But just know that I am here for you, and I do know your pain, more than you know." Mrs. Reed stood and grabbed Nina's hand. "So, what do you say?"

"Where are we going? I don't know you like that to be going anywhere with you."

Mrs. Reed laughed. "Are seriously trying to tell me that I pose a threat to you? That I am some kind of a murderer and may kidnap you?"

Nina laughed at how dumb the idea sounded. "Hey, you might. There are some lunatics in this world, both female and male."

They both shared a laugh, and then Nina agreed to go with the persistent counselor.

Chapter Eighteen

Nina sat in the passenger seat of Mrs. Reed's car and looked straight ahead. She felt kind of awkward because she didn't know where they were going.

"Mrs. Reed, where are we going?"

"Call me Nilda." She smiled at Nina.

"OK, Nilda. Can you please tell me where you are taking me?"

"I'm taking you to a meeting. A meeting where there are others in your same situation. You need to start attending these meetings. It will give you encouragement and help to keep you from backsliding," she said.

What can a meeting do for me? Nina wondered.

After parking in the very full lot of the church, they walked toward the building. Nina looked around at the people that entered into the church in street clothes. She was baffled at what was going to take place inside.

"So we're going to church?" she whispered to Mrs. Reed.

"No. We're going to a Narcotics Anonymous meeting."

Nina stopped. "Nilda, I don't need to go to these meetings."

Mrs. Reed stopped and faced her. "Nina, how would you know that you don't need to go to these meetings if you've never been before?"

"Because I've heard of these meetings. They told me about them in my program. Half of the people who come are high in the meeting, so how will that help me?"

"Listen to me, Nina. These meetings are necessary. They are therapeutic. NA will show you that you are not alone. It will encourage you and help rebuild your confidence. Just give it a chance like you gave heroin a chance," she pleaded.

Nina looked at Nilda like she was crazy. *The nerve of her! How would she know how and why I started using in the first place?*

"Just try it, please?" Nilda grabbed her hand.

Nina and Nilda sat in folding chairs in the basement of the church. At the front of the room were two men seated at table. Nina looked around at the many faces in the room. It amazed her how many people actually fit into the large room. It was packed to capacity. Some people stood in small groups and talked to each other. Others were lined up in front of the large pots of coffee. Nina was nervous and didn't know what to expect, so she looked at everyone, trying to see who was actually high. The rumors she heard about NA meetings were that they were a joke.

One of the men up front stood and yelled, "Quiet down! Can we all take our seats?" Everyone sat, although the room was still buzzing.

"My name is Ernest, and I am an addict," he said.

"Hey, Ernest," everyone said in unison.

"I am officially starting the NA meeting. Who would like to be the first to share with us tonight?"

A man in the audience raised his hand. Ernest nodded and the man walked up to the front. Ernest sat and waited for the man to speak.

He stood proudly in front of everyone. He was a short, stocky man with a full beard and a low-cropped fade. He licked his lips before he spoke.

"My name is Dave, and I am an addict," he said in a deep voice.

"Hey, Dave!" the audience replied.

"I've been clean for two years and three months to date." Everyone clapped. "I am a recovering crack addict. There wasn't nothing I wouldn't do for crack. I would steal new drawers that my mother had just purchased and put in her dresser to sell. I was the worst kind of crack addict. Why? Because if it meant that I had to hurt someone so that I could get that next blast, then I did it with no remorse."

Nina listened, but didn't really listen. She smoked crack, but that wasn't her high of preference. She could relate somewhat to the brother speaking, though. She preferred to look at everything and everyone in the room instead of focusing on the story he shared. Dave talked and talked and people in the audience agreed with him from time to time. Nina wasn't impressed, nor was she interested. *How is this brother telling his story gonna help me stay clean?*

Another man got up and told his story. He was more of an alcoholic than an addict, but when he didn't drink, he got high. Nina definitely wasn't interested in what he had to say. She twiddled her fingers and played with her hair while he spoke. When he finished, everyone in the room shouted, "Thanks for sharing!"

"OK, we want to ask that one more speaker come up and share their story. Is there anyone else that wants to share?" Ernest asked.

Mrs. Reed looked over at Nina. Nina looked at her like she was stone crazy and shook her head. Mrs. Reed smiled and patted Nina's hand.

A white woman, who looked to be in her forties, stood. The audience applauded. She walked slowly from the back of the room to the front. To Nina's eyes it didn't look at all like she wanted to go up there. When the woman walked past Nina, Nina noticed all the bruises on her face, neck and hands, which were the only areas of exposed skin on her body. She stood and looked at everyone for a few moments, dread evident on her face. Then she spoke.

"Hi. My name is Connie, and I am an addict."

"Hey, Connie!"

"I . . ." She lowered her head as if she was having trouble speaking.

"Take your time, girl! You can do it!" a woman yelled from the back of the room.

"I am a recovering heroin addict. I used heroin like my life depended on it, when in fact my life did depend on it," she said with her head still lowered.

"I lost my three children to heroin. I mean, I killed my three children because of heroin."

Nina sat up in her seat, interested in where the story was going.

Grumbles and whispers went around the room. The woman's head hung even lower.

"It's all right! You can do it! You'll feel better!" Several people shouted encouragement to her.

"I was high all the time. I loved to get high. I think I used every vein in my arms, legs and hands to shoot up until there was nowhere else to shoot. Then I began to shoot in my feet, and neck. Several times I skin popped in my face because I was so sick and needed that high. That's why I have these bruises and spots on my face. The spots are a result of infections from skin-popping the heroin." Connie ran her hand across her face for emphasis.

"There were times when I couldn't skin pop because my hands were so shaky or sore from all of the sores I had on my arms and hands." She rubbed her arms through the long sleeves she wore to cover the damage, even though it was summertime. "So what I would do was have somebody—anybody, whether man or woman—shoot me in my pussy veins. It didn't matter. I would lie down and spread my legs, waiting for the blast." Connie shuffled her feet in embarrassment.

"I can't tell you how I ruined my life with that junk. But I still had my children. Me and my kids lived with my mother, and one day I decided that I wanted to take them somewhere. So I begged my mother to let me use her car to take my kids to the park. She refused because she knew I did drugs. My mother gave me tough love. She let me eat there and sleep there, but trust that was about all I did. I was an honest addict. I didn't steal or whore for it.

"I showed my mother that I had money, still trying to convince her, but she wasn't convinced. She said I probably got it illegally." Connie laughed a little. "What do you know? She was right. I got the money from being the lookout for a robbery of a grocery store."

Connie stood there, remembering that night, and it became apparent to everyone in the room that she was having a hard time continuing. Her face became beet red. More shouts from the room helped her to finish her story.

"I have never spoken about this to anyone in public. My mother refused to let me use her car. Bright and early that next morning I woke my kids and got them dressed. I remember it was still dark outside. I snuck into my mother's purse and took the car keys, but I left a fifty-dollar bill in her purse. I guess that was my way to feel better for what I was doing.

"I decided to take a trip to Asbury Park. Don't ask me why I did that, because that wasn't the initial plan. And the crazy thing was, the park wasn't going to be open at five AM. But that's the mind of an addict."

More shouts of agreement came from the room.

"As I drove and the night became day, I knew it was gonna be a good day, and me and the kids were gonna have a ball. We waited until the park opened, and then we rode the few rides that they had left there, and we ate hot dogs and cotton candy. We had a ball that day.

"Before we left to come home, I went into the public restroom to shoot up before I took the drive back up north. That was the biggest mistake of my life. I nodded off on the road, doing seventy miles an hour, and ran up under the back of a semi. All three of my children were killed instantly. I sustained a few broken bones, but that was it. Why was I left to live?" Tears clogged Connie's voice, and she swallowed hard before she continued. "I would have rather died that day in that car with my children. But I lived, and you would have thought that experience would have sent me into recovery. No. What it did was push me headfirst into a life of destruction. I had to stay high twenty-four seven in order to escape the dreams. The dreams were what kept me getting high. The dreams haunted me horribly. It was those dreams . . . I couldn't get past those dreams." She cried, tears streaming down her face.

"For a long time I believed God saved me to punish me for killing my children," Connie said as the tears continued to fall.

Nina cried so hard that Nilda had to put her arms around her shoulders. Nina got up from her chair and ran out of the church. Mrs. Reed followed. Nina reached the car and slid down to the ground, crying.

Nilda sat down beside her on the ground.

"Nina, you gotta let it out. You gotta share. You can't keep holding it back," Nilda pleaded.

Nina continued to cry as she sat on the ground. The meeting was over not long after Nina ran out of the church. Ernest found them in the parking lot sitting on the ground.

"Is everything OK?" he asked, looking at Nina.

"Yes, it will be." Nilda looked up at him. "Hi, I'm Nilda, and I'm a counselor."

"Pleased to meet you, Nilda. Let me help you to your feet." He grabbed Mrs. Reed by the arm, pulling her to her feet. They both helped Nina to her feet.

"I'm Ernest," he said to the ladies.

"Yes, we know." Nilda smiled.

"Is there anything I can do to help?"

"Maybe you can help." Nilda realized that her tactics obviously weren't working, and if Nina wouldn't listen to her, then maybe she would listen to someone else. "I have been trying to tell Nina that in order to move on into recovery, she has to stop keeping everything inside."

Nina leaned against the car and wiped the tears from her face. She kept her gaze to the ground, not wanting to look at either of them.

"Miss." Earnest touched Nina's shoulder.

She looked up at him. "Nina. My name is Nina."

"Nina, please let us help you. I know it's hard, and probably even confusing. But this is the better way. You must talk about it. Listen, here's my card." Ernest reached into his wallet and produced a business card. "Let me be your sponsor. I can help you through this," he offered.

Nina reluctantly took his card and put it in her pocket without looking at it.

"Call me whenever. It doesn't matter what time of the day or night. If you feel the urge to use, call me. If you just need someone to talk to, call me. If you are going through a stressful time, call me. I will be there for you." He looked at her with strong eyes full of reassurance.

Nina nodded in acknowledgement.

"It was nice meeting you, ladies. Get home safely, and enjoy the rest of your night."

"Thank you. You do the same," Nilda replied.

"Nina," Ernest called out to her. She looked at him. "Anytime," he said, and walked away.

On the ride back to Nina's apartment, Nilda asked Nina if she would like to go for a cup of coffee. Nina agreed and they stopped at Don's Diner in Irvington. While seated in the booth for two, Nilda looked over a menu.

"Well, since we're here, we might as well have something to eat. Feel free to get something. It's on me." She smiled.

Nina looked at the menu and then put it down. She decided to just get a cup of tea instead, and when the waitress brought it to the table, she immediately began sipping on it.

"Nilda, you know that woman that spoke tonight?"

"Yes?"

"I can relate to her pain."

"That's good, Nina. There is always somebody that you will be able to relate to. That's what's gonna help you with getting through this."

"The dreams. I can relate so much to her dreams."

"Do you have bad dreams?" Nilda was careful not to push.

"Do I?" Nina chuckled. "I have nightmares."

"You know that most people who recover have crazy nightmares."

But Nilda didn't know that Nina had the dreams for a different reason.

Nilda wanted to probe more, but had to remain patient. She believed that maybe Nina was going to tell her what she had been holding back. They both sat there in silence for a few minutes until the waitress brought the food to the table.

"I did some things in my past that I am not proud of."

"We all have, Nina."

"No, I've really done some things in my past." Nina laughed nervously.

"You know, I thought I had it all figured out. I thought that since I still worked, kept myself looking good, never losing too much weight to make me look sickly, like most who use drugs. I thought I was something." She shook her head as she played with the spoon in her cup.

"Nina, that is perfectly normal for a user. You are what they call a functional addict—a person who still works, a person who still pays her bills on time, and a person who still lives life as if she weren't using. But in reality, you are still an addict, Nina. You have polluted your body with the same substance as the addicts who don't have better control over their addiction. It's the same thing. Your body still becomes dependent on the drug. That's what addiction means," Nilda explained.

"I know, and I thought I was so different. I used to quit for a few months and then go back. I really thought that I was different."

"It's a mind game. Using drugs affects your brains cells as well, Nina. You know, you should read up on your disease. You do know that being an addict is a disease, don't you?"

Nina shook her head in disbelief.

"Yes, it is," Nilda insisted. "I have some literature in my car. I will give it to you."

"OK."

Nilda looked up from her plate of food and noticed the scab around Nina's nose, thinking it was a booger. She handed Nina a tissue.

"Your nose is dirty, honey."

Embarrassed, Nina excused herself and rushed off to the bathroom with the tissue covering her nose.

Chapter Nineteen

Kurt showed up on the corner as Malik stood there leaning against the mailbox. He was tired and in desperate need of sleep, but he knew he wouldn't be able to sleep. He would just lay in his bed and look at the ceiling, wondering about how the block was doing.

Malik had been thinking heavily about getting his own place. It wasn't because of his mother, because he was proud of her. She hadn't drugged since going to rehab. He just wanted his own space. Sharing a room with his brother at the age of nineteen was wearing thin on him. He loved his brother, but two men should not be sharing a bedroom. One reason that stopped him from leaving at that point was that his mother still hadn't found a job, and he was pretty much taking care of all the bills. His bank definitely wasn't quite where he wanted it to be just yet, and he didn't want to leave his mother or brother hanging. Although the money was all right, he knew that in time, when he stepped out on his own, the middleman would be cut out of the profits and his pockets would be fatter.

The main reason Malik didn't leave was that he didn't like the fact that Jackie, his mother's best friend, was running through the crib every now and then. He didn't trust her. He bought a lock for their room and offered to put one on his mother's bedroom door, but she declined the offer. She said that Jackie wouldn't take anything. Malik found that funny. How could his mother trust a fiend?

"What it do, boy?" Kurt asked. He wiped his face with a dirty towel. The night was muggy, and it seemed that there was no relief from the stifling heat.

"Hey, what's up?" Malik looked around. "Where your carts at? I didn't even hear you come up."

"I took the night off." Kurt laughed. It was obvious that he was feeling good from whatever drug he had used earlier. He swayed from side to side and kept wiping sweat from his forehead. As quickly as he wiped it, more beads reappeared.

"How you like that hardware I put you and yo' boys up on?" Kurt had recommended a guy from whom Malik and his crew could buy guns.

"Yeah, man! Homeboy hooked us up with some nice toasters. Indeed." Malik smiled. "They're clean, right?"

"Aw, yeah, they clean. He a good dude. He don't fuck around. He don't want no repercussions from that shit, so he makes sure they are clean before getting rid of them."

"Yeah. A'ight."

"What did you get?"

"I got a tray-five-seven," Malik told him.

"Damn, boy! You tryna do some serious damage, huh?" Kurt exclaimed.

"Yeah, that's the purpose. I copped a nine and a four-five too."

"You a good kid, Malik. You got these boys working they asses off. These blocks doing what they do!" Kurt smiled.

"You groovin', huh?" Malik noticed Kurt's sleepy eyes and body swaying.

"Hell, yeah! I'm right tight tonight, baby boy. I got some of that shit

Luke got, and that shit is fire," he drawled.

"Fire, huh?" Malik inquired. He heard about how Luke and Death had been beefing lately. It was all over the streets. In fact, Malik knew about Death pulling men from the corners and putting them on security. He hadn't seen Death in a while. Just yesterday, Ibn came through the block and dropped off a brick that was already cut and prepared for bagging. Malik was informed that he would now have to package his own goods. He was shocked by the display of trust from Death. Death had never left his product with any of the runners.

Malik still had product from what was dropped off two days prior. Since no one came to pick up, he just took it home and brought it back out the next day. The brick was well hidden in his room since he didn't know where he was gonna bag it up. He knew his mother would air his ass out if she found out. It also wouldn't be fair to her to even know that drugs were in the house, especially now that she was in recovery.

"I heard your mother was in recovery," Kurt said as if reading Malik's thoughts.

"Yeah, man. She is doing good too," Malik said solemnly.

"That's good. Y'all still don't get along, huh?"

"We cool. I mean, it's better than before, but honestly, I think it's because she's not working and I'm holding it down."

"Yeah, well, you a good son. She know it, but she is stubborn as hell—always been that way. She still holding on to the past."

"What is she holding on to?" Malik was curious.

"Nephew, it's a lot about your mother that you don't know, son."

Malik stared into the distance. He checked his watch because the shift would be changing over soon.

"Yeah, and you know the little piggies are beefing too," Kurt mentioned.

"Who you talking 'bout?"

"Man, the piggies are getting restless in the pig pen." Kurt laughed at his own silliness.

"Conductor, what the fuck are you talking about?"

"You know how Death got the corrupt cops on his payroll?"

"Yeah."

"Well, Luke got his own set of corrupted cops, and they battling against each other. Shit gonna hit the fan soon."

"How you know so much?"

"I know all things. You'd be surprised. I'm everywhere, so I see everything." Kurt scratched his butt, but couldn't scratch it the way he wanted to, so he just shoved his hand down the back of his pants. He scratched and dug, trying to satisfy the itch he had in the crack of his ass.

"Wash your ass! You standing out here digging in your ass," Jeff said and laughed. Neither of the men had seen Jeff walk up.

"Hey, baby boy! What's up?" Kurt held out his hand for a shake.

"Come on, Conductor, I wouldn't shake your hand if you was holding the winning numbers to the lottery."

Kurt laughed and walked away from the action.

Malik let Kurt's information process in his brain. "Yo, Jeff, me, you, and Brian need to have a sit-down," Malik told Jeff in a low voice. "I think shit getting ready to get outta hand, and I don't wanna be caught up. Whether we got enough loot or not, we need to break out on our own. When these clowns take each other out, I want to be the last man standing. Feel me?"

"Yeah, I feel you, but what's up, though? I mean, I'm saying, our pockets light as hell. How we gonna swing that?" Jeff was curious.

"Yeah, I know, but we'll rap about that later. Right now I need to put y'all down on this product thing. There's been some changes, and we need to split the work load. Yo, call them niggas over here." Malik nodded in the direction of the runners who were ending their shift, and the two runners who were ready to start the next shift.

Jeff did as he was told and the four boys came over to where Jeff and Malik stood.

Kurt had worked his way over to a cement stump that sat in the ground. It used to be a light pole, but the pole had been removed and the stump still remained. He sat on the stump in the deepest dope nod anyone had seen in a long time.

"Damn, look at this nigga!" Hanif pointed at Kurt as they approached the corner.

Everyone looked. By then Kurt was in a nod that bent his whole body over in between his legs.

"Damn, our shit got him like that?" Money asked in surprise.

"Naw, he said he copped from Luke's squad," Malik responded. He stared at Kurt, thinking some more about Kurt's earlier comments. He snapped out of it and addressed his crew.

"A'ight, this is what's getting ready to go down," Malik said to everyone gathered around.

He began to tell them what he wanted to do to keep them on point when out of nowhere four masked men appeared from around the corner and started shooting. Everyone outside ran and dove to the ground. Malik and Jeff took cover as well and returned the shots with their recently acquired gats. One of the masked men caught a bullet in the back while trying to run for cover. Glass shattered from the windows of parked cars. Kurt responded to the gun fire and dove to the ground.

A car pulled up to the block and a semi-automatic echoed over the sounds of the handguns. When the gunfire stopped, silence fell over the area. Ibn stepped out of the car.

"Yo, Malik!" he yelled.

Recognizing the voice, Malik responded. "What up?" He peeked from behind the car he'd hid behind. He saw Ibn and Jamal holding their smoking guns, looking like gangsters from a blaxploitation flick.

"Y'all niggas a'ight?" Jamal asked.

"Yeah, I'm good," Malik said.

But all wasn't good. One of the runners lay in a pool of blood and his boy Jeff had been hit in the stomach. He lay there on the ground, breathing hard and fast.

"Oh shit! Jeff got hit," Malik shouted. Ibn came running to his aid while Jamal ran to check on the other boy.

Two of the masked men lay dead on the ground. The rest had fled the scene.

"Little man over here is dead," Jamal called out to Ibn.

"A'ight. We gotta let ya boy go and get the rest of y'all outta here." Ibn grabbed Malik by the arm.

Malik snatched his arm from Ibn. "Naw, man! We ain't leaving him here! Fuck is up with you?" Malik was furious.

"Yo, man, we gotta get the fuck outta here! The boy ain't gonna make it!" Ibn yelled.

"He is gonna make it! We gotta take him to the hospital," Malik tried to reason.

"Naw, young gunner, we can't do that, and we ain't got enough time to drive him to Staten Island to our doctor. Look at him. He can barely breathe. Let's roll. Now!" Ibn demanded.

Jamal sent the rest of the boys away, got the stash out of the mailbox, and headed back to the car.

"Let's go!" he yelled at Ibn.

Ibn grabbed Malik by the arm again and tried to pull him to his feet.

"D-don't leave m-me, Mal-ik," Jeff struggled to say.

Blood covered his stomach and hands. It drained onto the ground underneath him. He started coughing up blood, and it squirted from his mouth. Sirens could be heard in the distance while onlookers filtered out onto the streets, trying to see what had happened.

Malik felt all of the blood drain from his body. Jeff and Brian had been his best friends since childhood, and losing Jeff was like losing his own brother. He wanted to break down and cry, but his ego wouldn't let him.

Ibn practically dragged him to the car. Jeff stared at him while he was being pulled away, his eyes glazing over with death. Malik kept his gaze on Jeff until he got in the car. He hated Ibn for making him leave his friend. They sped off in the car, and several minutes later two police cars pulled onto the scene.

Nina and Marquis came running down to the corner. They heard the shots, but that was normal for the neighborhood they lived in, so they never thought anything of it. Then one of the local boys came over to the house to tell them about the shooting. Marquis didn't know if Malik had been hit or not. All he did know was that somebody got shot.

Nina could see the four bodies lying on the ground. The police kept everyone back from the scene area, so she wasn't sure if Malik was one of the bodies. She felt pain in her stomach and a lump the size of a lemon was in her throat. She broke down in tears, even though she didn't know if her son was one of the dead.

Marquis craned his neck, trying to see if any of the bodies on the ground were his brother.

"Ma, I don't think any of them is Malik," he told his mother while holding her in his arms. He wasn't lying either. He didn't recognize the clothing on the bodies as any of Malik's apparel.

Nina walked through the crowd trying to get a better look. A police officer grabbed her by the arm.

"Get off me! I need to see if that's my son!" she tried to breakaway from his grip. "Ma'am you need to step back." He continued to hold her arm.

Marquis ran over to help the police with his mother.

"This is my mother! Let her go! I got her," he yelled at the two officers.

"Young man, you'd better contain your mother before she gets arrested," one of the officers told him.

"How are you gonna arrest my mother? That could be my brother over there, on the ground, dead!"

"Well, you need to calm down your mother, and I will see what I can find out." He walked away.

Sergeant Tilmond drove in his unmarked police car. He got out and walked over to the scene.

Tilmond looked at the bodies sprawled on the ground and sighed heavily as he rubbed his hand over his face. He knew that this was his brother's territory, and things were falling apart at the seams. He would have to have another meeting with his brother to put everything into perspective.

Nina's crying had calmed to a whimper. She looked up at Marquis with hurt, reddened eyes. It was enough to make a grown man cry.

"Mark, if Malik is dead, I couldn't live with myself," she told him.

"Ma, don't say that! He's not dead." Marquis looked down at his mother. "Come on."

Nina felt extremely guilty. To an outsider one would think that Marquis was her only son with the way she treated Malik. Regardless, though, Malik was still her son, and although she had said some bad things about him, she loved him very much. She had allowed her shallow way of thinking to control the way she treated him, and drugs only cosigned that fact. She hated that Malik was like his father. He went against all morals and sold drugs instead of being everything his father was not. Nina hated that she had no control over Malik, and she hated how he disrespected her.

But now that she was clean and sober, she really saw the good in him and realized it was she who went against the grain by treating him unfairly. She prayed to God as she stood right there on the streets. She prayed that if he would just give Malik another chance at life, she would take every day of life with him one day at a time, and treasure each moment as if it was the last.

A neighbor from Nina's building came over and pulled Nina into her arms, rocking her back and forth. Marquis took this as a cue to go over and try to find out who the dead bodies were. Before he made it halfway across the street, he heard someone call his name. He turned to see who was calling him, and it was Brian. He walked over to him.

"What the fuck happened?" Marquis demanded to know.

"Man, Dap came to the crib to get me, and he said that some niggas ran up on them and started wild'n out. But Malik, he a'ight. He hit me up. Ibn and them snatched him up."

A weight was lifted from Marquis when he heard that his brother wasn't dead.

"Your brother weak, man. He said they killed Jeff and he can't take it," Brian said sadly.

"Aw, man!" Marquis was hurt. "Anybody else we know over there?"

"Dunno. He just told me about Jeff, man. Yo, he on his way home."

"Oh, a'ight! Let me get my mother and take her home. I'll get up with you later." Marquis rushed over to where Nina stood with their neighbor.

"'Scuse me, Miss Davis," he said to the neighbor while taking hold of his mother. He draped his arm around her waist and led her away. Nina rested her head on his shoulder.

"Ma, Malik is a'ight," he whispered to her.

"He is?" She looked up at him, hoping and praying he was telling the truth.

"Yeah. Brian told me he should be home in a few. Let's go home and wait for him."

They walked at a normal pace home. Nina was feeling relieved that God had given her a second chance with her son.

Chapter Twenty

Marquis paced the floor while Nina sat waiting for Malik. When Malik finally walked through the door, he was surprised to find Nina and Marquis waiting for him. They both looked up when the front door opened. Marquis walked over toward his brother, but Nina beat him to the punch. She embraced Malik tightly and Malik hugged his mother back, but looked at his brother with a perplexed look on his face.

"It's all my fault," she wailed. "It's all my fault! I am a horrible mother to you. I want us to have a closer relationship and I promise I'll be a better person."

"Come on, Ma, what's wrong?" Malik tried to pull away from the tight grip she had on his neck.

Nina released him. "What happened out there, Malik?"

"I don't know what you talking about." Malik downplayed the situation.

"Don't play me, boy!" Nina snapped.

As she looked up at him, Malik could see a scab on the inside of her nostril. "Ma, are you using that cream the doctor gave you?" he asked, trying to change the subject.

"Don't worry about my damn nose! What the hell happened out there?"

"How did you find out?"

"Are you kidding me? You didn't think I heard the shots? Malik, whenever I hear shots, I think about you. I worry about you every time you go out there on them streets. Every time the phone rings at night, I think it's a call to tell me you are dead or in jail—regardless of what I might say to you." Hurt was in her voice. She could feel a migraine coming on.

"Come on, Ma. Why you gotta think like that? I'm good, Ma."

"You're good?" Nina shook her head and walked away.

"You a'ight, man?" Marquis asked his brother.

"Yeah, man, I'm good." Malik still watched his mother.

"Tell me what happened later," Marquis whispered to him.

Malik nodded and walked over to Nina. She was standing in front of a picture she had on the wall of the boys all dressed up when they were little. *They look so innocent*, she thought. Nina loved that picture and looked at it often.

"Ma, I didn't do anything," Malik started.

She whirled around to face him, and anger had crept into her eyes.

"You didn't do anything? You didn't do anything?" Nina screamed. "Are you serious, Malik? You did everything! Do you realize what kinda pain you've caused me and your brother? Huh?"

Malik was at a loss for words, and his face reflected his confusion. *She must have multiple personalities*, he thought. She was just crying for him, and now she seemed to be against him. It wasn't his fault. He was just standing on the corner, and that was when the hit came. He didn't do anything to anyone.

"Malik, you are running those streets day in and day out," Nina continued. "I worry about you every day. Sometimes I sit and wait for the phone to ring because I know any day I will get the call saying that you're dead or in jail. I used to say that at least I'd know where you were, but tonight made me realize that's not what I wanted for you. You are doing everything wrong by just being in the street!"

Malik couldn't believe his ears. Did she just say that she wanted him dead or in jail? His head was still messed up about Jeff's death. He wanted to put his fist down her throat. Rage built in his body, but he held in all the things that he wanted to say to his mother. He wanted her to know the hurt he felt from her mistreatment all these years, but he didn't tell her. He held it in, like he had always done. The one thing he felt for sure was that his mother didn't love him the way that she did Marquis, and at that point, Malik didn't care anymore. He had just been shot at and could have died, but all she could do was stand there and go off on him about being on the corners.

"Yeah, well, you almost got your wish tonight! They killed my boy Jeff, and I thought I could come home and my family would feel my pain. But, no, my mother beastin' on me without even hearing me out. You ain't got to worry 'bout me, Ma. I'ma stay outta ya way till I can make this paper, and then I'm breakin' outta here!" Malik walked away to his room.

Nina looked after him. Her heart went out to Jeff's mother because she knew how she must feel. Nina felt the same way tonight when she thought Malik was dead.

ເຊຊເຊຊ

As the weeks passed, things got worse. Luke would hit Death, and Death would hit him right back. It came out that it was Luke who put the hit out to do Malik and the boys on the block. He heard that the block was one of Death's most profitable blocks. Luke had plans to kill

Death slowly, first, by hitting him where it would hurt—his pockets. Things were getting out of control, and the police officers actually started to turn on each other. It was precinct against precinct, as if they, too, were in a gang war.

The police finally found the body of Cutty. Cutty was the man Death had tortured in front of Justice that day, the man who tried to leave Death and go to work for Luke's team. His face had been bashed in with a blunt object, his eyes were missing, and his skull had been cracked to the point where brain matter oozed from the top of his head. He was unrecognizable. The murder weapon—a brick, covered in blood and flesh—lay next to his body. This incident was charged to the stream of murders that had been circling the city between the two rival drug gangs. Little did the police know that shortly after the man's wife filed a Missing Persons report, she received a package in the mail. It contained the eyes of her husband.

Bodies turned up dead, from street dealers to undercover cops. Death recruited more people for his team. He was so desperate that he forgot his age limit rule and put eleven-and twelve-year-olds on the team, so that he could take the older ones off the block and put them on the front line, all except Malik's crew. Malik's blocks brought in the most profit, and Death needed that to keep coming in.

Death knew he was going to have to win this war, because his connect was now concerned about all the publicity that surrounded the city.

ൟൟൟൟ

The lions lazed in the comfort of the shade from the trees in the Bronx Zoo. Not much action went on in the den due to the heat that blanketed the zoo. Even the cubs were in the shade as they cuddled next to their mother. Occasionally the lioness's tail would swat at the annoying flies that bit her. The lion rolled onto his back and then back to his side as he stretched his legs. He yawned, showing huge, sharp fangs while he tried to find a comfortable position.

"Yo, man, you done lost your mind this time." Death walked up to his brother as Tilmond leaned on the fence, watching the lions do absolutely nothing. It intrigued him how they looked to be the gentlest cats, similar in behavior to an ordinary house cat. However, this same animal could rip a chunk of flesh from a man's body.

Tilmond turned to Death, then turned back to watch the creatures. Death leaned onto the railing next to him. Tilmond held out his fist as he always did, and, as usual, Death tapped it with a fist of his own.

"The team is not going for the percentage of increase you offered them," Tilmond said without preamble. "They figured that Luke's deal was a sweeter deal. Not only that, it is becoming a grave disruption to the order of things at the precinct."

Death began to speak when Tilmond held up his hand and silenced him.

"Other precincts are jumping on the bandwagon, and it's creating friction between units. Greedy hands are digging into each other's pockets. Internal Affairs is being summoned as we speak because of the death of two police sergeants from two different districts. There are too many murders, and we know what the reasoning was behind this. Do you?"

"Naw, we had nothing to do with that," Death assured him.

"What do you take me for, Todd? This shit has got to stop or I'm gonna pull the plug."

Death told the truth. It had been Luke's team that had killed the two officers who sat in their patrol car one night. Luke's reason was because the cops were power-tripping over the increase. Unfortunately for Death, there was no evidence and no witnesses to confirm that Luke's camp did those two murders.

Tilmond turned and strolled down the paved path. Children ran by while mothers pushed strollers. They were all excited about being at the zoo. When a group of chaperoned kids walked past them, he and Death ceased their conversation. They were in the House of Snakes before they spoke again. Tilmond stopped in front of a display of a twenty-year-old anaconda. The head on the snake was larger than that of a child. The huge snake looked to be fake as it lay there, motionless. Its eyes sat deep into its huge head and seemed to be staring off into the distance. Death frowned while studying the unreal-looking creature.

"Rell, man, you be picking some crazy-ass spots to meet! Why are we here at the fucking zoo? It stinks in this joint!" Death rubbed his nose, trying to find relief from the animal smell.

"You know, Todd, I've never been to the zoo. I never even brought my kids to the zoo when they were younger. All the fucking money that has passed through these hands"—he looked down at the palms of his hands—"and not once did I do a simple thing like bring my kids to the zoo." Tilmond shook his head.

"Rell, you can take your grandkids to the zoo. So is that why we here, because you ain't never been to the zoo? Man, let's at least go back outside! These snakes are fucking with me. I ain't feeling this shit." He looked at the snakes crawling around

"Why, Todd? I mean, you crawl around with snakes every day. The people you deal with in the business that you're in aren't that much different than they are." Tilmond pointed to the snakes behind the glass.

"Rell, man, you losing your mind. I deal with *people* in the streets."

"You don't get it, do you? The mentality of some of the street niggas is like the mentality of snakes. There is enough paper out there on them streets for everybody to eat. But, no, there is always a motherfucker that can't get enough. So, what does he do? He begins to plot, scheme, snake his way around, and try to take the next man's bread and butter. A snake, Todd." He pointed to the snakes again before walking out of the building.

Death followed. "OK, I get it. But what the fuck is gonna happen with the protection I pay for?"

"Are you ready for me now?" Tilmond stopped and faced Death.

Death looked his brother square in the eyes. *Here we go again*, he thought. He started to wonder if the whole thing wasn't a setup in the first place. He thought about how his brother was always trying to tell him what to do, and how to run his business. *Maybe this is the way he's going to get back in. Who is the snake now, Rell?*

How could his brother do this to him? Naw, he wasn't going out like that. It was always the one closest to you who tried to stab you in the back. A family member, or a supposed close friend would be the one to take you out. *Not this dude!* He would have to keep a close watch on his brother. Death thought this in his usual selfish way. But not once thinking how he has done the same thing to his cousin Demetri.

"Naw, Rell. I'm good, man," he said nonchalantly and stepped back.

"Just checking. I told you before—if you need me, I got you."

Death felt something twinge in his gut, a feeling that he felt too often when he knew someone was trying to play him. He hated that he felt this way toward his brother, and he struggled with the idea. But business was business, and if Rell tried to get funky, then Death would have to serve him, just like the rest.

"We need to have a sit-down with Luke," Tilmond stated. "I'll set it up with my squad and the sergeant running the team that protects Luke's squad from the eyes of Internal Affairs. I'll call you with the details—time and place, you know, that kinda shit,"

Death looked at Tilmond like he was crazy. "Man, what do you think this is? This ain't the Mafia. Niggas don't have sit-downs. That's a death trap waiting to happen. We go hard, and the last man standing owns the city,"

"You just don't get it." Tilmond shook his head and walked away.

Death was right behind him. "What are *you* talking about? You don't get it. Times have changed, big bruh. This is a new day and age, and that old-school shit is dead, man."

"Owns the city? Is that how you think it works?" Tilmond laughed. "I thought you were smarter than that. I thought you had it under control?"

"I do."

Tilmond stopped to look at an albino white tiger. She was a beautiful specimen.

"Rell, man, I can't have a sit-down with Luke," Death reasoned. "There is no way that young nigga gonna play fair, or hold the white flag up so that we can have this meeting."

"He will," was all Tilmond said.

"How the fuck do you know? What, he got you in his pocket too?"

Tilmond stared at his younger brother. "Is that what you think, Todd?"

"Naw. I'm saying, you talking like you know this nigga personally."

"I got pull on the force, whether you want to believe that or not. I know what I'm doing. You just be ready to meet when I call you." He continued to stare at his younger brother. "So that's where your head's at, huh?" He laughed again at Death's belief that he, Tilmond, would side up with Luke.

"Always love," Tilmond said as he walked off, leaving Death standing there.

"Yeah." Death eyed his brother's back. But was he really feeling the love?

Chapter Twenty-One

It had been awhile since the last time Death had seen Nina, and now she was almost two months clean. He watched her as she walked out of the corner store. She looked clean and refreshed. He thought back to how she once had every male chasing after her, including himself. Death loved to be in control. It gave him a sense of superiority to be on top, to be in charge, to be able to decide someone's fate. As he watched Nina walk home, he decided her fate.

"Pull up next to her, Bear."

Bear did as he was instructed. Nina turned to see the Benz riding beside her. She stopped and put her hands on her hips.

"Look at this feisty bitch! I bet I know how to put that fire in her out, huh, Bear?" Death laughed.

Bear chuckled, sounding like an actual grizzly bear. Death got out of the car and leaned against it. He folded his arms across his chest and smirked at her. Nina looked at him with disgust. The two stood and stared at each other until Nina finally spoke.

"What do you want, Todd?"

"Easy." He held up his hands in surrender. "I just want to tell you how good you look, except you really should get that nose of yours looked at." He gestured at her nose.

Nina's nose had been peeling and she was self-conscious about it. She would pull the dead skin from her nose until it was raw to the touch. She administered the cream that the hospital gave her at least five times day, and still it peeled. The migraines that she suffered with were now coming more frequently as well, and nothing seemed to stop them.

She rolled her eyes at him and rubbed her nose. Some of the dead skin flaked away to the ground, which embarrassed her further. She shot Death an ice grill filled with hatred.

"Aw, poor baby," Death teased. "You embarrassed about it? I know what can make it feel better."

"Todd, I'm clean now, so miss me with the bullshit!" Nina snapped. She was offended at his offer. Death laughed. "Fuck you, Todd! I ain't gotta deal with this bullshit!" Nina turned to walk away.

"Oh, but you do, baby." He smiled a predator's smile.

"Do what?" Nina turned back and looked at him.

"How soon we forget. You owe me." Death walked over and stood in front of her.

Nina stared up at him in disbelief. "You crazy as hell! I don't owe you shit!"

"Sure you do." He continued to smile and moved a little closer.

Nina felt her space being violated and tried to push him back, but Death was a built man and her weak attempt did nothing to budge him. Nina stepped back a couple of steps, still peering up at him with hatred in her eyes.

"Todd, I paid you your money. So we even," she huffed.

Death laughed again. "Is that what you think this is about? Baby, it ain't 'bout the loot. It's never been about that. C'mere." He tried to grab her hand.

Nina pulled back to avoid being touched.

"C'mere. Why you acting like that?" Death softened his voice and spoke to her like one would speak to a skittish animal.

"Fuck you, Todd! You up to some shit, and I ain't buying it. I don't get high no more, so you can't use dope to get me to do what you want. I'm past that now." Nina's words were full of bravado.

Death frowned and the muscles in his arms flexed. He lunged forward and snatched Nina up by her arms.

"You listen to me, bitch," he snarled. "I tried to be nice to yo' funky ass, but you leave me no other choice. You are a drug addict and will always be one. Your body has tasted dope. Your body knows how dope feels running through it. You will always crave the drug, and as long as you do, you will always come to me. I own you because you owe me."

Nina felt his hot breath in her face. Her arms were turning numb where Death gripped them. For some reason Nina was not afraid. She stared right back at him, stone-faced and full of fire.

"You listen to me, you sorry excuse for a man. If it makes you feel like a man to hit on a defenseless woman, then go 'head. But let me tell you one thing, motherfucker, you bleed just like I do, so don't *you* ever forget that!"

"You threatening me, bitch?" Death squeezed a little harder.

"No more than you are threatening me. I don't owe you nothing, Todd. You've used that line to get me when I was sick and needed a bag. But I am a changed person, and that just ain't me. I only fear God, not you."

"You fear God? Naw, baby girl, you better fear *me*! How soon we forget about that favor I did for you years ago."

Death was so close to Nina's face that she could practically see his brain behind his eyes. She tried to pull back, but this time he grabbed the back of her head and held her in place, trying to instill fear in her. It was beginning to work.

Two women walked past. One of them frowned at the altercation between Death and Nina.

"Pick on somebody your own size!" the woman yelled.

"Yeah, leave her alone!" the other one chimed in.

Bear got out of the car and walked over to the sidewalk. The women were preoccupied with watching Death and Nina, and they didn't see Bear approaching.

"Keep it movin,'" Bear said. "There's nothing to see here," he bellowed, scaring the life out of the women. They screamed and scuffled away from him.

"What the fuck is that?" the first woman asked her friend.

"Hell if I know, but I ain't tryna to stay here and find out from his ugly ass," the second one retorted. She speed-walked away, leaving her friend to catch up to her. Bear sat on the front of the car.

Nina tried to reason with Death. "Todd, this doesn't make sense! You know damn well that you are as much at fault as I am on what happened. So stop tryna hold that over my head! I am not afraid anymore. Go ahead, tell the police! I don't care. I am at a point in my life where I can face what has happened in the past. I am on the road to recovery, leaving that mess behind me."

Death released her and just stared at her. It almost seemed as if the words of faith were defeating the devil himself. Then a wicked smile appeared on his face, resembling that of the Grinch from *How The Grinch Stole Christmas*.

"We'll see, Nina. So you're strong and confident now, huh? Let's see how strong you are. Did you know your son works for me?"

Nina looked at him sideways. She knew that Malik was out there in the streets, selling drugs. She didn't like it, but who was she to tell him that he couldn't when she had told him countless times that he was grown, and to get out and take care of himself? Who was she to tell him he couldn't when she had used that very same drug he sold? Who was she to tell him that he couldn't when she never treated him with the same love that she showed Marquis? Even knowing all that, not to mention the fact that he paid the bills, she would have never thought he would be working for Death.

"Yeah, I see that tough-guy shit just went right out the window, huh?" Death continued to gloat.

"That's bullshit, Todd." Nina's denial lacked conviction. The one thing she knew about Death was that he was a straight-up dude. He never lied about anything. If it was gonna hurt your feelings, oh well, because he was going to give it to you raw.

"Naw, baby, no bullshit. This is straight shit. Your son is my moneymaker. That little nigga grinds his ass off, caking me up lovely. You do remember my number-one rule, don't you? Oh, yeah, you remember. You was there when we made them up."

One night back in the day Death and Wiz made up their rules of the game while at Wiz and Nina's apartment. Nina sat right there when they were made. She didn't say anything about them then, but now that her son was involved, it was a whole different ball game.

"There is only one way out, and that's what?" Death asked, holding his hand up to his ear and waiting for her to answer the question.

Nina looked like she was about to freak out. She felt moisture seeping from her nose. She raked her hand under nose only to see blood on her hands. She backed away from him slowly.

"Where are you going, Nina? Talk to me. Let's make a deal. A deal with Death, that is."

Death pointed to himself and slowly walked toward Nina with a sinister grin on his face. Nina continued to slowly back away from him.

"I'll give you your son's life back for your own," he said. "And then let's say we call it even. Or I'll take your son's life and let you go. Either way, somebody gotta pay for my time and services. Deal?"

"Go to hell, Todd!"

"Deal or not?" he repeated.

"You can't have my son, so leave him alone!"

"OK, so we got a deal then. I still own you."

Nina ran down the street as fast as she could. Tears streamed down her face. She felt a burning sensation in her chest and pain in the pit of her stomach, and her head began to hurt. Death watched her run as he continued to smile. He turned to Bear, who stood and opened the back door for him to get inside.

Nina burst into her apartment. She ran to the kitchen and grabbed a paper towel. When she blew her nose, a huge blood clot landed in the paper towel. Nina went into the living room and fell face first onto the sofa. She cried with all of her heart. Then she prayed the Serenity Prayer over and over.

"God, grant me the serenity to accept the things I cannot change, the courage to change the things I can, and the wisdom to know the difference."

Malik came from his room. He had come home to get a couple hours of sleep when he heard the commotion. He had his gun in hand, not knowing what to expect. He saw his mother crying on the couch, holding a bloody tissue. He ran over to where she lay and got down on his knees beside her.

"Ma, you a'ight?" He examined her to see if she was hurt.

She looked at Malik as if he were the devil himself.

"You selling for Todd, Malik?"

Malik just looked at her. He thought about the night she thought he was dead and how she had told him that she was going to be a better person and a better mother. She told him she wanted to have a closer relationship with him. So far she had kept her word—until now. What he saw in Nina's question was the same woman who hated him for no reason in the world. Malik copped an instant attitude, one that he used to protect his heart from the one woman he loved more than life, even when he didn't get the same love in return.

"Why? What's up, Ma?" he asked nonchalantly.

"Answer the question!" She stood. "Do you sling for Death?"

"Yeah. So what?"

"Of all people to sell drugs for, why him, Malik?"

Malik was confused. "I don't get it. What difference does it make who I get money with? I'm paying the bills around here."

"Oh, so you grown now, huh? You been paying the bills for a few weeks, so that makes you a man? That makes you grown? That makes you the man of the house, and I should bow down to you?" she yelled.

"You the one who told me I needed to grow up and take care of myself!" Malik shot back. "You the one who told me that, Ma. You don't have a job to pay the bills, so what was I supposed to do? Let us get put out? I thought you appreciated that I stepped up to take care of everything until you got on your feet. You ain't satisfied with shit! Every time I think I'm doing something right, you bitch and complain that it's wrong. I can't do shit right in your eyes, Ma, and I'm sick of it. I'm done with tryna prove to you. I'm tired of tryna get your attention! Dancing around in your face, tryna get you to notice me! I have been doing that all my life, Ma, competing with my own brother because you loved him more than me!" Malik's eyes were red from anger and his words were full of repressed pain.

Nina stood there in shock. She had never seen Malik express so much emotion before. Malik was always serious. He was the distant one, but to see that he actually could express emotion overwhelmed her. It broke Nina's heart to see what she had created. Malik was the man he was today because of her behavior toward him for so many years.

She ran to him and pulled him into her arms.

"I'm sorry, son! I do love you. I really do," she said. She was on an emotional rollercoaster and didn't know how to get off.

"Get off me!" Malik pushed her away.

"Malik, I'm sorry."

"Just leave me alone," he snarled.

"Please, son, don't give up on me! I'm trying. It ain't easy for me."

"Then why do you kick me the way you do?" He pulled away from her.

Nina couldn't answer the question because she would have to reveal her past, and she didn't want to do that with her sons.

"Listen, Malik, stop slinging for Todd."

"Why, Ma? That's our bread right there, and until you get on your feet, I need to keep rolling with him. No ordinary square job is gonna do it. I didn't finish high school, so I can't get a good-paying job."

"You don't understand. It is much bigger than just selling the drugs for him, Malik."

"Why, Ma? Tell me why?"

She turned, sat back down on the sofa, and placed her hand over her mouth. She wiped the tears from her face and looked back at him.

"I can't," she said.

"Then how do you expect me to stop selling? That's not good enough for me." Malik sat down next to her. He was concerned. "Do you owe him money or something?"

"No." She shook her head in emphasis. "It's deeper than the money. Just trust me. You gotta get out now while you still can."

"I can't do that," he replied simply.

"Malik, that man will kill you."

"What for? I work for him. I make more money on my corners than any other blocks he got," he stated proudly.

"He will kill you over me," she whispered. She looked at him with reddened eyes as if seeing him for the first time. She realized that she really did love her son.

"What?" A puzzled frown crossed his face. He didn't understand what she meant.

"Malik, I've known Todd since we were teenagers. He knows something about me from the past, something that could put me in jail for life."

"What, Ma?" Malik asked urgently.

"That's not important right now. But what is important is that he says I owe him. He has held that over my head for years. I have done some things for him that I am not proud of, but I thought by doing those things, it would make us even. He is crazy, Malik, and you will never be able to beat him. Did you know that once you're in, you can't just walk away from it?"

"No. What do you mean?"

"Malik, didn't you wonder where he got the name from? I don't want nothing to happen to you. I think I'll just do what he says and give myself to him. I've been living with his ass chasing me all these years anyway."

"Are you crazy?" Malik exploded. "Hell no it ain't going down like that! What do you mean, you gonna give yourself to him?"

"Malik, listen to me! He will kill you."

"Fuck that! That nigga bleeds just like the rest of us." Malik stormed out of the room.

"Malik! Malik!" she called out after him. Nina got up and went to the boys room. She saw Malik rummaging through the closet. "What are you going to do?" she asked.

"I'm gonna handle that nigga! He ain't shit without Bear, and I'm gonna peel that niggas cap," he said with rage in his voice.

"Malik, just listen to me!" Nina grabbed his arm. "He ain't no punk. He don't need Bear. He is very educated in the streets. He plays hard, and he plays to win. Don't think he just a business suit sitting behind the desk. He can cut your throat in one swift move, and you would never know what hit you," she pleaded with him.

Malik looked at his mother in disbelief, then smirked.

"Well, he ain't went up against me," he said simply. He shoved the .357 down the front of his jeans.

Marquis walked into the room and stopped, trying to figure out what was going on. Nina was fed up and walked out of the room.

"Talk to your brother before he gets himself killed!" she said as she walked past Marquis.

"What's up?" Marquis was perplexed.

"Do you know that nigga Death threatened Mommy?"

"For what?"

"Mommy did some shit back in the day, and he holding that shit over her head." Malik's voice was muffled through the shirt he was removing.

Marquis sat on his bed and watched his brother change clothes.

"What did she do?"

"I dunno. She won't tell me. But this nigga told her that she either had to do what he say, or she had to give me to him if she didn't. Is that nigga nuts or what?" Malik laughed a sinister laugh. He pulled on a black, oversized T-shirt and removed his white-on-white Air Force Ones. He reached under the bed and pulled out a Timberland box.

"A'ight, hold up! You saying that he wants your life for Mommy's? That don't sound right." Marquis shook his head in disbelief.

"Right now, Mark, it don't fucking matter what that nigga want. I told you I didn't trust that motherfucker. And I didn't forget about the last time I saw him use Mommy. I refuse to let that shit happen· again. That nigga gonna have her back on dope, and probably will use her to trick for him or something. Fuck that!" He put on a pair of black Timbs.

"Yeah, I hear you," Marquis commented. "But you can't just be running out there in the streets, buckin' and wild'n out, because you heated with that cat. Naw, man, what you gotta do is plan this shit right. Get you a game plan, bruh," Marquis reasoned.

"You know what, baby boy? I hear you." Malik pulled a black fitted cap over his head. "But seriously, I ain't with that TV bullshit you spittin' at me right now. I'm a rebel, and I'm taking this shit straight to the head, no chaser!" Malik left the room. Marquis could hear his mother yelling, trying to stop Malik, but soon he heard the front door slam.

Marquis sat there and rubbed his head. He had to do something before his brother got killed. Malik was hotheaded and tended not to think before he acted, or reacted.

Marquis could hear his mother whimpering in the living room. He was afraid the pressure would send her back into using drugs. He jumped to his feet and went into the closet that he and Malik shared. Pulling out the duffel bag that was stashed in the back of the closet, he opened it and saw all of the drugs and money that Malik had stashed away. Marquis knew about the stash and simply moved the packages around until he found the snub-nosed .45 that he knew Malik had. He picked up the gun and held the hard steel in his hands, eyeing it. He fingered the trigger, holding it firmly, then he stood and shoved the gun into the front pocket of his jeans.

Marquis walked past his crying mother, and out the front door to search for his brother.

Chapter Twenty-Two

THAT NIGHT . . .

Death got a call from his brother on his personal line.

"What's up?" Death asked.

"We meet tonight at eleven PM."

"It's all set up?" He said looking at his watch and reading the time was 9:45pm.

"Yup. Get a pen and write this down," Tilmond ordered.

"A'ight go 'head," Death said, waiting to write down the information.

Tilmond rattled off the information so fast that Death could hardly keep up.

"Slow down, man."

Tilmond slowed his pace and gave his brother precise directions.

"A'ight, Todd, you can only bring one man with you to this meeting," Tilmond explained.

"What?"

"Yeah, that's how it's gonna go down. One man from your camp, and one man with Luke from his camp. Simple as that."

"So you really think this shit is gonna pan out like that?" an unbelieving Death asked.

"It will, and trust me, Todd, if you think you gonna come up in there and show your ass, think again. There will be several other officers and another sergeant present. If you so much as throw shade in this meeting, then don't look to me for backup, because this ain't that type of party. You feel me?"

"Come on, who do you think you're talking to?" Death wasn't feeling the discipline.

"Listen, little brother, this meeting is to bring peace and order, and that's what's gonna happen. So I'm just tryna let you know how it's gonna go down before we get there. Because rank don't mean shit at this point in the game."

Death was cocky, and he laughed at how his brother tried to pull rank over him. The fact of the matter still remained that he, Death, had the power on the streets that his brother wished he still had. Death didn't fear the badge Tilmond carried. If push came to shove, and Tilmond put his job before blood, then Death wouldn't have a problem bleeding him.

ರಾರಾರಾರಾ

Death chose Ibn, instead of Bear to come along with him. Ibn had brains and the experience to deal with situations like this. Although it may have seemed like Death didn't take any direction from Ibn, Death listened to his advice from time to time, and applied it to the game.

Ibn drove while Death sat and listened to the CD the older man had in the system to help him focus. "Shaft" by Isaac Hayes was followed by "Super Fly" by Curtis Mayfield. Then there was "Inner City Blues (Make Me Wanna Holler)," "What's Going On," and "Trouble Man" by Marvin Gaye. The mellow sounds of the music put Death in a zone. He was first turned on by this music when Three the Hard Way came on board with his crew. Since they still lived in that seventies era, that was the style of music that they rocked to. Death clowned them for a long time whenever they listened to it, but as time went on, and after many times listening to it, the music grew on him, and he learned to love it too. The music from back then had reasoning. It was relevant to society and it was what black people needed to keep them focused.

The three old heads used to tell him, "Y'all young cats listening to this jungle music with no meaning. What the hell are you actually getting outta this so-called rap music when you can't even understand the words?" Death would simply ignore them until he finally caught on and got the message. He still enjoyed gangsta rap because he lived it, but he understood the value of some seventies soul.

While Ibn drove he tried to look at the written directions scribbled on a piece of paper. He was getting frustrated because Death sat there with the seat laid back, his eyes closed, zoning.

"Listen, Superfly, I hate to bring you back to the present, but how the fuck am I supposed to read this chicken scratch you got down here and drive the fucking car? Come on, boy, get ya mind right and help an old man. It's foggy as hell, and I can't see shit in front of me." Ibn tossed the paper onto Death's lap.

Death was not happy with the interruption, but he knew that if he didn't help Ibn, there would be no peace. He adjusted the seat so that he could see, and then he looked at the paper and at the upcoming street sign to see what street they were on. They were in the town of Elizabeth on their way to Linden, and it was indeed a foggy night. Death became frustrated too as he tried to help Ibn find their location. This only added fuel to the fire that grew inside him toward the stupid locations his brother would pick for them to meet.

Traveling down interstate US 1/9 they drove past the White Castle that was listed as a landmark, and Death knew then that they had about a mile to go to get to Woodland Avenue.

"I've been watching how things have been unfolding," Ibn said out of the blue.

Death remained silent and continued to look straight ahead, looking for the next street listed in the directions.

"I think you need to let Terrell come on in and reorganize this here organization you got."

"What?" Death turned the volume down on the system. "What are you talking about?" Death wanted to make sure he had heard what he thought he heard.

"I talked to your brother. He has a good head on his shoulders. He's from the old school, back when I was around. He never did a day in prison. He was good to us. He had a good, solid rep. He took care of his people and in return, they took care of him. That's what gave him longevity. If he hadn't changed his game plan, he would still be running shit right now, to this day. That's where you lack, son. You treat your people like shit, and that's why you have a lot of trouble tryna keep order. You shouldn't be in the mix as much as you are."

Death didn't say a word. He was still in shock that Ibn would go behind his back to even speak with his brother. This was his business, and Terrell was his brother. Death did all the talking and made all the decisions. What gave Ibn, or Terrell, for that matter, the right to discuss anything that had to do with Death's business? As a result of Death's silence, Ibn had passed the street he needed to turn on.

"I'm not saying to give him the run of the business," Ibn continued. "I am simply saying, let him show you how to be successful in what you got. We got way too many bodies counts and with Rell's help, we can minimize the body count and up the revenue."

"Pull this motherfucker over!" Death shouted.

"Did we miss the turn?" Ibn asked, looking around.

Ibn quickly pulled the car into a gas station with a Dunkin' Donuts in it, and parked away from the front door of the establishment. Death reached over and grabbed a fistful of the older man's shirt.

"Let me tell you one fuckin' thing, old man. I run this shit, not my brother! You and my brother can kiss my ass! Matter-of-fact, if I ever find out that y'all motherfuckers is up to some shit, you gonna find yaself laying at the bottom of the Hudson River in a body bag filled with bricks! Death by lethal injection, motherfucker!"

"Let me learn you something, playa," Ibn said through clenched teeth. "I ain't one of them little punk niggas you put fear in. I don't fear you, nigga. I been in this motherfucking game before you traveled down that funky canal to life!" He jerked out of Death's grip and fixed the younger man with a lethal stare. "You are just as dumb as the day is long! Listen to me, and you listen to me good. If you think that I would go against you, after all the time I been down with you, then you do what you feel you need to do. But just know that I ain't no easy nigga to take out. Don't let the old age fool you, boy. Try me if you want, but trust and believe it will be the fight of your fucking life! I got fucking skills that you ain't even thought of, and *you* might just be the motherfucker that they will be sweeping the Hudson River for!"

Both men sat and stared at each other.

"Hear me when I say this, playa," Ibn continued. "You better open your eyes and see that if you don't get your shit together, you won't have a business, and any and everybody that is connected to you will take a fall. Frankly, I'm too old to let some young, hotheaded, stubborn motherfucker fuck up the rest of my life and have me sitting in a motherfucking box!

Now it's your call. What you wanna do?"

Death stared at Ibn for a few seconds longer and then sat back in his seat. He could spit fire, he was so mad. His mind raced and he didn't know what to think. Ibn had been with his team for quite a few years, and he, Dean, and Jamal had been the most loyal to Death, next to Bear. Yet they were cats who had been sent to him by his brother, and he didn't trust his brother any longer. Who was to say that his brother didn't have this planned from the beginning? Rell had always told him about patience. "Be patient and wait on the opportunity to make your move on the next man," he would say. As far as Death was concerned, the whole thing had been a setup from the rip. He tried to calm himself and made a mental note to watch Ibn, Dean, and Jamal more closely.

"So what's up, young blood?" Ibn asked again.

Death looked at the paper and then up at the street they were on. "Make a U-turn and go back down the street," he replied, looking straight ahead.

Ibn put the car in gear and did as he was told.

After driving up and down the highway for about ten minutes, Death finally realized that the street they were looking for was indeed US Highway 1/9, but it was listed on his directions as W. Edgar Road. When they both realized that the number of the address on the paper was a match to the number that was on the brick wall of the entrance to a cemetery, Ibn thought it was a mistake.

"A graveyard? Hell naw! You wrote down the wrong address, young'un." Ibn shook his head.

"No, I didn't. This was the address Rell gave me. I think we're at the right place."

"I'll be damned! Ain't no way in hell I'm going up in there."

"If I know my brother, this is the right place. Go 'head, man. Pull up to the gate."

"You ain't hearing me, boy. I ain't going up in there, period!" Ibn was serious. He was spooked by the idea of driving in the cemetery.

"OK! You ain't gotta go, but I do. So get out the car and I'ma drive up in there. I'll pick you up on my way out." Death smiled.

"The hell you won't! I ain't standing out here either!"

"It ain't nothing but dead bodies in there. You seen a thousand dead bodies before. What is the problem, man? They in the ground!"

Ibn didn't say a word. He just sat there on the side of the road, looking at the tombstones that lay behind the gate. The fog had engulfed them, creating a spooky look like something out of a horror movie.

"Look, the gate is closed and locked. There ain't no way we can get in there anyway. I'm telling you, I think this is the wrong place."

"Man, just drive the car up to the gate!" Death was tired of playing games with the old man.

Ibn reluctantly cruised to the driveway of the entrance. He pulled up to the black iron gates and they opened up as if on cue. Ibn looked around frantically.

"What the fuh?" he asked.

They didn't know that the cemetery's security guard had been instructed to open the gate for them. When the guard saw them pull up on the security camera, he immediately opened the gates.

"This is some sick shit," Ibn said. He was ready to bug out. Death shook his head.

"Just a few minutes ago you was gonna put me at the bottom of the Hudson River, and now you sitting here like a faggot-ass punk, scared to drive into a graveyard."

Ibn ignored Death's comment, and the car crawled through the entrance of the gate just before the black bars closed behind them. There was no light in this part of the cemetery. The car's headlights lit the path. Death looked down at the directions and told Ibn where to turn. They saw light poles scattered throughout the more remote sections of the cemetery, which lit some of their path. At the end of their journey, Ibn noticed several parked cars. He pulled the Benz next to a Jaguar. Death got out of the car and closed the door. Ibn still sat in the car, looking around anxiously.

"Ibn, get outta the damn car!"

Ibn opened the car door reluctantly. He stepped out and looked around in the darkness. The creepy feeling Ibn had intensified, and he dropped the keys to the ground in his nervousness. Death sighed with impatience.

Ibn looked up at the creepy stucco building that stood in front of them. He could have sworn he saw two bats flying around the steeple of the building.

"Come on, man!" Death yelled, scaring the shit out of Ibn.

Ibn bent down and picked up the keys. "Oh, my gawd!" Death was frustrated. He rushed to climb the steps with Ibn right behind him.

A sign inside the building read Rosedale Crematory. A burning, wood-like smell lingered in the air.

"Aw, damn! We in the place where they cook the damn bodies, man!" Ibn yelled. "Fuck this!" Ibn's voice bounced off the walls. He tried to walk out, but Death snatched him back. Just then the huge oak doors to the right opened with a creaking sound. They both looked up and Tilmond appeared in the doorway.

"Fellas, we're waiting on you." He turned and walked back the way he came.

Death and Ibn followed him through the doors and into a huge office with high ceilings. Floor-to-ceiling drapes covered ten-foot-high windows. Old paintings hung from the exposed part of the wall. At the huge oak table sat six men—Luke and his right-hand man, and four plainclothes police officers with their shields hanging around their necks. They watched Death and Ibn walk in. Everyone had their game face on, everyone except Luke. He wore his usual smirk. Death immediately knew this meeting was a big mistake.

Once Death and Ibn sat down, Tilmond took his seat at the head of the table. Death raised an eyebrow. He wanted to know how Rell got to be in charge of this meeting when there was another sergeant seated at the table as well.

Tilmond started the meeting. "All right, gentlemen, and my fellow officers, now that we're all here, let's get to the first order of business."

Luke looked over at Death with that stupid grin on his face, but Death never acknowledged him. He simply kept his eyes focused on his brother. He thought it was hilarious that his brother spoke to them like he spoke to his officers during roll call.

"All this shit is illegal, fellas, but for it to flow, there has to be some order," Tilmond continued. "Back in the day, none of the disrespect that y'all young cats display today would have been tolerated."

"Well, this a new day, old head. I'm a hustler who was taught by the best," Luke interjected.

"And I'm one by blood," Death spat as he leaned forward and eyeballed Luke. "So what's your point?"

"Hold on, let the man have his say," Tilmond said to Death, referring to Luke.

Death shot daggers at his brother. *How dare he side with this punk?* Before he could think any further, his cell phone vibrated.

Chapter Twenty-Three

Malik was on swole when he stepped onto the block. He had been looking for Death since he had the conversation with his mother earlier. His best friend had gotten killed behind Death, and now the incident that happened with his mother earlier. He took huge steps as he walked toward the corner and his crew. He didn't say anything to anyone. His face told it all. The young runners looked at Malik and thought it would be best to stay away from him. Brian saw him from across the street and came toward him. Malik went straight to the pay phone. He dialed the appropriate numbers and hung up the phone to wait for the return call. He looked at his watch and the time was eleven pm.

"What's up, man?" Brian asked.

Malik remained silent. He leaned against the phone box and just stared straight ahead. Brian knew him well, and knew he was pissed. He also knew how to handle his friend.

"So, who you gonna move on?" he asked, leaning up against the other side of the phone box.

"Yo, man, this nigga threatened my mother!"

"Who?"

"Death! I'ma squeeze off as soon as I see that nigga!" Malik paced in circles around the payphone.

Brian gave a head signal for the two young runners to clear the corner, and he watched as the boys quickly disappeared.

"A'ight, cool. I'm with it."

"Naw, man, this ain't your battle. I need you here to run the blocks."

"You can't go up against that dude by yourself. We a team, remember? Plus"—he lowered his head—"I ain't tryna lose another brother."

Malik looked at his boy with saddened eyes as the memory of their boy Jeff returned. He had been fighting to push it out of his head since it happened. Some days were good, and some days were bad. They'd all grown up together, and it felt like a piece of them had died with their friend that day. Things hadn't been quite the same since it happened.

"I feel you, but this is my fight. Ain't nothing gonna happen to me."

Just then Marquis walked up, glad to see that his brother was still there.

"What you doing here?" Malik asked.

"I'm here to try to stop you from doing something that's gonna get you killed."

"Word up, Mark, because I was gonna have to go with him to have his back," Brian chimed in.

"Well, if push comes to shove, I'm ready to do battle, 'cause it ain't gonna go down like that," Marquis said.

"Mark, what are you doing?" Malik stared at his brother. "Naw, man, I can't let you do this. If I lost you, I would go to the pen for real, because I would be out here wildin' out, tryna kill everybody."

"Well, that's how I feel about you too," Marquis shot back. "You wouldn't listen to me, so I figured I'd come out here to have your back."

Malik regarded his brother. If something happened to him, he wouldn't be able to live. "Yo, if the phone rings, holla for me," Malik told Brian. "I'ma be over here." Malik pointed to a spot a few feet away, and Brian nodded. Malik draped his arm around his brother, and they walked away to continue their conversation in private.

"So what the hell was you gonna do if I was out here battling?" Malik asked.

"I'm strapped." Marquis partially pulled out the gun in his pocket, then shoved it back.

Malik laughed. "Come on, B. You ain't built for this. I'm not gonna let you ride with me like that. If something happens to you, it's a wrap."

"You don't know what I'm built for. You may have always hugged the blocks, but you have no clue about what I been doing, or what I know. All I know is that you family, my brother, and I ain't gonna let shit go down like that. I love you. You always looked out for me, and I want you to know that I got your back the same way." Marquis was serious.

"I know man, but—"

"But nothing, Malik! I ain't no kid no more! Ain't nothing else to discuss. We ride together for life."

"A'ight, a'ight!" Malik saw that his little brother was dead serious. "I know you not a kid anymore, but I also know you can have so much more than this," he said, spreading his hands and gesturing at the streets. "I want more for you. You got brains, and I rather you use ya brains to be successful. And if you catch a bullet over me, ain't no coming back, B." Thoughts of Jeff swarmed through his head. "Ain't no coming back."

"Well, that's the chance I'm gonna have to take for family." Marquis's tone said that the discussion was closed.

The two of them stood lost in their own thoughts. Malik looked out over the blocks and Marquis looked at the ground with his hands shoved down into his pockets.

"You remember that time when I got into a fight with Danny in the eighth grade?" Marquis asked.

Malik smiled and nodded. He remembered that day clearly.

"Well, you have always had my back whenever I got into a fight. I would run to get you, and you would put them little niggas in their place."

"Yeah, I remember," Malik agreed.

"Well, that day I came running to you, you took me back to the schoolyard and we called Danny out. We were standing there, face to face, and damn near everybody in the neighborhood was there that day. Well, you told me to square up. I looked at you like you had four heads when you said that." He laughed. Malik laughed along with him. "I was like, huh? You told me that day that I had to man up and handle my own, because that was all a part of becoming a man. You told me that you were there just to make sure that Danny was shooting me a fair one. You said that you wouldn't let anything happen to me, and to handle mine, and feel confident that you were right there. Do you remember that?"

Malik nodded.

"Well, big brother, I am here for you the same way you were always there for me. I know this is your battle, but this is a battle that you can't fight alone, so I got your back like you've always had mine. I learned to fight that day, and I think I had a fight every week after that because I knew if I needed you, you had my back. So why won't you let me have yours?"

Malik simply grinned. He had nothing but love for his brother. True, he had always tried to protect his brother. He took care of Marquis. He helped raise him when their mother worked, and he was there for him. So, yes, he was a little overprotective, but Marquis was right. He wasn't that little kid anymore.

"You got that. I'ma give you that." Malik held out his hand for a shake. Marquis shook it before Malik pulled him in for a brotherly hug. "I love you, man."

"I love you too." Marquis hugged his brother back.

"So, what you getting ready to do now?"

"I ain't gonna move on the nigga tonight. I'll wait and set something up. But I think I'ma roll up to the bar to see if that shorty I met last week is there. She told me that she was gonna be there tonight."

"Yeah, maybe you need to go get with her and get ya head right," Marquis agreed.

"A'ight, baby. One." Malik gave Marquis dap. "Yo, Brian, I'll be back!" he shouted before stepping off.

"Yo!" Marquis called out after his brother. Malik turned around. "Here. Drop this off by the crib first." Marquis handed Malik the .45.

"Man, you shouldn't have brought this shit out here! You take it back."

"I'ma chill out here and kick it with Brian for a minute."

Malik shook his head, took the gun, and walked off.

"So what's up?" Brian wanted to know.

"He a'ight. He 'bout to go get with some chick he met."

"Oh, yeah, I know the broad. She came through here the other day and went into the store. She was fire too. She was dealing a nice little whip."

Marquis noticed the tennis ball in Brian's hands. "Let me see the ball?" Marquis asked.

"Oh, naw! Not this one. Hold up." He reached into his pocket for the real ball.

"What the fuck? How many balls you got in your pocket?" Marquis laughed.

"Oh, naw. One is the joint we use to move the shit." He showed Marquis how the ball had been cut and hollowed out.

"Oh word? Y'all doing it like that?" Marquis was impressed.

"Yeah, man. Ya brother came up with this move. It's tight too."

Marquis bounced the real ball just as two undercover narcs hit the corners, tires screeching. Brian threw the cut and hollowed ball into the bushes next to the store. He was pissed because no one spotted the Narcs moving in on them, so he couldn't get a warning out. He just hoped that the other runners got rid of their cut tennis balls.

"Come on, fellas! Y'all know the routine! Let's kiss the brick wall," ordered a young, black, good-looking undercover narcotics officer. He wore a bulletproof vest over a gray T-shirt. The other officer was white and wore similar attire. The two officers from the second undercover vehicle had gathered up the runners and marched them across the street to where Marquis and Brian were lined up.

"What's the problem, officer?" Brian asked.

"Put your fucking hands on the wall!" The black officer shoved Brian into the wall face first. "Everybody put your hands on the wall!"

They all did as they were told. Everyone was searched thoroughly, and they were all clean, but the officers knew they were dirty. Two of the officers searched around the building. They checked garbage cans and brown paper bags, and still came up with nothing. Brian looked over at the three runners and winked. They all smiled and turned their heads back to the wall. When the two officers came back empty handed, the black officer grabbed Marquis by the neck. He assumed that since he was the tallest of them all, he was the leader. He flipped Marquis around and slammed his back into the brick wall. Marquis never said a word. He kept the same stone face he had when the officers first arrived. The young officer stepped close to him, trying to intimidate him, but it didn't work. He looked down and saw Marquis's college ID card clipped to the belt loop on his jeans. The officer snatched the ID off and studied it, then looked back at Marquis.

"So you a college boy, huh? You ain't gonna last long in college hanging on these corners, boy."

"What do you mean?" Marquis asked, using his best diction.

"What do you mean?" the cop mimicked, and the other officers laughed. Marquis laughed too, on the inside, at the ignorant people that the city hired to protect its citizens.

"I mean, you out here selling drugs, boy!" Spit flew from his mouth.

"Just because I'm standing here talking to my neighbor doesn't mean that I am selling drugs," Marquis said calmly. He wiped away the droplets of spit that had flown onto his forehead.

"Listen, you piece of shit. I don't give a fuck that you attend college. Like I said, you ain't gonna last long anyway. I want all you little punks to get up off of this corner! Now!"

Marquis shook his head at the power-tripping officer. He was the only black one in this group of narcs, and it figured that he would be the one to show off and degrade his own people in the face of the white authorities.

"'Bout time!" Brian dropped his hands and fixed his clothing. "Let's be out, y'all."

"You better watch your ass, boy." The black cop pointed at Brian.

The crew walked two blocks, then looked back to make sure that the coast was clear.

"You know we can't go back down there," Day-Day, one of the lookout boys, said. "At least not tonight."

"Yeah," Tim chimed in. "What happened with the protection we used to have?"

"Man, I have no idea what's going on. I know Malik ain't tryna hear shit the way he tripping right now."

They all agreed.

"So what we gonna do?" Money asked. "We can't leave the stash out there, and we definitely can't step off. What if one of Death's people comes through and see we ain't out there bangin'?" Money was concerned.

Brian didn't know what to do. He didn't even have a number so that he could get in contact with Death. He didn't want to call Malik, because that would let him know that Brian couldn't run the shop without his presence. He looked up at the dark sky, thinking about their next move that would avoid getting any of them locked up.

"Yo, man, dig this. Why don't y'all just use little man's bike right here?" Marquis pointed at Day-Day.

"What do you mean?" Day-Day asked.

"Listen, y'all already sit on the old man's porch." Marquis nodded in the direction of the house across the street from the store. Since the runners occupied each corner, whoever was posted up in front of the old, run-down, one-family house would sit on the porch during downtime. The old man was cool, and he very rarely came out of the house, preferring to sit in front of his TV. He would often send one of the young runners to the store for him.

"A'ight, so where does the bike come in at?" Brian asked.

Day-Day's bike was a new edition mountain bike. He had saved his drug money to buy it. The back tire on each side had a metal bar protruding from it. This bar was used for another person to stand on so that two people could ride on the bike at the same time without having to share the small seat.

"What y'all do is instead of everybody working a corner, y'all work together as a team," Marquis explained. "Brian, you can be out of sight, in the cut, just watching over the blocks. Then one of y'all will be posted up as lookout. Like my man right here"—Marquis gestured to one the youngest boys out there named Peanut, who liked to hang around them—"he looks young as hell, and they may not fuck with him. Then the kid right here"—he gestured to Tim—"can serve when someone steps onto the block. He can get the packet from dude right here"—Marquis gestured to Money—"who will sit on the old man's porch, and the kid can ride his bike and serve the customer. The only thing is that you need to make sure you keep the customers from coming over to the house to get served."

Brian looked at him with admiration. The young runners nodded in agreement with the plan.

"I'm with it," Day-Day said.

"Bet. Let's try that," Brian told them. "Good looking, Mark," he said, giving Marquis some dap.

"You rolling with us?" one of the boys asked Marquis.

"Naw, I'm out." Marquis had had enough excitement for one night.

"Yo, man," Brian called out to him. Marquis turned around. "Yo, man, you should be out here. You got what it takes to run this block."

"Naw, man. I ain't built for this." Marquis smiled at his own words. His brother had said the exact same thing.

"Yeah, a'ight, nigga. If you say so." Brian didn't believe him.

Kurt was walking up the street when he ran into Marquis.

"Where you going, school boy?"

"I'm getting ready to go to the crib. I got class in the morning."

"You a'ight?" Kurt noticed Marquis's troubled look.

"Naw, not really," he admitted.

"Come on. Let's walk like we used to when you was younger." Kurt and Marquis walked off together.

Chapter Twenty-Four

"Like I was saying"—Luke smirked at Death—"I was taught by one of the best OG's. To hell with all the rules and shit. This ain't back in the day. I'm all for playing the game for keeps, everything else is null and void." He leaned back in the high-backed swivel chair.

"Hold up. Fuck that shit! Check this out, homeboy," one of the older black officers spoke up. "This here ain't no game, and how soon you forget that the shit you doing is illegal. I can bust your ass right now and send you up the river for the rest of your natural life with one snap of the fucking finger. So let's not get cocky and bite the hands that feed you, motherfucker!"

"You damn right," another officer agreed, "because y'all pussy-ass punks running around here today, thinking y'all got the game on lock when you ain't got shit on lock. If it wasn't for niggas like us"—he gestured to the other crooked officers at the table with them—"if it wasn't for us turning the other cheek every now and again, y'all sucker-ass niggas wouldn't be shit!" He slammed his hand on the table. He was fed up with the new generation's way of thinking.

The room fell silent and Tilmond sat back in his chair with a grin on his face. Death had an arrogant pose, and Luke looked like he just didn't give a fuck.

"So whatchu old motherfuckers tryna say?" Luke spat.

Tilmond leaned forward. "Today is the last day of the destruction you and your war is bringing to the city. It's bad enough we got petty criminals, car thefts, and bullshit traffic stops to deal with. We don't need the kind of heat y'all are bringing to the table. When you create this type of destruction, it gets all the high-ranked officials involved. That's money, manpower, and tons of fucking paper work that none of us care to deal with. Frankly, we've done our time. We are vets, and right now we're cruising into retirement. I ain't with that running down the street, chasing niggas no more. And as I can speak for the others as well as myself, ain't no fucking way I'ma let young, dumb punks like y'all fuck up my pension on some ol' bullshit."

"You damn right!" one officer yelled.

"Speak on it!" another chimed in.

Tilmond waited for the room to quiet down. "With that said, there are no more deals. We are giving you an ultimatum—either you play, or you pay. What I mean is, you play by the rules that we set, or you pay with your life. You can take that any way you want." He sat back and folded his arms, waiting for a response. The other officers sat there with equal confidence.

"I don't have a problem with that. Check your boy over there." Luke pointed at Death with an evil grin.

Death stewed in anger, but his facial expression showed confidence.

"So what are you going to do?" Tilmond asked Death.

"I'm good," he said while staring down Luke. In Death's mind, it was on. He didn't give two shits about nothing his brother and the others were talking about.

Tilmond stared at his brother and knew that he was going to have to have another conversation with him on the side once the meeting was over.

"Here's the deal, fellas. If anyone from your teams goes against what we have said here tonight, there will be hell to pay. So I suggest you have a meeting with your people as soon as this meeting is over to let them know. There will be no more favors. Your fee only covers issues that are discussed with one of us personally. So what that means is that neither of you makes a move unless we know about it, at least until the heat is turned down from Internal Affairs. Is that understood?"

"It's all good, baby. I ain't got no problems." Luke continued to be cocky. Death just nodded.

"Now while we're here, are there any issues or up-and-coming problems that either one of you have? We may as well put it on the table now to make sure we take care of it now."

Luke thought for a second and said, "Naw. Nothing that's gonna require your assistance, officer." He smirked.

"And you?" Tilmond looked at Death.

"I got a youngin' on my team who I think may roll over. So, yeah, I need to take care of him."

"You sure about this kid?" one of the officers asked.

"Not sure, but I ain't tryna wait to find out."

"So if you're not sure, maybe you should wait on it anyway, put somebody on him, and see where it goes from there," Tilmond suggested.

Death didn't respond.

"A'ight, so if that's it, and everybody understands where we are coming from, then you fellas can bounce. Oh, and just in case you're thinking about pulling a stupid move, everybody gonna have a personal official escort outta here." Tilmond smiled.

Tilmond wanted to keep Death behind so they could talk, but most didn't know that they were related, and he wanted to keep it that way. The men stood and left the crematory.

It was almost one AM and they were on the drive back to Newark, Death called the phone booth and Brian answered.

"Stay there," Death said simply and hung up.

Twenty minutes later Ibn pulled up onto the block. Brian walked over to the car.

"What's up, kid?" Death asked.

"Um ... Malik was looking for you earlier, but he stepped off," Brian told him.

"I was in a meeting. When he comes back through, tell him to hit me up."

"A'ight." Brian stepped back and watched the car pull off.

Brian called Malik on his cell phone but got no answer. He didn't leave a message.

Malik kept his word and went to the bar, except that there was no chick he was going to meet. This was a bar that Death and his people usually frequented. Word was that he was part owner of the bar, along with his uncle.

He nodded a greeting at several people he knew when he entered the bar. Malik was focused, and he had a funny feeling in his stomach that he was gonna run into Death. He didn't have any intention on stopping by the crib before going to the bar, so he still carried the two guns on him.

Malik surveyed the place, looking for any signs of Death or his crew members. From where he stood, he could see the entire room because of the small amount of people in the place. There were a few people on the dance floor, and several more sitting at tables. Most sat around the bar. Malik worked his way around the wall and moved into a dark corner where he could see the door and the entire establishment, but they couldn't see him. He leaned against the back wall for what seemed like hours, but he had only been in the bar for forty minutes the last time he checked his watch. Exasperated, he planned to leave and go to another bar when he spotted Justice standing in the opposite corner, eyeballing him. Their eyes met and the staring match began.

Finally, Malik had had enough. He decided to step to Justice. He crept along the wall like a wolf stalking his prey. Justice saw Malik approaching and gripped the hammer in his pocket. He had become quite paranoid since his reassignment. He barely showed up to his newly assigned blocks because of the abuse he had to take from AP. Justice knew that because he was falling off, he was going to raise some eyebrows within the organization. He also knew that AP would go straight to Death, and ultimately they would be coming for him. Justice had plans for them, though. He was actually at the club that night to deliver a message to Death as well. He had previously run into Shauna, and she told him how she believed that the crack they had was bad. She said that she herself eventually ended up going to the emergency room too, and had her stomach pumped.

Malik stood in front of Justice and mean-mugged him. "You got a problem with me?" He had his hand in his pocket on the grip that Marquis had handed to him. The other piece was still tucked away in the waistband of his jeans. Both young men were ready for a showdown. It seemed as if the crowd of people that gathered in the bar had disappeared. The noise seemed to fade away too. The two dealers focused on each other, each waiting for the other to make the first move. However, there was something in Justice's eyes that Malik seemed to recognize. This wasn't a man who was ready for war. This was a man who feared for his life and was ready to do whatever he had to do to defend it. Justice was on the defense. Although his face was hardened, the eyes never lied.

Justice thought Malik was there to do a hit on him, per Death's orders, and he was ready to beat Malik to the draw. Malik had no idea how close he was to losing his life.

"I heard you got set up across town," Malik said, still focused on the fear in Justice's eyes.

"Yeah," Justice replied. He still had not budged, but looked at Malik curiously. Why was he making small talk? Justice was not going to let his guard down. "And I heard you running my old blocks now."

"Look, I know what you thinking, but I ain't have nothing to do with that. Death told me to run the blocks until you got out of lockup."

"Yeah, right," Justice didn't believe him. He still fingered his gun while using his peripheral vision to keep an eye on his surroundings.

Malik could sense Justice's uneasiness, and it had him checking his surroundings. Maybe Death heard that he was looking for him, and sent Justice to body him? Paranoia was settling in on both of the young men.

"You a'ight, man?" Malik asked.

"I'm good. Just ain't never seen you up in here before. What's the occasion? You looking for me? I'm right here, so what's up?"

"Yo, chill, man! I ain't in here looking for you. Why you tripping and shit? What's up?" Now Malik became defensive. There was definitely something wrong with the situation, and he needed to figure it out. "Yo, I don't know why you're so jittery and shit, but one-on-one, man, let's take a walk."

Justice laughed. "You crazy as shit if you think I'm gonna let you walk me to my death! Naw, dude, I ain't going out like that. If I'ma go out, I'm going out blazin', and I'm taking you with me."

"What the fuh? Yo, you think I'm here to do you?" Malik chuckled. "Naw, kid, I ain't here for that. I'm here looking for that nigga Death."

"Word?" Justice was confused. "I'm here looking for him too. What's up?"

"Let's step." Malik and Justice walked outside.

Marquis and Kurt sat in front of Marquis's apartment building. They had been talking for a while like they used to when he was younger. Kurt had looked out for Malik and Marquis since they were kids, and in return, they never judged Kurt for his appearance or lifestyle. Marquis felt better after talking to Kurt. He was surprised that Kurt knew so much. The man was a walking library. He knew more about people's business than they probably knew about themselves. He even had information on cats he could have put away for life, but Kurt was a standup dude, regardless of what others had to say. He wasn't a snitch, and on the many occasions when he was offered money and the opportunity to do just that, he didn't.

Marquis was also surprised on how much Kurt knew about his father. Mark knew that Kurt had known his father and mother for many years, but the wealth of information Kurt revealed to him that night was overwhelming. Marquis found out that his father was a legend—a gangster, for real. *Maybe that's where Malik gets his temper from*, Marquis thought while Kurt continued to tell him how his father put fear into the hearts of many.

"Son your father was a bad motherfucker back in the day. Niggas would walk on the other side of the street when Wiz walked by. I mean the fear he put in them cats was the shit!"

"Word?" Marquis was surprised. He had heard bits and pieces throughout his life about his father mostly from Kurt. But Kurt had never revealed in detail the way he was telling now.

"Word, and what was so smooth about Wiz was he was that

pretty type a nigga. You know, dressed clean and his swagger had them bitches creaming in they panties," Kurt bragged as if he was speaking of himself.

"So it's true my father was a player huh?" Marquis had heard that part of the story from his mother.

"Well I mean hell we all where players in our time. I mean, yeah, Wiz could have any broad he wanted. And there were times he did his thing. But baby boy don't you ever get it fucked up. Your father loved your mother to death and took care of his family. He always put his family first!"

Marquis continued to sit there listening to Kurt give his parents praise.

"Oh I remember this one time this cat named Wags came through and thought he was gonna punk Wiz. Wags was from D.C. Yeah, he had some status but he really wasn't kicking up no dust like Wiz," Kurt scratched his matted beard. "But anyway, Wags pulled up to the curb in front of the strip club your father owned."

Marquis raised an eyebrow.

"Yeah boy your father had it on lock back then!" Kurt confirmed Marquis's doubts. "Yeah, so Wags pulled up to the curb in a Phantom! They wasn't even making them like that back then. This nigga Wags had one flown in from overseas! The shit was crazy!"

Marquis sat there still thinking how his father owned his own business.

"Wags and his boys walked up in the club and bought the bar! They tried to buy all the bitches that were dancing that night. They wanted to take them back to DC. Picture that shit!" Kurt stood to his feet and held his crotch. "Them motherfuckers wanted to take all the bitches outta the club that night!

"Wiz was in the back in the office and one of the workers came back to tell him what Wags was doing. I was sitting at the bar watching the whole thing. Wiz came out and approached Wags in a professional way. That Wiz is a smooth motherfucker boy," Kurt laughed.

"So what happened?" Marquis wanted to know.

"Wags started talking outta the side of his neck all slick and shit. Wiz told that nigga plain and simple that he wasn't taking his dancer's outta the club. Wags and his boys tried to surround your father, but his boys quickly came and stood behind him. Before Wags knew what hit him, Wiz had done pulled a switch blade from his pocket and slit that niggas throat from ear to ear!" Kurt laughed so hard he was bent over holding his stomach. "Them niggas was scared as shit! All wiz said to them motherfuckers was, 'thank you for your business and have a good night fellas!' Them cats hauled ass up outta there!" Kurt laughed so hard he began to cough.

Marquis didn't see the humor, but it did give him more insight on how ruthless his father was.

"After that day," Kurt stood upright breathing heavily trying to catch his breath. "After that day boy your father reigned supreme!"

Kurt continued to gloat in the past while Marquis stared at the ground in deep thought. They both became silent basking in their own thoughts when Marquis spoke again.

"Kurt did you ever find out the information I needed, so I can try and go see Wiz?"

"I didn't forget you, kid. I'm working on it."

ᖇᖇᖇᖇ

Nina sat in a diner with Ernest. She had given him a call when she couldn't reach Nilda for some much-needed counseling. Ernest was nice enough to come pick her up, although he didn't live near her and not to mention it was late at night. He made her feel comfortable because he could identify with her struggles.

Nina felt so comfortable with him that she told him more about herself than she cared to. She told him about the boys, about how she had been naïve and thought she was hiding her addiction from her sons when they knew all along. She told him about how she got high to escape the things she had done in the past, and to keep them from coming into her dreams at night.

"So how are the nightmares since you've been clean?" he asked her.

"Honestly, they are still there. The only difference is that they are less dramatized, but they are still there."

"So how do you handle them now, if you still have the dreams?"

"Most times I pray. Sometimes I may just turn on the TV. To be honest, I don't sleep that often anyway. If I was working, it would be better. I would probably be tired from working and could sleep better."

"Yeah, I know that feeling, and you're right, you do need to keep yourself occupied with positive things. I remember having dreams once I went into detox. I used to have crazy dreams." Ernest laughed when he thought of them.

Nina looked down at her nails and picked at them. They looked terrible. It had been a long time since she'd had a manicure. She quickly balled up both hands into fists to prevent Ernest from seeing them.

"Hey, I don't know if you're interested, but I have a friend who is a supervisor at a towing company and could use a dispatcher. You think that would be something you'd want to do?"

"At this point, anything is better than what I have." She smiled.

He grabbed his cell phone and dialed a number. He sat there patiently and when the voicemail came on, he left a message. He disconnected the call and turned his attention back to Nina.

"Now tell me what else is on your mind, because I know there's more."

"What do you mean?" Nina looked at him in confusion.

"I mean, I can see through those pretty eyes of yours, and I know that you are holding back." Ernest continued to look into her eyes until she couldn't look into his anymore, and she lowered her head.

Chapter Twenty-Five

Marquis had been struggling with school ever since all of the recent action in his household. Still, it was always a pleasure to spend quality time with Shea. He was growing to like her more and more each day. He even wondered whether he was falling in love with her. This was his last week working at Dr. Jay's. He no longer could handle the pressure of sleepless nights due to family drama, and school. It cut short a lot of the time to spend with Shea as well. Still, they had a small amount of time that they spent together at school. Malik had been a loyal brother and told Marquis that he didn't need to work anymore if he didn't want to, so Marquis chose to put in his resignation.

Money really wasn't an issue, and Malik made sure he had the finer things in life. He had the essentials—like clothing, footwear, and, of course, a cell phone. He splurged and bought himself and Shea some matching jewelry as well.

Since he and Shea had been seeing each other, Marquis managed to avoid meeting her parents. He felt that it would be better if he didn't at this time. He didn't want to put any more pressure on Shea than needed, which was why they spent most of their time on campus or at the local

McDonald's. That day Marquis wanted to spent time with her in private since there were no classes, due to a water main breakage on campus. He thought about renting a hotel room until Shea told him that her parents had gone to Atlantic City that morning and shouldn't be back until later on that evening,

Marquis sat on Shea's bed and stared at her while she lay on the bed and watched television. She looked over and noticed that he was looking at her.

"What's wrong?" she asked.

He shook his head.

"Come on. There is something wrong with you. You have been acting distant the last few days. Is it school?"

"Naw."

"Well, tell me." Shea sat up, scooted close to him, and rubbed his back.

"My family is falling apart."

"Don't tell me your mother is using again!"

"Naw, she still clean, but I don't know for how long. This cat my brother works for is threatening my mother. We don't know why, and my mother won't tell us. But my brother ain't having it, and he is running around trying to get at the cat. I don't want to lose my brother, but he's going about it the wrong way. I want to help him, but then again, I ain't tryna get caught up in the lifestyle. I'm tryna to get into my class work, but my mind is all over the place."

Shea could see the stress that Marquis was holding in, and she knew just the medicine that would help him to relieve that stress. She kissed him on the shoulder and worked her way up to his neck. He tilted his head to the side, exposing more neck for her to kiss. He turned his face to meet hers and they began to kiss passionately. Shea pulled him down on the bed and lay on top of him. They continued to kiss while Marquis slowly massaged her ass. His dick became rock hard and it pressed against Shea's clit. She ground into his manhood and he ground back. Their bodies began to heat up.

Shea removed her shirt and Marquis did the same. They kissed again and Marquis slid his hands down her pants and squeezed her bare ass. Shea helped him pull off her jeans and panties. He threw them on a nearby chair. She unbuttoned his jeans, he lifted his hips, and she slid off his jeans. Then she removed his boxers so that they were both totally naked. They kissed again as their private parts rubbed against each other, creating a wet friction. Marquis carefully rolled atop Shea, who opened her legs for him. He grabbed his dick and worked the head into her tight hole.

He sighed loudly when he was all the way in. It felt so good. Shea's pussy was tight and hugged his dick with its warm walls. Marquis worked it slowly with deep strokes, sending Shea into a frenzy. She wasn't a virgin, but it had been some time since she'd had sex. She held on to him for dear life. They meshed together as one while their bodies met with each rhythmic stroke. Once Shea was good and wet, Marquis grabbed her right leg and brought her knee up to her chest, and worked it a little faster. He stroked up and down, side to side, and then in circular motions. He watched Shea's facial expression as she reached her climax. He kissed her gently on the lips. Finally he was ready to bust off. His whole body went into a convulsion as he reached his climax. He unloaded inside Shea and then collapsed on top of her. They both were wet with perspiration and breathing heavily. It seemed to Marquis as if all the stress drained right out of his body with the nut he just had. They both drifted off into a deep sleep.

A little while later there was a knock on her room door, and both of them looked at each other.

"Shea?" her mother called.

"Oh my God!" she whispered. "It's my mother!" They both jumped to their feet and dressed as quickly as possible. Her mother knocked on the door and called her again. Malik was dressed in a matter of seconds flat, but Shea wasn't as quick. She kicked her panties and bra under the bed and opted to throw on an oversized T-shirt and a pair of sweatpants that were on the same chair as her jeans. She walked over to the door while attempting to fix her hair. Her mother knocked again. She whispered to Marquis to lay down like he was asleep. She unlocked the door and opened it partially, pretending to have been asleep.

"Oh, hey, Ma. I didn't hear you come in," she said groggily.

"Oh. You were 'sleep?" her mother asked.

"Yeah, I fell asleep. What happened? Why are y'all back so early?"

"Well, we missed the first bus, so we waited two hours on the next bus to Atlantic City when word came in that the bus had a flat, and it would be another hour before it got there. So, of course, you know Mr. Impatient didn't want to stay and wait."

"Oh, OK."

"Well, I'll let you get some sleep," Her mother said.

Shea was almost home free until her mother saw Marquis's Timberland boot.

"What's that?" She pushed her way into the room. Marquis knew he was busted, so he sat up and looked at her mother.

"Oh, no, you don't have a boy in your room! Are you crazy, Shea? If he sees this boy in here, all hell is going to break loose!" Shea's mother tried to whisper, but her voice was a little above a whisper. She was shocked that her daughter would even dare to pull something like that, especially knowing the type of man her stepfather was. Shea knew that her stepfather wouldn't dare touch her, but she didn't know that her mother would pay the price for her actions. Before her mother could close the door, her husband pushed his way into the room.

"Who the fuck is this?" Larry demanded. He had been eavesdropping on the conversation as he did so often.

"He's my friend, and he was just leaving," Shea stated.

"Oh fuck, yeah, he leaving! Why is he in here?"

"He was here to go over some class work with me, and we fell asleep," Shea lied.

Larry sniffed and frowned. "It don't smell like school work in here. It smells like pussy in here!"

"Ma!" Shea shrieked in panic.

"Larry, just give her a chance. She said they were doing school work and fell asleep. That can happen."

"Shut the fuck up! You know damn well this little whore was in here fucking." Larry was furious.

Marquis knew this wasn't going to turn out well, so he took it upon himself to try to explain.

"Excuse me, sir, I'm sure this doesn't look well to you as a parent right now. But Shea is actually telling you the truth, and if you would allow me a moment, I can tell you exactly the lesson her and I were discussing," he said in his best college-boy voice.

"Nigga, please! Don't blow smoke up my ass. I ain't new to this, boy. I know what pussy smells like. I ate enough of it in my time to know, and I also know how niggas are. Now you can kill that bullshit noise you talking. Matter-of-fact, get the fuck outta my house before I put my foot in yo' ass!" He stepped toward Marquis.

Shea jumped in front of Marquis to protect him at the same time that her mother jumped in front of Larry to stop him. Larry simply backhanded Shea's mother so hard that she flew to the floor.

Shea reacted out of pure reflex. "You motherfucker!" She charged at him only to be knocked to the floor as well. Larry looked down at the two of them weeping and crying.

"Now stay the fuck outta my way," he snarled.

He thought he was going to take care of Marquis as well, but when he looked up, Marquis had a Glock pointed right at his head. The menace in his eyes was convincing.

"What's up now? You can beat on women, so let me see what you got for my boy right here." Marquis fingered the trigger and held the gun with a steady hand. Shea's mother begged and pleaded with Marquis not to shoot her husband, whereas Shea gazed at her man with more love than she thought she could hold for a man other than her real father.

"Shea, pack as much shit as you can. I'm taking you outta here," Marquis ordered.

Shea scurried to her feet and began tossing items into a duffel bag.

"No, Shea! Don't go," her mother cried.

"Miss, you can stay here if you want to, but I refuse to let this clown touch Shea again. Because if he do, I promise you, I will bleed him slow." Marquis meant every word, and Larry knew it. Larry was no fool. He may have been a womanizer, and talked a lot of shit, but he was a straight-up punk. He knew that if he pushed Marquis's buttons. the young man wouldn't hesitate to fill him with hot ones. All he could do was stand there and mean-mug Marquis while gritting his teeth.

"Don't come back here when you find out your little boyfriend can't take care of you," Larry said to Shea while keeping an eye on Marquis.

"He can, and will, take care of me," Shea sassed him.

"You think this little nigga gonna pay for your schooling?" Larry laughed.

Marquis snorted with confidence, but paid Larry no attention. After all, he was the one holding the heat.

"You think this little punk gonna pay for your tuition? I pay for you to go to school! I pay for all them damn clothes you putting in that suitcase!" Larry fidgeted as he reprimanded Shea, who ignored him as she continued to pack.

"You stupid as hell! I'm on a scholarship, so you don't pay for my school. My godfather gives me money for my clothes, so stop tryna front like you do so much," Shea snapped and rolled her eyes at Larry.

Larry was furious. He rubbed his hand across his face, trying to keep himself calm.

"Homeboy," Marquis said. Larry looked at him with fury. "Stop moving," he said calmly.

"Put the gun down and come at me, straight up!"

Marquis laughed. "You would like that, wouldn't you? But that ain't gonna happen. Now I'm gonna ask one more time. Stop moving. Let's go, Shea."

"I'm almost done," she responded, moving around the room at the speed of lightning.

Her mother still sat on the floor, whimpering. She wanted to pack her own things and leave with her daughter, but she was afraid of Larry and knew he would come looking for her.

Ten minutes later Marquis and Shea walked out of her parents' house with two duffel bags and a suitcase on wheels. Marquis was still pissed, but Shea managed to calm him down. She reminded him that they were going to be together, and she knew nothing would happen to her, because he wouldn't let it. He assured her that she was safe with him. She didn't even ask him about the gun. All she knew was that she had a man who was willing to risk his life for hers. It reminded her of how her father had been there for her mother the same way.

Chapter Twenty-Six

Nina sat at the kitchen table, thinking about how she wanted to take a little hit of dope. She tried to convince herself that it would only be one bag, just to clear her mind. She was worried about Malik. She knew what Death was capable of, and she wished she did the right thing with her son years ago. He wouldn't be on the streets now had she done so. Her own selfishness and the craving for the drug had once again controlled her mind. She thought about the dream she had just last night about the little boy again.

He was four-years-old and they were both standing on the platform in the subway, waiting for the train to arrive. She had just purchased a gram of heroin. The little boy sat in his stroller. Nina was jonesing so bad that she decided to step behind a billboard and sniff a little before they got on the train. She wheeled the stroller behind a billboard that displayed an anti-drug logo, and she opened the package. In the meantime, the little boy ate some crackers. Nina turned her back so that the little boy wouldn't see her and handled her business.

Suddenly she heard the baby cry. When she looked up, he was gone from the stroller. She put her drugs away and ran from behind the billboard. She saw the other passengers looking down onto the tracks below. When she walked over to the edge of the platform, the little boy sat there on the filthy ground. Rats ran around him as they tried to eat the crackers he still held. He looked up at her with sad eyes and cried for her. "Mommy!"

Her heart began to beat two times its normal speed. "Help me!" she called out to the other passengers, but no one moved. They just looked at her like she wasn't saying anything to them. Some turned their backs and kept going with whatever conversation they'd been having.

Nina began to panic because she didn't want to jump down onto the filthy, rat-infested tracks. She began to cry. She willed herself to jump down there to save the baby, but her legs wouldn't move. The heroin took over at that moment and relaxed her instantly. The gram she had purchased from New York was good quality, and its potency was overwhelming. Nina nodded off right there at the edge of the platform. The little boy screamed louder for her, and stood up, reaching for her. But Nina could not move. She heard him, but her body wouldn't move. Then there it was, the whistle of the subway train. She saw the headlight of the train approaching in the distance and looked back at the handsome, wet-faced little boy. The train was not scheduled to stop at that particular stop. The little boy continued to reach upward for her. Nina looked at a man who was staring at her.

"Help me, please," she slurred.

The powerful drug took her deeper and deeper into her zone, making everything go in slow motion. The train whistled again, but when she looked up this time, the headlights were only several feet away. She leaned forward and made a slow attempt to get the baby, and she fell onto the tracks just before the train hit them.

That was when she awoke from her dream. She had been up for the rest of the night, thinking about the little boy. She wondered what the little boy would be like now. She picked at her nose for the better part of the morning, and was desperately trying to get the images out of her mind. She just wanted to take one small hit to relax, and then she would be OK.

She thought about confiding in Ernest about the part of her past that still obviously haunted her, but she didn't think she would be able to tell him. Would he turn her in to the authorities, or would he just stop dealing with her altogether? She didn't know what to do, but she knew she had to do something. She figured if she continued not to sleep at night because of the same recurring dream, then she knew she would turn back to heroin.

Nina always smoked a little weed back in the day but she thought about how Death had been the one to start her using heroin. He vowed to get even with her because he realized she had been toying with his mind, and had no intentions of ever giving him some play. Once Nina became pregnant with Wiz's baby boy, Death knew it was a wrap. He went into a jealous rage and decided to teach Nina a lesson.

One day Nina called Death crying looking for Wiz. Nina was stressing that day because she had just found out that Wiz was cheating on her again. The other woman had the nerve to call the house and ask for Wiz that morning. She told Nina that she and Wiz had been seeing each other for more than a month. She also told her that Wiz had spent the night with her the previous night.

Nina was pissed, because she was pregnant with their first child. When Wiz came home that morning, after not being home all night, Nina lost it on him and told him about the phone call she received from the woman. Of course he denied it. They got into a heated argument. It was the same argument that they'd had many times before when Nina suspected or heard that Wiz was cheating on her. Wiz walked back out of the house that morning.

Wiz loved Nina and took care of her, but the lifestyle that he led allowed him the advantage to be with any woman he wanted.

So after calling Wiz a hundred times and never getting an answer, she reached out to Death hoping he would be able to help her. Death showed up to the apartment. He sat and listened to Nina as if he really cared. Nina was hysterical and ready to kill herself because of the emotional rollercoaster she was on. Partly due to her hormones of being pregnant.

Nina laid in his arms and cried for what seem like hours. Death retrieved a baggie from his pocket. As Nina lay in his arms whimpering he told her he was gonna give her something to relax her.

"What is it?" she asked him.

"It's heroin."

"Are you crazy?" she expressed to him.

"Nina, a little heroin ain't never hurt nobody. I take a hit every now and then myself to relax me," he lied. "Look at yourself. You ready to kill yourself and Wiz right now. You're losing it, girl. You need to calm down. I promise you nothing won't happen," he assured her.

So Nina allowed him to scoop some on a bent matchbook cover. She snorted the substance in each nostril, therefore starting the cycle on the road to being a heroin user.

Death came over on two more occasions when Nina called him because she was stressing. Death gave her injections to calm her nerves. As time went on, Nina called on Death and inquired about more heroin. Death made sure he only came when Wiz wasn't around. Wiz never knew his boy was turning Nina on to heroin. Death also took advantage of the moments and had sex with Nina when she was doped. He came by frequently and gave her heroin until she was hooked. But then he stopped one day, and Nina began to crave the drug and went into withdrawals.

She became sick and began to vomit. She called Death and told him how sick she was, and wanted to know if he would bring her just a little dope to take off the edge. Of course he did so. After about another week of snorting heroin, Nina had a habit. She began to go to cop on her own. She made sure that drove completely across down when she purchased the drug. Wiz was well known and she didn't want to take any chances of him finding out. Wiz never knew what was going on, nor did he notice that Nina was using. He was so busy cheating on her and hustling that he hardly had the time to notice. Nina was good at hiding her addiction.

Death received a call from Nina one night about one AM. Wiz was out of town conducting business, and Death knew this. He could barely understand her because she slurred so much, so he went over to the house. When he got there, Nina was sitting in a pool of blood on the bathroom floor in a heroin nod. Death had seen some ill stuff in his life, but nothing this foul. He could see the baby's head poking out of her vagina, and his face was blue. Nina continued to nod off. He didn't know what to do, so he called her name. She opened her eyes and smiled at him.

Nina began to push as the contractions hit her again, and she looked down at the baby as it slid out some more. She reached down and pulled the baby from her vagina and left it laying there on the cold floor. Death knew the baby was dead. He immediately called a Jamaican woman he knew, who was a midwife, and told her he was bringing Nina to her. He cut the cord as he was seen on TV. He got Nina together and cleaned the bathroom floor as best he could. He helped her change her clothes and wrapped the baby in several sheets and a blanket. Nina snorted more heroin before leaving.

They arrived at the Jamaican's woman's apartment, which was located in the back of a Laundromat. The establishment was closed for the night. When he brought Nina in, the woman immediately had him put Nina on a folding table so that she could do what needed to be done. She cleaned out Nina, got rid of her placenta, and washed her body. When she was done,

Death handed her a stack of bills. He took Nina to the car and left her there. He went back to the Jamaican woman's door and knocked. When she opened the door, Death pumped a bullet in her head and walked away before the body even hit the floor.

Then he drove to Weequahic Park, opened the trunk, and took out a garbage bag that contained the baby's body. He added three bricks to the bag and tossed it into the lake.

Days later when Wiz finally came home, he noticed that Nina didn't look seven months pregnant anymore. She and Death had put the story together, and she told it to Wiz. She told him she had a miscarriage and when she tried to tell him, he never answered the phone. Nina did call him that night, but it wasn't for that. It was mostly to harass him about staying out late. Since she never left a message, it played out. As far as Wiz was concerned, Nina was taken to the hospital three days ago and had a miscarriage.

Nina overcame her addiction after that, afraid that Wiz would find out. Things weren't quite the same, though. Although Death had helped Nina that day, he held it over her head, threatening her if she didn't leave Wiz. When Nina stayed with Wiz and eventually gave birth to Malik and Marquis, Death had had enough. He did what he had to do when Wiz got sent to prison. Since then, Death had always had some sort of control over Nina, whether it was the heroin with which he supplied her, sexing her when he felt like it, or the secret of her killing her baby because of drugs. That was a secret the two of them held, but Nina knew Death's secret too.

Now she continued to pick at the scabs in her nose. It seemed that the infection had spread over to the other nostril. She was stressed and didn't know what to do. Having no more willpower left, she decided to go cop a bag of dope when Marquis came through the door with Shea in tow.

Nina looked at them and the bags they carried with questions in her eyes.

"What's up, Ma?" Marquis asked.

Nina didn't answer, she continued to stare at Shea.

"Hi Miss Boyd," Shea said.

They both stood there looking awkward.

"What's going on?" Nina finally asked.

"Ma, this is my friend, Shea. Ma, Shea . . . well her stepfather put her out and I said she could stay with us," Marquis said, bending the truth a little.

"Where's her mother?"

"Ma, it's complicated. We will tell you about it later. Just trust me. Can she stay?"

"I don't know, Mark. I think I need to talk to her mother," Nina was unsure.

"Ma, her stepfather hits on her mother and he hit Shea today. I can't have that, Ma," Marquis expressed.

"Really?" Nina looked surprised.

"Yeah, really," Marquis assured her.

"This ain't no hotel, Mark. I don't want no baby-making in here."

"Come on Ma, it ain't even gonna be like that."

"Yeah, you think I'm a fool, but I was your age once too." She looked at him sideways.

"So can she stay? Please?"

"OK, sure, she can stay. But remember what I said." She pointed at him.

Marquis helped Shea take her stuff into the room and Nina walked back into the kitchen. She decided to call Nilda instead of getting that bag of dope.

"Hi, may I speak to Nilda?" she asked the secretary.

"I'm sorry, she's gone for the day. May I take a message?"

"No, thank you." She disconnected the call.

Once again, Nilda was not around. Nina sat back down at the kitchen table and picked at her nose again until it became sore. She needed to keep herself busy. What was she going to do? She decided to call Ernest. He had been really nice to her and called every day, just to check on her. But as of yet today he hadn't called. That didn't mean she couldn't call him, though. She still hadn't heard anything about the dispatch job he was going to talk to his friend about. *That's it*, she thought. That would be her excuse for calling him.

"Are you OK?" he asked when he answered the phone.

"I could be better." She picked at her nose again, this time making it bleed.

"Do you need me?"

"Yeah, I kinda do," she said, sniffing.

"Do you have a cold?

"No."

"OK. I'll just let you hang with me while I take care of some business. I'll be there in a half hour."

"OK. Did you hear anything about the job?" Nina asked.

"No, but as soon as I get off the phone with you, I'll call my friend to see what's up."

"OK. I'll be waiting outside."

Nina ran to freshen up. She had to break down the other day and purchase some foundation. She never had to wear makeup before, but her nose was getting worse and the cream was no longer working, not that it ever had. She packed on the foundation to cover up what was starting to become an unsightly thing. For now, the makeup did a good job. She figured if she kept her face somewhat lowered, her nose wouldn't be as noticeable. She took Tylenol cold medicine before she left. Her nose had been very stuffy, but when she blew it no mucus came out, only blood.

While she looked out for Ernest, Kurt came walking up the street with his train. That day he didn't chant. He was down in the dumps. He wasn't able to get any work that day, and the junkyard owner didn't come to work. None of his workers would let him get an advance, so it was a bad day for Kurt the Conductor.

As he rolled up, he saw Nina standing out front and managed to smile. "Hey, Nina, my sister! What's up, babe?"

Nina scowled at him with her arms folded across her chest.

He walked up to her. "What's wrong with you?"

"You, Kurt! Who told you to run ya mouth? Don't be telling my sons none of my business!"

"Come on, now, sis, you know we go way back and I've always loved them boys as if they was mine," he tried to reason with her.

"I don't care, Kurt! They don't need to be hearing shit from you. I can tell them whatever I want them to know."

"But the boy wanted to know about his daddy. That ain't right to keep them boys from they father."

Nina opened her mouth in total shock. "Who the hell are you to tell me what they need, Kurt? I raised them boys, not him."

"I know you did, Nina," Kurt agreed, "and you did a damn good job. But it ain't like Wiz walked out on you. He got popped and you know if he was out, all y'all would be taken care of."

"But he ain't out here taking care of us, Kurt. I am."

Kurt was hurt by the way she talked about Wiz. "I hear you, but I'm my own man and I look out for them boys when you ain't around, and I'm gonna keep looking out for them. So you can take it or leave it but either way, I ain't gonna stop being who I am 'cause you feelin' some kinda way toward their father." Kurt walked back over to his train, saddened by her behavior. Since Nina had gotten clean, it seemed like she felt she was above him, and he hated the way she acted. But Kurt, being the good-hearted person he was, opted to walk away instead. As he was leaving Nina continued to yell at him and call him dirty names.

Depressed, Kurt continued to walk away. "You wrong for this, Nina," he said. He then stopped and turned back toward her. "You look good, by the way, Nina. You clean up well. Keep up the good work." He resumed his walking.

Nina never acknowledged the compliment he gave her and kept spitting obscenities instead.

Five minutes later, Ernest pulled up in his Nissan Pathfinder. Nina got in and they sped off. They spent the entire day together. Ernest had many errands to run, and Nina enjoyed being with him. They laughed and talked and bonded that day. She was very comfortable with Ernest. He was easy to talk to, and he made her feel like everything she had to say was very important, and he listened intently. He gave great advice and comforted her when she thought she did stupid things.

For instance, they talked about her nose problem. He asked her about it and she was embarrassed when he did. *The makeup obviously isn't good enough to cover it up*, she thought when he mentioned it.

"I have no idea why it's happening. You know, for a long time, I thought the heroin was making it scab and peel like it does. But I'm clean, and I've been using the cream that the doctor prescribed to me at the hospital. Ernest, it just seems like its getting worse." She held her hand over her nose to cover it.

"Have you been back to the doctor since?"

"No."

"I think you should go. Maybe that cream isn't strong enough. I'd hate to see that pretty nose of yours get any worse." He smiled at her and removed her hand from her face.

Nina held her head down low.

"Nina it's not that bad. It could be worse. You're still beautiful no matter what your nose looks like. At least see what the doctor says."

She thought about what he said. She had been getting stares from people who happened to notice that her nose didn't look normal, and that brought on a complex. That was one of the reasons she tried to cover it with makeup.

"OK, I'll go." She smiled back.

"I'll go with you if you want."

"You would do that?" She was shocked.

"Of course I would. Nina, I'm feeling you, and no matter what you think, you are a beautiful woman. You are just struggling with the idea of recovery, and that is normal. I am here for you, no matter what." He took her hand and kissed the back of it.

Nina felt chills go through her body. She hadn't felt that way since her and Wiz's relationship ended. She had been in other relationships, and they failed because her secret on-again, off-again addiction would always get in the way.

In the past she instantly shied away from the subject and didn't want to talk about it. But now he made her feel comfortable.

※※※

LATER THAT NIGHT . . .

Jamal was on his way to meet with Death, Ibn, and Dean. He was running late because he had been keeping company with a lovely lady named Tammy that he had met at a bar he sometimes frequented. They had been seeing each other whenever he had the time to get away from the others. She was just a few years younger than him, and he really enjoyed being with her. Tammy was mature and didn't question him about his occupation or whereabouts. That was what Jamal liked most about her. He hated dealing with young women, even though their bodies were an instant turn-on for him. He had learned in the past that the young ones were just that—young. Young in body as well as mind, and at his age, he neither had the time nor the patience for the drama that they brought.

Jamal had been laid up with Tammy for most of the night, and he hated to leave her, but Death's demand to meet up was serious. He didn't know what was going on, but the message he got advised him to show up. He knew he was gonna have to hear Death's mouth because they had to wait on him, but he was prepared to deal with Death in his usual manner.

Jamal wore an outdated, velour, jogging suit and a wide-brimmed hat. Stacy Adams shoes were on his feet, and he walked with a gangsta lean, his signature walk from the seventies.

With his brim tilted to the side, Jamal strolled over to his 1987 mint-condition Cadillac Seville painted in two-tone black and silver. He had many offers to sell the car, but Jamal knew what he had, and he refused to give up his ride. Besides, he had put a lot of money into the automobile to keep it in good condition. It was immaculate, inside and out.

Jamal tapped the unlock button on the car's alarm system and the electric door locks popped open. He reached for the door handle, but not before he observed his reflection in the window. He straightened his brim and smoothed his thick mustache with a finger.

Death and the others sat at his house in Maplewood, New Jersey where they usually had their meetings. The fellas sat around drinking and smoking weed while they awaited Jamal's arrival. Death was not in the mood to indulge in any of the substances because he had a lot of other things on his mind. He saw everything that he had worked for falling apart. The sad part was that he wasn't sure if the people he let in his backyard were the ones stabbing him in the back.

He was sure that his brother was behind a lot of what was happening to him. After the meeting the other night, and the way Terrell behaved, Death was dead set on believing that his brother was on a power trip and was eventually going to try to take over, not to mention the fact that his behavior was totally different now than in the past.

"Where this nigga at?" Death yelled suddenly.

Everyone stopped what they were doing at Death's outburst, but no one said a word.

"Hit him up again!" Death ordered. "You know what? Never mind. Ibn, you know where he be at. Go get him!"

ೞೞೞೞ

Jamal opened the car door.

"Yo!" someone yelled. Jamal turned around and a bullet hit him square in the middle of his forehead. He slid to the ground. Luke sat in the backseat of the Hummer parked across the street and watched Jamal die.

"Finish him," he said to the gunman. The young boy ran from the car to Jamal's body and pumped three more bullets into his corpse, then ran back to the Hummer.

The driver pulled off slowly, but not before stopping in front of

Tammy's place. She stood in the doorway. Luke rolled down the back window and waved to her. She waved back and closed the door. Tammy was Luke's aunt, and she was always glad to do her nephew a favor.

Ibn got into his Cadillac and started the engine. He knew the woman who Jamal was seeing and went to the bar where they'd gone earlier. The bartender told him that Jamal and Tammy had left together. Ibn drove to where she lived and tried to turn onto her street, only to find it blocked off by police barricades. He tried to see what he could see, but only saw the many emergency vehicle lights. He parked on the next block and walked back around the corner. He heard several people talking as he walked past them. Somebody had been shot, but as of yet, he didn't know who. He was sure that if Jamal had been over her house, he would've stayed inside. *Maybe that's why he's late*, he thought.

As Ibn got closer, he saw the police standing around Jamal's car. He also saw a bloody sheet draped over a body, which was being loaded into the back of the meat wagon. His heart pounded and he tried to get closer, but was stopped by an officer.

"My bad." Ibn held up his hands in a peaceful gesture and backed up onto the sidewalk. He got as close as he possibly could before he realized that it had to have been Jamal on the gurney. The passenger side door of Jamal's car was open, and an officer rummaged through the glove compartment. Ibn saw another officer carrying Jamal's hat in his hand. That was when Ibn knew for sure that Jamal was dead.

It hit him like a ton of bricks. Jamal had been his friend for many years, and to lose him was like a stab in the heart. He listened intently to the talk of two women who stood behind him.

"Yeah, girl, I heard the shots," the first woman stated. "I looked out the window, and this little skinny boy was standing over the dead guy with a big-ass gun. Girl, it was like watching a movie! He shot that man at least three times, and you could see the sparks coming from the gun. I ain't never seen nothing like it."

"Damn, it's getting worse around here," the other woman replied. "All I know is, I gotta get my kids from outta this city."

The women continued to talk and Ibn received the answers to his questions, all except one—who killed his friend? He looked over at the house where Tammy lived. She stood in the doorway, but when she saw Ibn, she closed the door. Ibn walked up the steps and rang the bell, but she didn't open the door. This aroused his suspicions. *She is guilty as hell*, he thought. He walked back to his car to begin the ride back to Death's house.

A short time later Ibn walked into Death's house with his head hung low.

"Where he at?" Death asked. He looked behind Ibn, expecting to see Jamal.

Ibn broke down and plopped down in the chair. "He's gone, man," he cried.

"What? What the fuck are you talking about?" Death yelled. The others in the room froze.

Dean stood slowly and walked over to Ibn. "You lying!" he yelled.

"No." Ibn shook his head, still not believing that Jamal was dead.

"Hell naw, man! I don't believe you!" Dean was disgusted, but there was a hint of fear underneath the disgust.

"Who did it?" Death asked through clenched teeth.

"I . . . I . . ." Ibn kept crying. He could barely talk.

"Man, get your mind right and tell me who did it!" Death wasn't concerned about Ibn's feelings at that point. He wanted revenge.

"I can't believe this shit!" Dean screamed. He held his head as the pain of the truth hit him.

Ibn tried to compose himself and spoke slowly. "I think it was that bitch Tammy he'd been fucking with."

"Who, nigga?" Death was now in his face and had lost all patience.

"He was fucking with this broad he met at the spot. I'm not sure if she did it, but I think she knows something about it. I saw her standing in the door to her house, and when I came over to talk to her, she closed the door and wouldn't open it."

"Nigga, you should have kicked that motherfucking door off the hinges and filled that bitch with lead! I should blow your fucking brains out!" Death pulled his gun from the shoulder holster.

"Death!" Bear stepped up, placed his hand over Death's arm, and brought the gun down to his side. "Man, that ain't gonna bring Jamal back. Calm down, man. We need to find out what this broad knows, and take it from there. We're all hurt by this, but you need to think with a clear head." He nodded at Ibn. "Give the man some respect. Ibn was closer to Jamal than you. Let the man grieve."

Dean had moved to the sofa and still had his head in his hands, rocking back and forth in sorrow.

"You're right, man." Death placed the gun back into its holster. He patted Ibn on the shoulder, walked over to the picture window, and peered out onto the quiet street.

"Dean, you and Bear get on this broad and find out what she knows. Either way, whether she knows something or not, do the bitch." Death's voice was cold.

"Got it," Bear replied, but Dean didn't say a word. He was still rocking back and forth.

Death turned around because he didn't hear a response from Dean. "Dean, man up! Did you hear me?"

Dean looked up at him slowly. His reddened eyes looked like they belonged to a demon. Death had never seen that look before. "Come on, man, you gotta find out what happened. We gonna set this shit right. A'ight?" Death asked in a softened tone.

Dean stood and looked at Bear. Bear nodded in acknowledgment and the two men left the house in search of answers.

Chapter Twenty-Seven

Malik and Justice sat in the park, going over their plan. They knew they couldn't get next to Death without having to deal with Bear or Three The Hard Way, so they planned to hit them one at a time, starting with Bear. He would be the one that would be the most trouble, so starting with him and then taking out the rest, one by one, was their best option.

"But how the fuck we gonna get next to that ugly motherfucker when he be playing Death close as hell?" Justice asked. "Shit, if they together, we might as well do them both."

"Naw, man, you don't understand. I want Death to be the last one standing. This way, it will leave him wide open. He will be exposed like the little bitch that he is. If we don't do it that way, then we gonna have all them motherfuckers coming at us at one time. It's just me and you, dog, and we can't take all of them out at once."

Justice listened to Malik's explanation, nodding to let him know he understood.

"Plus, if we hit the main niggas one at a time, all them other little motherfuckers ain't tryna fight for him. You said it yourself, half them niggas don't even like him. They just fear him because of the front line he got. Feel me?"

"No doubt, I feel you," Justice agreed.

"A'ight, look at it this way. He and Luke are beefing, so we can pull it off so smoothly that he would think that nigga Luke's coming at him."

"Yeah, that's what's up! Yo, didn't you say you had a cousin on his team?" Justice asked.

"Yeah, he was on his team, but he locked up now. He got caught with a key."

"Damn!" Justice shook his head. "A'ight, so when we gonna do this shit? 'Cause frankly, I'm tired of looking over my shoulder. I don't even stay at the crib with moms anymore, because I don't want to bring that shit around her and my little sister," Justice spoke with concern.

"Yeah, I feel you. A'ight, make the call to Death, and have him send Bear to bring some re-up."

"Naw, man, I can't do that. I ain't the man no more. This other nigga AP is running shit for the blocks I'm on. I'm telling you, man, there have been plenty of times I just wanted to put a bullet in that nigga," Justice said with hatred.

"Oh, we gon' take care of that nigga too, then. Shit, we might as well add him to the list. Anybody else you want to get got?"

"At one time, I wanted you to get got. But you turned out to be a'ight." Justice smiled.

"Your ass was on my list too, nigga," Malik laughed. "OK, so what we gotta figure out is how we gonna touch Bear."

"Why don't we start with one of them three old heads? I think they would be an easier hit. I know the spot they be at sometimes, plus neither one of us got wheels, so catching up with Death and Bear would have to take the back burner."

"Yeah, you right," Malik acknowledged. "A'ight. I'm with that."

As Malik and Justice continued to tighten up their plans to body

Ibn, Dean, and Jamal, they had no idea that somebody had already beaten them to Jamal.

ܡܠܡܠܡܠ

Bear sat in a bar that he and Death frequented when he overheard the loud, drunken talk of a nearby woman. Normally he tuned such talk out, but his interest piqued when he heard Luke's name.

It turned out that the loud woman was a good friend of a woman named Tammy, who was related to Luke. Apparently, Luke had hit Tammy off with a lot of money to do him a favor and, in turn, Tammy shared the wealth and gave her loud friend some money. The woman even went so far as to say that Tammy was in hiding because people were out looking for her. Bear sat there and soaked it all in as he began to put two and two together. He pulled out his cell phone and made a quick call.

About an hour later the drunken woman practically fell off the bar stool as she tried to stand. Bear helped her to steady herself.

"Hey, how you doing?" The woman rubbed his chest.

"I'm doing better than you, pretty lady," Bear flirted.

She giggled.

"I know you not driving in your condition, pretty lady?"

"No, I'm walking. Why? You driving?" She tried to keep her eyes focused, but they rolled around in her head while she swayed back and forth.

"Of course I'm driving. Do you need a ride home?"

"Fuck yeah! I can't walk home like this. Shit, I can't even stand up." She laughed hysterically.

Bear simply smiled at the inebriated woman and walked her out of the bar. Dean had come into the bar upon receiving Bear's phone call, and he was trying to see if he could get additional information on Jamal's death out of any of the other patrons. When he saw Bear give him a slight nod and walk out of the bar with the woman, he followed.

"How is Tammy doing?" Bear asked with mock concern. "I haven't seen her in a while."

"So you know Tammy, huh?" the woman asked drunkenly.

"Yeah. Me and Tammy go way back."

"Yeah, that's my girl. Did I tell you her nephew paid her thirty grand for helping him set up this sugar daddy she was seeing?"

"Naw, you didn't. Why don't you tell me?" Bear egged the woman on and she repeated much of what Bear had already overheard in the bar. She still hadn't told him the crucial piece of information, though, which was where Tammy was hiding out.

"So where Tammy at now?" Bear rubbed her ass while they walked.

"Ooh, that feels good, babe."

"You like that?"

"Mmm hmm," she moaned.

"Where you say Tammy hiding out at?"

"OK, I'ma tell you," she said as they arrived at Dean's Lincoln.

Bear leaned the woman up against the car while he waited for Dean to catch up. The woman massaged Bear's dick while she gave up Tammy's whereabouts. She concentrated so hard on Bear's dick that she didn't even notice that Dean had walked up to them.

"Get with Death and let him know that Tammy is hiding out over on Fifteenth Avenue in the second-floor apartment," Bear whispered to Dean.

"A'ight." Dean turned his back to them and made the call to Death from his cell phone.

When he finished the call, he turned around to find the woman down on her knees, sucking Bear off. Bear held the back of her head for guidance. Dean's mouth fell open.

Death had come to Nina's apartment because, as usual, he needed her to do his dirty work. Bear found out from the drunken, loud woman at the bar that the woman Jamal had been seeing was named Tammy, and she was definitely involved in the murder of Jamal. She was Luke's aunt and he had hit her off well for setting the stage for Jamal's murder. Death was so mad he wanted to just go through Luke's territory and spit bullets throughout the neighborhood. Dean was definitely down with the plan, but Bear talked some sense into them. Death and Dean calmed down and came up with an alternate plan.

Death walked down the hallway and knocked on the door to Nina's apartment. A female voice answered.

"Who is it?" Shea asked, looking at him through the peephole.

"Is Nina here?"

"No, she's not. Who should I tell her came by?" Shea continued to look at him. She got a bad vibe and had no intention of opening the door.

"Naw, that's OK. I'll come back later." Death turned and walked back down the hall.

Shea walked away from the door just as Marquis came out of the bathroom.

"Who was it?" he asked.

"I don't know. He didn't say. He asked for Ma." Shea walked over to him and wrapped her arms around his neck.

Malik and Justice sat across the street from the bar on the stoop of a business that was closed for the night. They were dressed in all black. When they arrived at the bar, Justice spotted Dean's Lincoln. They decided to squat and wait for Dean to come out of the club, but were surprised when Bear came out first, and with a woman. Then Dean followed.

That was when they decided to kill two birds with one stone, but there was a problem. The woman was an eyewitness. Justice noticed that the woman was drunk out of her mind and figured that she wouldn't be able to remember anything at that point. Malik begged to differ.

"Naw, B, if we gon' do them cats, then the bitch gets it too. We can't take no chances on leaving witnesses."

"So how we gonna do this shit with people still walking in and out of the bar? The car ain't that far away, and if they all get into it, then we fucked."

"Just chill for a minute." Malik watched Bear and the woman intently. When the woman fell to her knees and started sucking Bear's dick, Malik knew it was time to strike.

Before the trio knew what hit them, Malik and Justice sprayed them with bullets. Dean was preoccupied with his peep show and never saw the pair sneak up behind him. Justice caught him in the head at point-blank range.

Bear had his head back and his eyes closed while he was being sucked off. Malik pumped bullets into Bear until his clip was empty. Justice pumped two into the woman and had to use the rest of the bullets in his gun to finally knock Bear off his feet.

Malik and Justice ran down the street at top speed. They both wore black baseball caps pulled down over their eyes, but Justice had been spotted because a patron was coming out of the bar when they were just finishing off Bear. This patron happened to be AP. Justice made the mistake of looking back at the bar to see if anyone was out there just as AP walked out and recognized Justice.

Justice sat on the side of his bed in a room he had rented. He was trying to drown himself in the bottle of Patron that was now almost empty. He had never shot anyone in his life, and it was fucking with his head. Not to mention the fact that he thought AP recognized him. He didn't tell Malik, but he now carried a burner on him all the time just in case he ran into anyone from Death's team. He was so paranoid he pulled it out a few times, but up until now, he didn't have to discharge the gun.

Justice couldn't get out of his head how he and Malik just walked up on Bear, Dean, and the drunk woman and started buckin' at point-blank range. To see Dean's head explode sent chills up Justice's spine. He turned the bottle up to his mouth and killed the rest of the liquor in an attempt to shake the images. He kept seeing the woman on her knees with Bear's dick in her mouth when the bullets struck her in the eye and neck.

Justice staggered around the room, checking to see if he had another bottle of liquor. He found one in the small dresser, but it was empty too. He threw the bottle to the floor in anger and it crashed loudly. Glass flew and some struck him under his eye. He instantly felt blood running down his cheek and swiped it away with the back of his sleeve.

Justice made a drunken decision to go down to the bar that sold packaged goods after hours when the liquor stores were closed. It was the very same bar where he and Malik had killed Bear and Dean.

At the same time that Justice arrived at the bar to get some more liquor, Death sat in the office of the bar talking to AP. AP had gotten locked up on a warrant the night of the killing, and never got the chance to let Death know what he saw. When he got home, he made sure to come to the bar and find Death.

AP told him what he saw but didn't know who Malik was, so he couldn't describe him to Death. Death could care less about the description of the second shooter. He wanted blood, and Justice was definitely a marked man.

Death gave his new crew of bodyguards instructions on how he wanted Justice killed. He wanted the boy to suffer. He instructed a zombie-like Ibn to go with the men so that he could identify Justice and let them do the rest. Ibn reluctantly went with the goons.

"Good looking out, AP." Death handed him a stack of bills.

"Aw, man, you know you my man. Good looking out, Death." AP fanned the stack before he put it in his pocket.

The office door opened and Ibn returned with the two goons.

"What's the problem? Why are y'all back here?" Death asked.

One of the goons pointed at Ibn. "Dude say the nigga standing at the bar."

Death walked to the door, cracked it open, and peeked out. Sure enough, a drunken Justice was at the main entrance getting ready to pay for another bottle of Patrón.

"Get that little nigga and do it discreetly," Death demanded threw gritted teeth. He already felt some of his stress being lifted.

‭ ‭ ‭ ‭ ‭ ‭

OVER A WEEK LATER . . .

Marquis was finally on his way to see his father. Before he headed for the bus he went to the block to see if he could get Malik to come with him. He thought about taking Shea with him, but this was his first visit, and Marquis felt that he and his brother needed to go together, so he left her back at the apartment. Kurt had come through with the information Marquis needed to make it happen. Wiz was incarcerated at Allenwood Institute in Pennsylvania. Marquis had wrote his father a letter, letting him know he was going to come up for a visit.

"What's up, Mark?" Malik asked when Marquis walked up.

"What's up, man?"

"Whatchu gettin' into?"

"I'm going to see Wiz. You wanna roll with me?"

Malik looked at Marquis with a screw face. "How you sound?" he asked.

"Come on, man, just swing with me."

"Hell no! You know I ain't got shit to say to Wiz."

"Why?" Marquis wanted to know.

"I'ma grown-ass man. What can he do for me, Mark?"

"It ain't what he can do for us, Malik. I'm sayin', he is still our father."

"Well you go see him. I'm done."

"Come on, man! We ain't seen him in years. You know how happy he would be to see us," Marquis argued. Malik simply shrugged. He could care less.

"Don't you at least want to hear his side of the story about why he never contacted us?"

"It don't matter to me, because just as easy as you found him, he could've reached out to us."

"Come on, Malik, you don't know what his reason is. I mean, damn, why you so pissed with him when Mommy could have easily kept in touch with him too?"

"It don't matter to me no more, Mark. He ain't been in our life for, like, almost fifteen years. What can he do now? He can't raise us now, 'cause we already grown."

"Yo, what happened to you, man?" Marquis asked.

"Ain't nothing happened to me."

"I mean, you seem real different. We used to be cool."

"We still cool. I'm just on some other shit right now," Malik told his brother seriously.

"I don't know, man." Marquis shook his head doubtfully. "Well, I'm out. I gotta get to the bus to go see him. Anything you want me to tell him?"

"Naw." Malik shook his head and looked straight ahead.

Marquis left, disappointed.

Death rolled up on the block an hour later. He walked over to Malik, and if looks could kill, everybody would be dead. Death had three other dudes in the car who Malik had never seen before. Two of the men walked behind Death. Malik figured they were Death's new security.

"What's up?" Malik extended his hand. *There he is, standing right in front of me, and I can't even take the shot,* Malik thought.

"What's up, kid? I'm gettin' low for a while. I got some business to take care of, so I'm gonna offer you a deal right now. You can purchase weight from me at an increased price, and do what you want with the product once you get it. Or I'ma have to close down shop and move in another crew. Now I ain't sure if you got the bread, but that's my offer." Death still had a murderous look on his face.

Malik was unsure of this so-called deal Death was trying to make with him, so he didn't respond at first.

Death noticed Malik's reluctance. "Listen, Malik, I usually don't let niggas get off this easy. I have rules that I enforce, but at this point, I'm offering you the deal 'cause you my moneymaker and I ain't got time to be sitting out here, babysitting y'all young asses. But just know that if you take the deal and I find out you copping from anybody else, it's a wrap for you, baby boy. You only get your product from me. I increased the potency, so you will make a grip," he assured Malik.

Malik nodded. "That's cool."

"So, you wit' it?"

"Yeah, I'm wit' it." Malik was calm.

"I'ma send some boys through here. When do you think you can get the bread up?"

"How much you charging?"

"What you tryna do? Crack or dope?" Death asked impatiently. He'd expected Malik to just jump at his offer the same way AP had, but Malik was different. He was about his paper, and didn't trust the offer on the surface. He wanted to make sure that he was going to get the best offer that he could. Besides, in his mind, Death's days were numbered.

"Oh, that heroin. I'ma just rock the dope."

"The price just went up another three Gs." Death waited for his response.

"Damn!"

"I mean, it is what it is, Malik. I'm giving you a free ride in my territory." Death shot Malik a meaningful stare.

"It's cool. Send your boy through here in three days. So what's up with what I got left?"

"Pay me the usual for what you got left, and when you finish, it's all you. You renting these corners from me right now."

"So what's up with the protection? I'm losing bodies," Malik complained.

"You and me both." Death's eyes suddenly looked tired, as if he hadn't slept in days. "You're still covered out here, because these still my blocks." Death walked away. "Three days," he called over his shoulder, holding up three fingers.

Malik was relieved to know that Luke was stirring up shit. That way, it would make his and Justice's jobs that much easier. Ironically, the deal he had just made with Death was somewhat what he wanted anyway—to get his own product.

ന്ദന്ദന്ദ

Marquis sat in the waiting room with lots of other people, waiting for the inmates to come out. The doors opened and the inmates flooded the room. Marquis stood on nervous legs. He was trying to see his father. All he had was a vague memory, and a picture of him and his brother when they were younger. He had no idea what Wiz looked like now. Marquis knew from that picture that Wiz and Malik looked alike, but he wondered if that was still true. He looked around and still didn't see anybody who resembled his brother, nor did he see a man who appeared to be looking for someone. He never got a response to the letter he sent, so Marquis wasn't sure if Wiz even knew that he was coming.

When he came to register his visit, Marquis was surprised to find out that he, his mother, and his brother had been listed as visitors for Wiz. Marquis was about to sit back down when a tall, built, dark-skinned man appeared in the doorway. He looked like a older version of Malik with gray hairs sprinkle throughout his low cut hair. His shoulders looked like he had on football shoulder pads. The man looked around and spotted Marquis standing by a table in the corner. A smile came across his face as the man walked over to Marquis.

"Mark," Wiz said as he embraced his son. His arms engulfed Marquis's slim frame. He patted Marquis on the back, almost knocking the wind out of him.

Marquis hugged his father back. They released each other and Wiz stared him up and down, checking him out. They both sat down at the table.

"I knew one of my sons would come to see me." Wiz smiled.

"It's good to see you. Ma said you and Malik look alike, and she was right."

"Where's Malik?"

"He couldn't come."

"Oh, OK. So what brings you all the way down here to see me?" Wiz asked.

"You're my father, and I wanna get to know you again. There are so many unanswered questions, and I feel like you're the only one who can answer them."

"Yeah? Well, we got two hours to talk. What's on your mind?"

"Damn! I came all this way and I don't know where to start." Marquis laughed nervously.

"How about at the beginning?"

"Well, I'll at least let you know I'm in college."

"Word?" Wiz was proud.

"Yeah. I'm taking summer classes to get a head start." Marquis blushed.

The two men talked and talked for the entire two hours, mostly starting from when Marquis and Malik were kids. Those were the memories that Wiz kept of them, because those were the last memories he had. Marquis admitted to his father that Malik was out on the blocks, following in his footsteps. He told Wiz how Kurt told him all about the legendary stories from back in the day.

"Yeah, Kurt been around a long time. He's a good man. He still walking the streets, talking shit?"

"Yeah. That would be the Conductor." Marquis laughed.

"Damn! He still calling himself the Conductor?" Wiz laughed as well.

"Yup."

They both became silent and Marquis looked around at the other inmates having conversations with their loved ones. He thought about how he wished his brother were there to see their father.

"Listen to me, son." Wiz recaptured Marquis's attention. "I already knew about Malik bangin' out on them streets."

"You did?" Marquis asked with raised eyebrows.

"Of course I know. There isn't much I don't know in here. Son, trust me, I hear more shit in here than you do on the streets. Listen, I want you to see if you can get your brother to come up here the next time you come. I need to talk to him. I want him to know that that life ain't the life he wants to live. You see what happened to me?"

Marquis nodded his head in acknowledgment.

"Before I started hustling, I had no purpose in life. I didn't know what I wanted out of life. All the other kids talked about being doctors and shit like that. I didn't want that, because that meant I would have to go to school for at least seven years or more after high school. Naw, that wasn't for me," he laughed. "My mother, your grandmother, worked two jobs just to keep food on the table. My father walked out on her when I was young, so I never wanted to struggle again. But I didn't want to do the legal things that needed to be done in order to succeed, because I saw how hard my mother worked for honest pay, and we still struggled. Son, you figured out what you wanted to do in life, and that's the key. You gotta know where you at to get where you going. And if you don't stand for something, then you'll fall for anything."

Marquis listened intently as his father gave the best advice he'd ever heard.

"I just want to tell you that even though you weren't there, I know it wasn't because you walked out. I know if you weren't here, you would be with us. I still need you in my life for things like this. Us . . . you and me, having a man-to-man conversation. I need this." Marquis was honest.

"Son, you have no idea how I have dreamed of spending my life with you and Malik. It was hard for me at first, but I had to learn not to cloud my mind with the outside world. I tried to contact your mother for several years after I came here, but she never reached out to me. It was a hard reality for me to face, but the kinda numbers I got, it made no sense for me to focus on that."

"So you're saying that Ma kept us from you?" Marquis couldn't believe his ears.

"Well, I don't want to put it that way, or bad mouth your mother, because I see she did a damn good job raising y'all. But at the age y'all were when I left, she would be the only one to have brought y'all up here."

"Damn!" Marquis lowered his head.

"Mark, it's all good. You're here now. It ain't never too late to move forward together."

"Ten minutes!" one of the guards announced.

"Well, it's about that time," Wiz said. "You gonna do like I asked and try to get your brother to come up here, right?

"Yeah, I'll try."

"Listen, I need to rap with him. I hear he running for Death. Express to him that I need to see him soon." Wiz was adamant.

"A'ight. Hey, did you get the letter I sent you?"

"Yeah, I got it. Just didn't know what to say. That's why I didn't write you one back," Wiz admitted.

"So you put all of our names on the list. You were hoping we all came up, didn't you?"

"Son, y'all names been on my list since day one, and never came off."

"Inmates!" the guards yelled.

"I still have more questions for you!" Marquis stood because Wiz stood.

"Next time, baby boy." Wiz embraced Marquis one last time. "Stay focused, baby boy. You look good." He backed away.

"You too, man. I'll be back."

"I know you will, and bring your brother. Oh, yeah, tell your mother I said, what's up," Wiz shouted as he blended in with the other inmates.

Marquis watched his father walked back through the doors into the bowels of the prison. Wiz turned and waved to him one more time. Marquis waved back. He stood there feeling like a young child that had lost his parent in the mall. He wanted to cry.

ၷၷၷၷ

THREE DAYS LATER . . .

Brian and Marquis watched as the police put Malik in the back of the patrol car. Brian shook his head because he was mad as hell.

"I thought we was supposed to have protection! This shit is for the birds," he complained.

"Chill, man, It's gonna be a'ight. We got the loot to get him out,"

Marquis said.

"We out here like sitting ducks, and that nigga Death ain't even warn us!"

They didn't know that their protection had been lifted two weeks ago when Tilmond and the others discovered that the killings and shootings hadn't stopped as requested.

Malik looked at his brother from the backseat of the police car and nodded. Marquis nodded back, letting Malik know that he knew what to do.

"Our stash got robbed twice since we started buying our own weight. It's like it don't matter what we do. We keep getting burnt," Brian stated. "Then, last week, we got straight-up robbed at gunpoint. And the fucked-up thing is we don't have no idea who these cats are that jacked us! Since the narcs keep riding through here, we don't even be holding no hardware on us. We stash our hammers. That's why your brother got popped tonight, because after the last robbery went down, he was sick with it, so he kept his burner on him. Now he got caught with his pants down." He shook his head in dismay. "He the one who suggested that he be the only nigga with a hammer, because we all needed to grind to get this paper back we lost. Man, it's like we take two steps forward and some shit go down to knock us three steps back. I ain't about hustling backward!"

"So, my brother got his own product?"

"Yeah, man! For, like, three weeks now. He made a deal with Death, and we buy weight for a straight-up price, so the product is ours. I swear, man, I'm telling you, I think that cat Death be sending niggas through here to lift our shit so we can't make no bread. That's why your brother stashed the shit at the crib now."

Marquis was confused. "I don't get it. I thought Malik had a solid system?"

"Yeah, he did at one time, but he ain't been around much. He left me to do everything, and I ain't gonna lie, I can't watch everybody and everything at one time." Brian continued to bitch.

"A'ight, man, just chill. He'll be out soon, and I'll talk to him."

"Naw, man, that ain't good enough. I'm tired of going into the loot I got stashed to replace the shit we keep getting jacked for. I ain't making no bread like that. Shit, it's like I'm working for free. Yo, for real, Mark, we need leadership out here. I need help, man."

"What? You looking for me to help you out?" Marquis looked at Brian sideways.

"Come on, Mark, you are definitely built for this. I know this. Step up while your brother is down. I mean, I ain't tryna dog my man, because I have nothing but love for Malik, and you know this. But his head ain't been in the game lately," Brian admitted.

"I'm getting ready to break out, man. I gotta go home and get this loot so that I can get my brother outta jail. Plus, I got a test at school, and I got a lot of studying to do." Marquis did not really want to hear about what Brian was trying to convince him to do.

"Listen, man, at least come back out here with me for tonight. This is your brother's shit too. It's everything that he talked about grinding for." Brian looked exhausted, and his eyes pleaded with Marquis.

"Yeah, but you ain't hearing me, though. I gotta study for this test at school."

"A'ight, man, forget it. I hear you." Brian shoved his hands in his jeans pockets and lowered his head in disappointment.

Marquis stared at him for a moment, thinking. He was torn between his responsibility to his schoolwork and his loyalty to his brother.

"A'ight. Let me at least go see what's up with him, and maybe he'll be out tonight and can come back out here with y'all. But if he don't, I'll be back through for a minute." Marquis walked away and prayed that Malik was going to get out on bail that night.

"That's what's up, Mark!" Brian called to Marquis's retreating form.

Malik was just one of the few dealers who were arrested that night. Several others from Death's camp had also been arrested.

Marquis walked into the house and the smell of burning crack cocaine hit him as soon as he crossed over the threshold. He knew what it smelled like and immediately thought his mother had relapsed. He rushed into her room and found her sitting on her bed, reading a magazine. He stared at her, trying to see if she looked high, but she didn't.

"What's wrong?" Nina immediately became alarmed when she saw Marquis's expression. The first thing she thought was that something had happened to Malik. "Where's Malik?" she asked as she swung her feet off the bed and onto the floor.

"He's outside," Marquis lied, not wanting to tell her the truth. "Ma, what's that smell?"

Before Nina could answer, the door to the bathroom opened and Jackie walked out. She was butt-ass naked except for her bra. She carried the rest of her clothes in her hand. Her eyes were stretched wide and she stared at the floor like she was looking for something. Marquis looked at his mother like she was a creature from the dead.

"Ma, please tell me you ain't letting her get high in here?"

"She ain't bothering nobody. It don't bother me," Nina tried to tell him, but he cut her off.

"Are you serious?" He stared at her in disbelief and shock.

"Mark, I said she could do it as long as it was in the bathroom."

"I can't believe this!" He stormed out of her bedroom and right past Jackie, bumping her out of the way. He walked into his room and slammed the door, scaring Shea, who lay across the bed, studying.

She sat straight up in the bed. "What's wrong?" She sat straight up in the bed.

"You know my mother let that fiend bitch smoke crack in the house?" He was pissed. He punched the closet door chipping the paint away.

"Is that what that smell is?" Shea rubbed her tired eyes. She watched him snatch the closet door open with force. He began to rummage through the closet throwing clothing and shoes out of the way and finally he pulled out a duffel bag. He removed stacks of money from the bag. Shea's eyes widened.

"Where'd you get that money?"

"It's my brother's. He got locked up tonight, and I have to see if I can bail him out. Hand me the phone."

Twenty minutes later Marquis got off the phone with the bail bondsman that his brother told him to use if he ever got arrested. The bondsman told Marquis that there wasn't anything he could do for Malik tonight, and that he would give Marquis the information on the bail first thing in the morning.

Marquis put everything back in the bag and threw the bag back into the closet. He went over to Shea and kissed her. "I'll be back."

"Where you going now?" She didn't want to stay in the room by herself. "You got a test tomorrow, and you need to study."

"I gotta take care of some business," he said simply and left. He walked past the kitchen and Jackie was still bottomless and in her bra, looking out the kitchen window. Her butt was tooted in the air. Marquis shook his head and left the apartment, removing the gun from his pocket and placing it down the front of his waistband. He had managed to slip the 9 mm gun from the duffel bag and conceal it in his pocket without

Shea noticing. He would have to deal with the Jackie situation later, but right now he was on his way back to the corners to help protect his brother's investment.

Chapter Twenty-Eight

Malik was finally released two weeks later, due to difficulties with the release process. His court date was in a month. When Marquis couldn't get him out of lockup the night he was arrested, Malik was heated. The bail bondsman met Marquis down at the station the next day to get the money, but from the records the clerk pulled up, Malik had a warrant for possession. When the news got to Malik, he went off. He had never been arrested a day in his life, until then. It was bad enough he caught a gun charge, but now they were trying to pin a controlled substance charge on him too.

As a result Malik had to sit until Marquis was able to get a lawyer for him. The lawyer found out that someone had used Malik's name when they got arrested, and when that dude was bailed out of jail, he never showed up for his scheduled court date. The picture the courts had of the male that was supposed to be Malik didn't look anything like him. The lawyer was able to get the warrant dismissed, and Malik was released on bail.

He was happy to be home, though. While in lockup he was comfortable because he knew most of the inmates in the county. Still, there was no place like home. When he came on the block that afternoon, Marquis was happy to see his brother. They embraced.

"Yo, why you ain't get at me to let me know you was coming out?" Marquis fussed.

"I wanted to surprise y'all. Where B at?"

"He home. He'll be out here tonight."

"Wait! Hold up. Who watching my shit?"

Marquis smiled and looked at Malik like he was crazy.

"Oh, my gawd! Don't tell me you out here running my shit." Malik laughed.

"Yup! If it wasn't for me looking out for your investment, big bruh, you wouldn't have shit."

"Good looking out, man. So you gave up going to your classes to hold me down till I got home?"

Marquis didn't say anything for a minute, and it was minute too long for Malik.

"Yo, please tell me you're still in school?" Malik looked at him seriously.

"Yeah, I'm still in school. Come on, man. I just took off a few days to hold you down, like I said."

"Oh, a'ight." Malik didn't quite feel comfortable with Marquis's answer. "Well, I'm back now, Mark, so you can get back into your classes and do ya thing. Good looking out." Malik shook Marquis's hand but stared at him, trying to get to the truth about his brother's school status.

"What? Man, why you looking at me like that?" Marquis was instantly defensive.

"Nothing," Malik said. He knew something was up with his brother, though.

"So let me put you up on some things that I've done in your absence, big bruh." Marquis explained to him how he changed the order of things because of the conflict they'd been having with the police. Malik listened intently and was impressed with his brother's way of thinking.

"Oh, yeah, remember I went to see Wiz," Marquis said nonchalantly.

"Yeah? And?"

"And you look just like him, dude. I swear, he big as hell too!" Marquis spoke proudly of their father. Malik wasn't impressed. He didn't even look at Marquis when he spoke about Wiz.

"Real talk, he is cool as hell, man. I'm telling you! He asked for you too."

"Fuck he asking for me for?"

"Damn, Malik! That is our father!"

"Man, fuck him, for real!" Malik frowned.

"Naw, man, it ain't even like that with him," Marquis argued. "He ain't even do all that shit Ma said he did. He was a straight-up cat. I'm talking a legend on the streets and the whole nine. He told me that Moms kept us from him."

"Yeah? And what did you expect him to say?" Malik gave him the serious look. "Come on, man, don't let him brainwash you like Mommy already did."

"That's some fucked-up shit to say, Malik!"

"My bad." He felt bad for hurting his brother's feelings. "I'm just saying, man, they both gonna lie to us, so what are we supposed to do?"

"On everything that I love, I believe Wiz, because we was kicking it hard and he is as real as they come. A real gangsta. You need to go see him, at least once. He said he really needed to talk to you, man, and all I'm saying is, give him a chance."

Malik was silent. He looked around at the scene, thinking about

Marquis's words. He loved his brother, and trusted only him, but he didn't know if he could bring himself to go see a man who his mother said walked out on them years ago. Wiz wasn't there for him when he wanted a bike. He wasn't there for him when he wanted to play basketball and needed someone to teach him. For as long as Malik could remember, he had to be the father to Marquis, so to have a father now was null and void. Nina had made sure she instilled in their heads that Wiz walked out on them before he went to prison. But Wiz didn't.

"At least think about it, Malik."

"I don't think so, but I'll think about it."

While Malik thought about things, Marquis walked off. He was disappointed in his brother, but he wasn't going to give up. He believed that Malik and Wiz would connect once they met.

Chapter Twenty-Nine

Nina and Ernest had become an item. They were sitting in her living room when someone knocked on the door. Nina got up from the couch and answered the door. When she opened it, Jackie rushed right in. She whizzed right past Ernest and didn't even speak. In fact, she didn't even speak to Nina.

Ernest looked at Jackie with strange eyes. Jackie had lost more weight, and to the naked eye it was now apparent that she was an addict. She was still a bit chunky, but because she still wore the clothes she had when she was fat, they hung from her body, three sizes too big. She had a rope tied around her waist as a belt to hold up her pants. And Ernest saw something that Nina nor anyone else in the house saw on Jackie. It was the fiend look in her eyes.

Shea was in the bathroom, and Jackie practically broke down the door, kicking and banging on it for Shea to come out. Shea was tired of Jackie and the way that she pushed her around. She didn't trust her, and she told Marquis how she caught Jackie going through the drawers in Nina's room one time. Marquis told his mother. They both approached Jackie with this information, and of course Jackie denied it, and Nina took her word. Nina did love Shea. She thought she was the perfect girlfriend for her son. However, she knew that Shea was a little naïve, so Nina just assumed she didn't know any better.

Shea barely got the bathroom door open when Jackie barged in, knocking her into the door. She literally pushed Shea out of the bathroom and slammed the door behind her.

Shea walked into the living room, looking upset.

"What's the matter, sweetheart?" Nina asked.

"Ma, I know that's your friend, but I ain't gonna let her continue to push me around. Plus she is rude as hell."

"Don't pay her any attention, honey. She all right. Just ignore her." Shea didn't like that answer, so she excused herself and left the room.

Ernest frowned at the exchange and the entire situation. "Nina, not to get into your business, but I'm gonna say this anyway. You really shouldn't have your friend here."

"I knew you was gonna say that. Her smoking don't bother me, honey. I am past that."

"You don't understand. Nina, you will always be an addict. Your body has tasted it. There is always the possibility of relapsing. It is not impossible. It happens every day. One of the rules is people, places, and things. Do not associate yourself with people, places, and things of your drug use, including past and/or present drug users." He stared deeply into her eyes with deep concern written on his face.

"But she is my best friend and has no place to go," Nina reasoned. "It really doesn't bother me, seriously."

As the burning smell of cocaine traveled into the living room, Ernest stood to leave. "You need to figure out what's more important to you—your best friend, who has no respect for the fact that you're trying to recover, or the people that care about you and who don't want to be around it. Just keep it simple, Nina." He looked down at her in disappointment. "Now, if you will excuse me, I'm leaving because I don't want to be around it." Ernest left the apartment.

Nina was still dumbfounded as to why everybody was tripping off Jackie. She never bothered anybody, didn't eat the food in the house, and was barely there. Half the time she was actually in the apartment, she was so high that she couldn't talk anyway.

Marquis walked into the house and straight to his mother. She was lounging on the couch as if nothing was wrong. He had passed Ernest on the stairwell and Ernest told him about what he had just witnessed. He advised Marquis to try and talk some sense into his mother, because he had no tolerance for stupidity. Ernest had been quite understanding with Nina through her recovery process. He was a very good sponsor and treated her case differently because he had personal feelings for her. But Ernest was serious about his recovery, and he had lasted this long in the process because he surrounded himself with positive things.

Nina looked up at Marquis as if she had just noticed him standing there. "What's wrong?" she asked.

"Ma, Jackie gotta go," he said simply and with no remorse.

"She has no place to go, Mark," Nina protested. "I mean, what's the big deal? If it was me, I would want someone to help me out too."

"You could easily wake up one morning and she could be dead from an overdose or something, right here in this house. Do you want that on your conscience for the rest of your life? Or do you want to try and help her the same way you helped yourself?"

Nina just stared at the television, ignoring him. Marquis couldn't believe his mother. What was wrong with her? He was beginning to think that the drugs she used for so many years had started to affect her brain. Not only was she acting differently, it seemed as if she lacked common sense.

Marquis made up his mind. "Jackie needs to go, Ma."

"Go where?" She looked up at him like he had lost his mind. "Marquis, Jackie is my friend, and this is my apartment. So I say what goes on in this house. By the way, where is your brother?" She just realized that Malik no longer stayed in the house. He just came by to change his clothes. She couldn't even remember the last time she saw him before that night he got locked up.

No one, not even Ernest, knew that Nina had been sneaking and getting high off and on. She made sure she did it when everyone was gone, and she gave herself enough time to sober up before anyone came around. As a result, she couldn't remember things. She thought that she hadn't seen Malik in a few days when in fact Malik had been locked up for two weeks.

Jackie stumbled into the room, tripping over the throw rug on the floor. This time she was topless as well as bottomless.

"Yo, you gotta go! Get up outta here!" Marquis gestured with his thumb toward the door.

Jackie looked at Marquis. Her lips twisted as she tried to speak, but nothing came out except grunts.

"Mark, leave her alone!" Nina came to her defense. "Jackie, put on some clothes."

"Are you crazy, Ma? She gotta go, so you can get her outta here, or I'm gonna do it."

Nina glared at Marquis, her hands on her hips. "Let me tell you something, Marquis! I don't know what has happened to you, but you better check yourself. I mean, you getting you a little pussy now, so you think you can talk to me any way you want?"

Marquis couldn't believe his mother. He frowned and got ready to rip into her, but he had too much respect for her. Instead, he decided to leave. Nina sat back down on the couch as if nothing had happened. Her mindset was to hell with everybody. All she wanted was a hit.

ᖇᖇᖇᖇ

"I'll be back, Malik," Brian said as he walked over to the car that pulled over across the street. A light-skinned beauty was behind the wheel of the brand new Chevy Malibu. Malik had never seen her before, and he wondered if she was copping drugs. When Brian got in the car on the passenger side, his question was answered.

The car pulled away from the curb. Malik leaned against the building and watched the area. It felt funny to be back on the blocks. He hadn't seen Justice since he got out. He tried to call his cell, but the phone went straight to voicemail.

When Malik came into the house he saw his mother with her sponsor Ernest, and he immediately knew that Ernest was more than a sponsor. He was cool with the idea of Ernest being with his mother, because he thought Ernest was a cool cat. He was especially pleased because he knew that Ernest would keep his mother in line. He stayed in the house long enough to take a shower and change his clothes.

Since everything looked to be OK on the block, he decided to run into the store to buy a soda.

"Hey, Miguel! ¿Que pasa?"

"Hey, Malik! Where you been?" Miguel was happy to see him.

"I had to go away for a minute, but I'm back." Malik smiled. He really liked Miguel and would do anything he could for the older man and his wife.

"Ah, me know why you leave. You be careful, no?"

"I'm cool." Miguel was not stupid. He knew why Malik and his crew stood in front of his store, day in and day out. Malik brought his soda over to the counter and waited for Miguel to ring him up. He flipped through the day's paper.

On the front cover, the headline read MURDERS CONTINUE. Malik read about the ongoing murders that had been occurring for the past two months. Just yesterday the police found the body of Jerome Baker. Malik scooped up the paper and read intently.

The body of Jerome Baker was found yesterday in the dumpster of the Dunkin' Donuts on Springfield Avenue in Irvington. The sanitation department came to empty the dumpster when they discovered Baker's body. Police stated that the young man had been brutally murdered. Baker's body was partially nude.

Police believe this murder is associated with those stemming from an ongoing drug war between two rival drug gangs. Police have been investigating these murders for quite some time, but have made little progress. If anyone has information to help solve these murders, please contact Crimestoppers at 1-800-TIP-3333.

Malik slowly lowered the paper. Jerome Baker was Justice's government name. He couldn't believe the way they took out his boy, and he believed that he knew just who did it. Were they coming for him next? Could it have been him dead had he not been locked up? How could anyone have known that Justice and he committed the murders?

Paranoia began to settle in. Malik was a sitting duck on the corners, and he knew it. How come nothing had happened to Marquis? How come his brother was able to step into his spot so easily while he was incarcerated? How could Death allow his brother to fill in for him without a fuss? Maybe this was why Kurt told him that the niggas that will stab you in the back were the ones running around in your own backyard. Did that mean his brother would stab him in the back?

He shook his head to dispel the thoughts he was having about

Marquis who, at one point, he would have given his life for.

"You OK?" Miguel broke him out of his reverie.

"Yeah, I'm good." Malik replaced the newspaper.

Why didn't anybody tell him that Justice was dead? Were they keeping it from him because they were out to get him? Was it that everybody on his team may have been down with Death? Once again Malik shook the thought from his mind and walked out of the store. Miguel looked after Malik in confusion.

Malik was back in his usual spot in front of the store. But this time he wasn't so confident. He was hyper-vigilant and watched everything that moved.

"Yo, man, do you know Moms got that fiend up in the crib walking around high?"

Malik jumped and reflexively grabbed his gun. He was startled by Marquis's sudden appearance. He never heard him walk up.

"Yo, man, chill! What's up with you?" Marquis looked at Malik curiously.

"I didn't hear you walk up," Malik said defensively. "What did you say?"

"I said, Mommy got that fiend living up in the crib, and she getting high in the house. Man, I tried to get her up outta there and your mother protected her like she was her own child."

Malik frowned. "Ma getting high again?"

"Not that I know of. I tried to see if she looked like it, but she don't."

"That don't mean nothing. She didn't look like she was getting high before. We just knew." Malik kept eyeing the area. "I'll get her outta there."

Marquis noticed his strange behavior, but didn't say anything.

Malik took his normal, four-block walk back home when he noticed a Hummer driving slowly behind him. He peeked over his shoulder, but couldn't see who was driving because of the heavily tinted windows. He continued to walk while fingering the gun that he had carefully removed and stuck in the pocket of the tri-colored, zippered hoodie he wore. He pulled up his jeans and checked over his shoulder once again for the vehicle. It had slowed it pace.

Malik made a sudden left and cut through the backyard of one of the houses. He was now going in a direction away from his apartment building. He looked back before he hopped the fence in the backyard and saw the Hummer speed past the house. Malik doubled back, ran across the street, and disappeared into the yard of another house. He jumped several fences until he ended up just two blocks from his apartment building.

Malik slowed down, thinking he had lost the Hummer. But before he could make it up the street, bullets echoed. Several bullets hit him in the back as shock crossed his face. He fell to his knees, then onto his face. He didn't know that a man had jumped out of the Hummer before Malik saw it take off down the street. That man had followed him on foot.

The few people who were outside began to yell and scream. The gunman ran through the backyards, hopping fence after fence. When he came out onto the street, he realized he had run right back onto Malik's block where Marquis and the rest of the crew stood. This wasn't the gunman's neighborhood, so he had no idea where he was going. He ran because he had been spotted. He slowly backed up into the yard and stayed there for about five minutes while he placed a call on his cell phone. He jumped the back fence into an adjoining yard and ran onto the next street over. The Hummer picked him up and they sped off.

FOUR DAYS LATER . . .

The morning was cloudy and threatened rain. Nina sat up in bed when reality hit her again, and she began to cry. Ernest came into the room and sat down on the bed next to her. He pulled her into his arms as he'd done every night since Malik's death.

"You gotta pull yourself together baby," he said, kissing her on the forehead. "You gotta be strong. I know it hurts."

"I can't. I wished this on him."

"How can you say that? You didn't wish this on him. It happened to him because of the lifestyle he led. You tried to talk to him, but he didn't listen. There is nothing you could've done to prevent it."

"No, Ernest. I said to him, on more than one occasion, that the streets were gonna kill him or land him in jail." She sobbed.

Ernest didn't say a word. He just continued to hold her. He knew that at this point, she wasn't going to listen to him. What he needed to do was be there for her, and make sure that she didn't turn to drugs to get over this.

THE FUNERAL

Marquis and Shea walked toward the small church. He wore a black suit with a white shirt. Shea had helped him pick the outfit, and the Italian suit was custom fitted. He got a haircut the day before and picked up a new pair of shoes. Distress showed all over his face. He knew this was going to be the last time he'd lay eyes on his brother and best friend. It had been hard for him to identify the body down at the morgue and sign the papers. He desperately fought back tears. Shea held on to his arm and remained silent, because she knew what it felt like to lose someone you loved so deeply.

The weather was a bit breezy and she huddled a little closer to Marquis. *He looks handsome,* Shea thought as she looked at him. He wore a trench coat for the rain that was expected to come.

"Well, I better go say goodbye to my brother." He sighed.

The two climbed the flight of steps leading to the church doors that stood open, as if they were waiting for him to arrive. They walked slowly, one step at a time. It was as if Marquis was trying to prolong the inevitable. Suddenly, as if God wanted it, the sun peeked through the clouds. They both looked up at the sky and watched the clouds move away from the sun. The sky lit up brightly and a rainbow appeared.

Marquis raised his face toward the sun and closed his eyes. The warmth from its rays felt good. He began to climb the stairs again. As he and Shea reached the top of the steps, Shea suddenly stopped. He looked down at her.

"What's wrong?" She looked at him with horror all over her face. "Babe, what's the matter?" he asked again, now concerned.

It was a living nightmare for her. The reality of her father's death came back. Shea was that young girl again, climbing the stairs with her mother, going to see the man they said was her father. Shea's eyes welled up with tears and she had difficulty breathing. Marquis put his arms around her.

"Shea, tell me what's wrong!"

"I . . . I can't go in there, Mark. I just can't do it." Tears stained her face. "I'm sorry, but I can't go."

He pulled her into a hug and held her. His tears once again threatened to fall, and yet again he held them back. He knew he had to be strong for his mother and Shea. He would have to cry about it another day, but for now, he would be strong.

"I understand, babe," he said.

"Do you really?" She looked up at him. "Mark, I'm sorry, but this reminds me of the day my father died, and I don't know if I can handle this."

Marquis really did understand, as it wasn't easy for him to go in either. The organist began to play. The sad music poured from the open doors of the church. No one was outside. All who had come were seated inside the church. Marquis kissed Shea on the forehead.

"Where are you gonna go?" he asked her.

"I will be right here when you come out. I am not going anywhere," she assured him.

Marquis kissed her on the lips this time and entered the church. Shea watched him. She wanted to be by her man's side, but it was difficult for her to go into the church, so she stood there and watched him walk inside.

Marquis paused in the back of the church. He could see the ivory and pearl coffin with gold trim, gold drop handles, and eggshell white velour interior. He saw the body lying in the casket from a distance. Several viewers stood around. They acknowledged him, but Marquis didn't return the acknowledgment.

He took a deep breath and pushed forward. Looking straight ahead, he kept his focus on the coffin. His attire and demeanor made him seem like a gangster as he walked down the long aisle.

Once he reached the front row of the church, he could see clearly. He slowly approached the casket. Misery filled his lungs. There he was, his brother and best friend. He looked so good in his eggshell white Christian Dior suit. Malik appeared to be sleeping. He looked peaceful to Marquis.

The church was so huge it didn't look as if there were many people in attendance, but there were about eighty or so people there to see Malik off.

The pastor waited patiently in the pulpit to start the service. He was a recovering addict of over fifteen years, and a personal friend of Ernest. When Ernest asked him to preach the eulogy for a good friend who didn't have a church home, the pastor was more than happy to do so, especially for a fellow recovering addict.

Nina sat in the first pew, dressed in black. Next to her sat Ernest with his arm draped around her shoulder. She laid her head on his shoulder and stared at her son's body. Her nose looked burnt red against her light brown skin. It almost seemed as if her nose was dissolving. Nina wore a black hat with a veil to cover her face and hide her decaying nose.

Marquis peered down at his brother. After close examination, it looked as if his brother had been stuffed. He reached over and touched Malik's hand. It was cold and clammy. He tried to hold back the tears and force the lump in his throat back down, but this time he failed. The river overflowed and Marquis finally cried for the loss of his brother. He sobbed loudly, like a baby. He couldn't move, nor did he want to move. He never wanted to be without his brother. He wanted to stay beside Malik forever.

"I'm sorry, big brother. I should have been there for you, like you've always been there for me. I'm so sorry! Please forgive me. You said you would always take care of me. How can you just leave me?" he cried.

A man walked down the aisle with short steps, followed closely by two other men. Everyone turned to watch him walk past. Some whispered while he continued his journey to the casket.

A shackled hand rested on top of Marquis's hand, which was still resting on Malik. Marquis looked up to see Wiz standing next to him. Wiz lifted his shackled arms enough for his son to come into his arms.

Marquis continued to cry as his father held him. Nina raised her head from Ernest's shoulder and looked at Wiz. Wiz turned and looked at Nina. Their eyes met for the first time in over fifteen years. It was like meeting for the first time all over again. Nina felt all the love she once had for him return. She rose to her feet and walked over to where the father and son embraced. Ernest looked on intently, wondering what was going to happen. He knew that was the boy's father. Nina had told him so much about her past that the picture he had of Wiz in his mind was almost accurate. Besides the shackles, Ernest still would have been able to pick Wiz out of a lineup as Malik and Marquis's father.

"Wiz," Nina whispered as she stood next to the two men. Marquis turned to see his mother standing there. Wiz removed his arms from around his son and faced Nina. The two police escorts stood close by, watching him like a hawk.

Because of the good behavior status Wiz held in prison, he was allowed a free pass to come to his son's funeral. It was hard for Marquis to tell his father that Malik was dead, and Marquis couldn't bring himself to do it face-to-face, so he wrote Wiz a letter instead with all of the details of the funeral arrangements.

Kurt was seated in the second row when he realized Wiz was standing there. Although he was inebriated, he sat straight up and looked at his old friend. He became full of sorrow. He began to feel like he had failed Wiz because Wiz had asked him to look out for his family, and now his son was dead.

Nina lowered her head and whispered, "I'm sorry."

Wiz grabbed her hand. She stared at him from behind the black veil. "We all make mistakes, but it is the forgiveness that means the most. I'm sorry for leaving you to do it all by yourself." He brought her hand up to his mouth and softly kissed it. Nina's insides melted. She laid her face on his rock-hard chest and silently cried. Wiz laid his head on top of hers.

Ernest didn't like what he saw, but what could he really do? The two parents had lost their son. That was the only reason why Ernest let things go down like they did.

The pastor walked up to the podium and cleared his throat. The organist continued to play, but softer. The two prison officers walked over and gently grabbed Wiz by the arms. Ernest leaned forward and grabbed Nina's hand. She looked at Ernest, then back at Wiz, who was being escorted to another part of the front row, in the next pew over. The officers sat on either side of him. Nina obviously preferred to sit with Wiz instead of Ernest.

Ernest fumed silently. After all he had done for her! He'd been there for Nina and her nightmares. He'd been more of friend than a sponsor to her. He'd helped her in many ways, and this was the thanks he got? He noticed Nina looking down the row at Wiz instead of at her dead son in front of her.

As the pastor gave the eulogy and the choir sang mournful songs, Marquis couldn't keep his eyes dry. He was mad. He turned to look behind him to see Brian in tears, looking lost. Marquis turned back around and looked down the row at his father. Wiz looked back at him and saw how much Marquis was really hurting. Wiz held up his fist and put it over his heart, signaling Marquis to man up and be strong. Marquis nodded and looked back at his brother. He thought about what he could do to find out what happened, and why Malik was murdered.

It was now time for the last viewing of the body by the immediate family. Marquis walked up to the casket and the tears flowed again, despite what his father told him. He looked down at Malik and continued to cry. Wiz was escorted back over to the casket and stood next to Marquis. He, too, wanted to cry, but didn't. Nina performed when Ernest and one of the ushers tried to help her over to the casket. She screamed and cried, and could barely walk. They practically carried her. Once at the casket, she held her head low and continued to cry loudly. There wasn't a dry eye in the place as the lead singer of the choir sang "His Eye Is On The Sparrow." Ernest looked over at Wiz and Wiz gave him a nod of approval. Ernest simply nodded back and they both turned their attention back to the casket.

Once they were all seated again, the funeral home employees prepared to close the casket.

ᖆᖍᖆᖍᖆᖍ

The pallbearers—Marquis, Brian, Kurt, and some recovering addict friends of Ernest—carried the body out of the church. The rest of the funeral attendees followed the casket. After the casket was placed in the hearse, Marquis went over to speak with his father when Nina walked over.

"Wiz, how are you?" she asked.

"I'm well, Nina. Are you going to be able to maintain?"

"I have no other choice." She lowered her head.

"Mark, you take care of your mother. She's gonna need you now more than ever. She gotta stay clean."

Nina looked up at him with wide eyes. "How'd you—"

"I hear things, Nina. I pray for y'all every night. I ask the Higher Power for His forgiveness, and that He can allow you to forgive me."

Nina didn't know what to say, but Wiz knew her heart.

"All right, Wilkes, we gotta get you back," one of the officers said.

"Can he stay for just a while longer?" Nina asked the officer.

"Sorry, ma'am. The funeral is over, and our orders are to get him back as soon as it concluded."

"Come see me sometime, Nina. Mark can bring you with him the next time he comes."

Nina was in love all over again. Wiz was even more handsome than she last remembered him. Ernest spoke with his recovery friends a few steps away and tried not to look over at them.

Wiz read her mind and shook his head. "Stay with ol' boy, Nina," he said, referring to Ernest. "He a good dude. I can tell."

"Thank you, Wiz." She still didn't want him to go.

"Wiz, what's up, man?" Kurt walked over to them. He held his head low in shame.

"Kurt, my old friend." Wiz held his hand out for a shake. Kurt shook his hand.

"I'm sorry, Wiz. I failed you."

"Naw, Kurt, you didn't fail me. Why would you say that?" Wiz asked.

"Because I didn't look out for your family like I promised you."

"Kurt, you did what you could. Don't blame yourself. You done good, man," Wiz told him.

Wiz turned to Marquis. "A'ight, son. I'll see you next week, right?" Wiz held up a shackled hand for a shake.

"No doubt," Mark said sadly, and shook his father's hand.

"Keep your head up, and stay away from them corners. Keep your head in them books and do better for yourself. Feel me?" Wiz tried to get the message into Marquis's head. He had a bad feeling about Marquis. He believed his son would try to pick up where his brother had left off in the streets, out of a misguided sense of loyalty.

"Yeah."

"Peace, Kurt. When you coming to see me?" Wiz asked.

"I'm coming, Wiz."

The three of them watched as the officers escorted Wiz to a prison van. Some of the men who attended the funeral knew Wiz from back in the day and yelled out to him in acknowledgment. Wiz simply nodded or pointed at them as they called out his name. He appeared to be a celebrity to them.

THE FOLLOWING WEEK . . .

Marquis and Kurt rode the bus to see Wiz. Kurt had put on some decent clothing that Marquis had bought for him, but he failed to bath before putting on the new clothes. The new clothes did nothing to camouflage his dirty skin and fully matted beard. It made one hell of a bus ride to Pennsylvania. Everyone on the bus complained, and they had all the windows open. The bus had air conditioning, but no one cared about that. They just tried to escape the funk that lingered in the air. During the ride Marquis told Kurt that he was going to step up his game and take his brother's place on the blocks. He had been talking to Brian about it, and the money was definitely rolling in.

Kurt shook his head in dismay. "Aw, naw, Mark! Not you! That ain't for you. You was doing the right thing by going to school. I thought it was only temporary until Malik got outta jail, man. Why don't you leave that shit alone? You see what it has done to your brother!"

"I ain't my brother, though, Kurt. I handle things differently."

"Mark, it don't matter how you handle it. There have been some legends way before your time, and they all got dropped some kinda way or another. Whether they got canned or killed, either way it's a dead-end street."

"Yeah, but the difference with me is that I'm gonna take the bread I make and go legit." Marquis thought he had it all figured out.

Kurt snorted. "How many niggas you think said them same words you just did? Plenty! The game is like quicksand. Once you step into it, it sucks you deeper and deeper into the ground. I'm telling you, youngin.'"

"Not me, Kurt." Marquis was confident.

Kurt stared at him. "Where we going now?"

"We going to see my father. Why you ask me that?"

"Because your father is doing life because of what you tryna get into."

"My father got time for a murder."

"Murder comes with the game, boy!"

Marquis turned away from Kurt and stared out of the bus window in silence.

ﾍﾟﾍﾟﾍﾟﾍﾟ

The two of them sat and waited as the inmates filled the visiting hall. Wiz stood out in the crowd as he made his way over to the table with a smile on his face. Marquis stood and the two embraced. Kurt waited his turn and he and Wiz shook hands and shared a brotherly hug.

"Good to see you, Kurt," Wiz said.

They sat at the table and Wiz placed his elbows on the table and interlocked his fingers. He looked at Marquis with a serious face.

"What's this I'm hearing you dropped outta school and now you out on the corners banging?"

"Huh?" Marquis was flabbergasted.

Wiz didn't respond. He just eyed Marquis in a fatherly way. Marquis felt uncomfortable, and the way he fidgeted it was obvious that he was caught.

"Listen, son, I told you everything runs through these walls. I know shit before you do."

"I . . . didn't drop out," Marquis stuttered and lied.

"Listen, Mark, I'm the last person to judge, and I'm not here to judge you or try to tell you how to live your life. I fucked my chances up at being a father by being in this hole for all of your life. But what I'm tryna tell you, son, is don't make the mistakes that your brother and I made. It fucks me up that I wasn't in y'all lives to prevent this. Then again I wonder if I was still out on the streets would I have walked away from the game."

"Listen to your father, Mark. He talking real shit to you. Wiz is the smartest cat I know," Kurt interjected.

"Look at me," Wiz told Marquis. Marquis looked into his father's eyes.

"Walk away from it, son. Trust me, don't feel obligated to be loyal to Malik because he's gone. That was what Malik chose to do. Life is all about choices. With each choice you make comes a consequence. With each consequence comes a result. Think about the choices you make. You feel me?"

"Yeah, I feel you," Marquis answered in a low tone.

"I love you, Mark, and you are all I have left. I blame myself for Malik's death. I don't blame you, Kurt, so stop beating yourself up over it." He looked at Kurt to reassure him, and then looked back at his son. "Walk away and go back to school, Mark. Don't do it for me, your mother, or nobody else. Do it for you," Wiz said.

Marquis looked at his father with admiration and respect. He loved his father and wished he was out of prison so he could have him around to guide him all the time. He made up his mind that he was gonna tell Brian he was out of the game as soon as he got back to the block.

"I feel you. I'm gonna go back to school," Marquis assured him.

"That's my man." Wiz grabbed him by the back of the neck, pulled his head over, and kissed Marquis on the top of the head.

"Now back to you," Wiz said, referring to Kurt. "What's up with the new clothes?" He smiled at Kurt.

"Hey, you know I had to do a little something-something to come see my man. You feeling my threads?" Kurt smiled and stood to show off his new clothes.

"Yeah, but you couldn't wash your ass before you put on the new threads?" Wiz asked.

They all burst into laughter.

Chapter Thirty

When Marquis and Kurt returned from visiting Wiz they walked up the block together. Brian was there with Death when they arrived.

"What's up, Death, my man?" Kurt smiled a dirty-toothed smile.

Death nonchalantly nodded at Kurt.

"I'll see ya later, youngin'," he told Marquis and left.

"A'ight, Kurt," Marquis said but kept his eyes on Death.

Death shot daggers at Kurt and turned his attention to Marquis. A smile crept across his face.

"What's up, baby boy? Where you been at?" He held out his hand for a shake.

Marquis reluctantly shook his hand.

"I was just talking to my man right here about the loot he owes me for that last package."

"What about it?" Marquis asked.

"I'm sayin', it's too bad what happened to my boy Malik and all, but business is still business."

Marquis raised an eyebrow. "Yeah, it is too bad. I don't remember seeing you at your *boy's* funeral, though."

"Aw, I was outta town and couldn't make it, but give Nina my sincere regards." Death placed his hand over his heart.

"Yeah, mighty funny your out-of-town business trip happened on the same day as my brother's funeral. And mighty funny nobody knows who wasted my brother. Do you?" Marquis grilled Death with untrusting eyes.

"Naw, baby boy, I have no idea." Death looked at Brian. "So back to you, my man. What we gonna do about our little situation?"

Brian had no answers. He was still mourning Malik's death and had it not been for Bird, the new kid they had on their team, the work wouldn't have gotten sold that week.

"Don't worry about the bread. I got it," Marquis interjected.

Death raised his eyebrows and chuckled. "Oh, you got that kinda bread?" Death couldn't believe his ears.

"Fuck is so funny?" Marquis was offended.

"I'm just saying, I know you ain't into this kinda shit, and I can't figure out where you would get that kinda paper from."

"Listen, man, don't count my money. Count your own. I'm taking over my brother's business, and like I said, you will get your bread," Marquis said with authority, totally forgetting the promise he had made to Wiz.

"Woooo!" Death laughed and held up his hands in mock surrender. He looked back at his two bodyguards and they all laughed at Marquis.

Marquis simply lifted his shirt to expose two chrome Glock 9 mm guns with black handles.

He and Kurt had stopped by his house before walking over to the block. Marquis hadn't felt safe out on the streets since his brother's death, so he had begun carrying the armor.

Death's laughter died. "Oh, word?"

"Word," Marquis confirmed.

One of Death's bodyguards reached for his own gun when Death stopped him.

"Chill, man, it ain't necessary." He looked at Marquis with new respect. "So now we do business. Have all my bread by nine tonight. I'ma send somebody through to pick it up. If you ain't got it, get ready to start using your new little toys you got there."

Marquis shook his head. "Naw, B, I ain't passing no paper off to nobody but you. Somebody done told you wrong, or you got me fucked up with somebody else. Ain't no way I'ma pass off that kinda paper to somebody I don't know. So it's on you, playboy."

Death was pissed but tried not to show it. "Not a problem. Have my shit." He walked away with his bodyguards backpedaling to the car. They didn't trust the young boys standing in front of them.

LATER THAT NIGHT . . .

As promised, Death came back for his money, and Marquis was waiting on him.

"So, you takin' over your brother's business?" Death asked.

"That's what you heard earlier, didn't you?"

"Yeah, OK. Don't bite off more than you can chew, baby boy."

"Just send another package through here by the end of this week," Marquis said.

"Oh naw, baby boy. The rules have changed. That was a deal me and your brother made. Now I got a new deal. One, the price just went up another two thousand. Two, you pay before you get the package, and three, like I told your brother, these are my blocks. You can't push nobody's shit but mine. So now it's on you, playboy," Death smirked as he tossed Marquis's line back at him.

"Come through here at the end of the week with my product, like I said, and your bread will be here waiting on you."

Death was pissed all over again. He hadn't expected Marquis to go for the deal. He stormed to his car and drove away.

Chapter Thirty-One

Jackie sat at the kitchen table in Nina's apartment. Nina stood at the counter and poured powder cocaine into a large glass jar. She opened the refrigerator and stuck her hand into an open box of baking soda and pinched a large amount between her fingers. She tossed the baking soda into the jar and added enough water just to cover the mixture.

Jackie cut a steel wool scouring pad into pieces and laid them out on the table. One by one she gripped each piece with a pair of small pliers and carried it to the stove where a spare burner glowed with blue gas flames. She held it in the flames until it turned silver, then removed it from the flame. Nina was at another burner holding the jar over the flame until it boiled. She removed it from the flame, then shook it to mix the separated oil from the melted cocaine together. She poured a little ice water from a glass into the jar, shaking it to make sure it was mixed until the cocaine mixture molded together into a rock.

The women worked as if their lives depended on it. There was no talking. They were serious about the hit they were about to take, and time was not to be wasted. Nina sat down at the table with Jackie, who had squeezed a piece of the burned steel wool into a ball and placed it at the end of the stem of the glass pipe. She used a screwdriver to pack it into the stem. Nina poured as much of the water out of the jar as possible without pouring out any crumbs of cooked coke. She dumped the rocks—one large one and several smaller ones—onto a paper towel to dry. When the moisture from the rocks had soaked into the towel, Jackie handed Nina a fresh, newly packed stem. Neither woman hesitated to grab one of the smaller rocks and slam in into the stem. They lit up with brand new lighters and began to smoke.

The smell of burning cocaine was strong as they blew the smoke from their lungs. The smoke hovered over their heads like dark, angry thunderclouds. Nina closed her eyes and allowed the drug to take over her body, whereas Jackie went into her usual ritual of foot tapping, eye stretching, and lip twisting. Nina opened her eyes when she heard the tapping. It annoyed her at times that Jackie did this. Most times Nina was already grooving from the heroin, but she hadn't taken a hit of it yet. Nina went into her cleaning spree and cleared the table of anything that didn't belong there. She wanted to get it out of the way before she snorted the heroin that sat in a pile on the table.

When she got the first call from the doctor's office about her results from her tests regarding her nose, they told her that she needed to come to the office. This scared the hell out of Nina. She knew from experience that when the doctor's office told you to come in for your results, something was wrong, and in Nina's case, she didn't want to know. The first thing that came to her mind was that she had AIDS. She knew she had slept with quite a few people in the past without protection, and it could be a possibility. At first she was concerned about dying. Then she figured with AIDS she was going to die anyway, so why not go out with a bang? That was when she began to dabble into the drugs again. Nina had gone down to the doctor's office that morning and was hit with the horrible news that she had paranasal sinus cancer, and the doctor wanted her to start cancer treatments immediately. She was sick to her stomach when she found out. Nina agreed to show up for treatment, but didn't. For the past several weeks she had been ducking the phone calls from the doctor's office about scheduling her cancer treatments.

Depression settled deeper into her soul. She'd lost her son, and now she was going to lose her nose from nose cancer and possibly her life. When she got home, she decided to go into the boys room to go through Malik's things. She cried while she cleaned out his closet and dresser drawers. After Malik died she and Marquis had discussed whether he wanted Malik's clothes. He picked out what he wanted to keep for sentimental value, because Marquis couldn't fit any of Malik's clothes. She packed his clothes and shoes in boxes for the Salvation Army, then she found the duffel bag in the back of the closet. Jackie was asleep on the couch in the living room.

Nina opened the duffel bag, expecting to see clothes, but saw the cellophane bag filled with cocaine. Then there was another bag filled with heroin. She held the two bags in her shaking hands. Tears streamed down her face at a rapid pace. Her stomach began to bubble. Gas passed through her rectum and the urge to use was stronger than anything she had ever felt before in her life.

She had been sneaking hits here and there for over a few months without anyone knowing. But she never before had an urge like she had at that moment.

She thought about calling Ernest, then she thought about flushing the substance down the toilet. Instead, she woke Jackie and they got ready to get high. Nina made sure that she didn't take a noticeable amount from the stash, but what she did take was enough to get them high for hours. She didn't know if Malik had been holding the stash for someone else, and she didn't want to create any problems if they came looking for it.

Jackie started to move things around on the table as if she was looking for something.

"What are you doing? I just cleaned that table!" Nina snapped.

Jackie grunted. She got up and started looking through the drawers and the cabinets. Nina was used to this behavior. Jackie wasn't looking for anything, so Nina kept cleaning. When she finished, she sat down and snorted some heroin. She tilted her head back and felt something warm running from her nose. She saw Jackie staring at her with big eyes. Nina wiped her nose, looked at the tissue, and saw that it was covered in blood.

She packed her badly decaying nose with tissue while Jackie frowned at her in disapproval. Nina's nose was a sight to see. She no longer could wear makeup to conceal the damage. There wasn't enough makeup on the planet that could cover the sight of her nose as it was being eaten away. As a result, she simply placed an adhesive bandage over the decayed part of her nose.

Twenty minutes later Marquis walked into the apartment with Shea trailing behind him. They both stopped short when they saw his mother and Jackie in the kitchen getting high. He was beyond hurt. He thought his mother had been clean for months. After all that had happened to them, after everything she promised, there she was, getting high all over again.

Marquis was pissed. The two women didn't even know he was there. Jackie finally looked up and saw the couple standing in the kitchen doorway. Nina turned around and saw them too.

"Hey, Mark," she said in a drug-induced haze.

Marquis walked away and went into his room. Shea followed.

"Pack what you can," he ordered.

"Where we going, Mark?"

"For tonight we gonna go to a hotel. I'm not gonna stay here and deal with this bullshit."

Shea did as she was told, and Marquis packed his own bags and added the duffel bag from the closet. He walked back to the kitchen and watched his mother get high. It still hurt him to do things this way, but at this point he couldn't help her any longer.

"Ma!" he yelled.

"Boy, you ain't gotta yell. I'm right here," she slurred.

"I'm outta here. Find your own way to pay the bills."

"Mark, where you going?" Her high was suddenly blown and Nina was concerned.

"I'm getting away from you. I told you I ain't want her in here"— he pointed at Jackie—"and this is the reason why. You sitting up here, getting high after all everybody has done to support you. You ran Ernest away too. I can't deal with this bullshit no more!"

"Can you just leave me some money to pay the bills till I find a job?"

Marquis was incredulous. "Are you outta your mind? You gets no more money from me so that you can put it up your nose." He went back to the room, grabbed his and Shea's bags, and left with Shea in tow.

THE NEXT WEEK . . .

Marquis stood on the corner waiting for Death to come through with the product, but he never showed up. Marquis still had some product left from the last package, but the supply was low. He got Death's number from Brian and tried to call him. He stood out on the block for another hour before Brian showed up to take over the watch. Still no call from Death.

Later that night, Marquis walked into the bar that Death frequented and asked for him, but he wasn't there and the bartender said he didn't know when he was going to come in. Marquis left the bar and went back to the block to kick it with Brian. Thirty minutes later Death and his two bodyguards pulled up. They jumped out of the car like they were going to war.

"Listen, you little punk, don't you ever walk up in my establishment looking for me!" Death snarled.

"Yo, man, we had a deal, and you reneged on your end of the bargain," Marquis shot back.

"I don't give a fuck! You wait on me," Death said.

Marquis shook his head. "Naw, bruh. Like I told you before, you got me fucked up. I don't wait on nobody. You can keep your product. I got me a new connect, so your services are no longer needed here."

Death laughed. "Motherfucker, your brother ain't tell you who I am? No, matter-of-fact, your mother ain't never told you who I am?"

"No. Did anybody tell you who I am? Matter-of-fact, do you know who my father is?" Marquis challenged him.

"Yeah," Death chuckled. "Sure, I know who your father is. Your father worked for me," he lied. "So let me put you up on some shit. I am not the one to be fuckin' with, because your mother will be burying her younger son next to the older one. Now fuck with me if you want to."

"It don't mean shit to me," Marquis said nonchalantly.

Death reached for the gun in his shoulder holster, but Bird had a MAC-10 pulled on Death before he could get the gun clear of the holster. Behind Death three more runners trained their handguns on him and his bodyguards as well.

Death looked into the eyes of the young boy Bird and knew that he was heartless.

"A'ight, y'all, chill out," he told his two men. Marquis remained silent and his crew never lowered their guns. Brian and Marquis stood with their arms folded across their chests, confident in their young, ruthless crew.

Death and his bodyguards walked off. Death turned and yelled to Marquis, "Watch yourself, baby boy!"

"I will!" Marquis yelled back.

Brian looked at Marquis. Marquis watched Death's car as it traveled down the street.

ᖇᖇᖇᖇᖇ

TWO WEEKS LATER . . .

It was well into the fall, but the weather was still a bit warm on some days. The kids were already back in school, and Nina was on her way back from a trip to the store. She had seen Marquis, and he broke down and gave her money to put food in the refrigerator.

This was Nina's second time in detox during the last two weeks. She vowed that this time she was going to stay clean.

"Ma, I can't do this with you no more," Marquis told her.

"Mark, I did the two-day detox program at East Orange Hospital. I'm gonna stay clean this time," Nina said.

"Yeah, you said that the last couple of times. I'm done with this."

"Mark, don't do me like this. I'm your mother."

"Yeah, you are, so act like one. You been manipulating me all my life and I couldn't see it. Well, I see it now. I know I told you I would help you if you detoxed, but I see you still tryna take advantage of me. This is it. If you slip and relapse this time, don't come to me, because I ain't got no words for you, Ma." He was serious.

"Mark, please, don't do me like this," she begged.

"I paid your light bill after I moved out because I felt sorry for you. I'm not paying your bills this time. I didn't want to give you the money for food."

"Mark, I promise you I'ma stay clean this time. Just trust me. But at least give me something on the rent. You don't even have to give me the money. You can pay the landlord yourself."

"Naw, Ma, I'm finished. That's it. You need to find a job. If you get a job, and I see you really tryna do something with yourself, and you need my help, then, yeah, I won't have a problem helping you. But as far as me giving you anymore money for the bills, naw, that's a wrap."

Marquis was fed up with his mother. He had become hardened and simply ignored her request for help. Nina was hurt because Marquis was her baby. He was her favorite, and they were the closest. She now saw what the streets had done to her son.

Marquis became hardened when everything he loved was destroyed. The dream he had of going to school was destroyed by the time he invested in trying to save his family. He was hardened and didn't care about life, because he tried to live right and do the right things, and he was constantly being disappointed. He was hardened because in his mind there was supposed to be a God, but why had God taken everything that he loved away from him, everyone except Shea? No, the streets didn't harden him. The streets opened their arms and embraced him. The streets pulled him in and made him feel loved.

Marquis and his crew were bigger than Malik could have ever imagined. He had a bigger crew, more blocks, and a solid team of soldiers. Death tried to come at him a couple more times, but two of his team members were killed in the process, so he backed off, or so Marquis thought.

∾∾∾∾

Nina sat down at the table and looked at the mail that fell out of her jam-packed mailbox when she opened it. The first thing she saw was a letter of eviction. She threw that letter to the side. Next she saw shut-off notices for her lights and gas. She saw the disconnection notice for the phone, but she tossed that aside too because the phone had already been shut off. Each letter she opened, she tossed in the trash because it was somebody asking for money she didn't have, nor had a means to get. One letter caught her attention. The return address showed it was from Ernest. Her heart began to beat faster. Nina did miss him. It had been a couple of months since she'd seen him. He was a good man and she had been too blind to see it. She opened the letter and began to read. It was a short letter.

> *Nina,*
>
> *By the time this letter reaches you, I hope it finds you in the best of sprits, mentally and physically. I must say that I have missed your presence. I have missed your smile, but most of all, I have missed your spirits. However, I am not writing you this letter to tell you such. I am simply writing you because I tried to call and your phone is disconnected. I am not sure if you are still cleansing your body or, as I have heard, that you started using again. I will not judge you, as I am in no position to judge. The judging is left up to the Higher Power. I simply want to extend an invitation to you. Every Wednesday night at seven pm, there will be an NA*

*meeting at the church where I originally met you, on Martin
Luther King Blvd. I've taken the liberty of contacting Nilda,
as she has been asking about you as well. Every Wednesday
night she plans on being there, just in case you show up. It
would be good to see you.*

   Best wishes,
   Ernest

Nina sat there and stared at the letter for quite a while. She got up
and went to the mirror. She peeled off the bandage that the nurse put
on her nose at the detox center. The staff at the hospital she went to in
East Orange had advised her that she needed to see a doctor about her
nose. On every occasion she came in for the two-day detox program and
the subsequent follow-up visits, she was told to see a doctor, but Nina
ignored them every time.

Nina looked at the gruesome sight of the inside of her nose. She
had been extremely nasally and suffered with migraines, but she just
didn't care anymore. She had lost a considerable amount of weight, and
everybody knew she was on drugs. No job would hire her. She no longer
cared too much about life. She tried to, but on most days she looked at
herself in the mirror, looked at her nose, and reminded herself that she
wouldn't have long to live.

Nina tossed Ernest's letter aside. She had no intention of going to
the NA meeting. She didn't want anyone to feel sorry for her because of
her cancerous nose, so she decided that she would just stay indoors and
hide.

はいはいはい

The meeting was winding down and Nilda kept looking back at the door, waiting for Nina to walk in, but she never did. When the meeting was over and the Serenity Prayer recited, the audience broke off into smaller groups for conversation. Ernest walked over to Nilda and gave her a hug to comfort her.

"Don't worry. She will show up one day," Ernest said.

"I should just go over to her house to see if she still lives there," Nilda said.

Ernest shook his head. "No, Nilda, don't do that. You never know what her position is right now, and you should know from experience what could possibly happen with an addict." Addicts were known to get violent occasionally, especially if they felt you were there to stop them from getting high.

Nilda nodded and resigned herself to the fact that the only person who could help Nina right now was Nina.

"So she didn't come again," a woman said as she approached Ernest and Nilda.

"No, Shauna, she didn't."

Shauna had gone into a rehabilitation program for three months after Juanita and Patrice's deaths. When she had her stomach pumped, she found out that there had been a deadly chemical in the crack that killed the women. Shauna had spoken with Justice before he was killed, and he told her that Death had given him the vials to give to Juanita the next time she came to cop, because he knew they'd stolen his stash. Shauna was afraid that Death would come after her when he found out she was still alive, so she decided to turn her life around. She checked herself into the program in upstate New York. When she returned to the city she ran into an old friend, who had also rehabilitated himself. He went into a one-month program and was set to leave for a follow-up program for three months. He and Shauna had spent time together going to the meetings where they met up with Ernest.

"So what are y'all talking about over here?" Kurt asked as he smiled and walked over to the three of them. Kurt was Shauna's new friend. He had finally decided to clean up his act after all these years.

"Just talking about Nina and how she hasn't shown up again," Ernest answered.

"Just give her some time. She will one day. I gotta be catching my train in a few hours, so what are we gonna eat? I'm as hungry as three monkeys at feeding time!"

The group laughed as they left the church.

Chapter Thirty-Two

SEVERAL WEEKS LATER . . .

Despite all of the drama during the last couple of months, Marquis was thrilled to learn that Shea was six weeks pregnant with his child. She seemed to have a different look about her. She appeared refreshed. Shea told him that just because she was pregnant, that didn't mean she wouldn't finish college. She was determined to do that, and with Marquis now taking care of her, she knew things would be better. She didn't care that he sold drugs. She knew that it was only temporary, and he was going to go back to school and finish his degree so that they could live a normal life. Shea didn't understand that Marquis was getting deeper and deeper into the game each day. Of course he told her that he was going to finish school. He told her that this was only temporary to get a few dollars in the bank for the future. In his heart, he meant every word, but the way the bread flowed in each week, his plans for returning to school were put on the back burner, and he thought less and less of them as time passed.

Marquis and Shea decided to make a trip to the prison to see Wiz. They told him about their soon-to-be new addition.

"So how's everything going?" Wiz asked as he smiled admiring the two of them sitting there.

"It's all good," Marquis responded.

"That's what's up."

"I do have some good news to tell you though," Marquis said.

"We sure do," Shea sang.

"Really? OK so what's up?"

"You 'bout to be a grandfather," Marquis smiled.

"Word?" Wiz was surprised.

"Yup, I'm pregnant," Shea added.

"Aw man," Wiz sat back in his chair smiling at the two of them. He was at a lost for words.

Wiz was proud. He was going to be a grandfather. His smiled suddenly dissipated when he realized that he would only be able to see his grandchild while still in prison. That is something he didn't want to happen. He did tell Marquis to marry Shea and not string her along, like he did to Nina. He told him to be a better man than he was, and to do the right thing with his life and family. But what really troubled Wiz was the fact that Marquis had broken his promise.

"Shea, can you excuse me and Mark for a minute? I really need to talk to him alone," Wiz said.

"Sure. I need to go to the bathroom anyway." She smiled.

"Again?" Marquis asked. "Damn, you went at least three times on the road. Now you gotta go again?"

"Boy, leave me alone." Shea hit him playfully.

"Yeah, leave my daughter-in-law alone. She's carrying my grandson," Wiz said.

"Granddaughter," Shea corrected him with a smile.

"OK, I'll take a granddaughter too."

She walked off, leaving the two men to sit together. Wiz's face became stone serious.

"You broke your word," he said simply. "I know you still out there banging. Like I said before, I'm not gonna judge you, and you have to be a man and make your own decisions. But I want you to know that I'm disappointed in you."

"Who told you?"

"That's neither here nor there. Just know that I know. I still got eyes and ears on the streets, Mark."

"Well, I'm sorry I disappointed you, but I had to do what I had to do. I'm good at what I do. Trust me."

Wiz sat back in his seat and stared at his son. He saw a lot of himself in Marquis as far as his business sense. But what could he do? How could he expect his son to do the right thing when the example he had set wasn't a good one. His name was a legend in the streets.

"I don't buy it, Mark, because I thought I was smart too. One mistake,"—he held up his index finger—"one mistake is all it takes."

"I know, but I'm gonna be long gone outta the game before that happens," Marquis said, not quite believing his own words.

"If you say so," a disappointed Wiz said. He looked up to see Shea returning from the bathroom. "I still love you, son, and if that's what you gotta do, then if there is anything that you need, advice or anything, you make sure you get at me before you make a move."

"No doubt," Marquis said, feeling somewhat relieved.

ฌฌฌฌ

The couple pulled up in front of the bodega. Brian was on the block, surveying the area. He walked over to the passenger side of the car and bent down. Shea rolled down the window with a smile on her face.

"Hey, Brian," she sang.

"Hey, ma." He leaned in and kissed her on the check. "What's good, new money?" He reached over and shook Marquis's hand.

"How's it looking out here?" Marquis looked around at the runners working expeditiously on the corners.

"Oh, it's all good. I just stopped through to check out ya boy, Bird, to make sure he was doing his job. He got this shit on lock out here." Bird had recently been put in charge to run the block. "So now I'm about to step over to the other blocks to check them out. What y'all getting into?"

Since Marquis had stepped up and made things happen for the crew, Brian was able to play the position he should have been playing from the beginning—partner.

"Well . . ." Shea smiled and looked at Marquis for approval to tell Brian about the baby. He nodded.

She turned back to Brian and said excitedly, "We're having a baby!"

"Oh, word?" Brian raised his eyebrows and smiled with approval. "That's what's up! Congratulations! Get outta the car. Let me see you." He opened Shea's door for her.

"Boy, I'm not showing yet." She laughed.

"So what? I still want to see." Brian helped her out of the car. Marquis got out of the car and walked onto the sidewalk. Brian stood back and examined her. "Yeah, I see something!"

"Boy, stop!" She hit him playfully. "You don't see nothing."

They all laughed and Marquis kissed Shea on the lips. "I need to go holler at Miguel. I'll be back. B, stay with her till I come back."

"A'ight."

"Mark, get me some cookies and cream ice cream and garlic chips," Shea told him.

"Aw, damn. Here we go. Damn, baby, we just found out yesterday, and you starting to eat crazy already?" He smiled at her.

"Just go get my stuff." She grinned.

He winked at her and walked to the store. Brian and Shea leaned against the car and continued to talk about the baby.

Inside the store Marquis held a conversation with the store owner as he always did when he went into the store. The store owner was good to the residence of the neighborhood and they in turn protected him.

As they spoke suddenly shots sounded from outside of the store. Screams came milliseconds later. Marquis pulled his nine from his waistband. "Get down," he yelled at the owner before peeking through the store window, bending low, and exiting the store. The sidewalk was chaos. What he saw next changed his life forever.

Shea and Brian lay on the ground by his car. Blood leaked from them both. Brian's gun was on the sidewalk next to him. He had tried to retaliate, but it was too late.

Shea was face down with three holes in her back. All the blood drained from Marquis's body. He ran over to her body and fell to his knees. The love of his life and his unborn seed were now gone. He'd loved Shea with every ounce of his body. He turned her body over as the tears fell fast and hard from his eyes, down his chin, and onto his shirt. He looked at his precious love. Her eyes were closed and her mouth was partially open.

"Baby, don't leave me," he whispered as tears fell onto her body.

Marquis felt like he couldn't breathe. He felt like someone had put a piece of plastic over his face and was suffocating him. His chest was tight and his throat was dry.

He held Shea in his arms and cried silently. People gathered around, talking about what had happened, but Marquis couldn't hear a thing.

There was no sound. All he heard was his own whimpers and the beating of his heart.

Miguel came out of the store and stood with his hand over his mouth in shock. Marquis suddenly screamed at the top of his lungs, startling everyone who was there.

"Noooooooooo! Nooooooooo!" he cried. Everyone who stood there felt his pain. Some of the females started to cry with him. Even the young kids began to cry for Marquis.

Marquis held Shea and looked at the sky. He cried even harder. "Why her? Why not me? Why didn't you take me?" he yelled angrily to the sky. "Give her back and take me! Don't take my babies!"

Marquis closed his eyes and continued to cry silently. He felt someone touch his shoulder, but he never moved. It was the old man who lived across the street, whose porch they used.

"Come on, son. You gotta get outta here," he said.

Marquis opened his eyes to see a crowd of people surrounding him, and the two dead bodies. He could see his workers—Bird, Money, Day-Day and Tim—all standing there. His vision blurred from his tears. He looked at the old man and realized who he was. He was shocked to see him standing there. The old man never left his house.

"Come, young man, get up. They gone. You can't stay here. The cops will be here soon."

Marquis looked back at his best friend Brian, who lay sprawled and twisted on the concrete. The old man kept trying to get Marquis to get up and leave, but Marquis ignored him.

"Come on, son. Snap outta it!" The old man shook him. "Them cops come, it's gonna be over for you."

"Why? I've done nothing wrong."

"You know how them crooked motherfuckers are. Come on, get up."

He grabbed Marquis by the arm.

Marquis kissed Shea on the forehead one last time before he rose to his feet. He looked down at his clothes and saw all the blood that had stained them. He noticed his car windows had been shot out. The old man removed the gun from Marquis's tight grip and put it into his own pocket.

A black Buick LeSabre with deeply tinted windows cruised by the scene slowly. Everyone was preoccupied with looking at the dead bodies and didn't pay the car any attention, but Marquis did. The window slowly lowered and the car drove slower, almost coming to a complete stop. Death held up his hand and stuck it out the window in the shape of a gun. He lowered the thumb finger to mime a gun shooting. He grinned a wide-toothed grin and the Buick sped down the street.

Marquis's whole body tensed and he clenched his fists. He heard the sirens in the distance. The old man tried to pull him away from the area, but Marquis wouldn't budge. He thought about how he had lost his brother to a bullet, his mother to drugs, and now his most precious possession. He began to cry again.

"Mister, I ain't leaving," he finally said in a hoarse voice.

Police and an ambulance arrived. Marquis still stood over the bodies of his friend and beloved girlfriend. He stared straight ahead. The police questioned them.

"What happened?" one of the officers asked him.

Marquis didn't say a word. The officer asked him again, and he still didn't respond. The officer noticed the blood on Marquis. Another officer walked up to them and the two cops had a brief conversation. They continued to try to get Marquis to talk, but he would not open his mouth. The old man stood in the background of the crowd and observed. Moments later Marquis was in handcuffs.

His crew members all began to shout.

"Yo he ain't do it!"

"A-yo Mark man tell them!"

The crowd reacted angrily and began shouting in Marquis's defense. But their shouts went on deaf ears.

Marquis was placed in the back of a patrol car and hauled off to the precinct.

Several hours later Marquis walked out of the precinct a free man. The police interrogated him, trying to find out if he was the actual killer. Marquis told them he went into the store and when he came out, Shea and Brian were dead due to a drive-by shooting. The police tried get him to say it was a drug-related retaliation drive-by because they thought he was a dealer, but Marquis kept it simple and gave them minimal information. In his mind, he was out to get Death.

Chapter Thirty-Three

Marquis was out of control. He was on a man hunt to find Death. He had hired new men to be just straight muscle. He put Bird in charge of the whole operation while he did what he felt he needed to do to get at Death. Since Death's whole crew had been destroyed, there wasn't anybody that he could get at that would bring Death out of hiding.

Even Kurt had been missing in action. Marquis desperately wanted to find Kurt to get some much needed advice. After coming up empty with Kurt, he decided to visit his father. He didn't want to take the drive because he knew his father was gonna lecture him, and now wasn't the time for lectures. But Marquis did remember that his father told him if there was anything that he needed to come to him before making a move. Marquis knew that he didn't want his father to tell him to get out of the game, because that wasn't going to happen while he was seeking revenge. What he needed was some seasoned advice on how to take care of the one they called Death.

When Wiz walked through the doors and saw the expression on Marquis's face, he knew what he heard was true. Marquis didn't even stand and give Wiz a hug like he usually did. He simply held out his hand and Wiz shook it as he sat down.

"What happened?" Wiz asked.

"How well do you know that nigga Death?" Marquis asked with venom seeping through his voice.

"I took him under my wing and started him in the game," Wiz said. "Why?"

"I want his heart in my hand." Marquis was pissed. He held out his hand and made a tight fist.

"Relax, son. Was he the one that bucked off?" Wiz could see the deep hurt in his son's eyes.

"Yeah."

"Do you know that for sure, or is it hearsay?"

"I saw that motherfucker with my own eyes. He made sure that I saw him, and then he played me out," Marquis said a little too loudly.

"Mark, calm down. Remember where you are," Wiz warned him.

Marquis sat back in his chair breathing heavily.

"Now tell me everything that has happened up till now. Don't sugar coat shit. I wanna know every move that coward ass nigga has made," Wiz said through gritted teeth. "Then I'm gonna tell you how to pull his skirt up and expose his pussy."

Marquis and his boys went on a wild goose chase looking for Death, but what they found out was almost as rewarding as finding Death. They discovered that Luke was the one who had killed Malik.

Marquis began some recruiting of his own. He went out and found some fearless young teens. They went on a war path. They hit Luke's blocks killing several of his runners in drive-bys. They would come through on motorcycles spraying up the blocks. Then there was a time Marquis had his boys run up in the nail salon because he was told that the four girlfriends of Luke and his top men where in the salon. The young teens walked up in the nail salon in broad daylight with ski masks on and killed the four women along with two nail technicians. It was chaos on the streets for over a week.

When Marquis learned the identity of his brother's killer from a reliable source, he was even madder at himself because he had been buying his weight from Luke. The day he and Death had it out, Marquis went to Luke and got a better deal, and better quality drugs. Luke had no idea that Marquis was Malik's brother. Luke didn't even know who Malik had been. All he knew was that he had worked for Death. Marquis could never get close enough to Luke to kill him and this frustrated him even more.

One day Marquis had gone to pay the old man and just sat with him for a while, keeping him company.

That day the old man told Marquis how he saw Luke in his backyard hiding out. He watched Luke jump the back fence and then jump into a Hummer on the next block. Which he could see through the neighbors backyard onto the next street.

"I don't know what was going on," the old man said in a raspy voice. With trembling hands he scratched his balding head. "I knowed something wasn't right cuz my bones was aching me something terrible," he said rubbing his knees as if remembering.

"I got them storying telling bones. I knows when there's trouble. When something just don't sit right on my stomach like sour milk."

Marquis sat patiently waiting for the old man to finish the story.

"The day your brother got shot my bones was ailing. I knew something was getting ready to happen but I didn't know what. Then there it was, I heard the shots. Pop, pop, pop, pop," the old man said emulating a gun with his old wrinkled crooked fingers as he made each sound.

"I sat straight up in my chair and a sharp pain hit me in my knee. I could feel this bad feeling cover my whole body."

Marquis sat there while his blood began to boil listening to the old man relive the day his brother was shot.

"I went to the kitchen to get my medication cuz I'd knowed this was gone be one of them there days. I's standing in the kitchen over the sink getting some water to wash the pills down, when I saw something out the window in my yard. Sho''nuff there he was crawling round in my yard with a gun in his hand," the old man was referring to Luke.

Marquis placed his hands over his face and rubbed them across his face before standing to his feet. He paced the floor while the old man talked.

That day the old man heard from the boys outside in front of his house that Malik had been shot and killed, and that was when he put two and two together and fingered Luke as the killer.

The crew never knew how much the old man knew. But he didn't sit in his front window for nothing. He has heard many conversations and he knew exactly who was who. That's how he was able to let Marquis know it was Luke's camp that did Malik.

Marquis now had the information that he wanted, and he needed to plan things out carefully.

ༀༀༀༀ

Sergeant Tilmond had been reviewed by Internal Affairs. It had been a month-long investigation and he had once again escaped being imprisoned for his wrongdoings. Unfortunately for the other officers with the other precincts, they weren't so lucky. Tilmond realized that he was just that close to serving time himself, so he made sure he used the connections he had on the inside to keep him from serving prison time for the moment.

He gave Internal Affairs all the information he could muster without actually giving them too much information that would backfire and incriminate him or his team. They all walked that day, but he knew that they would have to keep their noses clean for a while until everything blew over.

Tilmond was pissed because not only had Death gone against the grain and continued his war with Luke, but he had been ignoring his calls for over a month. Finally he was able to reach Death, and they agreed to meet. Tilmond wanted to warn his brother for the last time. There were now new men in place to take over a lot of the cases because Tilmond and his team had been placed on restricted duty, pending further investigation. This meant that Tilmond would no longer have total control over any investigation, and could no longer help Death.

ಬಬಬಬ

Death drove his old Chevy Monte Carlo, which he kept stored in one of his garages. He traveled alone.

This was a meeting that Death had been avoiding since they all met over at the cemetery. After that meeting he no longer trusted Terrell, and that was why he pulled his team from the corners and recruited them to security. Dean, Bear, and Jamal were all dead. They had been his main men, and he missed them. Ibn was falling off and had no more fire to him because of the loss of his two close friends. Death gave him a pass. Ibn had had a good, long run, so instead of keeping him on the team, Death paid him a grip to just retire. He felt better that way. He still talked to Ibn from time to time, seeking some of his wisdom, but the flame had burned out and Ibn was of no use to him anymore. Death got a new team of henchmen who were young and hungry.

He had to admit to himself that it felt funny not having his old crew around anymore, but sometimes change was good, and in his case, change was real good. He still had one problem, though, and that was Marquis. He smiled to himself when he thought about the young man. He believed that Marquis was young and inexperienced in the game, so he figured if he backed off Marquis for a minute, he would start believing their interactions were over. In the end, though, Death knew Marquis would be making a deal with him.

Death frowned as he turned the corner. He knew his brother was going to have him come to some crazy place, but when he pulled up to the construction site, he was pissed. It was a pile of junk and dirt. Death wore all beige, shoes and all. He knew he was going to leave from the site with his shit all fucked up.

He stopped outside the gate and called his brother on his cell.

"Yeah," Tilmond answered.

"Yo, man, I ain't coming up in there! I ain't tryna get dirty. I got somewhere to be after I leave here," Death complained.

"That's why they have cleaners, and I know you got more gear at home. This won't take long. Drive all the way to the back." Tilmond hung up.

Death wasn't feeling the way his brother just spoke to him. Something wasn't right. He started to just drive off and meet him somewhere else, at another time, and bring security. But curiosity was damn near killing him, so he drove into the site anyway.

He saw his brother parked in the back of the site, in the corner, and in the dark. Death killed the headlights and parked next to the unmarked patrol car. He rolled down his window and Tilmond did the same.

"Get in," Tilmond ordered.

Death sucked his teeth and stepped out onto the dirt road. Dust kicked up as he walked. He rolled his eyes, not wanting to look down at his eight-hundred-dollar shoes.

He checked the backseat of Tilmond's car to make sure no one else was in the car. Once in the passenger seat he removed his piece from the shoulder holster and laid it on his lap. He was going to be ready in case anything popped off. Tilmond looked at him and laughed.

"Why are you so paranoid?"

"I ain't paranoid! It's uncomfortable to sit with this in the holster with this suit jacket on," Death lied.

"Listen, Todd, I'm sure you know by now that your blocks are not protected anymore."

"Yeah, I figured that shit out when my peoples were getting popped and I started losing bodies from my team 'cause your boy Luke was running amuck out on the streets, and nobody was stopping him."

"Slow your roll, Todd. I tried to call you several times and you never answered my calls, so point the finger at yourself."

"It don't matter. I'm here. Now what do you want?"

"You need to lay low for a while because I'm still being investigated by Internal Affairs, and I don't need no more heat on me than there already is."

"You killin' me, Rell! You know this shit is for the birds, and frankly, I'm tired of it," Death snapped.

"What are you talking about?" Tilmond was confused.

"I'm talking about how all of a sudden Luke has more control than I do. My crew is being picked off one at a time, and nothing is happening to stop it. You are my brother, and you are a sergeant on the force, and I can't get no better play than what you giving me?"

"I told you at the meeting that if you fucked up again, it wouldn't be nothing I could do for you."

"Well, that ain't good enough for me. So since I feel like I'm out here on my own, and I got family with authority on the force who is not helping me, then I'm gonna have to take matters into my own hands to protect me and mine." Death was serious.

"I wouldn't do that if I were you, Todd," Tilmond warned.

"See, Rell, that's the difference between you and me. I'm me, and you're dead." Death pumped four bullets into Tilmond's face. Blood splashed onto his beige suit, creating red splatters. "Now look what you did! You done fucked up my suit," Death said, and got out of the car.

If Death only knew that Terrell was innocent and really had his back.

Chapter Thirty-Four

Luke lay in bed with Lana and Lani, two beautiful Hawaiian twins. He didn't discriminate. Pussy was pussy to him, and a broad who could suck a mean dick was definitely ranked at the top of his list. He was exhausted. The Hawaiian women possessed outstanding stamina that surpassed his any day of the week. The sisters were in perfect shape. Their physiques were those of professional athletes, yet their astonishing beauty softened their appearances. Although Luke was young and very much still had his sex game, after each orgasm with the women, he became more and more drained.

He'd met the women just two days ago at Newark airport when he had flown home from Florida. He saw them at the airport and it seemed as if they were waiting on him. They told him that they had just flown in from California and were going to meet some friends in New Jersey and then do some sightseeing in New York. After the sisters practically threw themselves at him right there in the airport, Luke decided to take them with him.

Both women lay under each of his armpits with one leg draped across his body. Luke was sound asleep. He was able to sleep this deeply because of the amount of protection he knew he had. He had two bodyguards stationed in the lobby of the hotel, two posted in the back parking lot, and one posted on each side of the hotel. Lately Luke felt the need for such a great deal of protection after all the turmoil he had created. He was taking Death's squad out left and right. Death had hit his squad a couple of times, but it was nowhere near the damage Luke had done.

Luke stirred in his sleep and opened his eyes. When he saw the twins, a broad smile appeared on his face. He kissed them both on their foreheads. They simultaneously looked up at him.

"Damn, y'all got the prettiest skin I have ever seen." He peered down at both women.

They simply smiled up at him in silence. Both sisters looked at each other and narrowed their eyes, then got up and went into the bathroom. When they were done cleaning themselves, they both kissed Luke on the cheek and left the room.

Luke rolled over in the king-sized bed and fell into another deep sleep.

He was awakened by hissing sounds. He opened his eyes and looked around, but didn't see anything, so he closed his eyes again. Within minutes he felt the stinging sensation of a bite on his calf. He pulled the covers back and saw three black mamba snakes in the bed with him. He yelled as the snakes went to work on him, biting him all over his body. Luke tried to get out of the bed, but he fell to the floor where there were more black mambas waiting for him. The snakes continued to bite him until his skin swelled. He finally collapsed on the floor after several failed attempts to run. Before he died he looked at the entrance to the living room and saw the Hawaiian twins standing there with Marquis behind them.

The two sisters where the daughters of a well known Hawaiian drug lord. The girls were flown in from Hawaii to handle the job. They were ruthless beauties who handled their father's organization. Their father is the longtime cellmate of Wiz's. They've been cellies for ten years and have created a bond like brothers. Wiz has done many favors for the Hawaiian king pin since he first stepped foot into the penitentiary. Wiz protected the Hawaiian from the other inmates. He was happy to assist Wiz with his son's situation.

They watched Luke become paralyzed. Within several minutes he was dead.

Marquis kissed each woman on her forehead and they closed the bedroom door as snakes continued to crawl all over Luke's body.

Marquis's cell phone was blowing up. His head was pounding from the amount of alcohol he consumed trying to drown out the fact that Shea was gone. He looked at the number and saw it was the block's pay phone number. He sat up in his bed and stretched. He hadn't planned on sleeping so late, but he needed the rest. He looked over at Lana and Lani and felt guilty that he allowed himself to get drunk and had slept with the two women. The women were gorgeous and drove a hard bargain and in the end, his manhood took over.

He got out of bed. He dressed and walked out into the sunlight, and squinted from its rays. It was three o'clock in the afternoon. He got into his car and drove the fifteen-minute ride to his territory. When he got there Bird ran up to the car before it came to a full stop.

"What's up?" Marquis asked when Bird jumped into the car.

"We got jacked," he said.

"What? How the fuck that happen?"

Bird lowered his head.

"What the fuck, man?" Marquis yelled.

"I know who did it," Bird said.

"Who, nigga? Stop playing these games with me!"

When Bird told him who had stolen the stash, Marquis banged his fist on the steering wheel. "Fuck!" he yelled. He sat there for several seconds with his face screwed up as if he was in pain. He shook his head. "Why?" he finally whispered.

Bird just looked at him. He felt sorry for him.

"How?" Marquis finally asked in a calm tone.

"Only thing I can think of is that they been watching us. They came out here to cop a couple times. The last time they was short, but that's about it." Bird shrugged.

"But how do you know?" He looked at Bird closely.

"Because Money saw them running with it in their hands."

"Is he sure?"

"No doubt," Bird confirmed.

Marquis laid back his head on the headrest and stared straight ahead.

"So what you wanna do?" Bird asked.

"Was that all of it?" Marquis wanted to know.

"Yeah, it was all we had left. I mean we was gonna call you to re-up, but it was still enough to last us a couple of hours."

"A'ight, get out the car. Let me think for a minute."

"Oh, yeah, we know where they at," Bird added. "That's why I called you, because we didn't want to make a move unless you told us to."

"Good looking out," Marquis said softly, still staring straight ahead.

Their eyes met. His eyes showing disappointment and sorrow. Her eyes showing no life to them. The dealer raised his gun as his eyes began to tear. *BOOM!* Her blood splattered all over the floor. The crew members collectively shook their heads at the pitiful pile of flesh.

Marquis cried while Nina's body lay twisted on the floor. He'd fought himself on what to do before he decided to kill her. He had tried to work with her several times. She had constantly been in and out of detox, yet she still couldn't remain clean. The drugs had finally caught up to her after all the years she was able to control it. She was the woman who had brought him into this world. She was the woman who had loved him unconditionally. She was the woman who'd thought her oldest son would do her in, and she never thought that her baby would be the one. But Marquis did it to save her. He did it to save her from herself. He did it because he could no longer watch his mother kill herself with the very poison that he sold. He didn't know if that made it right, but he knew that her soul and body could now rest peacefully.

"Let's break out, man," Bird said to him.

Marquis wiped his face and straightened up. Bird, Money, and Marquis began to walk out

of the basement of the abandoned building. Before they left Marquis noticed that his mother's belongings were sitting in the corner of the basement. She had been living there.

Marquis knew she had gotten evicted because she came to him asking if she could stay with him, but he turned her down. He hated what she had become. He was embarrassed by how she looked, but not once did he ever think that what he did for a living only helped to get his mother the way she was. Drugs had destroyed her life.

Marquis picked up the picture of him and his brother when they were younger, all dressed up. His mother loved that picture. He took the picture with him and left the basement.

Later that day Marquis had one of the boys make an anonymous call to the police to report a dead body in the basement of the abandoned building. He knew no one would find his mother's body in that basement unless it was called in. All that occupied his mind for the next several days was his mother's dead body lying on the cold, hard, cement floor.

Chapter Thirty-Five

Marquis sat in the front row alone. He was all the family that showed up for the funeral. Ernest finally arrived and sat down next to him. They shook hands and embraced. Marquis was glad he came, but he felt guilty sitting there, knowing he was the one who ultimately put his mother in that box. The casket was closed at his request. Marquis didn't want to remember Nina the way she looked when she died. She was all skin and bones, and her nose had been eaten away by the heroin and cancer. He didn't want anyone else to see her that way, so he had the picture of his mother when she was a dime piece blown up and placed on an easel next to the pretty white coffin. He spent eight thousand dollars for her coffin. He wanted nothing but the best for his mother.

Marquis had talked to his father about Nina'a death, and he said he would see if he could get another pass to come to her funeral, but he didn't think it would be possible because they were not married.

A few of Nina's get-high buddies sat in the back of the church, crying, but Marquis didn't pay them any attention. He guessed they had to grieve too, so he left them alone instead of asking them to leave. His boys sat in the row behind him while four more posted up around the church and four outside the church as lookouts. He was still on point, watching out for Death. Marquis had not seen or heard from him in quite some time, but if Death was a smart man, then the two of them thought alike. It paid to be patient and catch your opponent off guard.

Marquis and Ernest didn't talk. They both just looked at Nina's astonishing picture. Ernest was mesmerized by her former beauty and sad that she had to die so young.

The organ music played and more people came into the church. Shauna walked over to Marquis and gave him a hug and a kiss. Marquis smiled at her because she looked so pretty. She was clean and sober. This was the first time he had seen her in a good while. The last time he saw her she was skin and bones.

"I'm sorry for your loss. You know we loved your mother," she said, kissing him again. He just nodded his head in acknowledgement.

Nilda walked up next and shook his hand.

Ernest introduced them. "Mark, this is Nilda. She was your mother's drug counselor before I became her sponsor."

"It's nice to finally meet you, despite the circumstances," Nilda said, giving him a sympathetic smile.

"Same here," Marquis said, partially smiling at her.

She patted the back of his hand and sat next to Shauna in the second row with the crew.

"It's so sad," Nilda said to Shauna. She reached into her purse for a tissue to wipe her eyes.

"I know. I can't imagine what that poor child is feeling. He lost his mother and his brother just months apart." Shauna shook her head in sympathy for Marquis.

"Ernest told me he lost his girlfriend too, and she was pregnant with his child," Nilda added.

"Oh my God!" Shauna whispered in shock. "Are you serious?"

Nilda just nodded as the tears continued to flow.

Marquis sat there with his head hung low when a man came and stood in front of him. Marquis looked at the brown, shiny shoes and followed the length of the man's body up to his face. He stared at the man in shock. It was Kurt. He stood and they embraced each other tightly. Kurt was not only clean, but sober as well. He released Marquis and looked him in the eyes. Kurt had shaved his beard and now sported a mustache and a short afro.

Marquis was so proud of Kurt. They hugged again. By this time Shauna was crying hard as she watched them. Marquis was sad because everyone there that used to get high seemed to have gotten themselves together, everyone except his mother. Although she had been a drug addict, though, he still missed her.

The two men hugged again for what seemed like an eternity before they finally sat down. Marquis sat between Ernest and Kurt. The two people he knew cared about his mother were now his family.

Shauna got up from her seat and Nilda followed her. Shauna sat next to Kurt. Kurt kissed her on the lips. Marquis looked at the two of them with wide eyes. Kurt winked his eye at Marquis.

After Kurt had returned from his rehab program, he met up with Shauna at an NA meeting, and the two of them hit it off instantly. They had known each other for years, but only as addicts on the streets. When Kurt left to go to a three-month program, Shauna stood by his side and waited for him. Now they were an official couple.

An extremely skinny woman dressed in a filthy pastel-colored sundress approached the closed coffin. She seemed to be drunk because she swayed and reeked of the odor. Her skin was blotchy with black liver spots. Her feet were crusty. She wore run down flat sandals with scotch tape placed on the straps to hold them in place. The woman then walked in front of Nina's picture and gazed at it for a long time. She wiped her tear-filled eyes with the palm of her hand. She then turned and walked over to Marquis. He looked into her hazel eyes, he knew who she was. He didn't recognize her when she first walked in. It was Jackie.

"Marquis, I wanted to apologize for the things I've done in the past. I'm gonna miss your mother. Can you forgive me for invading y'all home and starting your mother back on drugs?"

"Jackie, my mother was a grown woman. She did what she wanted to do."

"Well I still wanted to apologize."

He just shook his head.

After the brief ceremony they all went over to the gravesite where Nina's body was to be buried beside Malik. Marquis, Kurt, Ernest, Nilda, Shauna, and a small crowd watched as the casket was lowered on top of the cement wall that separated Nina's casket from Malik's. After Malik was killed, Marquis bought the family cemetery plots so there was enough room for all the family members to be buried there when their time came.

Marquis never thought that death would happen this soon. He knew that in time if he kept living the way that he did, they would be placing his casket on top of his mother's. But that was something he would be ready for, because at that point, he was ready to join his mother and brother. Well not quite. First he had to take care of one more problem, and that was Death.

After the casket was lowered, some of the crowd left. Marquis remained, looking down into the hole. He tossed a couple flowers into the hole. Kurt walked up next to him and put his arm around him.

"You look good, man," Marquis said, smiling at him.

"I do, if I say so myself." Kurt clowned as he straightened out his suit jacket.

"What's up with you and Shauna?"

"That's some crazy shit, ain't it? Who would have thought? I ran into her before I went into the rehab program. She had gone to a recovery program too. She was looking good as hell, and you know a playa like me had to step to her. And check this out, she waited for me until I came out," Kurt bragged.

Marquis laughed. "So you hitting that?"

"Am I?" Kurt smiled. "Seriously," Kurt said as his smile disappeared. "I loved your mother, and I loved y'all like you were my own sons. I'm sorry that I couldn't be there for Shea's funeral. It liked to kill me when I found out what happened, 'cause I know how you felt about her. But I was in rehab and just couldn't get out," Kurt said sincerely.

"Come on, Kurt. You ain't Superman. You can't do everything. I know if you could have, you would have been there."

"But it don't matter what Wiz say, I still feel like I've failed him. I made a promise and couldn't keep it. Now Nina's gone too," he said, looking down into the hole.

"Listen Kurt, you were good to us, regardless of what you think, man. You can't hold on to that. Let it go." Marquis was sincere.

"Hey, when's the next time you gonna go see your father? I want him to check me out."

Marquis laughed. "Yeah, he would like to see this. I'll probably go up there this week."

"Good. I'm gonna give you my number, and you call me so I can ride with you. Do you need anything?"

"Naw, man. I'm good."

"So, you still out there pushing that shit, huh?"

Marquis didn't answer. He turned to look back into the hole.

"I ain't here to rag on you, son. Just be careful."

"Kurt, will you take a ride with me? I really need to talk to you about something," Marquis said.

"Sure. Anything for you. You my man." Kurt grabbed him around the neck and threw a playful punch to Marquis's stomach.

The two of them walked off, play fighting, when Marquis suddenly stopped. "Kurt, meet me at my car. I got one thing I need to do."

"OK." Kurt walked quickly to catch up with the others.

Marquis walked through the cemetery, looking for Shea's grave with two of his boys in tow, watching his back. He had been to her grave at least twice a week since she was killed. He didn't go to her funeral because he had been too ashamed to show his face. He knew her mother would have been there. He'd taken her only child from her home that day, and he allowed her to be killed. Marquis was devastated by this, and he couldn't bring himself to go to the funeral. He secretly watched from afar, and when everyone left, he went over to her gravesite just like Preach did in the movie *Cooley High*. Every week after that he made sure he brought flowers to the grave.

That day Marquis would talk with Shea briefly and admit to her what he had done.

ಌಌಌಌ

TWO MONTHS LATER . . .

Death was relieved to hear that Luke had been killed. He wasn't sure who did it, but he was glad that it was done. With Tilmond out of the way as well, maybe he could come out of hiding. Death had been down under since he finished off his brother. He was currently posted up at his main house in South Jersey that only one person knew about, and he was no threat to Death. Death was close to Atlantic City and often went over to the lavish casinos to try his hand at the craps tables. Death would also pick up a chick here and there to spend time with in a room he would rent in one of the hotels. That night he decided to go to the hotel and try his hand at the blackjack tables.

After sitting there for two hours and making small talk with a beautiful, chocolate-skinned woman, Death decided to quit for the night. The two of them had conversed for an hour, not really paying any attention to the game. Death broke even and didn't lose anything. However, the young lady had lost about a thousand dollars. Death decided that they should go over to the bar and finish their conversation over yet another drink, although they had already finished four drinks while sitting at the blackjack table. However, the beauty wanted to go back to his room instead. Death was impressed by her forwardness and accepted her offer graciously. The two traveled in the elevator to the sixth floor and felt each other up the whole time. They burst through his hotel room, kissing and groping and ripping off their clothes.

They fell hard onto the bed. While grinding on each other, they removed the rest of their clothes. Death shoved his tongue down her throat and palmed her ass. They rolled back and forth on the bed when Death fell off it in a drunken stupor. He hit the floor hard. The woman laughed drunkenly, and so did he. He stood, and his erection stood at attention. The woman's eyes were fixed on it. Death was cocky and knew he was holding, so he grabbed his dick and massaged it. She licked her lips and played with her clit.

Death heard the sound of a bullet being chambered and froze. He was literally caught with his pants down and his dick in his hand. He tried not to move. The woman never heard the gun click because she was drunk and playing with herself, moaning with her eyes closed.

Death's gun was in the shoulder holster that he took off in the adjacent sitting room of the hotel suite, but he did have a smaller gun in the pocket of his dress pants, which were on the floor near his foot. He could have kicked himself for not watching his surroundings more carefully. More importantly, he wanted to know who knew where he was when he'd told no one. He began to turn when the gunman spoke.

"Easy now," he said.

The woman heard the male's voice and jumped up, startled. She began to scream when the gunman pumped two into her body with a silenced nine.

Death looked at the woman with no remorse. He turned and looked at the gunman and was shocked to see Marquis standing there looking like a gangster.

He wore a black, pinstriped, three-piece suit with a white doo-rag and a black, wide-brimmed hat. Marquis actually held two guns. Death smirked. He had to give it to the boy. He was good. Death had totally underestimated Marquis.

"Can I at least put on my pants?" Death asked while slowly reaching for his pants.

"Come on now, that shit is played out." Marquis figured that Death was trying to go for his weapon. "Turn your dumb ass around slowly. If you make a fucked-up move, I got some hot ones for ya."

Death did as he was told and slowly turned his entire body to face his predator. His legs weakened due to shock when he saw who had just entered the room. He, too, wore a tailor-made pinstriped suit, but in navy blue.

"What's good, Death?" Wiz asked and smiled.

"Wiz," Death said, still not believing his eyes.

"Damn, I see my son caught you with your pants down. Didn't I teach you anything, boy?" Wiz chuckled. "It's good to see you, though."

"When did you get out?" Death asked. He knew it was all over for him.

"Oh, about a week or so ago. Why? You miss me?" Wiz toyed with him. "It's a shame when you can't even trust your own boy to have your back. Oh, yeah, I know all about it, homeboy."

"What are you talking about?" Death played dumb as sweat ran down his spine.

"Oh, so now you gonna play stupid? OK, I know how to play that game." Wiz grinned. "They got your fingerprints off the gun. A witness came forward from that day I killed that nigga on the porch, way back when. You remember that, right? Remember when I gave you the gun to get rid of? See, the thing is, my man, I had on driving gloves that day. Although I shot that kid for fucking up my work, I handed you the gun. So your fingerprints are on the gun."

"But you got arrested because you off'd that nigga. Not me!" Death tried to defend himself.

"Yeah, I did one, and you did the other. But I did over fifteen years for both of them. I can even say that I got some rehabilitation from it. But I think seeing you standing there, knowing you about to die is rehabilitation enough for me. Death, I know you snitched, partner. I know all about it. You see, you wanted me out of the way 'cause you couldn't have Nina. Well, you destroyed her, and now I'm gonna destroy you."

"Come on, Wiz! I don't know what you're talking about," Death protested.

"Oh, don't bitch up on me now, nigga! You broke all the rules we ever made up as a team. You dropped a dime on me because you gave them the gun that I used to kill that one cat. The slugs matched what they pulled from the body, and I got sent up. You canceled the other nigga. But you forgot I had on gloves, so when the eyewitness confessed to witnessing the shooting, my son here got me the best lawyer, and my case got dropped, setting me free." Wiz's smile was gleeful.

"No! That's bullshit! Whoever told you that shit is a lying motherfucker!" Death stayed defensive, although he knew that what Wiz said was the truth.

"Naw, homeboy. It's the truth, and you know it. Matter-of-fact, why don't I let him tell you himself?"

As if on cue, Kurt walked through the door wearing the exact same ensemble, but in burgundy. He, Wiz, and Marquis stood there, looking like Three the Hard Way of the new millennium.

"That nigga don't know shit!" Death yelled.

"Oh, but I do." Kurt smiled.

Death couldn't believe his eyes or his ears. He knew he was dead meat, because Kurt was indeed the one to whom he had given the gun that day. Wiz had told Death to get rid of the gun, but he didn't. He decided instead to carry the gun around in his pocket.

One day when the cops rolled up on the corner to search them, Death panicked and passed the gun off to Kurt, who at the time was reading a newspaper. Kurt rolled up the gun in the newspaper without touching it and stood on the sidewalk, waiting for the police to finish their search. When they were done, he gave the gun back to Death. He and Death stood out on the corner for a few moments and talked. Back then Death bragged about everything. That day he bragged about the shooting. But with Kurt on drugs, he never put two and two together.

Then when Kurt started going to the NA meetings he met up with Ernest. When they talked about Nina, Ernest told him everything that Nina had told him. That was when Kurt realized that Death had snitched on Wiz. Death was the only person other than Nina who could have known what happened that day. Not only did Nina tell Ernest about Death, she told him about the baby she miscarried and how Death was the one who introduced her to heroin.

When Kurt went into rehabilitation and got himself together, he knew he had to do the right thing to get his old friend out of jail. Kurt believed in the no-snitching law of the streets. But his conscience wouldn't let him rest until he got even with Death.

"The main reason I wanna see you dead is because you destroyed my seed," Wiz said.

Death's eyes became wide.

"Oh, yeah, I know all about it," Wiz continued. "You destroyed my family. After all I did for you, that's how you repay me?"

"OK, so now you know," Death said with newfound courage. "One question, though."

"Is this gonna be your dying wish?" Wiz asked with cold eyes.

Death gritted his teeth. "How did you know where I was at?"

"Ibn!" Kurt called out.

Ibn walked through the door dressed like Bill Cosby in *Let's Do It Again*. Kurt shook his head. "Man, you killing me with them damn colors!" He squinted his eyes as if the colors were too bright.

Death was furious. "Oh, that's fucked up!"

"Yeah, it sure is, boy," Ibn agreed. "But don't nobody want to deal with a snitching-ass nigga."

"Me and ya boy Ibn go way back," Kurt added.

"I'ma kill you, nigga," Death growled at Ibn.

Ibn just stood there and smirked at Death.

Marquis had had enough. He shot Death in the kneecap. You could hear the crunch when the bullet hit it. Death yelled out in agonizing pain.

"Stop acting like a bitch and man up!" Ibn said.

"Take it like a man. It'll all be over with soon," Kurt added.

"A'ight, son. Finish him off," Wiz ordered. "This little bitch is crying over a little pain." Wiz looked Death in the eyes. "I should have finished you off when I found out you was screwing my woman behind my back, you snake-ass nigga," Wiz said through clenched teeth. "Looks like you fucked around and made a deal with death!"

Marquis finished the job, making sure he riddled Death's and the woman's bodies with holes.

Marquis thought he would feel better when he killed Death, but he didn't. He had never considered himself a gangster, and never thought he would be able to take another person's life. In the last month, though, he had done just that, many times. Killing those people did nothing to mend his heart. It didn't bring back his loved ones, and it didn't relieve his pain. He missed his mother, brother, girlfriend, and best friends deeply. Now that Wiz was home, Marquis hoped that they would be able to build the father-son relationship he'd missed with his father.

Later they all met up at a diner to get something to eat. It was odd to Marquis when he thought about it. How could they eat after they had just killed two people in cold blood? He couldn't do it. He wasn't hungry in the least, so he stood to leave.

"Where you going?" Wiz wanted to know.

"I need to go take care of business," Marquis said.

"OK. I'll meet you at the crib later."

Marquis shook hands with Kurt and Ibn. He was grateful that Ibn had helped them find Death. He had no idea that Kurt had so much pull. When Kurt told him he knew everything, he wasn't lying. It was obvious that Kurt had some status back in the day as well. It was just unfortunate that he loved to get high, and that was his downfall. Ibn had been fed up with Death and his unfair treatment. He had lost his two best friends, and decided enough was enough. When Kurt came to him for help, Ibn graciously participated.

Marquis drove up on the block and saw his team serving customers. He sat there for a few moments, thinking about his life. In a matter of several months he went from graduating high school, registering for college classes, meeting the love of his life and turning into a drug dealer, to losing his entire family. He didn't like the way he felt. He knew most young men of his status would be tricking off their money on the bling and finer things in life. But not Marquis. He'd never been impressed with that way of life, and it still did nothing for him.

He got out of the car and walked over to the old man's house where they stashed their dope and posted up. The old man had been good to them and allowed them to do this. They paid him and he kept to himself and minded his business.

The old man opened the door and smiled at Marquis. He didn't have his teeth in his mouth, so only his gums were visible. Marquis walked in and took a seat. He reached into his suit jacket and handed the man an envelope. Inside was ten thousand dollars.

"Young man, this sure is a lotta money," he gummed.

"It's just a little something for the information you gave me. But, nothing will bring my brother back." Marquis held his head low.

"Son the type of lifestyle you living is always a gamble. I've been on this here earth a long time. I've seen people come and go. I'm Ninety-seven years olds and I can still get around with the best of 'im. But if you don't get yaself together, you gonna be next."

Marquis listened intently to the old man speak.

"I knowed what y'all kids been doing. I sees things. I lived in this old house for a longtime. I've watched several generations of drug pushers stand on them very same corners. When they go, another generation take up where they left off." The old man adjusted the pillow that was placed behind his back. "There's gonna be plenty a pushers after I leave this earth. Trust me when I tell you, leave it all behind you. Your wife and child are gone, your mother is gone and your brother is gone. What's it's gotta take for you to get the picture," his claw like finger pointed at Marquis.

After about an hour, Marquis left the old man's house. He turned and shook his hand before descending the steps. The boys from his crew spotted him and ran over to talk to him. Marquis was giving them all pounds when he spotted Bird pulling up to the curb.

Marquis went over to his friend.

"What's good, Mark? You take care of that problem?" Bird asked.

"No doubt," he confirmed.

"So, what, we gonna celebrate now? I mean we free and clear to do what you always wanted to do from the rip!" Bird was amped.

"Really, B? Do you really think we free? Or will there be some other nigga tryna be kingpin, tryna get at us? Will there be other hating motherfuckers out here to fuck with us every chance they get? Or maybe they will pick us off one by one like we did Luke's and Death's camps. Will we ever last long enough to enjoy all this paper we making? Is it all worth it?" Marquis looked at him seriously.

Bird was confused. He couldn't understand why Marquis was talking like that.

"Naw, B, I don't think it's worth it," Marquis said, answering his own questions. "I'm tired. I've had enough." Marquis walked away.

"So, you out, man?" Bird asked, running up behind him. "You just gonna throw it all away like that?"

"Yeah, man, I'm out. It's all yours. I'm done, man." He said it and meant it. Marquis got in his car and drove off, leaving Bird standing there, perplexed. He scratched his head and walked back toward the corner.

Marquis drove down the highway doing ninety miles per hour. He thought about running into a brick wall. He thought about driving off the bridge. But most of all, he thought about his mother, brother, two best friends and Shea. Was it all worth it?

MELODRAMA PUBLISHING ORDER FORM
WWW.MELODRAMAPUBLISHING.COM

Title	ISBN	QTY	PRICE	TOTAL
Wifey	0-971702-18-7		$15.00	$
I'm Still Wifey	0-971702-15-2		$15.00	$
Life After Wifey	1-934157-04-X		$15.00	$
Still Wifey Material	1-934157-10-4		$15.00	$
Sex, Sin & Brooklyn	0-971702-16-0		$15.00	$
Histress	1-934157-03-1		$15.00	$
Den of Sin	1-934157-08-2		$15.00	$
Eva: First Lady of Sin	1-934157-01-5		$15.00	$
Eva 2: First Lady of Sin	1-934157-11-2		$15.00	$
The Madam	1-934157-05-8		$15.00	$
Shot Glass Diva	1-934157-14-7		$15.00	$
Dirty Little Angel	1-934157-19-8		$15.00	$
Cartier Cartel	1-934157-18-X		$15.00	$
In My Hood	0-971702-19-5		$15.00	$
In My Hood 2	1-934157-06-6		$15.00	$
A Deal With Death	1-934157-12-0		$15.00	$
Tale of a Train Wreck Lifestyle	1-934157-15-5		$15.00	$
A Sticky Situation	1-934157-09-0		$15.00	$
Jealousy	1-934157-07-4		$15.00	$
Life, Love & Lonliness	0-971702-10-1		$15.00	$
The Criss Cross	0-971702-12-8		$15.00	$
Stripped	1-934157-00-7		$15.00	$
The Candy Shop	1-934157-02-3		$15.00	$
Cross Roads	0-971702-18-7		$15.00	$
A Twisted Tale of Karma	0-971702-14-4		$15.00	$

(GO TO THE NEXT PAGE)

MELODRAMA PUBLISHING ORDER FORM
(CONTINUED)

Title/Author	ISBN	QTY	PRICE	TOTAL
Up, Close & Personal	0-971702-11-X		$9.95	$
Menace II Society	0-971702-17-9		$15.00	$
			Subtotal	
			Shipping**	
			Tax*	
	Total			

Instructions:

*NY residents please add $1.79 Tax per book.

**Shipping costs: $3.00 first book, any additional books please add $1.00 per book.

Incarcerated readers receive a 25% discount. Please pay $11.25 per book and apply the same shipping terms as stated above.

Mail to:

MELODRAMA PUBLISHING

P.O. BOX 522

BELLPORT, NY 11713